DISTANT RELATIONS

FINN O'BRIEN CRIME
BOOK 5

REBECCA FORSTER

ACKNOWLEDGMENTS

As always, I would like to thank Jenny Jensen, fabulous editor, for putting up with all stages of my writing angst, Bruce Raterink for his boundless energy and ability to read a full novel in less than 24 hours, and Glenn Gallo for his fine eye for detail.

A special shout out goes to Rebecca's ARC Angels who take time to read the Advance Reading Copies. You are awesome.

It goes without saying that my supremely patient family should be thanked over and over again.

For my sister, Beth Barnes

May the past remain distant, and the future you deserve be at your fingertips

"It is not the broken heart that kills, but broken pride..."
—Gilbert Parker

DISTANT RELATIONS

By

REBECCA FORSTER

1

SAN FRANCISCO 12:30 P.M

He traveled light: his best suit, shirt, a silk tie, and shined lace-ups for the meeting; jeans, a light jacket, and trainers for comfort during his flight.

He did not check a bag.

He flew coach.

He had booked a room at a mid-level hotel.

He had learned discipline at his frugal mother's knee, and priorities from his father who believed a man should be the last to benefit from his own hard work. The community mattered. The whole should thrive. His father was a smart man. He had raised a smart son. As much as he hated the extra cost of all this, in the end it was money and time well spent. Everything had been accomplished so professionally, so neatly, and that pleased him.

He zipped up his carry-on and checked the room again, just to make sure he hadn't forgotten anything. That done, he put one key card on the bureau next to the sign that informed him Suzanne had been happy to clean his room. He hadn't been there long enough for Suzanne to clean the room, and if she had, he doubted she would have been happy to do so. Even if he had extended his stay, he would not have left a tip. Management could afford a living wage and if the hotel chose not to give it to Suzanne, and she chose to work for miserable wages, then that was on her.

He texted the home office to check on deliveries and received confirmation that everything was complete. There was a post-script; the vendor was waiting for a check to be cut. He gave his permission. He then clicked on a link in another text that had come in the middle of the night. He double-checked the information and saw everything was on schedule. The man appreciated the efficiency of the provider even as he regretted the need for it.

Putting on his suit jacket, he confirmed the boarding pass in his pocket, and then looked at his watch. It was time to go.

Suzanne was just coming out of room 207 when the man walked down the hall. She had seen him early that morning checking into room 220. He did not acknowledge her then; there was no indication he saw her now. He was an in-and-out. No smile. No humor. No tip.

She had long ago suspected that people who stayed in hotels like this were the stingiest ever. In the cheap places folks gave to insure they got fresh sheets; in the fancy places rich people left ridiculous tips as a way to prove their superiority. She needed to find a job at a fancy place. Suzanne had no problem being inferior.

Still, stingy, or not, that man was easy on the eyes. Too bad he had a stick up his ass. The elevator door opened. When he was gone Suzanne took a couple of towels off her cart with one hand and grabbed the vacuum with the other. She went into room 211.

DOWNSTAIRS, the man from room 220 put his carry-on on a bench in the communal dining room. On the far end of the room was a long counter upon which stood gleaming silver bins. They were all empty despite the fact that the hour was early, and breakfast wouldn't end for another four hours. At one time, those bins held breads and pastries, clumps of something akin to scrambled eggs, and strips of bacon. Now happy little signs pointed to the brown bags lined up neatly on the counter. A sign with an elf pointing toward them read: *For Your Convenience, Grab and Go!* Brilliant management: save on service, hot food, and labor and still make it sound like a perk.

He filled a cup with coffee. Next to the urn was a basket and on the basket was a handwritten sign begging for tips: *Karma insurance.* In the basket were assorted coins. The man dug in his pocket and came up with a few dollars and a plastic card. He put the folding money back in his pocket and picked up one of the bags. He put his hand inside and then, as if deciding a banana and a bagel was not to his liking, refolded the top of the brown paper bag and set it near the coffee urn.

A woman walked in, saw what he was doing, and thought he must be a very nice man to set aside a bag he had touched. Before she could tell him how much she appreciated his concern for his fellow man, her ride came and she went out the door.

The man turned around in time to see her get into a cab. A black car pulled up behind. He left his coffee, picked up his carry-on, and went out the door taking no notice of the man who held it open for him. He did not watch the man walk inside, enter the dining area, and go directly to the breakfast bags. He did not see this man pause as if he was trying to decide which one to choose. Instead, he went to the black car and leaned down to look at the driver.

"Mr. Cain?" the driver said.

He nodded and got in the back seat. He was long gone by the time the man who had passed him at the door picked up the brown paper bag near the coffee urn and went on his way.

SUZANNE WAS GATHERING SHAMPOO, conditioner, and two tiny bars of soap when the elevator dinged. She wandered back to the hall and saw a man studying the plaque that would direct him to his room. He was tall but not handsome like the other one. He looked a little like her cousin George who still lived at home and swore he would be wealthy when his app hit the market. The man in the hall was a little nerdy, a little not. His hair was definitely weird. It almost looked like it belonged on someone else's head.

She went back into the room she was working on and gave the mini-bar one last look. As she straightened up, Suzanne saw the guy pass out of the corner of her eye. When she looked out the door, she saw him stop at room 220 and wave a key card at the reader. When he did it again and nothing happened, Suzanne went to help.

"'Scuse me," she said.

"What?"

The man nearly jumped out his skin. He didn't seem angry, but he sure wasn't happy she was talking to him.

"What room are you looking for?"

He looked at the room number, he looked at her.

"220. This room. Right here. 220."

"I haven't cleaned it yet," she said. "The guest who was in

there just left. Check-in isn't until noon. I mean, it's not freshened up."

"That's okay." He turned his back on her and swiped again. "Don't worry about it."

"Okay."

Suzanne lingered. Something didn't feel right, but then again what was right with the world these days? When she heard a click and the door opened, he looked at her, irked that she was still staring at him. He raised a brow. She shrugged and went back to work.

Inside room 220, the man threw the deadbolt. He put his back against the door, blew out a deep breath, put a hand to his head, and scratched hard. His head was damn hot. He pushed off the door, walked into the bathroom, checked himself out in the mirror, and decided he looked like an idiot. The wig seemed like a good idea but he couldn't stand the itching, so he tossed it into the trashcan. His own hair wasn't much more attractive, but at least it was his. He was still giving his head a good rub as he looked around the bedroom.

It took him a minute to find what he was looking for. When he had it in hand, he smiled. This was a good one. Heavy. Very cool. He was already having a ton of fun and the next part was going to be even better. Everyone would get their money's worth.

Before the man left, he took a napkin from the little tray on the bureau, patted his forehead with it, and put it in his pocket. There must have been something in the wig because he was still itching and sweating. He glanced at the clock. There was no time to mess around anymore. Hitching the case, he let himself out of the room and headed for the elevator.

Not more than five minutes had passed between the time he went into the room and the time he left it. Suzanne was doing the origami of hospital corners on the sheets in 213, so she didn't see him go. It took her fifteen more minutes to get to room 220.

Receiving no answer to her knock, Suzanne opened the door. She called 'housekeeping' until it was clear the room was empty.

There wasn't any luggage. The bed covers were drawn up neatly. Bothered, Suzanne called down to the front desk where her friend was working. She asked if the new guest in 220 had left luggage with her. The woman at the front desk was busy and said no one was expected in that room until three that afternoon. She implied that Suzanne was dumb for not knowing that. Suzanne started to object, but her friend hung up. Sometimes her friend pulled rank and that sucked.

Since she wasn't paid enough to go the extra mile, Suzanne set about her chores. She changed the sheets, cleaned the bathroom, and vacuumed. When she was done with the big stuff, Suzanne swept up the two key cards on the bureau and put them in her pocket. She looked in the brown paper bag that had been left near the TV. Suzanne took out the banana and bagel to keep for lunch before crumpling the bag.

There was nothing in the trashcan in the bedroom, but the can in the bathroom was another matter. For a minute she thought there was a dead animal inside. She picked it up with two fingers, but it was only a wig. A stupid, ugly wig. That explained the weird guy's hair, but it did nothing to explain why he had been in this room. She hoped he wouldn't come back if this was the kind of stuff she was going to have to deal with.

Suzanne took the thing and tossed it in the big garbage bag hanging from the side of her trolley. She closed the door to room 220 and thought no more about the man who had gone into the room, the wig in the trashcan, or anything else. When they paid her to think, she would —if she could remember how.

2

FLIGHT 4236 ON APPROACH TO SAN FRANCISCO

Dawn Berry opened the door to the cockpit just wide enough so she could slip through. She closed it behind her, leaned down, and gave the pilot a kiss on the head before collapsing into the co-pilot's seat.

"Tired?" she asked.

"I'm fine. You?"

"I'll be ready to hop in bed when we get where we're going." She extended one long leg and nudged his knee with the toe of her shoe.

"Sounds good to me." He flipped a switch; he checked the log.

"Well, don't get too excited." Dawn's smile faded.

She turned in the seat, eyes forward, leaving Jimmy Mustafa to chores he could have done with one hand tied behind his back.

It was a beautiful day: the sky was clear and blue, the clouds fluffy. There wouldn't even be a shudder when the plane started its descent into San Francisco. Forty-five minutes later they would be fueled and on their way to L.A. After that, she and Jimmy were free for four days before they had to pick up the

German charter. That one was going to be tough. A year ago, she had serviced a rock band that booked that route. Not only were they a disgusting group of human beings, but they were also cheap.

Dawn closed her eyes, leaned her head back, and smiled. It didn't matter if she had some annoying flights. This gig with Platinum Wings had set her up for life: she'd made some serious money, traveled, and enjoyed more adventures than she could count. Wild times. Dawn opened her eyes and swiveled her head. She started to speak, thinking to share all this with Jimmy, but he was not looking happy.

"Anything wrong?" she asked.

"No."

Dawn took a deep breath. He could be such a child. She was beginning to think she'd made a huge mistake hooking up with him. Jimmy made a great first impression: smooth talker, quick on his feet, tall, dark, and handsome. She knew he wasn't exactly divorced, but that was fine with her. What wasn't fine was the fact that Jimmy's ex popped into his brain at the weirdest times. When that happened it sent him on a rant that ruined everything, including a romp between the sheets. There were the occasional temper tantrums too. Those were tedious, sometimes scary, but mostly just stupid. Not that Dawn thought he would hurt her, but he had broken a lamp and punched a hole in the wall in the hotel in Germany. It took some fast talking to convince the management that it had been an accident. They were dark folk, those Germans. Good for business, but hard nuts to crack. As for Jimmy, he was proving to just be a nut. Still, he had introduced her to the right people, the kind who threw money at her and asked little in return.

"What are you looking at?" he snapped.

"Nothing," Dawn said, surprised to find she had been staring at him.

"Thirty-seven minutes," he said.

"Then I guess it's time to get back to work. See you on the ground." She started to get up, but he clamped a hand on her arm.

"We're okay, right? I mean everything is in order. Right? I want this all to go like clockwork when we land in L. A."

"For God's sake." Dawn pulled her arm away and stood up. "Everything is fine. I know what I'm doing. You're the one with the problems. Get it together, because this paranoid act is getting a little boring."

Dawn left the cockpit. Despite Jimmy's snit, this had been one of the easiest flights ever. There were only two passengers, both grateful for her minimal effort and unaware they could ask for the world. She smiled and gently shook the old man awake.

"Time to buckle up, Mr. Murphy."

He woke slowly, blinking, a bit confused, but happy when he finally focused on the beautiful woman speaking so nice to him.

"We're there then, are we?" he said.

"Not quite, but I need you to fasten your seat belt. We'll land in San Francisco to refuel and then on to Los Angeles. Only a little while longer."

"Yes," the old man said. "I'll be glad when it's over."

Dawn gave him a pat. When she moved on, he closed his eyes and fell back asleep. It really didn't matter if he was buckled in. Not really.

The other passenger, a silent, brooding woman who hadn't said more than ten words during the entire flight, was next. Dawn had tried to engage her. The old man had given it his best shot. Jimmy had even greeted her, but lost interest when the woman's eyes didn't light up at the sight of him.

"We're going to be landing in San Francisco soon," Dawn said.

"Thank you," the woman answered.

Dawn didn't linger. The woman took out her phone. She texted:

L.A. two-thirty. Platinum Wings.

She put her phone away, and looked out the window, thinking of nothing except the challenge ahead of her. It was not going to be pretty, but she had made up her mind. It had to be done.

HE GLANCED in his rearview mirror to see if anyone had followed him off the freeway. You never knew who was watching, who had signed on as back-up, who had gone rogue. That was the thrill of it all, the cat and mouse, the cloak and dagger.

But today it was just a straight shot, business as usual. No one followed him off the freeway and onto the auxiliary road that would take him to the airfield. He was a little disappointed that the job was so easy. Then again, he had to get back to the city before three, so it was probably a good thing this contract wasn't more challenging.

He drove past the first building, and the second, and parked near the hangar.

He got out of the car, walked around to the trunk, and opened it. There were only two things inside: his tennis bag and the briefcase. He took the briefcase. He paused before entering the hangar so he wouldn't make the same mistake he had made at the hotel. The maid had flustered him. This time he had to be on his *A*-game.

Make it real.

Make it believable.

He put a smile on his face, went inside, and found hog

heaven. It was like a movie set: big space, big machinery, big plane. There was a ladder laid up against the side of the plane just beyond the wing

"Hey. Anybody home?"

"Yo," came an answer.

A man climbed down the ladder, revealing himself slowly: big boots, big legs, big guy.

"There you are," the man with the briefcase said. "Hey, my man."

"What can I do for you?"

"Are you the one in charge?"

"I am right now. James is going to be back in a minute. Marv's over at the terminal."

"Well, then, I guess I'll be talking to you. I have a favor to ask. My partner is on a plane that's coming in and …."

The man with the briefcase told the man in the coveralls what he wanted to do. *A prank on his partner. A lesson his partner needed to be taught.* The big man started to shake his head, and the man with the briefcase was beginning to sweat. If he didn't pull this off, he would be out a shitload of money not to mention the damage to his pride. There was only one thing left to do.

"Of course, I'd be happy to pay you for your trouble…" he said.

The man picked up a rag and started to wipe his hands. His lips were twitching. His mind was working. His greed was showing.

"What do you have in mind, Mr.…"

"Stuart," he said. "Just call me Stuart."

3

PLATINUM WINGS TERMINAL, LOS ANGELES, 2:17 P.M

"Your uncle has friends in high places, O'Brien. Private jets for an old guy like him? Impressive. "

Finn gave a nominal swing of his head toward his partner, Cori Anderson, but he never took his eyes off the horizon. For the last fifteen minutes, he had been looking for the plane that was bringing his uncle from Ireland. It wasn't due for another ten minutes or so, but he kept watch just the same. Cori huffed. She puffed. Finn tried to ignore her because he was as jumpy as a cat waiting for this reunion, but then Cori took the Lord's name in vain and said:

"O'Brien? Do you know how to make this darn thing work?"

This time Finn looked over his shoulder to see Cori glaring at a fancy machine that offered her ten kinds of coffee, but no direction on how to get the brew into her cup. He abandoned his post, took her mug, and asked:

"What is it you're wanting?"

"Coffee. Black."

She put her hip against the polished granite counter, and crossed her arms. Finn punched one button and then another.

An elegant mechanical burp was followed by a whispery hiss, and then a rush of dark liquid. He handed her the cup.

"Coffee. Black."

"I hate you." Cori took the mug in both hands.

"'Tis a gift."

He gave her a small smile before he went back to his watch. Cori chuckled. The man had a talent for cutting through the clutter, but he was an amateur when it came to being in a snit. Cori left him to his thoughts, picked up a slice of cheese from the buffet, and nibbled on it while she wandered around the lounge of Platinum Wings, California's premier private airline.

While the building itself was a simple box —three walls and one giant glass window that counted as a wall—it was the most elegant place Cori had ever seen. The interior was decked out with deep navy blue carpeting, grey paint on the walls, lush white sofas, wood tables, and pewter lamps with silk shades. Framed photos of the Platinum fleet hung over two sleek desks in a business center. Hot and cold food, cocktails, and coffee, were all free for the taking. There was a marble bathroom off the main room with a full-size tub and shower, white towels, expensive shampoos, and soaps. Behind a door marked private Cori found a stunning bedroom suite.

"You could have an orgy in there," she said as she closed the door. "There's just no accountin' for how the dice fall, is there O'Brien? I mean how come some no-talent folks have enough money for this, and those of us who serve selflessly couldn't scrape up enough in two lifetimes?"

Cori settled herself in a chair just behind Finn. She plucked at the upholstery then looked around hoping to find something interesting that she hadn't already checked out ten times over. When that proved impossible, she did the only thing left to do, she made Finn O'Brien talk.

"So, what's the real scoop on Uncle Hugh?"

“Is it too much to ask for some quiet time, Cori?” Finn said, but she could see a smile on the edge of his lips which meant he wasn’t all that bothered.

"Delightful as all this is, I want to know if my time is being well spent. I mean, I could be back at the office listening to Fowler lecture me about overdue reports...” She ate the last of her cheese. “And just to remind you, last I looked, I was doing you a favor coming out here.”

Finn hung his head and laughed a little. Then he turned around and put his back up against the window.

“I believe the way it went was this: I said I was picking my uncle up, and when you found out he was traveling in style, you said ‘I’m coming with you’. I’m not recalling a choice in the matter, nor that I was begging.”

“Details.”

Cori took a drink of her coffee, closed her eyes briefly and fluttered her lashes. Her eyeshadow was particularly blue today which made her eyes all the brighter when she looked at him again.

“I should have left you at work,” Finn said. “But since you’ll give me no peace about this, what is it you’re wanting to know?”

“Everything.” Cori settled deeper into the chair. “If you had a rich uncle who could afford to fly Platinum Wings, then I think you should have told me a long time ago. So, spill it. What’s the deal with this guy?”

"The man is eighty and some, and according to my mother he was kind, and fun, and handsome as a young man. She has great memories of him even though the last time she saw him she was just a little girl."

"How come they haven't seen each other if he was such a good guy?"

"Ah, it’s an Irish tale to break your heart,” Finn teased.

“Truth be told, he had the misfortune of falling in love with a Protestant girl."

"Well, there's an annoying pimple on your uncle’s butt," Cori drawled.

"It was the times. Uncle Hugh's bride would not promise to raise the children Catholic, so his parents banished him. It was hard on ma's heart," Finn said, not even trying to explain the inexplicable.

"But she's happy that he's coming now. No hard feelings, right?"

"You would think the pope was coming on that plane. But on the off chance that he has horns and a tail, she wanted me to pick him up." Finn turned back to the window. "That and she's cleaning the house again."

Cori got up and joined him for the watch. Now she was the one leaning on the plate glass, her shoulder up against it.

"So, where's the Protestant wife?"

"Dead, she is. No children, so there never was any reason for the estrangement. He lived in Cork, and we stayed in our village 'till my da moved us."

"Do you know what he looks like?" Cori asked.

"No, but unless this plane is full of eighty-year-old men I shouldn't have a problem recognizing him," Finn said.

"I guess we'll know soon enough if you can pick him out of the crowd."

Cori raised her mug. Finn turned his head and then full-on faced the window. In the distance the plane came into view, glistening like a silver ingot under the bright sun, seeming to float in the outrageously blue sky. Finn took two steps to the right, Cori stood upright, tensing as she saw the wings dip. Finn did the same, but a moment later it leveled out. The door to the office opened, and the receptionist joined them, clipboard in hand. She smiled and said:

"Sorry it's a little late. Something held it up in San Francisco."

"Not by much," Finn said.

Cori put her mug on the counter, and by the time she joined Finn again the plane had touched down. It rushed forward only to slow before taxing lazily toward the private terminal. It was a thing of beauty with its sleek design and Platinum's blue and silver logo emblazoned on the tail. Five windows pocked the side of the metal skin, but they were tinted so Finn couldn't see if anyone was looking out. He sidestepped again, following along as the plane rolled to a stop.

"May I go out to greet my uncle?" Finn asked the woman with the clipboard. She shook her head.

"Regulations. You'll have to stay here."

Finn stayed put, though it was difficult because he suddenly found himself excited. Perhaps his mother's anticipation had rubbed off on him, perhaps he was nervous being in this rarified space, or maybe he suddenly realized how much he missed Ireland now that a piece of it was coming to his doorstep.

The ground crew appeared, three in all. Two pushed a portable stairway toward the plane while a third drove a luggage dolly under the nose and around the backside. At the same time, the door of the plane opened, and a beautiful young woman in a white shirt, short grey jacket, and blue pencil skirt appeared. Her blonde hair was pulled back in a ponytail. Her legs were long and her posture impeccable. One of the crew waved at her as they secured the stairway. She smiled brilliantly and then turned that smile on the people inside the plane. She held out one graceful hand and nodded, inviting the passengers to disembark.

"There he is," Finn called. "'Tis Uncle Hugh."

Finn stepped back and back until he was behind Cori. He put a hand on her shoulder and bent to eye level as he pointed at a pale-as-parchment old man with rosy, red cheeks. Hugh Murphy wore spectacles and a hat. He leaned upon a cane. Finn chuckled. He had expected a raging Irish bullfighting the tides of time, but Uncle Hugh looked like a parish priest.

The stewardess took Hugh's arm. Her lips were moving, reassuring him no doubt as she guided his hand to the safety railing. He shuffled on, careful of every step. Finn was watching to make sure all would be well, when his attention was caught by someone standing behind Hugh. The stewardess moved just enough for Finn to catch a glimpse of a tall woman. Though he only saw a flash of burnished hair, a quick peek at eyes that he knew to be green, his heart skipped a beat. He didn't see her lips, but if he had there was no doubt her smile would not have changed with age.

"Maura? Maura Shaughn. . ."

Finn let go of Cori and headed to the door, ignoring the warning to wait until the passengers had deplaned. Cori laughed. Knowing there was no stopping her partner, she called out:

"Who in the heck is Mau—"

Before Cori finished her sentence, before the receptionist could stop Finn from putting his hands on the glass door, and before he could push it open, the world as they knew it ended in a fireball of brilliant orange and gold.

4

The glass wall imploded, spewing shards into every corner of the room with no mind if they tore through flesh or furniture. The sound was instantly deafening, leaving those who survived in a profound, dense, suspended silence. After a time that couldn't be measured, that silence was sliced into irregular pieces by the shriek of alarms, the moans of people inside the terminal, and the raised voices of those outside. There was no way to tell how long it took, but eventually, the distant wails of sirens were added to the mix.

Finn was thrown back, landing hard on his hip as he crumpled to the ground. Dazed, he raised his head and peered through the cloud of dust and dirt, choking on the smoke that filled the room, gagging on the smell of fuel. The white-hot core of the explosion had seared one side of his face, and the flying debris had pocked it leaving his skin smeared with blood. He blinked and wagged his head. The plane came into view, distorted through the haze of dust and wreckage.

The center of the beautiful silver aircraft was gone, disappeared into a deep black hole. Nothing moved save for the flames licking at the metal. The pretty stewardess was gone.

Uncle Hugh was gone. Maura Shaughnessy — if indeed that's who Finn had glimpsed — was no more. He shook his head once, and then again to keep himself from falling fully to the floor. It seemed no use. He was injured, he was stunned, but then there was another flash, a bang of understanding inside his head.

"Cori," he muttered. Finn raised his voice. "Cori!"

Frantically he turned this way and that, until he finally saw her lying on her stomach, unmoving, pushed up against the fancy sofa like a forgotten doll. Pulling his weight forward on his elbows, leaving a trail of blood as he went, Finn kept low in an army crawl just in case there was more to come. Throwing one arm over his partner, he protected her with his body.

"Cori," he said again as he pushed back her hair. For a second, he thought she was dead, and then she gasped. She coughed. She moaned. She bolted upright and barked.

"I'm okay. I'm okay."

"Don't move. Stay put," he said.

Finn pulled at her neck scarf and wrapped it around the wound at her temple. When that was secure, he ran his hands over her, top to bottom. Her arm was askew, but she only cried out when he touched her leg. The blood pooling around her seemed to come from her head, but he couldn't be sure. Finn prayed he wouldn't find anything worse once she was turned over, but that was not for him to do.

"Don't move, Cori," he said. "Please, for once, do as I say. Help is coming."

She didn't fight him as he felt for her pulse. It was strong, so Finn looked toward the landing strip again. Rescue vehicles were moments away. He squeezed Cori's shoulder, and let her be as he got to his feet, unsteady, stumbling

The metal that had framed the double doors was twisted

into a grotesque shape. The picture window was all but gone. Beyond that, the plane burned under a beautiful, bright sky.

Suddenly aware that someone was crying, Finn's eyes went around the room. He found the source of the sound in the corner near the door to the reception room. The girl who had moments ago admonished him not to leave the waiting area was sitting on the floor, her back up against the wall, sobbing. Her arms were limp by her side, her eyes were closed. Pushing aside a table, Finn stumbled toward her and hunkered down by her side. She opened her eyes when he touched her shoulder. She shed no tears and yet she sobbed and sobbed, gulping air that was filled with the same dust and ash that made her hair and skin grey.

The top buttons had torn off her shirt. She was missing one shoe, but she appeared unhurt. Carefully Finn pulled her head to his shoulder and gave her a pat.

"I have to call someone," she said. "I think I'm supposed to do that."

'They know; everyone knows," Finn said.

When he thought she had calmed enough, he pushed off only to have his leg give out as he tried to stand. In his shock, Finn hadn't noticed that his jeans were ripped and a shard of glass was embedded deep in his thigh. Getting to one knee, he pulled aside the fabric, saw that no bone was exposed and, while there was a great deal of blood, no artery had been severed.

He took off his jacket and threw it aside. Next, he ripped off his shirt, and wound it around his right hand. Setting his jaw, grinding his teeth, Finn grasped the piece of glass and pulled it fast, yanking it out of his leg. His head fell back as he cried out, but his jaw was clenched and only a muted sound of despair could be heard. Tossing aside the glass, he unwound his shirt from his hand and wrapped it around his thigh. It was no tourniquet, but it would do until help arrived. Breathing hard, managing the hot flashes of pain and the frigid throes of shock, Finn set his mind right. He was not crippled, nor was he near death, so the pain would have to wait.

Favoring his good leg, Finn gave a hand to the receptionist. She grasped it with both of hers. Finn raised her up, and pointed her toward the front of the building. He had no idea if that's where safety lay, but it was as good a guess as he could make. When she was gone, he limped back to Cori, wiping blood from his eyes. He got to his knees, and grasped her hand as he fell back on his heels. It had taken everything he had left to get to her side, so it was just as well that she didn't respond to his touch. He had nothing more to give, no idea what to do, and this – the room, the plane, the destruction – was not a thing he wanted her to see. He sat with her, watching the last of the dust and debris dance in the sunlight that came through the shattered window.

Workers from nearby hangars had gathered, standing, pointing, unsure of how to help. The sirens that had been nothing but sound in the distance were screeching now as the rescue vehicles arrived in full force. What had seemed like hours of isolation were really only minutes. First responders poured out of the trucks.

The fire had almost burned itself out by the time they put foam on it, but they covered the hot metal for good measure. Two men entered the plane itself, looking for survivors. Finn watched with little curiosity. He knew they might find someone alive, but it wouldn't be his uncle, the stewardess, or the red-haired woman who stood behind Hugh.

"Hey. Buddy. Hey!"

A shiver ran through Finn. He looked at the hand on his shoulder and then up at a young man's face; so young he looked fresh out of high school. Finn smiled. He sighed. The man gripped Finn's shoulder tighter.

"Can you hear me? I need you to move away, so I can get a good look at you. Can you do that?"

Finn nodded. Given the commotion outside, it was a surprise when help came to him. He rolled onto his hip, giving the young man access to his partner.

"Her first," he said, indicating Cori.

To his credit, the young man did as he was told. Finn watched, admiring the speed of his ministrations: the collar on Cori's neck, vitals recorded. A woman came to help lift Cori onto the gurney. Finn winced when the woman pulled up and locked the thing into place. She covered Cori with a light blanket, and wheeled her away. It took him a minute to realize that the man was touching his face. Finn didn't know when it had happened, but the wound in his leg had been bandaged and a mylar blanket had been put over his shoulders. The young paramedic was asking if Finn could get up, if he could walk.

Finn O'Brien wanted to tell him that he couldn't do either of those things just yet. He was praying for an uncle he had never met, a young woman whose last act on this earth had been to offer a helping hand to an old man, and a special prayer for the little girl he had loved when he was a young boy. The last bit he edited. Finn prayed that the woman he had seen wasn't Maura, and if it had been he asked God to rest her soul. His own soul, on the other hand, would always be restless after this day, and there was nothing God could do about that.

5

Dennis Cain parked his vintage Aston Martin in one of three spots nearest the elevator. Having access to these spaces meant that he, Dennis Cain, was damn important, but that wouldn't last long if this meeting didn't go well. Looking into the rearview mirror to adjust his tie, Dennis saw a young man slowing to eye the car. The man's admiration was heartfelt but the daydream of owning such a thing was fleeting, so he moved on quickly. What few people knew, was that Dennis wouldn't have this fine car either if it hadn't been a family legacy left by his grandfather. In fact, if it weren't for his father and his father before him, Dennis would not be the man he was today. Those men had built Wolfhound Distillery; Dennis was the one they entrusted with its future.

There were older Irish distilleries, but none finer than Wolfhound. Generations lived their lifetimes proudly making the brew that touched the lips of prime ministers and presidents.

Some said distilling the whiskey was a religion for the Cain family. Dennis did not disagree, but he understood that each family member worshipped at the altar differently. Dennis loved the institution and the history. He had devoted himself to keeping Wolfhound exactly as it had been for generations, but times and fortunes had changed. When he sold Wolfhound to Hammet Industries, many were unhappy, some were disgusted. Dennis believed he had grasped a helping hand, been given a leg up, and that the deal would stay in place only until Wolfhound could stand on its own again. But good intentions and his long thought-out plan for redemption had gone awry. The smooth path he had foreseen was now rocky and treacherous.

The gentleman's agreement between the conglomerate and the small distillery stated that Wolfhound would use the mother company's assets while retaining the distillery's unique personality. The reality was that Wolfhound's heritage was subordinate to the power of Hammet. The encroachment into decision-making had been slow and steady until, finally, Wolfhound had begun to dance to every tune Hammet played. Dennis's brother, Brian, had said it would come to this. Now he was being proved right. That alone made Dennis Cain sick at heart.

Drawing a hand over his eyes, Dennis knew there was no putting off the inevitable. He got out of the car, and put on his jacket. His suit was bespoke. Fine clothing, like fine whiskey, was a passion. He had one other passion, but that was personal and would remain so until Wolfhound's future was secure. No one could make Dennis change his mind in that regard.

Dennis walked the few steps to the elevator and waited less than a minute for it to arrive. The ride to the thirtieth floor was smooth. He felt strangely calm and ready for this meeting, yet when the doors opened Dennis hesitated. A hole had opened up in the pit of his stomach. In that minute of hesitation, the doors of the elevator started to close. Dennis put his hand out. The heavy metal punched his wrist. Instead of crushing the bone, the doors retreated. Dennis shook his head. Lesson learned. Sometimes it was the timing of the punch that mattered.

Squaring his shoulders, Dennis stepped out of the elevator and into the rarified world of Hammet Industries' corporate offices. He walked down the wide, carpeted hall toward the marble reception desk. The woman behind it, not quite young but definitely not old, smiled. He said:

"How are you, Pamela?"

"Good, Mr. Cain. Thanks for asking." She raised a hand to direct him even though he knew the way quite well. "They're expecting you."

"He's already here then?"

She nodded. The news didn't surprise Dennis. He could never beat his brother except in one thing: he, Dennis, had been named CEO of Wolfhound Distillery and Brian CFO.

Behind him, the receptionist watched him walk away. Dennis Cain was one of the most handsome men she had ever seen. There was something about the way he moved, the way he looked at a girl, sexy and warm without coming on. She could imagine him in the countryside, dressed in a kilt— except that was what men wore in Scotland. She wondered what a man like Dennis Cain wore in Ireland? If she had her way, he wouldn't wear a damn thing no matter what country he was in.

Her phone rang and Pamela went back to work, amused by her silly thoughts. She should actually be feeling sorry for the man. Everyone knew what was going on, and she thought it was sad. Still, sad stuff happened every day and this was none of her concern. She liked being one of the worker bees. Let Dennis Cain and his brother duke it out with Harry Lauder. One of them would lose big time, and she doubted it would be Harry. No matter what happened, she would still collect a paycheck, and the Cain brothers and Harry would all be fine.

Rich people always were, even when they failed.

6

Dennis nodded to the executive assistants, secretaries, and the secretaries' assistants. All of them had offices that rivaled Wolfhound's, but that was befitting American business. Everything was bigger and seemingly better. Brian thought optics a waste of money; Dennis thought it part of the marketing mix. Brian had won that fight and the offices in Cork remained modest. Now it seemed a silly disagreement, but that's how life was. Everything was irrelevant when death appeared inevitable.

Mrs. Farrow's office was at the end of the hall. She had neither secretary nor assistant because, as Harry's right hand, all of the company's resources were at her disposal. Mrs. Farrow saw him, rose, pivoted, and opened Harry's door. She moved aside to let Dennis pass.

"Here he is," Harry said, coming around his desk and meeting Dennis at a mark the older man had calculated. They shook hands. They smiled.

"Good to see you, Harry. " Dennis's eyes went to the bank of windows where his brother stood. "And Brian. You beat me here. I would have picked you up."

"No need for you to go out of your way."

Brian gave Dennis the smile of a disciplined man, but then he always played things close to the vest. Ex-Irish Army Ranger, he could be counted on to be tough, strong, and stand his ground. That was exactly why Dennis's half-brother was not given charge of the company. Their shared father understood the need for heart and soul, not just discipline and strategy.

"Well, shall we—" Harry began only to be cut off by a low ring from the phone on his desk. "Excuse me a moment, will you?"

"Of course."

Dennis knew Mrs. Farrow would never put a call through if it wasn't critical, so he joined Brian while they waited for Harry to finish.

"Did you have a good flight?" Dennis asked.

"I did." Brian's heavy accent underscored the many differences between them.

Brian was the product of their father's second marriage, entered into as soon as the ink was dry on the divorce papers from Dennis's mother. American to the core, she had taken Dennis to California— a land of perpetual sunshine, great space, and a happy lethargy. California never suited Dennis though his mother flourished in Los Angeles.

Dennis blossomed when he spent summers in Cork with his father's family. Cork, Wolfhound, and tradition were not the tedious things his mother thought them to be. His father gave him all the attention he needed, his stepmother was kind enough, and Brian was what Brian would always be: insular, serious, unknowable, but he was still Dennis's brother.

"I wanted to have a few minutes alone before this meeting." Dennis lowered his voice.

"There's nothing new to tell. We're still in arrears, but I've managed to move a few things around. I've given the go-ahead to purchase the casks we need and to replace the bottling line."

Dennis turned on his brother, his back fully to Harry.

"You gave the go-ahead to replace the line? Are you crazy?"

"'Twas necessary. The old line is falling apart. We're losing too much money to breakdowns and inefficiencies," Brian said. "I had to deal with this when father passed and we were fine because I had managed. We were fine until five years ago when you decided I couldn't—"

"That was then. What's done is done," Dennis said. "And where is the money coming from to pay for this? And what about approvals? Hammet's terms are specific: we pass major expenditures by Harry—"

"I've read the contracts," Brian said. "We are to detail all expenditures, not go crawling for permissions. I've managed the money. We'll have it. That's all you need to know."

"And I told you to wait for my go-ahead. I have a plan—"

"Gentlemen, I'm sorry," Harry said. "My time is yours now."

The brothers turned away from the window, but not without a last warning from Dennis.

"Don't forget that I'm still the last word where the company is concerned."

With that Dennis settled himself on the sofa while Harry took the wing chair across from him. Brian lingered, looking at his half-brother, wondering what he could possibly have planned that would save Wolfhound. He didn't dislike Dennis; he just didn't respect him as a leader. The roles should have been reversed, but the decision of who would run the company had been made in secret, revealed only when their father died. Still, it wasn't all bad. Dennis lived in the states now leaving Brian to run things at the distillery. Dennis was fooling himself if he thought he was in charge

"Brian? Join us."

Harry indicated the long sofa; the gesture was a command, not an invitation. Brian took one last look out of the wall of windows. Straight on he could see the first five letters of the Hollywood sign, open space, and clear skies. Through the other, he looked into neighboring high rises where men and women labored in sad and predictable ways. Their heads were down, their lips were moving, buttons were being pushed on phones, keys pressed on computer keyboards. More than one looked off into a distance. Few, Brian was sure, took pride in their work; fewer still knew what they were working for.

Brian looked back at Harry. That man knew what he was working for. Greater return on investment. A double truck obituary in the Wall Street Journal. Money. Wealth. Both were worth the fight. And Dennis? He knew what he was working for too. He labored for the ghosts of his father and grandfather. No one knew what had pleased those two in life, so Dennis' efforts were an exercise in futility.

"Brian?" Dennis said, unable to hide his annoyance.

"Sorry. Yes."

Brian sat on the sofa with Dennis, relaxed, his arms draped over the back while Dennis sat on the edge of the cushions. He looked too eager.

"So, what's on your mind gentlemen?" Harry said and Brian almost laughed aloud.

They all shared the same balance sheet. There were no surprises here. The only thing Brian was unsure of was Harry's price to let them go. Still the game had to be played. At least the brothers had agreed that they would save Wolfhound at any cost —all costs. They were united on that front. Brian, though, was surprised at the strategy Dennis brought to the battle.

"Harry," Dennis said. "We've come begging."

7

Brian's spine stiffened and his eyes slid toward his brother, disgusted by what he heard, but that was as far as he engaged with his brother. Dennis spoke only to Harry.

"If you shutter Wolfhound, you'll be throwing entire families out of work. There's no similar situation to absorb them in all of Ireland. There would be no protection for our heritage," he said. "Here's what I'm thinking. If we discontinue Wolfhound 24 and get back to our premium products, we can change the bottom line in a year."

"I don't see it, Dennis."

"I'm just asking for three million to put into a new marketing campaign that will be true to our brand. I want to partner with —"

"Dennis." The slight movement of Harry's fingers cut him off. "Another cash infusion will be a tough sell to the board. You know that."

Harry's eyes went to Brian.

"Do you think Wolfhound 24 is a lost cause, Brian?"

"Wolfhound 24 is garbage," Brian said. "That doesn't mean

there isn't a market for it. I've been known to drink my fill of garbage."

Harry laughed. He liked Brian, just in a different way than he liked Dennis.

"And if I gave Wolfhound another three million and let you spend it as you wish, do you think it would change the bottom line?"

Dennis looked at his brother. Brian didn't look back, but there was no doubt he was speaking to Dennis.

"It might," Brian said. "Ten would be better."

"Brian isn't the one to address this, Harry. I am," Dennis said. "I've consulted with a

firm that specializes in such communications. We'll use GEO fencing and target our customers in their clubs and their mansions. I am not averse to using digital advertising, but it must be tethered to traditional means. Our influencers are politicians, old monied families, not movie stars."

Harry looked at Brian once more. The man was enjoying pitting the brothers against one another. He would do the same with his own team because that was how business worked. You had to find out who had the mettle and who had the dreams.

"Fashions have changed," Brian said. "Wine and clear spirits have cut into our market share. Heritage is not a selling point. We could do better with Wolfhound 24 and a celebrity endorsement."

Dennis scoffed, but Harry was engaged.

"Our folks approached Liam Neeson," Harry said. "He was interested, but Dennis said no. Now Neeson is going with Bold Barrel, so that window is closed."

"Bold Barrel is a start-up distillery," Dennis scoffed. "Their brew is a joke. Even Wolfhound 24 beats them."

"The U.S. is the market you need to own, and here we like celebrities." Harry's brow beetled, but his impatience with the conversation lasted seconds. It did no one any good to be annoyed. "The market is fragmented and complicated, Dennis. It moves quickly what with one thing going viral, then another. Wolfhound can't be heard because you refuse to compromise on how your message is delivered."

"We have a website and social media accounts," Dennis said.

"And they are boring. Wolfhound is the dowager countess looking down her nose at the young royals. The dowager will die, and the young royals will keep on dancing and drinking someone else's product. So, here's what I'll do. Three million to market Wolfhound 24 as the bad boy brew, the party liquor. You can still sell the good stuff to people who care, but the money goes into Wolfhound 24."

Harry's expression indicated that negotiations were over, but he had not delivered the final blow.

"If that doesn't work then we sell to Kentucky Spirits, or shut you down and take a loss. Per our agreement, the recipe remains with you, but the name remains with us."

"Harry, you can't. Kentucky Spirits is bargain basement—" Dennis said.

Brian was on his feet, towering over his brother.

"You sold the name, Dennis?"

It was the first time Harry had seen anything akin to emotion from Brian Cain. The man recognized his mistake in the next moment, and sat back down. Dennis ignored him, and his outrage.

"You promised to protect the name in case anything went wrong, Harry," Dennis said. "Well, it's gone wrong. Selling the name to Kentucky Spirits breaks that promise."

"I've done nothing to undermine the name or reputation of Wolfhound. Conversely, you've done nothing to expand the line and make our acquisition pay off. Cut production costs, agree to get behind Wolfhound 24, and we're good, Dennis."

"We've won gold medals precisely because we don't cut corners. We've...we've..."

Dennis's voice trailed away. His shoulders sagged. Harry's expression didn't change.

"I won't change your mind will I, Harry?"

"No, Dennis," Harry said. "On this side of The Pond, as they say, we're all in agreement. We can give Wolfhound another year to turn things around."

"That's a hundred years thrown away with the snap of corporate fingers," Dennis mumbled.

"It was the snap of those fingers that pulled your ass out of the fire a few years ago, Dennis. We're not a good fit, but we tried hard," Harry said.

Dennis sat back. He bounced a fist against his lips, thinking, trying not to scream. He looked over Harry's shoulder, as if there was some answer written on the wall. Harry knew the power of silence, so he waited for Dennis to fold. Before he could, Brian spoke up.

"What if I could buy back, Wolfhound?" Brian asked.

Harry smiled. He knew every penny in Wolfhound's coffers, but he also knew Brian was a fighter and resourceful. Harry was also aware that the brother's relationship was strained which meant Brian might be getting ready to oust Dennis. That, Harry decided, wouldn't be a heavy lift.

"Harry, I think I should have a word with Brian," Dennis said, but Harry talked past him.

"Yes, if you could meet our price," the older man said.

"Would the price reflect your understanding of what we're facing? No upsell? You take what we can afford," Brian said.

"Within reason, given Kentucky Spirit's offer," he said. "It's clear you're going out on a limb, Brian, but Dennis is still the CEO. Work this out between you, but remember that the family doesn't have the resources — and now I'm also talking marketing talent, not just money— to get through a year. It's a huge personal risk. Admiration on my part is one thing, but I can't make this a fire sale."

"I understand," Dennis said. "Brian?"

"Yes. It's doable."

Dennis licked his lips. They had suddenly gone dry. He looked at his brother, but Brian did not engage. There was nothing for Dennis to do but play along.

"We'll have a proposal for you, Harry," Dennis said. "Wolfhound's legacy is mine to protect."

"And Hammet's fiscal health is mine."

The meeting was over. The three men stood at the same time. Harry put his hand on Dennis's shoulder, but spoke to both brothers.

"We gave it a good run. If you two can't pull this out of the fire, I know you'll build something better. You're still young."

"There is nothing better for us," Dennis said.

Harry had no idea the weight that history put on a man's shoulders. Dennis, on the other hand, would sacrifice his soul to make sure Wolfhound survived. And Brian? Dennis had thought his brother a good soldier, but today he realized that he was laying the groundwork for a coup. That would be a fight for another day.

"Talk to the board," Dennis said. "Brian and I will—"

A discreet knock interrupted him. All eyes went to Mrs. Farrow who hovered behind the half-open door. When she had her boss's attention, she summoned him with a slight tilt of her chin.

"I'll be with you in a moment, Mrs. Farrow," he said. "We're almost done here."

"I need to speak to you now, Mr. Lauder."

Mrs. Farrow's voice was tempered as always but when her eyes subtly cut to the brothers, Harry noticed. When she fell back, drawing Harry into the outer office, Dennis turned on Brian.

"Don't ever do that. Don't ever make an offer like that without talking to me. You don't buy the company back. We do. I do. Not you." Dennis paced, pivoted, and then did it again. "I had a plan, and now you've put us on record matching price to Kentucky's offer."

"And your plan was to beg for what is rightfully ours?"

"If I recall, the sale was a decision we both made," Dennis said.

"Then you've a faulty memory, brother," Brian said. "It was a done deal before you even mentioned it to me. Your request was for a rubber stamp, not a good-faith discussion of what should be done."

Dennis put his hands to his head and drew them through his hair.

"What was father thinking when he put us in this position? It should have been you or me. Both of us trying to run the business has never worked."

"It's a good thing we don't live under one another's feet," Brian said.

"That's going to change," Dennis said. "I'll be back in Ireland as soon as this shakes out, and you know what? I'm not leaving, so maybe you better rethink how you're going to work at Wolfhound. You're going—"

"Dennis? Brian?"

Harry had returned a changed man: his jaw was tight, his mouth twitched, he was pale and somber.

"Harry?"

Dennis started for him, but Harry kept him at bay, gesturing toward the sofa.

"Sit." When Dennis didn't, Harry raised his voice. "Sit down. Both of you."

Surprised by his tone, they did as they were told. Mrs. Farrow was back, waiting to be needed. Harry composed himself. He clasped his hands together and then, uncomfortable standing, sat on the arm of the chair he had so recently occupied.

"Mrs. Farrow has brought some news," he said. "There's been an accident. The plane you chartered? There was an explosion, a fire. I'm so sorry."

Harry pulled his lips together. One of his shoulders rose and fell. He had no words.

"There must be some mistake. I mean that plane wasn't supposed to..." Dennis looked at his watch. He blinked as if he couldn't quite see the numbers. It was later than he thought. He stood up. Harry did too, but only long enough to put Dennis back down.

"Mrs. Farrow has confirmed it. There might have been a fuel leak, but no one knows yet. The pilot is in serious condition. A stewardess died."

"Only the stewardess?" Brian asked.

"Neither of the passengers made it either. I am so very sorry."

Dennis put his face in his hands; Brian who dropped his own onto his brother's shoulder. A tremor ran through Dennis. He raised his head, sat up, and swiveled first toward Brian and then back to Harry.

"Passengers?"

"Your team from Cork," Harry answered. "They are both gone. That has been confirmed."

"There was no team," Dennis said. "I mean, yes, I was expecting someone but ..." He swiveled toward his brother. "Brian? Did you have someone coming?"

"If there's anything we can do..."

Harry kept talking, distracted, trying to find his footing in this awkward, sad situation. Brian shook his head. It was a gesture Dennis couldn't interpret. Was it denial of what had happened? Surprise that there were two people from Wolfhound on the plane? Or was it something else? A warning to stay silent, perhaps.

Numb, Dennis got up and walked to the bank of windows. He looked out at the heart of the big city. He felt alone, cold, and hopeless even though, deep inside, he knew he shouldn't be feeling any of those things. His brother, what was left of his family, was here with him.

8

Cori held her hair back. Finn dutifully eyed the staples closing the wound on her temple.

"'Tisn't as bad as I would have expected. There will hardly be a scar," he said.

"Easy for you to say, bucko." She let her hair fall over her brow again.

Finn smiled, though it wasn't his best effort. In truth, he didn't find the split in her head as disturbing as the other damage his partner had suffered: bruising that blossomed from the top of her head to the rise of her cheek, her left eye swollen shut and so purple it was almost black. The cut on the edge of her lip was crusting over with a scab that made it painful for her to smile. Her leg was encased in a soft cast, and her left arm was bandaged from wrist to elbow.

"I wouldn't let them cut my hair," she said, oblivious to Finn's scrutiny. "I told that baby-faced doctor he better just slow his roll when he got out those sheers. I'd rather bleed to death than have a bald spot."

"Sure, you must have put the fear of God in him," Finn said. "He did a fine job. Not a hair out of place. And the leg?"

"Just a precaution." Cori raised up a bit so she could look down on it. She winced with the effort. "The cast is to keep the swelling down. It will be off in a day or two. But this..." Cori touched her bruised face gingerly. "I'm gonna be a hot mess for a month of Sundays. What about you? I mean besides the face. You look like someone forgot you in the fryer."

"I should be happy I've no hair, otherwise I would have lost half of it in the heat." He shrugged and laughed. "But I'm not too bad. A shard in the leg."

He stood back so Cori could see.

"Ruined your favorite jeans. That's a bummer."

And my hands." Finn held them up. "It looks like I took a razor blade to them."

Cori took hold of them. Her lips pulled tight as she pretended to examine the damage. She found it as hard to look at him as he did at her. They were both exhausted, Finn's heart was broken, and Cori's broke for him. They both knew it could have been worse. One of them could be dead leaving the other to pick up the pieces.

"It's all right now, Cori. We're here. All this will heal."

He pressed her hands tight. She gave a curt nod and let him go. Her lashes lowered and then she pushed her chin up.

"It would take more than this to get us to the cemetery," she said. "Just not our time, O'Brien."

"As you say."

Cori's head fell back on the pillow. Sleep was coming on, but she fought it.

"I'm so sorry about your uncle," she mumbled. "How's your mom doing?"

"She's as good as can be expected," Finn said. "She is happy we've not been hurt worse. I think that would have killed her for sure."

"Did anybody else make it out?" Cori asked.

"The man collecting the luggage was behind the plane, so he's fine. The two with the stairway were already at a safe distance," Finn said. "The door to the cockpit was closed when the damn thing went up, so the pilot fared pretty well. He's here in the hospital."

"Have you talked to him?" Cori asked.

"I'd like to hear something of Hugh's time on the plane, but I won't disturb him now. 'Tis strange being on this end of things, knowing my family will have to wait for an investigation instead of me being the one investigating."

Finn took a breath, and let his gaze roam over her face.

"I'm sorry, Cori. I am. You shouldn't have been there."

Cori waved him off, not wanting to think about what could have been: Amber orphaned, Tucker without a grandma, Finn with a constant burden of guilt, Lapinski with no one to keep him in line. None of this was Finn's fault, and there were no apologies needed. They were friends. They were partners. They were more than any word could describe.

"No caterwauling, or I'm going to put you on the porch," Cori said. "Besides, I've got about five minutes before I'm off to La-La Land. I gotta know. Who is Maura?"

"I can't believe you remember that," Finn said. "Not that it matters. I think it was my imagination playing tricks. Sure, it would be too much of a coincidence to have her on the same plane as Hugh and a double tragedy had she been."

"Okay, but who did you think it was?"

"Maura Shaughnessy," Finn said. "We were terrors from the time we could walk."

"I figured you for terrorizing the village grocer with a gang of boys."

Cori put her fingertips to her swollen eye and pressed down, trying to quell the throbbing. Finn, seeing her pain, fussed over her. He straightened her pillows, talking all the while, hoping to help her get to sleep.

"'Twas the priests I terrorized," Finn said. "The grocer had a long memory and my family had too many mouths to feed to get on his bad side. The priests, on the other hand, were bound by God to forgive my pranks. As for Maura, she could hold her own with any bully, but she was a pretty girl too."

Finn fluffed Cori's pillow.

"Ribbons in her hair."

He smoothed the case.

"She was smart. I thought her a goddess."

Finn's hand rested atop her head, well away from her wound. She turned her eyes upward, but they were dull with the effect of the painkillers.

"Please tell me she had pimples or something," Cori mumbled.

"Skin as pale as the morn. Hair as red as the sunset." Finn's Irish came thick and his voice went softer to soothe her.

“Figures.” Cori sighed. “Maybe you should have married her.”

“I think not.” Finn laughed. “Now go to sleep.”

“Still...” Cori mumbled.

“No,” he said.

America was home now. His family was here. The man who killed his little brother, Alexander, was somewhere. Finding that murderer kept Finn rooted as nothing else could. He mentioned none of those things. Instead, he said:

“Had I not come here I wouldn't be an officer of the law and have a fine partner. I wouldn't be with my family. Besides, Maura was a bossy thing just like you.”

“Only when you need it.” Cori's voice was a whisper, a mumble, a garble.

Finn slid his hand to the pillow, letting it rest there until Cori's breathing deepened. When he thought she wouldn't wake, he put his lips to her brow on the one place that wasn't swollen or bruised. He pulled the thin blanket up over her shoulders, checked her heartbeat on the monitor, and moved quietly away from the bed. He was halfway to the door when Cori rallied with a last word.

"It's nice to be back at Wilshire Division. You tell the captain."

"I will," he said. "Sleep now."

In the hall, Finn checked with the nurses and confirmed that Cori would be discharged the next day. Before he finished, Finn saw Amber, Cori's daughter, coming down the hall. Her step was brisk, her expression tight. Finn went to meet her.

"Where is she?" Amber asked. "How is she?"

"There," Finn cocked his head toward the door. "It looks worse than it is. Nothing broken. There are no internal injuries, but she's bruised badly."

"Okay." Amber nodded. "Okay. I'm sorry I couldn't get here sooner. I was in finals, and it took a while for the message to filter down."

"Don't worry. She's being well cared for."

"Thomas? Does he know?" Amber asked.

"I called him," Finn said. "He'll be here as soon as he can. It's the end of the day. Court is running late."

"Okay, good," she said. "Tucker is with the sitter. Who do I talk to?"

"Right there. The nurses will give all the information you need and her personal things. I've taken possession of her weapon and will manage work." Finn put his hands on Amber's shoulders, dipped his head, and looked her squarely in her eyes. "Are you going to be all right? I can stay with you for a bit."

Amber had been looking past Finn to the room where her mother lay, but now she got a good look at him. Clearly, he was in no shape to help. In fact, she was surprised he was still standing.

"I'm fine, Finn. I'm good," she assured him. "And you need to get home too. Is there going to be someone to help you?"

"'Tisn't that bad, Amber. I'm fine on my own, but thank you for thinking of me."

"Mom would kill me if I didn't. I know we've been through worse, but it's always terrifying when one of you is hurt."

"You're a good woman. Right now, we both need to take care of our families." Finn gave her a pat. "No matter what, you call if you need anything."

Amber smiled, grateful for his concern, but the blood on his jeans and the bandages beneath the tear hadn't escaped her notice. He was not as well as he made out. She put her fingertips to his face.

"Take care," she said.

"Now that you're here, I'll rest easy. Go on. See to your mother, and I will see to mine."

With that, they parted ways. Finn watched while Amber spoke to the nurse. She was given the bag that held Cori's belongings, signed for it, and conversed a bit longer. Knowing Cori was in good hands, Finn went on his way, he just didn't leave the hospital.

9

On the fourth floor, 'Jimmy' Mustafa, Platinum Wings pilot, was sleeping thanks to a morphine drip. He didn't look great, but then who did in a shapeless, washed once-too-often, pea-green, cotton gown? It had been pulled off his shoulder to accommodate the leads to the machine that monitored his heart. His face was swollen, his lips so big they looked like a new appendage. The pilot's arms lay by his side. One leg was in a cast and raised in a sling.

A woman stood beside the bed, and it was clear that she had come quickly when called, taking no time to worry about her appearance. She was attractive, but not beautiful. Her hair was chin-length and dark. She wore a sweatshirt, jeans, and tennis shoes. When she turned her head, she showed Finn a tortured face. Her chin went up, not in welcome but as a prelude to an attack. She left her purse behind as she came toward him, forcing him back as she stepped into the hall.

"Can I help you?" she said.

"I'm sorry," Finn answered. "I was told this is the pilot's room. The pilot from the plane that..."

"Yes, that's him," she said. "If you're here to make trouble for Jimmy, get in line."

"No. No. My uncle was on the plane. Your husband was the last to see him. I thought..." Finn paused to gather his thoughts. "To tell the truth, I don't know what I expected."

The woman pulled up her chin, the aggression was gone, replaced with exhaustion.

"I know the feeling," she said. "I'm sorry. These days being pissed off is my default mode. So, how is your uncle?"

"He didn't make it." Finn looked past her and back again. "My partner was hurt also. She's down one floor."

"Jesus." She took a deep breath. "What a mess."

"That it is," Finn said. "Are you his wife?"

"Unfortunately."

"I was hoping your husband would be well enough to tell me something about my uncle," Finn said. "That was selfish of me. I apologize for intruding. This is difficult for everyone. Is there anything you need? Anything I can help with?"

The woman pulled back as if Finn had slapped her. Her lips curled into a crooked, ugly expression that passed as a smile. The anger was back in her eyes.

"What are you? Some kind of do-gooder? Do you work for this place? Do you work for the charter? Oh, God. Are you an ambulance chaser? Are you trying to make a buck off this?" Suddenly she raged and moved in on Finn. "We don't need shit from anyone. I don't know what you're pulling, but I'm not going to say anything about anything so just leave."

"No, no." Finn pumped his hands, palms down. "Please, missus, I just..."

Finn's voice trailed off. He didn't know what to say because he didn't know what he was doing. He only knew he wanted to do something.

"I'm sorry. This day was a shock. I must not be thinking clearly. I was there. I..." he paused, knowing he sounded the fool. "You're right. I've. No reason to be here. I'm a police officer, and I feel badly that I couldn't do anything to stop what happened. I suppose I want to make right. It can't be done. I should know that."

He turned to leave, but she stopped him.

"Hey. I'm sorry. That was uncalled for. I'm just not used to a man doing something nice for no reason." She stuck out her hand. "I'm Franny Mustafa. Jimmy's going to be fine, and the only reason I'm here is because I am still his 'In Case of Emergency'. I guess he hadn't changed it even though we're divorcing."

"Then it's good of you to come," Finn said.

"Yeah, I'm a saint." Franny laughed sadly. "I don't mean to be such a bitch. I am glad he's going to be okay. We've got three kids. They still need their father."

"Children give their parents strength. He'll be well for them," Finn said.

"Boy, you are a glass-half-full kind of guy," she chortled. "But my kids probably would be better off without him. Jimmy lives for Jimmy, and no matter how he screws up he comes out smelling like a rose. That's some role model."

She gave a little shrug. Finn hooked his thumbs in the pockets of his jeans.

"You'll probably be able to talk to him in a few days," Franny said. "But don't hold your breath. Jimmy isn't what I would call compassionate. He probably never said boo to your uncle."

She turned away and started to walk slowly down the hall, making no objection when Finn followed. They dodged a food cart. In one of the rooms, someone moaned. In another, someone laughed. Franny crossed her arms, rubbing them as if she was cold, speaking quietly to Finn as she put one foot in front of the other.

"So, you're a cop. Were you really at the airport for your uncle or for Jimmy?"

"No, as I said, for my uncle."

"I know what you said, but I've heard so many lies when it comes to Jimmy that I'm not sure what to believe. He's not the most upstanding citizen."

"I have nothing to do with this investigation, or any other." Finn waited a beat. "Do you think he was doing something illegal?"

"I honestly don't know. He's been cheating on me since the day we got married. He got fired from his job at Ace Charters for a stupid stunt. He never told me why he left the one after that. I just found out that he's got a bank account I didn't know anything about. He was always nickel and diming me. I suppose he could have squirreled it away from his salary, but I doubt it."

"I supposed you'll be doing some talking when he wakes, then," Finn said.

"Only to tell him that I know he's got it. If he misses one alimony payment, I'll put a forensic accountant on him so fast his head will spin."

She did a slow pivot. Finn did the same. They stood side by side as tired, hurt people do when there is nowhere for them to go. Finally, she looked straight at Finn.

"The divorce will be final in a few weeks, I'm exhausted, I need this like a hole in the head, but I'm not a monster. I'll help him until he gets on his feet because there is no one else." She laughed a little. "I should say no one else that I know of. If there is, she's probably twenty-two and wondering why he hasn't called her yet. I doubt a little girl is going to want to play nurse unless she's wearing a white garter belt, stockings, and nothing else."

There wasn't much to say to that. Finn dug in his pocket and pulled out a card. Both were aware that it was crumpled and dirty; both knew it hadn't been when he left his house that morning.

"If there is anything I can do," he said.

She sighed deeply when she took it. She said:

"Got another one?"

He gave her another. She went to the nurse's station and asked for a pen. When she was done, she handed the card back to him.

That's my number. If you want to check in, maybe he will remember something about your uncle. Don't wait too long, though, 'cause I'm throwing him out as soon as he can stand up."

"I appreciate it." Finn held up the card.

"Take care."

Franny Mustafa went back into her husband's room. Finn followed slowly. He stood in the hall, watching as she picked up her purse, looked at her husband, and left without a kiss or a touch. When she was gone, he went to the open door. He remembered when he slept like that, drugged and oblivious after he'd been beaten by his fellow officers. There were more than one of his brothers in blue who hoped Finn would not wake up considering he had killed one of their own. That it was in self-defense didn't matter. On that score, the pilot was lucky. The wife may not want him around, but she didn't wish him dead.

Finn put a hand to his face. Suddenly the day crashed in on him with full force. He felt as if he couldn't walk another step much less make it home. Talking to the pilot's wife exacerbated his exhaustion. It took energy to harbor such feelings as she did — love and hate, kindness and the desire to inflict pain. No human ever made the right call that tipped the scale between one or the other.

"Excuse me."

A nurse stood behind him. She was small and pretty, yet formidable as nurses always are.

"Are you family?"

"No," he answered. "Not family."

She nodded and waited, wanting him to leave. Finn wished her a good evening. The people getting into the elevator didn't hold the door, which was just as well. Finn rode the next one alone and was happy for the quiet.

By the time Finn got outside, he was sorry he had not taken the doctor up on his offer of crutches. Still, there was a bright side. Captain Fowler had sent a black and white to transport him home, and it was waiting at the curb.

He said his hellos to the driver, Officer Gilles. Finn was aware that his clothes smelled of smoke, there was dust in every crease of him. He apologized for his appearance as he handed his car keys over to the young officer who assured him that his own car would be delivered to his home ASAP. With that, Officer Gilles, a compassionate man, went quiet and drove.

Once home, Finn climbed the stairs slowly. In his apartment, he undressed carefully, covered the wound on his leg, and showered as best he could. Towel wrapped around his waist, he sat on the edge of his bed for a long while, thinking of nothing and everything, putting off the inevitable, regretful chore of facing his mother.

She would fuss over him, thank God for his and Cori's survival, and then lecture the good Lord on being distracted when it came to Hugh. Finn would tell her that he had seen Hugh Murphy, that he had been happy in that moment, and that he did not suffer.

After that, he would go home, have a drink, and get a good night's sleep. Sadly, his plan fell apart when he lay down on his bed for just a minute, thinking to close his eyes briefly. He did not wake until the next morning. He couldn't remember falling asleep, he vaguely remembered answering the phone and hearing his mother's voice and his own answering.

In that deep sleep, he was embraced by the darkness, at peace until he saw the first flame licking like a candle at the edge of the blackness. And then there were two, and four, and six wicks until he floated above a bed of flame. He was hot, but not burned. Hugh was there standing in the fire, his face melting under his hat. His walking stick was kindling. He pointed at Finn with the charred wood.

"Come on, boyo," the melting Hugh said. "Save me."

Before Finn could take hold of the stick. Maura floated by.

"Finn O'Brien, come along. Come along." She put out her hand. He reached for it, but she was gone before he could make contact.

Finn tossed and turned. He sweated, and he groaned, and tried to wake up. He tried to reach Hugh's stick, he tried to follow after Maura. He could not do both so he did nothing.

"Don't be a laggard," Hugh said, his eyes twinkling even though they were covered by his melted flesh. "You can save us both."

"For the love of God, you can," Maura said, her voice that of a commanding child.

Finn cried because he could do nothing at all to help them. Just as he opened his mouth to apologize, to beg their forgiveness they exploded and the fire leapt higher. Bits of them floated around him: Hugh's hat, Maura's green eye, Hugh's spectacles, and Maura's long, long hair. As the fire-roasted Hugh, Maura's shank of hair wrapped around Finn's throat until he could hardly breathe. And then he saw Cori's face. Her beautiful hair was gone, her blue eyes were watching him. She fell into the fire, too.

The last thing Finn remembered was hearing a voice that sounded like Alexander's, calling to him. Finn couldn't get off his bed to go looking for his brother.

He could not help anyone at all, not even himself.

10

Brian Cain tossed his room key on the credenza, and set the bag he carried next to it. He opened the mini-bar, put in the few groceries he had purchased on his way back to the hotel, and then shut it with the heel of his shoe.

He took off his jacket, loosened his tie, sat on the end of the bed, and looked at his phone. There were a number of messages from Wolfhound, but none were urgent, and the offices were closed. He would deal with it all tomorrow. Brian was about to set his phone aside when he stopped the scroll. There was a message from the Intrepid expeditor asking for confirmation of the names, policy numbers, and written confirmation from the CEO regarding the claims Brian had submitted. He sent the first two pieces of information and would get Dennis to sign the forms that were coming through.

Rolling up his sleeves, he sat at the small desk and got to work, pouring over employee records, planning for the future, identifying where Wolfhound might incur losses and how it could affect the company. When Brian looked up hours later, he had identified two more employees that interested him: Emily Gan had cancer and insurance was denying her an experimental drug, and Sean Brady was going in for open-heart surgery. AS CFO that meant that Wolfhound would incur lost efficiencies, lost time, lost expertise, the cost of training and replacement. In the end, though, the scales would be tipped in Wolfhound's favor, but only if those two could hold on a little longer.

Tossing his pen on the desk, Brian stood up and stretched. He was tired. The meeting with Harry, Dennis's meltdown after he heard about the plane, and even his own surprising sense of shock and sadness had taken more out of him than he could have imagined.

Brian went to the bathroom and put cold water on his face. He was surprised to see that his reflection in the mirror showed an exhausted man. That, he supposed, was to be expected after a day like this. Still, he was unsettled both by his reflection and the feeling in his gut that he had somehow failed. He knew that the reality was the polar opposite, but still the nagging remained. Brian put it down to the spare hotel room, the fact that he hadn't eaten, that Dennis had not bothered to thank him. He put it down to missing his home territory. Brian Cain did not like the United States. In need of fresh air, he left the hotel, and crossed the street to the public park. It wasn't Ireland, but it would have to do.

The park was a larger space than he had thought and he walked the concrete path through it. He passed a tent and then two. A man wearing only a pair of dirty pants was propped up against a tree. Two other men and a woman —or Brian thought it was a woman— sat upon a berm. Each was dressed in layers and layers of clothing. A cart full of *things* was next to the woman. Inside were things that *might* be of some use, and broken things of *no* use. Brian understood how precious they were to the woman. Everyone needed to own something, even lost souls with no names.

"Hey! Hey! I told them it was dumb and then they said it wasn't and..."

Brian looked at the three, thinking that he was being spoken to. He was not. The man with the straw hat was talking to an imaginary friend, carrying on, feeling greatly put out by something. The other two were paying him no mind. Brian thought the person with the imaginary friend was a bit like Dennis. Talking and talking and no one listening. Suddenly, the woman took notice and told him to shut up. In answer, the man with the imaginary friend hauled back and punched her full in the face. The woman toppled backward, rolling a bit before righting herself. She shook off the blow.

The half-naked man by the tree woke just in time to see what had happened. His head lolled. The woman looked at the man who was still talking to no one. She moved out of reach. Finally, she put both hands on the ground, pushed herself up, took the shopping cart, and went on her way. Her nose was bleeding.

"Better if he would a kilt her," the man beside the tree said.

"Is that so," Brian said.

"Ya git a bed if ya killt somebody. Bed, food, clean clothes." The man's head fell back against the trunk. He closed his eyes. "All you gotta be is a crazy killer. Punchin' don't get ya nothing. Gotta finish it. Ya gotta finish it to get stuff worth having."

Brian squinted into the dying light, appreciating the man's words. The man on the berm was quiet again. The man at the tree, the urban philosopher, had nodded off once more. Brian stuffed five dollars in the man's hand. He hoped he would find it before someone else did. The man deserved something for his wisdom.

When he got back to his room, Brian's phone vibrated. A text had come through from DQ Enterprises.

CONGRATULATIONS!

Your order #A356Q1 has submitted proof of completion
Can you take a minute to tell us how we did?
Were you satisfied with the outcome of your challenge?

Brian typed.

Extremely.

He added.

Thank you. You have been very helpful.

A reply came back.

Can we set up another challenge for you?

Brian typed.

No.

He put aside his phone and readied himself for bed, thinking the world was a funny place.

11

There were times that Finn O'Brien took exception to the weather in Southern California: the perpetual sunshine, the mild temperatures, the sporadic rain that seemed to fall in a romantic patter only at night. This weather was the envy of everyone in the world except Finn. In California a person's soul floated on the surface of life's waters, its face turned skyward, the sun's warmth lulling it to laziness. Ireland made a soul search for its peace. You put your head down against the rain and your shoulder to the wind to keep the heart pumping. A cold day made the skin tingle and pushed a person to work for their warmth. A burly, thunderous storm gave one the courage to brave it. Gloom and pall tamped the mind down, so that when the sun finally came out the spirits were lifted.

But all this sun? Today? Yesterday?

The brilliance was unfair, unwanted, and unseemly. There should be dark clouds overhead, a hard rain, a brisk wind forcing him to zip his jacket and raise his collar. Since there was no changing the turn of the earth, Finn set aside his annoyance and parked in front of the Platinum Wings terminal.

The place looked as it had yesterday. The pretty little hedge still stood at attention beside the brick walkway. The welcome mat was at the door. The windows flanking that door were etched with the Platinum logo and were unscathed. Surprisingly, the glass sparkled as if freshly washed, and the shine of that glass felt like a personal affront.

Rationally, Finn knew there was nothing he could have done to save anyone on that plane, but his dream of the night before was still vivid. That he blamed himself was laughable, so he left his hubris behind and got on with what could be done.

At least the night's sleep had done some good. The skin on his cheek felt like he had been in the sun too long, and nothing more. The stitches in his leg were annoyingly tight, but his leg was serviceable, and he favored the other one only slightly.

In the distance was LAX, a mess of traffic and commercial airlines. The private terminals at the edge of that massive hub were unimpressive from where Finn stood. The three buildings were spaced equidistant from one another. There were cars parked in front of a number of them, but no signs of life. Then again, there was no sign of the tragedy that had occurred the day before either.

Unable to put off the inevitable, Finn tried the front door of Platinum and found it locked. Cupping his hands, he put his face against the glass and peered inside. The outer office had suffered no damage; the interior was silent as a tomb. The receptionist was probably home still shaking in her boots, and some executive was doing damage control with his celebrity clients via cellphone.

Finn walked around the building and kept going until he stood on the runway, kicking at the dirt. Every last little piece of the damaged plane had been taken away. A great black patch of burned ground told a story, as did the idle Platinum plane at the end of the far end of the runway. Finn knew that every nut and bolt would be checked and rechecked before that plane took to the air. God help Platinum should they have a repeat of yesterday with a rich person onboard instead of an old Irish man.

Finn raised his face to the sun and closed his eyes, thinking he might somehow connect with the spirit of his dead uncle. No such thing happened. Even so, Finn whispered a short prayer for the old man's soul before facing the building. The next prayer he said was one of thanks that he and Cori made it out alive.

The damage to the back of the building was brutal. Large pieces of cracked glass were still attached to the framing, but the middle of the huge pane had been blown clean through. The double doors that stood beside the window were completely gone leaving only a few mangled pieces of metal. From where he stood the furniture did not appear damaged only askew. One lamp was turned over. The coffee machine that had given Cori fits was on the ground, the silver still shining, a light blinking.

Finn took his time walking toward it, pausing before stepping over the lip of the blown frame, wincing at the pain in his leg as he did so.

No glass crunched under his heavy boots, but he could see the glint of small pieces embedded in the creases of the sofa. One pillow had been ripped open. The chair upholstery was black with soot. The paint on the walls was scratched, the drywall gouged. The pictures of the Platinum aircraft had been taken down and were set against the wall near the door to the reception area. The glass was broken on both. The desks were still standing, but the printers and computers in the business center were gone. The place smelled like smoke, fuel, and disinfectant. Finn ambled across the room, pausing at the place where he had made a stand with Cori. The blood had been cleaned, the stain remained, and the —

"Hey there, friend. You need something?"

Finn looked over his shoulder. A man in grey pants and shirt stood in the doorway between the main room and the private bedroom that had so entranced Cori. His hair was long, his face worn, his expression that of a working man who had been at his job so long it no longer gave him any satisfaction if it ever had. He held a cloth and a large spray container. Finn gave him a small smile and then nodded at nothing in particular.

"I was here yesterday," he said.

"Sorry about that." The man's eyes flitted over Finn. "You look pretty good, considering."

"A scratch or two." Finn held up the back of his hand, he turned his cheek.

"God Bless," the man said, and then in a nod to Finn's accent: "That's the luck of the Irish."

"For me at least," Finn said.

“I heard there were a couple of folks who didn’t make it. God bless,” he said again as he walked into the room. "I've been working all night because they want to get things up and running fast. Clean-up will be finished today. We'll do the structural repairs, repaint, everything. Give us a week, and you'll never know that anything happened here."

"I expected someone would have to inspect the place before you touched it," Finn said.

"I don’t touch nothing until I get the go-ahead from the top," he said. "I guess the inspection's done, 'cause I got the call."

"Seems strange to erase something like this so quickly." Finn touched the couch. He rubbed his fingers together to rid them of the dust.

"It would take a whole lot more than one accident to make the whole world stop. Know what I mean?"

"That I do," Finn answered.

Both of them fell silent, thinking about the world and how it worked. In the grand scheme of things — war, famine, crimes against humanity — this hardly deserved a footnote. For every one small tragedy there would be ten more on its heels. Every murder, every assault, every vile crime was nothing more than a sliver of human misery to be swept into the dustbin of time. Finn knew this because he wielded that broom often enough on the job. What really was the difference between grief and joy when the world kept turning?

"It's all good."

Finn's newfound friend hung his spritz bottle in a fabric loop at the hip of his pants. He spoke as if he had been reading the detective's mind.

"They're going to need all the business they can get after this. You know how it goes."

He rubbed his fingers together.

"Payday. Everybody's going to want a piece of the pie. It'll be like 'wow, we liked our brother before, but we really love him more now that he's dead and going to be worth a million bucks'. Know what I mean?"

"That I do," Finn said.

"Funny, ain't it?"

"Tis," Finn answered, moving around as the man did. It was a strange little dance of solidarity that was somehow comforting. When it was clear Finn was not going to engage further, the man said:

"So, what can I do you for?"

"I'm wondering if you know where the wreckage is? The investigation of the aircraft?" Finn took his badge from his jacket. The long-faced man raised one eyebrow.

"Oh man, late for work, huh? Sorry, I've been talking your ear off."

He pushed the big sofa out of the way, walked over to an industrial vacuum, and dragged it toward what had been the picture window. He swung his chin up and over as he plugged in the machine.

"Out there, make a right. Two hangars down. You can't miss it."

"Thanks."

Finn retraced his steps and went on his way. He hadn't gone more than five feet when he heard:

"Hey."

Finn looked over his shoulder. The man seemed concerned, so Finn walked back to see what the problem was.

"I didn't mean nothing about the families," he said. "If you talk to any of them...you know. It's just that seems to be the way it goes, you know? In the end something like this comes down to money in my experience, but I was just commenting."

"Not to worry, my friend. No offense was taken. The families won't hear of it from me."

“God bless,” he said.

12

Finn went on his way, raising a hand over his head in farewell. Still, he couldn't help but think about what the man had said. His ma was a firm believer that the Lord worked in mysterious ways, and this time Uncle Hugh had been in His path. She would not sue Platinum Wings, but what of Hugh Murphy's other family? There were no children from his marriage, but there might be in-laws inclined to argue that he was as close as a brother. It would be interesting to see who crawled out of the woodwork.

Finn walked to the hangar and what he saw inside took him aback. The hobbled plane sat in the huge space with its nose pointed forward, the wings spread, the tail rising majestically. From where he stood the plane seemed as if it were ready to roll out and take to the sky, but the activity inside the place told a different story. This was a mechanical autopsy, and the investigation underway was impressive.

To Finn's right long tables ran the length of the building. Boxes of all shapes and sizes were on the floor at the far end just past the last table. Each was uniformly identified with a written code. Large pieces of debris from the plane were laid out on the floor in another quadrant; smaller pieces were spread over the table tops. Two people dressed in jeans and white coats picked through those boxes. Their hands were gloved, their shoes covered in booties, their hair covered with plastic caps. They went from boxes to tables and back again.

As Finn walked into the hangar, he caught sight of the gaping hole in the side of the aircraft and paused. It was both horrific and fascinating. Yesterday he had been aware of it, but not truly cognizant of the depth and breadth of the damage.

The edges of the cavity were jagged, the metal peeled back like a cheap tin. The black char on the perimeter smudged into shades of gray and then disappeared altogether into the bright silver skin of the plane. The destruction was a testament to the heat of the fire and the force of the blast. Those closest to the explosion died quickly, and that was some comfort to Finn.

Hearing the muted sounds of voices, he tore his eyes away from the plane and saw a knot of men standing near the tail. One noticed him. His head went up like a prairie dog.

Finn pegged him for a Platinum Wings executive given his fine suit and the level of controlled distress etched on his face. The other two men were not executives. The middle-aged man with the thinning hair was the boldest of all. Rather than step back to welcome him to the circle, they stood shoulder to shoulder, creating a wall.

"Can we help you?"

It was the middle-aged man who took the lead. He was tall, but not as tall as Finn; in good shape, but not as good as Finn. In a fight, he would move fast and have a strategy. Since Finn was not there to fight, nor to intrude, he smiled, hoping the man would stand down.

"My name is O'Brien. My uncle, Hugh Murphy, was on this flight," he said. "I was here yesterday when all this happened."

By unspoken agreement, the man in the suit became the

designated hitter. He broke the chain and stepped up to bat. He extended his hand. Finn took it.

"Dennis Cain." He kept hold of Finn's hand, put his other one on the detective's shoulder, and walked him away from the other two. "The charter was mine. Your uncle was my guest. I am so very sorry."

"As am I."

Finn moved a step back, and released the man's hand. The energy coming off him was unsettling, but not unexpected. Responsibility for such a thing as this was a terrible burden.

"You're Irish?" Dennis said.

"I've been here since I was fifteen. You think it would be long enough to tame the accent, but no such luck."

"And I was born in Ireland, but grew up here. I spent my summers with my father in Cork," Dennis said.

"We are two sides of the coin then."

"True," Dennis said. "How can I help you today?"

"I came to collect my uncle's belongings."

"I don't think that's possible, but it's not for me to say," Dennis said. "The investigators are working now. They're sorting through everything. I'm afraid you've made the trip for nothing. If you had called my office—"

"We didn't know who to call," Finn said. "My mother received a letter saying Hugh would arrive on this flight, but not why he was coming."

"That doesn't surprise me. Hugh was fond of tales, but kept his own business to himself. He was a bit of an enigma, actually." Dennis chuckled. He touched Finn's elbow. "Let's go where we can talk more comfortably."

Outside Dennis steered Finn to a rickety picnic table planted between the two hangars and beneath a lone tree. Near the table, a large green metal barrel, dented and rusting, was half-filled with trash. Flies flew in lazy circles above it. Cigarette butts had been squashed into the dirt around it. Finn sat; Dennis did not.

"Now that you're here, I realize how remiss I've been. I didn't reach out yesterday to any of the families," Dennis said. "I should have and I apologize."

"I wouldn't have expected it." Finn held up his hand to stop the man from saying more. "Everyone is in shock. You must have been devastated."

"The Platinum team has been taking the lead, but in Hugh's case it should have been me talking to his family." Dennis Cain pushed back his suit jacket and buried his hands deep into the pockets of his trousers. "I'm ashamed to admit that I didn't even know he had family. I knew his wife, of course, and that he had no children"

"No reason you should know about us. He's been estranged from my side of the family for many years," Finn said. "That's why my mother was so pleased when she received his letter. A reunion was long overdue."

"Well, that's a mystery solved. I thought Los Angeles was a strange choice," Dennis said.

"And what choice was that, Mr. Cain?" Finn asked. "Why was he even on such a fancy plane?"

"Ah." Dennis put a hand to his brow. "Of course, you wouldn't know unless Hugh told you. Your uncle worked for Wolfhound Distillery in Cork—"

"Wolfhound Whiskey?" Finn said.

"You know it?"

"What whiskey drinker does not?" Finn said. "The finest there is."

"I'm happy to hear you say that since it is my family's business. Much of that excellence is due to your uncle."

Dennis sat next to Finn. He loosened his tie, comfortable now that he was dealing with a reasonable man.

"Hugh was hired by my grandfather some sixty years ago. He worked under my father until he passed away, and then I had the pleasure of working with him before he retired. Distilling was a religion for Hugh."

Finn breathed a sad chuckle. Dennis paused.

"I'm sorry. 'tis your choice of words," Finn said. "It is religion that kept Hugh away from us for so many years. He married a protestant woman and that caused a bit of a rift with the Catholic side. I'm happy to know that he had a third option for his worship."

"Ah, yes. The Troubles. History. Thank goodness that's behind the Irish now," Dennis said.

"One can hope," Finn said.

"Irish passion is hard to tame. I'm glad Hugh and your mother made their peace," Dennis said. "Selfishly I'm happy Wolfhound had him for as many years as we did. He was our Master Distiller. There wasn't a batch that went out without his approval. My family is indebted to him in more ways than one."

"Surely he wasn't still working," Finn said. "I had a brief look at him. He was on his feet, but there was no doubt age had taken its toll."

"Oh, no, he wasn't working, but he fought retirement with everything he had," Dennis said. "Hugh consulted for us up until a few years ago when we merged with Hammet Industries here in the U.S. He wasn't happy with the buy-out, I can tell you. I felt like I was fifteen again with the way he lectured me."

"My mother has the same talent," Finn said. "She can reduce a grown man to child with a well-placed word."

"Long story short, it was brought to my attention that Wolfhound had never celebrated Hugh's service and retirement. We had a party, and as a gift we told him we would send him anywhere in the world he wanted to go. Private plane, best hotels. Everything paid for."

"That is generous of you," Finn said.

"Not as generous as we should have been. I thought Los Angeles was a modest choice, but I was pleased. I live here, so I thought we'd see one another."

"And he didn't say a word about visiting family?"

"If he had, I would have included your mother in the plans—or you or anyone he wanted. Then again, he might have told our travel staff while making the arrangements." Dennis smiled, tight-lipped, exhausted, disturbed, but rising to the moment. "Would you like me to forward his itinerary?"

"No, need. The fact that you did so much is a testament to Wolfhound."

"I'm sorry Hugh will never know how much we appreciated his sacrifice for Wolfhound.," Dennis said. "Not to mention, I wanted to stay on his good side so he wouldn't go to a competitor."

"Business is business. I would have kept an eye on him too," Finn said.

"I'm glad you understand." Dennis stood. "I'll be heading back to Ireland soon. Now that I know he has family, would you prefer to handle the arrangements? I'd be happy to do that, but it's your decision."

Finn stood up, too.

"That's very good of you. I'll let you know."

"Here's my information."

Finn took the man's card, and together they walked back the way they came. When Dennis stopped to say a final goodbye, Finn looked at the car.

"You've a nice ride, Mr. Cain."

"Another legacy of Wolfhound. There's not much in my life that isn't tied up in the company," Dennis said. "Legacy is what life is all about."

"'Tis true. I'm happy to hear that my uncle left one with Wolfhound."

"You have no idea, Mr. O'Brien," Dennis said. "You might say he was our savior. That's what I hear from our executives in Cork."

"There is one more thing. I saw a woman on the plane. I thought I knew her—"

"I can't help you." Dennis Cain opened the car door. The action was as sharp as his words. A moment later his tone softened. "These are shared charters, Mr. O'Brien. Perhaps they picked up someone in San Francisco."

"I see. Well, thank you. I was probably mistaken anyway."

Dennis went to his car. Finn started for the hangar, passing a tall, dark-haired man as he went. Finn glanced his way only to be distracted when Dennis Cain called to him.

"Mr. O'Brien. You can't go back in there. The investigators don't want unauthorized people inside."

Dennis Cain was hanging on the open car door looking like a model in an advertisement. Finn reached into his inside pocket, retrieved his credential, and held it up. Dennis Cain could not read the words imprinted on it, but he understood the flash of the badge.

"It's Detective O'Brien, Mr. Cain, and I know my way around an accident scene. I promise, I won't be a bother."

He waved and went on his way. Dennis Cain watched until he was out of sight. Brian reached the car and looked after Finn too. He opened the passenger door.

"Is there a problem, Dennis?"

"I don't think so."

They got in and when Dennis's seat belt was buckled, his sunglasses on, and his hand was resting on the gear shift, he still stared at the hangar.

"Who is he?" Brian asked.

Dennis threw the car in gear.

"He's a policeman, Brian. Hugh Murphy was his uncle." Dennis drove to the edge of the property, stopping before he turned on the boulevard that would take him to the freeway. He didn't look at his brother when he said:

"Is there something we should do?"

"What is it you're thinking should be done?" Brian asked.

"I don't know. He's a cop."

"And Hugh was his uncle," Brian said. "What cause is there for worry?"

"None, I suppose." Dennis drove on, and muttered once more. "None."

Brian settled down, comfortable in the car. He appreciated the ride for the fine piece of machinery that it was. Dennis thought he was jealous of him for owning it, but Brian didn't fret. It was only a thing after all. He also didn't fret about the people who perished on the plane. Sad as it was for the families, those people were gone. If Dennis was unsettled by the thought of dealing with Hugh's family, then Brian would see to it. These things did not need to be complicated.

"I contacted Sharon," Brian said. "She'll let the rest of the employees know."

"How did she take it?" Dennis said.

"It was a surprise, but Hugh hadn't been working for five years. He was already a memory."

Brian waited for a response from Dennis. There was none. His handsome brow was pulled together in that way it did when Dennis was overthinking things.

"You're handling everything, aren't you? I mean settlements and such," Dennis said.

"Yes. The insurance claims are being processed," Brian said, but that still didn't seem to satisfy his brother. "Dennis, what is it you're worrying about? Wolfhound will go on. That's the point, is it not?"

Dennis didn't answer. He wasn't Brian. The victims wouldn't be forgotten. Not by him. Never by him. All of this would torture him until the day he died.

"When are you going back, Brian?"

"I'll be staying on a bit. There's a lot to do," Brian said.

"I..." Dennis shifted in his seat, torn between wanting Brian to go and not wanting to face what might coming down the road alone. "That might be a good thing. We'll need to hammer out a deal with Harry. You're sure we can do that?"

"Yes, now we can," Brian said.

"Yes, now," Dennis muttered. "There will be lawsuits of course. We have to prepare for that. It may change the terms of our offer to Harry."

"We're not liable for this. The only suit we'll care about is ours against Platinum. Negligence, certainly," Brian said. "That should bring a tidy settlement and settle they will. They won't want a trial, so we can add that money to our coffers."

"Jesus, Brian, have you no feelings?"

"Haven't you enough of feelings, Dennis? I mean considering they've gotten you in a bit of trouble already," Brian said.

"Shut up, Brian. Just shut up. Don't even talk about that. You never understand—"

"I do. All too well," Brian said, but then he changed the subject. "What exactly does the constable want, Dennis?"

"Hugh's things," Dennis said.

"Give them to him, do your mourning, and let's get on with business. Remember what father would have said: 'tis the whole that is important, not one or two. I thought that was one thing we saw eye to eye."

"We do. I do," Dennis said.

Dennis took a sharp turn onto the freeway onramp. He

stepped on the gas and the car accelerated, smooth as butter. Eyes turned to watch as he threaded through the traffic. No matter how fast he drove, Dennis couldn't stop thinking about his father or his mother. Brian was right about their father. He would have said the explosion was a tragedy, but the possibility of buying Wolfhound back took the edge off. Dennis's mother, on the other hand, would say life's a bitch and then you die, but better if the bitch goes first.

As for Brian, he gave Dennis no more thought than he gave old Hugh Murphy or anyone else on that plane. They had served their purpose in life. Dead was dead. That was more than a silver lining; that was the pot of gold at the end of the rainbow.

13

The hangar was still cold, the plane was still an abomination, and the two people in the back worked their boxes like bees at a hive. The men who had been with Dennis Cain were nowhere to be seen, but there was a woman at the front table who appeared to have authority. She was middle-aged, short of stature, and elegant in posture. She moved precisely and with purpose as she chose an item from the table, examined it, and tagged it. Her hair was short and cut in a style that would be difficult to describe other than serviceable. She wore a white coat, her hands were encased in latex, and she had eyes in the back of her head.

"Other box! Other box!"

She barked at the worker-bees even though she hadn't so much as turned her head to see what they were doing. One of the men jumped, twirled away from the box he had been leaning over, and deposited a piece of metal in another one. Since Finn's objective was to talk with someone who could get him what he needed, this woman seemed the right choice.

She gave him no mind as he approached. Even when Finn stood at a respectful distance from her workstation, she was not distracted. He cleared his throat. She looped a tag over a jagged bit of metal. He licked his lips and gave his nose a rub. She took a Sharpie and marked a code. All her machinations were interesting to a point, but that point was now past.

"Sorry to be bothering you," he said. When there was no response from the woman, he pressed on. "Could you be telling me who's in charge here?"

"Depends on what you're here to talk about."

She continued with her code: a dash, a letter, four numbers. Finally, she set the item aside and looked at Finn. The light glinted off her glasses. She had lovely eyes. He was sure that if she managed a smile there would be mischief in them. She didn't smile. She wasn't amused, impressed, or curious about Finn O'Brien. Her eyes moved a click. Her helpers were off track again.

"Mark! That one," she barked. "Come on. Get in the game. Good grief."

Finn didn't bother to look and see how poor Mark was managing. Instead, he took note of the nametag on her white coat: *J. Sterling.*

"Sorry." She gave Finn her attention. "Those codes are a misery. If I talk, I screw up; if I screw up, it goes down the line."

She looked Finn over from the top of his shaved head, to his leather jacket, boots, and back to his eyes. He passed some sort of muster.

"If you're talking forensics, then I'm the boss; if you're talking the investigative team. Not me."

He offered his credential in the hopes it would impress. All it did was satisfy her.

"Investigative. In there." She pointed to the plane.

Finn thanked her, his eyes sweeping over the long tables as he turned away. The one on the far end caught his eyes. There he saw a book, luggage, a coat, a shoe. The shoe belonged to a woman. The heel was too high for the stewardess to have worn. It was...

"Is there anything else?" J. Sterling was annoyed that he was hanging around. Finn smiled at her.

"No. Thank you, missus."

She almost smiled, or at least the edges of her lips tipped up a bit.

"Josephine," she said.

“Josephine,” he reiterated.

With that, Finn confirmed there was mischief in her eyes, but only barely. He saluted her with two fingers to his brow and left her to her sorting and tagging.

Charter though it may be, private and small by comparison to a commercial liner, the plane was still an overwhelming presence. A ladder was stationed beneath the gaping hole. Finn climbed it, swinging himself up and over into the interior. A shiver ran up his spine the minute he was inside.

It was one thing to observe a violent event or to be collateral damage, but to stand where the violence had occurred was another matter. To his left, the cockpit door was twisted, hanging off its hinges, but not blown completely. Wires hung from the ceiling like Spanish moss. He stood where Hugh had, and Finn wondered if the old man experienced a split second during which he understood what was happening. Had he been terrorized or accepting? Had he taken the moment to pray to the Maker he was about to meet, or rail against Him? Finn hoped he would never find out. His own greatest wish was to die peacefully in his sleep.

He swiped a dangle of tangled wires away from his head, looked around and saw that the two men who had been with Dennis Cain were huddled in the back, looking into a space beneath the cabin floor.

"Excuse me." Finn walked toward them slowly, careful of his surroundings.

They both faced him squarely. The shorter one, the one Finn had taken notice of earlier, appeared annoyed. The second was watchful. The first stepped forward.

"Authorized personnel," he said.

"I appreciate that," Finn said. "My name is Finn O'Brien. LAPD. Detective out of Wilshire Division."

"A little out of your jurisdiction."

"Service has no borders," Finn said, but his goodwill did nothing to charm the man.

"We don't need anything, but thanks."

He pointed over the detective's shoulder, indicating there was only one way for him to go and that was out.

"Sorry not to be clear," Finn said. "I wasn't sent to assist. I'm hoping for a bit of professional courtesy. As you heard, my uncle was killed on this plane. I'd like to collect his things."

The man didn't say a word as he looked at Finn, weighing his options.

"Perhaps you could tell me your name," Finn said.

"Agent Lowery." He pulled a thumb over his shoulder. "Agent Franks in the back."

"Agent Franks," Finn repeated leaning right and raising a hand. Then back to the man in front of him. "Agent Lowery. I've not dealt with the FAA before, and I don't pretend to know the protocol, but I see there are personal things on the table out there. If there's one thing I could take away, I'd be grateful."

"We won't be releasing anything," Agent Lowery said. "Give me your contact info, and I'll keep you up to date — just like the other families."

Finn inclined his head. Point taken. No rank would be pulled; no professional courtesy to be had. Finn dug for a card and handed it over.

"And the remains?"

"Already with the coroner," Lowery said. "We'll let you know when you can—"

"I've dealings with the M.E. I can check on that myself," Finn said. "Since you cannot accommodate me, I'll leave you to your work."

Before Finn could go, Lowery was on him. It was an oddly aggressive move. Finn paused, curious to see where it might lead.

"The M.E. won't give you any information no matter how friendly you are," he said. "We keep a pretty tight lid on things. You wouldn't want to compromise the medical examiner or our investigation."

"I resent the implication, Agent Lowery, but I'll put it down to the stress of your job," he said. "Thank you for your time. I'll look forward to hearing any news —along with the other families."

"Good. Glad we're on the same page," Lowery said. "But since you're here, maybe you could tell us something about your uncle."

"What would you be wanting to know about him?" Finn inclined his head, wary of this cold man.

"We understand he was on the flight as a belated retirement gift."

"That's my understanding also," Finn said. "I'm not sure what interest that would be to you."

"We're trying to piece together victim profiles. What kind of man was he? What has he been doing since he retired? That sort of thing," Lowery said. "It might expedite matters."

"You are oddly thorough," Finn said, knowing an interrogation when he heard one and was surprised to find himself on the wrong end of it. "It seems that would have no bearing on discovering the cause of this acci—"

Finn paused. He had seen the subtle change in Lowery's expression, so he retreated and regrouped.

"Perhaps you could tell me who else was on the plane first. I would like to know who my uncle was traveling with."

"The captain, one stewardess, and a woman."

"And have you a name of the woman?"

"I can't release that information pending notification of next of kin," Lowery answered.

"If it is the woman that I am thinking of I'll be grieving twice today, Agent Lowery," Finn said. "Maybe the FAA might bend the rules a bit given that I'm an officer of the law, same as you."

Agent Lowery smiled, barely showing his teeth. Whatever the man was about to say it seemed he would relish speaking it. Finn, on the other hand, had no doubt that he wouldn't like hearing it. A breath later, he was proved right.

"I don't imagine the FAA would have a problem telling you anything, but we're not FAA," Lowery said. "We're ATF."

"Alcohol, Tobacco, Firearms—" Finn began, but Lowery finished for him.

"And explosives." His eyes cut to the cavity in the side of the plane and then locked onto Finn again. "This wasn't an accident and everyone is suspect until we say they're not. That includes your uncle."

Lowery turned away, and then thought again. He had one more thing to say.

"And a local dick isn't even close to being the same as us. Are we on the same page?"

14

Finn stepped forward, unwilling to be dismissed after the man-made such a vile suggestion about Hugh Murphy and dismissed Finn O'Brien as a lesser professional. Finn had been relegated all too often to a place where he was expected to hold his tongue, and take his licks. It was one thing to be disrespected by his fellow officers, quite another from this arrogant man.

"My uncle was a victim—"

Before Finn could say another word, a woman's cry pierced the air, echoing and amplifying inside the plane. This was not Josephine Sterling calling someone to heel; this was the sound of aggression and anger. Finn's own fury was forgotten as all three men instinctively reacted.

Franks started down the aisle. Lowery put a hand out to push Finn aside, but Finn had the advantage. He was the first one out of the plane, scrambling down the ladder with Lowery on his heels. Agent Franks stationed himself at the edge of the hole high above the hangar floor, drew his weapon, and gave cover.

At the far end of the building, two women were going at it.

One of them was Josephine Sterling: short, solid, the defender. The aggressor was tall, young, and well-dressed. Her arms were flying, her body language was threatening. She pointed at Sterling, punching at her with a finger. Josephine slapped it away, but the woman went at her again, stopping just short of laying on hands. Behind them, Sterling's two male counterparts watched, unsure of what to do.

Finn and Lowery moved, trying to see if the woman had a weapon. The agent went under the plane, sheltering behind a wheel. Finn fell back to get a clear view outside. When he returned, he stayed low, moving at a diagonal until he was at Lowery's side.

"One car that was not there before. A white Mercedes," Finn whispered. "No one else outside."

He meant no one to put a bullet in their backs. Lowery nodded, accepting that information but wanting nothing more.

“Stand down, detective,” Lowery said. “We’ve got this.”

“Like hell,” Finn said, his eyes on the altercation the same as Lowery’s. “The plane is yours; the city is mine.”

“Take it down a notch.”

Josephine Sterling raised her voice, curtailing the men’s turf war.

The younger woman kept at it. Everything she did was louder and bigger than Josephine managed. She moved forward, backward, flailing, screaming. Josephine’s eyes cut toward the plane. She tagged Finn and Lowery. Those eyes flicked up, and she saw Agent Franks. Sterling knew what to do. She engaged the woman, keeping her attention as the men started to move. Lowery stored his weapon, and pulled his windbreaker over his holster. Finn did the same. They covered the space quickly.

Lowery pulled out ahead lest Finn O’Brien thinks he was on the team, but the detective wasn’t more than a half a step behind. Franks was halfway down the ladder when the screaming woman tried an end-run around Josephine. Sterling did a box step to corral her, but the woman was young and quick. Formidable as Josephine Sterling was, she was no match for white-hot hysteria. The woman shook Josephine off, and threw herself at the table where the personal effects were laid out.

"Get out of my way, you *langer*. I swear I'll pan you out, you *gowl*. You *eejit*—"

Sterling, lunged for her, but she wiggled away, knocking things off the table, scrambling to catch them as they fell.

"Hey!"

Agent Lowery called out in a great, deep, booming voice that surprised Finn and stopped Josephine cold. While it should have struck fear into the fancy woman, it had the opposite effect.

Super-charged, she scrambled up. Slipping once on her high heels before turning on him. Her green eyes were ablaze, her pale, freckled skin was spotted with the high color of rage. Her red hair was long— a fall of corkscrews and curls— and it flew about her face. Strands of it caught on her lipstick. She swiped at them, but missed her mark. Frustrated, she spat them out and all the while she screeched and crowed.

"Hey, what, you freakin' *plonker*! Are you startin' with me? I'm not the one being a bitch here. This sow... This..."

She huffed and puffed. She tossed her arm out at Josephine, and poked at Lowery. The woman fisted her hands, and stomped her elegantly shod foot. Finally, she stood away with her hands on her hips, trying to catch her breath, looking for someone to stand with her. There was no one.

"You're done," Lowery said. "And next time you talk, watch your language."

He reached for her arm to move her aside, but she pulled back.

"Feck away off, you *comquat*," she said. "I have rights...I have..."

Her eyes went from one to another: Lowery and Finn, Franks and Sterling then back to Lowery. She wouldn't go down easy, and those fists came up. She faltered, unsure of where she should take out her rage. Before she could act out again, the woman did a quarter turn, and took another look at Finn. Her interest was fleeting. She was back at Lowery.

"I came for my sister's things, and she..." she pointed at Josephine. "She's bein'... Oh, forget it. Just give me what I've come for, and I'll be on my way."

With that, she surrendered. Out-numbered, worn down, she tossed her hair, filled her lungs, and then raised herself up like a majesty.

"This is truly screwed." Her voice was low, and beautiful in defeat. "Let me talk to the man in charge. I'm sayin' it's not right. I called this place, and got no answer. I come here and a janitor tells me the friggin' plane blew up. It's enough to blacken your arse and go mad. Then this..."

She threw out her arm, pointing at Josephine Sterling. The woman's eyes narrowed.

"Yes, you, my girl. Doing the dog on it. Not even a word of condolence."

The woman snapped her head back to the men.

"This banshee tells me to get out like she's asking me to leave the grocery because I've no shoes on. Who in the hell says something like that? Everyone's dead? That's how you say such a thing? *Eejit. Scaldy...*"

She dropped her arms. Her head swung like a pendulum. Tears came to her eyes and her bottom lip quivered. Still, her shoulders were back, and her spine straight. Finn gave her credit. She was a force, she was Irish—for no one swore like the Irish— and she deserved something for her effort.

Lowery reached for her, but she shrugged him off. His next words were for the team.

The man stood back, but he kept his eyes on the woman while he said:

"Everybody, take a break. Good job, Sterling."

The team faded away. Lowery started in again.

"That lady is helping make things right. Until we identify the victims, we can't notify the next of kin. Do you understand?"

Her head went up, sharp words were at the ready, but she couldn't get them out fast enough to satisfy Lowery.

"I will take that as a yes," he said. "Now, I'm going to have someone escort you out. This is a crime scene and. . ."

"Crime? Crime!" The surrender of moments before was gone. "My sister was murdered?"

"Hey! Hey. Miss..." Lowery raised his voice, hoping to get her attention, but Finn beat him to the punch.

"Shaughnessy," he said. "'Tis Shannon Shaughnessy, is it not?"

At the sound of her name the woman did a slow turn, and looked at Finn. She inclined her head, and studied his face. Her expression softened. The sound of an Irish voice meant an ally. But then her eyes went to his waist where his jacket had not quite covered his gun and those eyes changed again. Before she could decide whether to rage or not, he said:

"It's Finn O'Brien, Shannon. Maura's friend."

"Oh, my God. Oh, Finn."

With that, she fell into his arms and put her head against his chest. Over the riot of red hair Finn caught Lowery's eye. He gave the man a small smile. Disaster averted. They had done it together, they had—

Gotten nowhere.

"Get her out of here," Lowery said. He looked Finn in the eye. "And don't come back.'

15

Finn and Shannon sat on opposite sides of the picnic table where earlier he had spoken with Dennis Cain. Shannon's back was against it, her legs were splayed in front of her. She smoked her cigarette like it was a punching bag. Finn counted this as a victory since it had taken five minutes to convince her to leave the hangar. She spent another five pacing, flailing, and swearing at the people inside before raging at her sister's death and cursing Finn, God, and airplanes in that order. Cori at her worst could not pull up such a litany as Shannon reeled off. It was only after she wore herself out, twisting her ankle one too many times on the uneven ground because of her high heels, that she threw herself down on the splintery bench.

Finn waited her out, admiring the woman she had become. Shannon was slim, but her figure lush. Her legs were long as were her beautifully manicured fingers. Her hands were elegantly expressive in stark contrast to her words. She had crossed one arm under her breasts. The other was at an angle, close to her side, used as a lever to move her cigarette back and forth. As she calmed, her motions became efficient. They were those of a woman who hated to waste time on anything, pleasant or not.

"Better now, Shannon?" Finn asked, deeming she was played out.

"Passable."

Shannon shook back her hair, tossed the cigarette, and ground it out under the pointed toe of her boot, the gold filter shining like a little nugget amidst the other discards. She turned around and threw her legs over the bench like a schoolboy, but when she settled Shannon sat like a proper lady, back straight, her hands clasped together in front of her. She crooked her elbow and cradled her chin in the palm of her upturned hand. Her lashes lowered. Finn could almost fool himself that it was Maura he was looking at, but Shannon was less wholesome than her sister. She was Maura, but not as genteel. By the look of her, Shannon was doing well. From her expensive clothes and fine boots, she was fancier than any woman Finn knew. Delicate gold chains hung about her neck, diamond studs were in her ears, and a Rolex watch, its face paved with diamonds, graced one slim wrist. She wore a sapphire ring on the middle finger of her right hand but nothing on the left, so it wasn't a husband keeping her in such finery. Whatever her work, it was lucrative and didn't seem to need her attention any time soon.

"'Tis been a long while," Finn said.

"I was four the last time I laid eyes on you," she said, giving him a close look. "You've changed a bit too. For the better, to be sure."

Finn chuckled. He'd been just shy of his teenage years when last they met. Shannon's late arrival had miffed Maura greatly. The thought of her parent's doing the deed and getting pregnant were both folly in Maura's estimation. Finn— in his eleven-year-old wisdom— had agreed. He and Maura had been arrogant little bits of humanity then. They knew nothing of real love or loss, death or the crimes people could commit against one another on a whim. Yet they were so confident that they alone understood the way the world turned. It had been a wonderful time. Perhaps he and Maura should have stayed put as Cori suggested. He wondered if the same could be said for Shannon. Looks could be deceiving, and the trappings of wealth could be forged.

"How long have you been here?" Shannon dropped her hands, not so much undone by his scrutiny as tired of it.

"We left Ireland when I was fifteenteen," Finn said. "You?"

"I've been here four years. Before that England for a bit. Oh, and a stint in Dubai. That was interesting."

"And your parents? Are they well?" he asked.

"Depends who's sayin'." Her gaze held his, and he saw that little girl she had been. The illusion shattered in the next instant. "They're dead, so there are no worries for them, now is there? I suppose that makes them well."

Shannon reached for her purse and pulled out her cigarettes, thought better of it, and pushed the pack back inside.

"Ma had the cancer. Da? I don't know. Something with his heart. Maura told me, but I forget now."

"I'm sorry," Finn said.

"Me, also." Shannon spoke with a nonchalance that didn't fool Finn. She hurt deeply, but would rather die herself than have his sympathy. Beverly had been like that. And, like Finn's ex, Shannon shrugged to toss off the pain. "That's the way it goes. And yours?"

"Ma is here. All my brothers and sisters. My father passed," he said.

She smiled ever-so-slightly. Now they were caught up as far as she was concerned. Finn not so much.

"What took you away?"

Shannon barked a laugh.

"Ah, Finn, you've not changed. So polite, you are," she said. "If I'd waited for something to take me away, I'd still be on that island. Opportunity presented itself, and I went with it. I made my own way, thank you very much."

Finn's lips twitched. He felt a stab of sadness for the Shaughnessy family. Maura might have been a bossy little thing, but Shannon was a harsh one. Whatever road she took had made her comfortable, but not happy by the sound of it.

"And Maura? What was she doing all these years?" he asked.

"She did well for herself, I think." Shannon's fingers tapped the table. Her eyes darted past Finn.

"You don't know?"

"I know enough," Shannon said. "She was in Cork, went to Trinity, and back to Cork again. She could have gone anywhere in the world to work. She was smart, but you knew she was smart."

Finn laughed. "Smarter than me, certainly."

"Book-smart, I meant. 'The executive', ma would call her. She and da were so proud," Shannon said. "Everyone wanted me to be Maura, too, but the business life wasn't for me. They never understood how different we were."

"Where was she an executive?" Finn asked.

"Lots of places, I think. She was in finance, or economics, or something. Marketing, perhaps. For the last few years she was on her own. A consultant of some sort. I wasn't around. I wanted more of the world, and she waved me off with a fare thee well."

"It seems you made the right choice." Finn smiled, but there was no settling the woman.

"Worked for me," Shannon muttered.

"Did Maura ever work for Wolfhound Distillery?" Finn asked.

"She did," Shannon answered.

"And was she working for them now?"

"I don't think so," Shannon said. "Last I heard she had clients of her own and such. Maybe she still had something to do with the place, but Maura was always looking ahead for the top spot. And it's not like we were close, so I've no real knowledge of her circumstances."

Shannon pulled her purse close, opening it only wide enough to retrieve her cigarettes and a gold lighter before snapping it shut. She cupped her hand around the small flame even though there was no breeze. The tip of the cigarette glowed crimson as she inhaled. She tossed the lighter back in her purse, put her head back, and let out a mushroom cloud of smoke. It was then that Finn saw her eyes were shadowed in blue like Cori's. Unlike Cori's, Shannon's choice was an elegant, soft blue-grey. Everything about her was subtle, expensive, and beautiful, yet it was Cori Finn found more interesting. Shannon was still looking skyward, still holding her cigarette between her long fingers, when she said:

"Why?"

"Why what?" Finn took off his leather jacket. Even under the shade of the tree it was too warm a day for such a thing, yet he always felt at odds without it.

"Why did you want to know if she was working for Wolfhound?" Shannon dropped her head and her eyes were on him again.

"Because the plane was chartered by Wolfhound. Because my uncle died on that plane, and he had worked for Wolfhound. Because a connection seems reasonable, but the man who made the arrangements said if anyone else from Wolfhound was on the plane, he didn't know who it was," Finn said. "If Maura was still working for the distillery, I would expect him to know she was on the flight. If he lied about such a thing, I would be curious to know why."

"Maybe she was consulting. One thing about Maura, once

she made a good connection, she never let it go. Like a bulldog she was. Very obstinate if you fit into her plans. You're lucky you got out of her way when you did."

"There was no choice. You moved away," Finn said. "She let me go easy enough."

"You were children," Shannon said. "Children grow up into people who want what they want."

"Truer than you know," Finn said. "When did your parents pass?"

"I was thirteen. Still under age. Maura was working."

"She took care of you then," Finn said.

"She paid the bills," Shannon shot back.

"I'm happy to know she was successful," Finn said.

"That she was," Shannon said. "Now ask me if she was happy."

"Was she happy?"

"She should have been, but I don't think so. Nor did I care," Shannon said.

Again, the aside; the grudging tone. The dynamic of sisters could be curious, but in Finn's family those relationships were at least affectionate. The Shaughnessy sisters' estrangement brought up a question that bothered Finn.

"And yet she was coming to see you. You were distraught when you found out what happened—"

"I was shocked—" Shannon said. "There's a difference."

"Did she not give you a reason for coming?" he asked.

"No."

Shannon hung her head, miserable for so many reasons. Shock was one of them, perhaps regret now that she was truly orphaned. To Finn, it seemed more complicated than that.

"Maura texted me with her arrival time, and that she was flying on Platinum. She wanted to stay with me for a few days. She didn't ask. She told me what was going to happen, and what

I was going to do." Shannon smoked and talked. The smoke drifted between them, back and forth. "I told her fine, but I would be busy. She texted back that she would see me soon, so I suppose it wouldn't have mattered had I said no. Nor do I care what business was bringing her. It's all done now. Just like ma and da. Gone."

Shannon took another drag and dropped her hands on the table. Her arms crossed at the wrist. The cigarette was held between two of her outstretched fingers. Her nails were painted the same color as the lazy smoke winding its way into the still air. It smelled exotic. Rich. Like a Turkish blend.

"Look, Finn, you're remembering that little girl who everybody thought was amusing because of her big vocabulary and her smart ways, but she became entitled. Instead of stamping her foot when she didn't get what she wanted, Maura put that foot on your back and pressed her heel. I didn't like her much, but she was still my sister. When she texted her arrival time I was away. I left a key. I'll admit that I did think she might want to patch things up, but I'll never know now, will I?"

She started to put the cigarette to her lips, but she had let it go too long. The tail of ash fell off onto her lovely skirt. She brushed it away without much consideration and ditched the butt.

"Is there no husband? Did she have no children?" Finn asked.

Shannon shook her head.

"The Shaughnessy sisters are not the marrying kind," she said. "But, sure, Maura had someone. I think that was why she was coming. To decide what to do with the relationship. God knows why she should be seekin' me out."

"'Twould have been better if you had been close," Finn said. “For both of you.”

"'Twould." She laughed, mocking him in a lovely way. "Understand, Finn. I'm not blind, nor am I selfish. Maura had some goodness. She took care of my parents when they were ill, but I was so young and so afraid. Every time I tried to help, it upset Maura's plans and that would upset our parents in turn. It was impossible for me to wrap my head around what was happening. When they passed it was as if the world collapsed. No one to comfort me, only Maura telling me what to do, where to go, what to think. It was all legal, and it was all unhappy."

"I'm sorry for that," Finn said.

"Don't be. Life happens. We were two different people. She didn't want me as a baby, and I was a yoke as a young girl. Maura wasn't mean, she just had a way of letting me know I was temporary. Still, the rough years had their moments. I'll try to think about those times. She deserves something akin to mourning. In the end, she did fine without me, and I did well without her."

"It appears so, Shannon. I'm glad for you," he said. "It is a pity you don't know who Maura was involved with, though. It might be helpful to talk to him."

"Whoever he was, he must have been something. Maura wouldn't waste her time on just anyone." She smiled. "Maybe it was you she was coming to see."

"That would have been a surprise," Finn laughed.

"And is there a wife who would have been surprised, too?" Shannon teased.

He shook his head. "Divorced."

"Ah, a disappointment."

"More so because it wasn't my choice. And you?" Finn asked. "Did you never find someone special enough to think about tying the knot?"

"I've found many, but I've also learned there is always one better after that."

She laughed and tossed her curly hair. It glistened bright red and shiny gold in the stray beams of sunlight that came through the leaves above. Beneath the make-up, behind the cloud of smoke and the fine clothes, she was a true and natural beauty.

“At some point, there are diminishing returns," Finn said.

"Right you are, but as the village women would say, ‘That Shannon is a hard-headed one." She hung her head and let it loll back and forth, a sad pendulum of regret, or wistfulness, or both. She raised her eyes and looked at him with some affection. "Taken then are you, Finn?"

"I've many friends." Finn thought of Gretchen and of Cori. He even had a kind thought for Beverly, his ex who hadn’t had the courage to see him through his hard times.

"Well, there you go, we're in the same boat. I've many friends too."

"I've no doubt, Shannon," he said. "And what is it you do when you're not with your friends?"

"Sure, I'm always with my friends, Finn."

Shannon looked straight at him. The color of her eyes deepened seductively. A smile teased her lips, and suddenly she was transformed in a way that was unsettling. Her movements were more graceful, her fingers lingered on her purse before she opened it. When she did, she put the lighter and cigarettes away and brought out a card. It was an elegant thing made of eggshell linen and adorned with golden script.

In the center was Shannon’s name. Beneath that were the words *One Night* and a phone number. When he looked at her for an explanation, Shannon leaned over the ancient picnic table. A bit of paint flaked off the wood and stuck to the sleeve of her jacket. Shannon put her fingers on Finn's arm, and the connection was stirring. He could not look away from her gaze, nor stop thinking about the way her full lips parted and her green eyes sparkled with golden flecks.

"'Tis an escort service," she said in her sweetest Irish lilt. "Sure, are you needin' a date for the evening, Finn O'Brien?"

16

"How's it going here?" Agent Lowery asked the question when he was still ten feet from Josephine Sterling's workspace. She waited until he was closer before she said:

"It would have been better if that woman hadn't gone psycho. Wasted a good twenty minutes on her nonsense."

Josephine was tagging what looked like a faucet. Her lips were drawn into a thin line of annoyance, creating an equator that separated the all-business top of her face and the ticked off part below.

"We all have our crosses," Agent Lowery said.

Behind him, Franks snorted. Sterling shot him a look, impressing Lowery with her gift of shaming.

"Sorry." Agent Franks mumbled like a schoolboy.

"Your mother should have taught you better."

Josephine leaned across the table, and got as close to the men as she could. Plain speech was called for.

"Look, I'm not happy right now. I like my job precisely because I don't have to deal with the victims. It gives me the creeps to see the families. The cop was okay, but that woman. . . That was rough."

Sterling shook her head, took a deep, cleansing breath, straightened up, and tugged at the sleeves of her white coat. She adjusted the piece of metal she had been tagging, lining it up as precisely as she could with the other small debris.

"Now that we're clear, let me show you what we've got so far."

She made a sharp turn and started walking. Franks and Lowery kept pace with her on a parallel path, careful not to touch anything on the tables between them. When Sterling stopped, so did the agents. She motioned to the second table.

"All this is headed to the lab. Those to the reconstruction team. Those." She pointed to two large boxes on the floor. "Those go to storage. I'm thinking I can get to them in two, maybe three, weeks."

She moved on, calling a halt when they reached the end of the hangar. She pointed to a partial seat leaning against the wall. The stuffing inside had erupted through the back. With both hands, she turned it to show them that the leather on the front was only scorched.

"Power to the cow it came from. Not a scratch on the front of this thing," she said. Josephine tilted it against the wall so that they could look more closely at the back. "This is the telling part. Whatever blew came from inside the plane, not the luggage compartment. But you probably already know that. I'm thinking it was under this seat, first row. "

She pointed to the scratched and bent chrome frame.

"It's hard to see, but the mark is 1A. You can see the blast impact here. The fireball blew out—forward—tearing this seat off its mounting and splitting it in half vertically. This part went up into the ceiling toward the cockpit. It was found in the galley, and I've got ceiling material scraped off this part here."

She pointed to the gusset in the upholstery construction.

Sterling crooked her finger and led them to a smaller table where there was a little mountain of debris. Bits of plastic, microscopic pieces of metal and glass. Skin and bone would be found when it was sifted through, but now the three were focused on two small pieces of charred wire.

"We found parts of a power supply, initiator, and evidence of the explosive. I'm still looking for the switch component. It's a fine job, I must say."

"So, we're dealing with a pro?" Lowery said. Josephine shrugged

"The internet makes everyone a pro if they apply themselves. The lab guys will have to determine if there's a signature or if it was a one-off."

Josephine snapped off her latex gloves and leaned back against the wall, posture perfect like a dancer.

"It actually shouldn't have done as much damage as it did. I think it was designed to implode, killing the people inside. It took out that building because the blast was exacerbated by the proximity to the fuel tank. If that plane was taking off or in flight with a full fuel load there wouldn't be anything left to look at."

"Do you think the detonation time was a mistake?" Agent Franks asked.

"There could have been a malfunction in the timer or the switch. Or, it could have been that there wasn't a timer and whoever detonated it was inside the plane. Maybe whoever was supposed to pull the switch got cold feet. Maybe he—or she—didn't find their balls until the plane landed. You know, a now or never kind of thing." Sterling's palms went upward. "It would be nice if you guys got a handle on a person of interest fast. That would save my team a whole lot of time if I could point them in the right direction."

"It won't be long." Agent Franks puffed out his chest. He was an eager beaver, and Sterling liked that.

"What about the casing?" Lowery asked.

He was the old pro and knew there was no magic. Sterling admired that too. It took all kinds to figure out who the bad guys were. Sometimes the trick was intuition, sometimes boring, meticulous probing. Eventually, they'd figure it out —or not.

Sterling pushed off the wall and simultaneously put her gloves back on. They were on the move again, retracing their steps. At the middle table she picked up an L-shaped piece of metal, fabric, and leather. She held it gingerly between her palms, turning it slowly.

"This is part of a briefcase. Four metal feet were on the edge, here." She used her nose to point the agents' eyes in the right direction. "That's the bottom. The depth is ten inches, the width is sixteen, height is fourteen. It was a substantial case."

She held on to the edges of one side, and dropped her other hand. This time she pointed with her finger.

"There was a metal bracket that attached the sides to the bottom piece meaning it was hard-sided: an attaché not a messenger bag or a duffel. It was well made, and expensive. It would be impossible for anyone to figure out what was inside because it provides rigid support. No jiggling or rattling, perfect dimensions to pack your hardware tight. Slide it under the seat. Choose your time, and boom." Josephine twisted it one more time, and held it toward the agents. "We've got a lot of stuff melted into the lining. This is off to the lab, too."

She put the item down. Lowery turned to his counterpart.

"Does this thing match up with what we've got on the luggage manifest?"

"No, but that doesn't mean anything," Franks answered. "It's not like Platinum did a sweep of the luggage."

"That will change now," Sterling said.

"Don't hold your breath," Lowery said. "Money talks. Private transportation won't take a chance on upsetting the clients. If they don't want their luggage scanned, it won't be."

"They won't have to worry about checking for bombs if they're out of business," Sterling countered.

"Wrongful death is the least of Platinum's worries. If the pilot or the stew were involved, then Platinum might be complicit in terrorism," Lowery said. "Can you tell who this case belonged to?"

Sterling put the piece back onto the table and arranged it just so.

"I might be able to pull DNA from oil residue; we might find a fingerprint. All that will tell us is who touched the case, not who torched it."

Agent Lowery rubbed his eyes, but they still felt dry and scratchy. He was getting too old for all-nighters.

"We've got what looks like a scrap of a watch face. I want to send that to the repository to see if they can bring up a manufacturing number," Josephine said. "I just don't know if it was part of the mechanism or came off someone's wrist."

"Sounds good," Lowery said.

The ATF's Arson and Explosives National Repository was the best in the world. If there were something to find, some connection to be made, they would make it.

"Let's share with The Terrorist Explosive Devise Analytical Center too."

"You want to bring the FBI in on this?" Josephine said. "This isn't even going to make above the fold in the Times. I doubt they'll give it a look anytime soon."

"She's got a point," Franks said. "They're gonna be ticked if this is just a personal grudge thing. There's not much glory in that."

"Nobody bothered to mention that a bunch of guys were taking private flight lessons but didn't want to know how to land before 9/11," Lowery said. "What if this was a dry run? I'm covering my butt with a heads up, that's all."

"Is the flight origination bothering you? Ireland?" Sterling asked.

"Ireland has a political history, but then again so does San Francisco." Lowery sighed and wagged his head. "We should have heard something by now if someone wanted to claim it."

Lowery put his hands in his pockets and glanced over the organized chaos.

"Whatever this was, I want to close it out fast and that's why we'll go wide. If the FBI reads the outreach as anything other than what it is, so be it."

"You're the boss," Josephine said, only to stop them before they went on their way. "FYI. I didn't find a flight recorder."

"They aren't mandated for charters," Lowery said.

"There's one thing that bothers me, though," Franks said. "It was a long haul— Ireland to San Francisco to L.A.—why wasn't there a co-pilot for the first leg? Maybe there's some guy in San Francisco who was lucky he got off when he did, or he got off because he knew what was going to happen."

Sterling and Lowery exchanged a look. She hadn't given Franks enough credit.

"Follow up with Platinum on that. "Agent Lowery did a half-turn and put a hand on his hip. He set his gaze outside. "What about cameras?"

"Two on the side of the building were damaged. Platinum is accessing the backup," Franks said, scoring another point.

"And I've got the damaged hardware ready to go over to the lab for recovery," Josephine said.

They fell silent, each running checklists in their mind, each concluding they were on track. When Lowery spoke again it was to no one in particular.

"A fancy plane and a big bomb, but nobody passengers. It

blew up on a runway removed from LAX so it wouldn't disrupt commercial travel. If this was supposed to be a statement, it's not translating."

"And if you wanted to take out one person, there are easier ways," Josephine said.

"Yep," Lowery said. "I'm betting whoever did this missed their mark, or it was an amateur who didn't think it through."

"They sure blew it then." Agent Franks snickered. Sterling gave him a cold eye and Lowery rolled his. Franks doubled down. "Come on, it's funny."

"Not if you've heard it a million times," Josephine said.

"Okay. No more jokes, but maybe it didn't have anything to do with the people on board," Franks said. "Maybe it was business. You know, it could be another charter wanted to sideline Platinum, or maybe Platinum torched it for the insurance."

"Whatever it is, it sure feels hinky," Lowery said. "Come on. Let's get back to work. I want to be home before dark."

Lowery and Franks left Josephine Sterling to her work and ambled toward the front of the hangar.

"You know what would be really bad?" Franks said.

"What?"

"If there was no good reason for all this. That would be bad."

"You think there's ever a good reason for blowing something up?" Lowery asked.

"No, but it's worse if it's just some hot dog. I hate it when it's a hot dog. I can at least understand if someone thinks they have a reason."

Lowery shrugged. He was not given to philosophical discourse. When you'd been around as long as he had, you knew the truth. The truth was even assholes had their reasons for being assholes.

Outside the two agents separated, each staking out half of the runway. Slowly, carefully, they paced, looking for missed fragments from the plane, the bomb, or the bodies. When they came together again both were empty-handed.

"I'm going to head back to the office," Agent Lowery said.

"I'll finish up inside. See you tomorrow," Franks said.

When Lowery got in his car. Franks gave him a wave, and disappeared into the hangar. Franks was a good guy, but Lowery hadn't bonded with him. For all he knew Franks didn't think Lowery was hot shit either. For sure the ATF brass didn't hold Lowery in high esteem. They were easing him out gradually, subtly, firmly. His assignments weren't high profile anymore. Lowery's input at the agency was minimized. His spit and polish attitude, wasn't considered cool. He was assigned Franks. That said it all.

The agency wanted younger agents who could play to the media, and they wanted them diversified: women, blacks, Hispanics, gays. Lowery didn't check any box. If that cop, O'Brien, worked for the ATF he would have been a star because he had an accent and a leather jacket.

That wasn't quite fair, though. O'Brien couldn't help the way he sounded and how he looked. Lowery might have even liked O'Brien if they met under different circumstances, but they hadn't. Finn O'Brien had crossed one too many lines to ever get on the right side of the agent's balance sheet. He entered Lowery's crime scene without permission, he assumed he would be welcome, he asked for a God damn favor because of his badge. In his entire career, Lowery had never asked for a favor or expected special treatment.

Tired, Lowery started the car and went on his way. He was a pro and always would be. Dwelling on a cop who would mean nothing in the long run, was a waste of time. He had to focus on some dude who thought he was a man when he really was a coward; who thought he was smart when he was the stupidest ass on the planet. He had a pile of crap on this one, and it was up to him to figure who pooped it out. Him and no one else.

Lowery swung onto Rosecrans, considering all the possibilities. The crew could have a beef with the company, the old guy could have been tired of living, the lady might have been involved with the pilot who wouldn't leave his wife, Platinum execs might have been between a financial rock and a hard place.

Or it was something else entirely.

Or it was just an asshole showing off.

17

Thursday was Mexican night at Mick's Irish Pub. Two-for-one Margaritas and free nachos until seven meant the place was packed.

Cori and Finn had snagged the last table, the one near the window under the neon Guinness sign that had hung there for twenty years. It spritzed and fizzled every time someone opened the door. Geoffrey Baptiste, the proprietor who hailed from Trinidad, was running his skinny ass off seeing to his customers, so Finn had bagged himself a Guinness and Cori a Margarita at the bar. He threaded his way back to her, put the drinks on the table.

"I'm sorry for not making it back this afternoon," he said, as he settled in.

"Anything I can help with?" Cori said.

Finn shook his head.

"No. I'm finding it difficult to get my bearing is all. I stopped home for lunch, and called Agent Lowery to see if there was an update.

"And what did he have to say?" Cori asked.

"I never got through," Finn said. "I tried Agent Franks. I even left a message for Josephine Sterling."

"You left a message for the tech?" Cori said. "What did you expect her to tell you?"

Finn shook his head, he smiled a little, and pushed a glass toward her.

"I've not got a clue, Cori. Sure, I'm feeling at odds and ends, and all this over a little old man I never knew."

"And an old friend you were in love with as a kid." Cori touched the rim of her Margarita and then put her finger to her tongue. That first taste of salt was the best. "Geeze, O'Brien. You grew up hearing your mother talk about Uncle Hugh, and Maura's always been in the back of your mind. Give yourself a break. Distance does make the heart grow fonder. Tell the captain. Take some time off. Grieve for God's sake. I can handle the work until you settle."

Cori took a healthy drink of her Margarita, but kept her eyes on her partner, trying to figure out what was different about him. There was a hard boil roiling inside him, but she couldn't figure out what specifically was popping his top. Anger? Disappointment? Maybe this incident stirred up a lot of old scores: resentment at the abuse he had taken from the department all those years ago, Bev's betrayal, his little brother's murder. Maybe Finn had turned the other cheek one too many times, and this... Who knew what Lowery's affront had triggered.

"You know, you're the one who should be asking for the break," Finn said. "You were hurt worse, and you're back to normal."

Cori almost spit out her drink. "Oh, honey, you are having problems if you're calling me normal."

Finn took a swig of his Guinness.

"Then I'll see the psychologist in the morning if that will

make you feel better," he said. "Until then, let me see what you've brought."

Cori was amused. There was a snowball's chance in hell that O'Brien would see the psychologist. At least his lie was smooth, and she appreciated the delivery. She pushed a sheaf of papers his way, thought of munching on the Nachos, and decided to pass.

"That's Paul's report on the body we checked out behind the parking lot near Grauman's Theater a couple of weeks ago."

Finn flipped to the body diagram. Neat markings indicated knife wounds on the victim's torso: two on the lower left and one just below the shoulder.

"I doubt the man could have done this to himself, and I further doubt we'll ever find who did this to him," Finn said.

"It wouldn't matter if we did," Cori said. "Look at page three. Our victim died of a heart attack."

"Then we can set this aside. Even if we found the person who assaulted him, the D.A. wouldn't prosecute."

"And that's a crying shame," Cori said.

"Criminals running the show," Finn lamented. "What else do you have?"

"Captain Fowler gave us a rousing talk on making sure we've updated our benefits information since the window is closing to make changes."

"Always fascinating," Finn laughed.

"Well, don't forget to look it over. Your packet is in your locker." Cori licked the salt off the rim of her glass and finished her cocktail. "If you need help, you just give me a holler, and I'll guide you through it."

She was about to tell her partner what other excitement rounded out the afternoon when she nudged Finn.

"Meg's here."

Finn turned to see his sister blow in with two guys hot on

her heels. The men went for the bar, and Meg beelined for Finn and Cori. She bumped into a man's chair and spent thirty seconds apologizing to him.

"She is cuter than a bug's ear," Cori said.

"That she is."

Finn stood so that Meg could throw herself at him for a quick, ferocious hug before holding him off to say her hellos twice for good measure. It did Cori's heart almost as much good as Finn's to see Meg.

They shared the infectious O'Brien family grin, but Meg used it more often than her brother. Other than their smiles, they were as different as night and day: Finn's eyes were blue and Meg's dark; Finn was tall and fit, Meg round and soft; Finn kept to himself and Meg was everyone's friend at first meeting. She had been a kindergarten teacher before having her own babies. As the youngest of the brood, she was all-American, born in the States unlike, her brother who was nearly grown when the family left Ireland. When she let go of Finn, Meg was on Cori.

"Oh, Cori. How nice to see you." Meg's brow furrowed as she looked at Cori's face. "How are you feeling?"

"Like a Macy's parade balloon." Cori puffed out her cheek, knowing her make-up could hide neither swelling nor bruising.

"Very funny, but I still think you're crazy doing the work you're doing." Meg made a clicking noise with her tongue. "I'm grateful you do it, but honestly, it's so dangerous." Finn pulled out a chair for her, and she was still fussing when she sat down. "Still, I'm glad you're Finn's partner. I mean selfishly, I'm happy for that."

"Can I get you a drink, Meg?" Finn asked.

"Oh, no. Thank you. I've really got to get home and get dinner started. I was at mom's all afternoon and Dave is going to be home by…" She checked her watch. "Oh, my goodness. He'll be home at six. I'll be late, but it can't be helped."

"We wouldn't want Dave to go hungry, so what is it that brings you here?" Finn said.

"I'm really sorry to bother you with this, but I honestly didn't know what to do." Meg pulled her big purse onto her lap, opened it, and took out an envelope. She started to hand it to Finn, but pulled it back against her chest before he touched it. "Maybe I shouldn't give it to you at all. I don't want to implicate you."

Meg's voice lowered, and her eyes narrowed. She was almost whispering when she said:

"Opening someone else's mail is a crime, and that's what I did. Maybe I should have shown it to ma first. Maybe that's what I should do instead. Give it to her."

She started to put the envelope back in her purse, but Finn took her wrist in one hand and the envelope in the other.

"Sure, Meghan, I'm not going to be turning you into the feds," he said.

"And I'm sworn to secrecy." Cori crossed her heart, before resting her chin on her upturned fist.

"Okay, then," Meg said. "Well, take a look."

Finn gave the envelope a once over, but saw nothing unusual. It was eight-by-ten and manilla colored, heavy in the hand, and important looking. He noted the return address, flipped the envelope, opened it, and withdrew a sheaf of white paper that was stapled to the light blue cover stock of a legal document. He perused the first page and then flipped to the next. That's when his expression changed from confused, to curious, and finally amused.

Meg held her hands to her heart. Her eyes were wide as she waited for her brother to speak.

"Well? What do you think?"

"How did you come by this again?" He spoke even as he read, turning a page and then turning it back.

"I've been trying to help ma out a little. You know, tidying up, just keeping her company," Meg said. "When Sean took her to church on Sunday, I saw the mail had piled up so I sorted it. I threw away the junk mail, and was putting the bills in a pile. I thought this was one of those mailings to sell her insurance, but just in case it wasn't I opened it and—well—you see. I mean, wow."

Meg hunched over the table, despite the fact that no one in Mick's was paying them any mind. She lowered her voice and listed toward Cori.

"It was all I could do to zip my lip, Cori. I just don't like to be responsible for things like this, so I decided to call Finn because he's the law." She swayed the other way, closer now to Finn. "What do you think? Should we tell her?"

"Tell ma what?" Cori asked.

Finn cut his eyes her way. She saw the twinkle in them, and knew that he was trying to hide his amusement from his sister.

"It would seem our mother is an heiress," he said. "According to this, Uncle Hugh has kindly left her ten million dollars."

18

"Dennis? Honey?"

Katherine Cain paused in the doorway that led from the lovely living room of her home to the equally beautiful yard. She was backlit by the low lights. Had her husband looked her way he would have seen only her long, lean silhouette, not her annoyed expression.

When he didn't respond, Katherine thought about leaving him to his deep, miserable thoughts, but changed her mind. Done with being the understanding wife, she headed for him, walking past the teak table where they entertained in the summer and the pots of herbs and tomatoes that she meticulously tended year-round. She took the wide steps to the lower patio in stride, and walked the apron around the exquisite pool.

The concrete was cool under her bare feet, the night was warm, and the water in the pool was inviting. When the family first moved into this house, they lived in the pool: the boys cannonballing into it, Dennis swimming laps, she twirling on a float only to have Dennis surface for a kiss before diving under again. Sometimes they skinny-dipped at midnight. Katherine couldn't remember the last time they had a swim –midnight or not. It was hard to remember when Dennis had come to her for a kiss instead of her begging for one from him.

These last days had only made things worse. Once she thought she heard him crying in the shower. Tonight, though, he looked peaceful. His eyes were closed, his hands were crossed over his stomach. She touched his shoulder. He turned his head and watched as she slid her hand down his arm.

"Where are you tonight?" she asked.

"Right here."

"Liar." Katherine did her best to smile. She made a motion and Dennis reluctantly made room for her. When she was settled beside him, she said, "I know Hugh meant a lot to you, but it's not like he was family, Dennis. "

"He was family," Dennis said.

"Oh, honey, come on. You hadn't seen that man in years."

"You're right. Move on."

Katherine clenched her jaw to keep from snapping at him. She hated this act, this weird mood, this romantic, tragic nonsense. She tried again.

"Why don't you tell me what I can do? Do you want me to follow up on the people who are hurt? Send flowers to Hugh's family? Would it help if Brian moved in here until this business is settled?"

"No." Dennis was quick and sure. "Brian prefers the hotel. You know him."

"Yes, I do," she said. "And I think you need him now to—"

"I don't want to talk about, Brian," Dennis said.

"Then let's talk about the investigation."

"It's being taken care of," Dennis said. "Katherine, really, I just need to work some things out. You don't know what it's like. I'm responsible for Hugh's death—"

"Oh, stop," Katherine said. "You made him very happy giving him this trip. I'm sorry it ended the way it did, but you have a family that needs your attention and Hugh has a family to take care of him."

Dennis dropped his head back.

"If it hadn't been for Brian, I wouldn't have known that we just let him retire without some sort of fanfare."

"Well, then, good for Brian, but you made it happen. Take some credit, sweetie." Katherine took her husband's hand in both of hers. "Have you seen Hugh's family?"

"Only a nephew."

"Then contact him. Tell him you'd like to pay for the funeral expenses even if it means flying the whole family back to Ireland."

When Dennis shrugged and stayed silent, Katherine dropped her husband's hand.

"Dennis, listen to me. I know Wolfhound is failing. I know you've done everything you can to save it, and I know Hugh's death is another blow. There will probably be lawsuits. Settle them, leave Wolfhound to Hammet, and be done with it. If you don't, you're going to lose more than the business."

When Dennis stayed silent, Katherine pulled her lips together.

"I see. I didn't realize I was expendable."

She started to rise, but Dennis clamped his hand on her arm and kept her down. She pulled away again, but he was surprisingly strong.

"I am sorry," he said.

She turned her head. He sat up. Now he had both her hands, and Katherine had no choice but to look at him.

"You didn't see that plane. I had no idea it would look like that. I mean, it never occurred to me..."

"You never thought anything bad could happen to your precious Wolfhound family?"

"Jesus, Katherine."

"I'm just saying that life can be shit. Sometimes you have to suck it up," she said.

"Okay. Fine. Fine."

Dennis let her go and swung his legs over the side of the lounge. He got up so abruptly that the lounge teetered. He paced the edge of the pool. When he turned around again, Dennis Cain saw his wife so clearly: beautiful, tenacious, strong, so objective about everything. In that instant, he hated everything about her even though that was unfair. She was fighting for him the same way he fought for his company. Sadly, she didn't know it wasn't just Hugh's death that was torturing him. The fact that he couldn't tell her the whole truth about this nightmare made him feel low and dirty.

"It's not like television, you know. What happened to that plane was horrific."

"You're preaching to the choir, Dennis," she said. "Just because I don't talk about it doesn't mean I've forgotten all those horrible things I saw."

"That was different. That was..."

Katherine heard a catch in his throat. He licked his lips and lowered his eyes, and Katherine saw the sad truth. Dennis would always feel responsible for the accident in the same way he felt responsible for Wolfhound's legacy. Guilt was built into his DNA.

"You'll learn how to handle this. I can help you." Katherine slid off the lounge, speaking softly as she walked toward him. "The worst thing you can do is internalize this."

She stood in front of him. He looked as if he wanted to speak. Instead, he pulled her close. One hand stroked her hair. Katherine could hear his heart beat, steady and strong. Her arms went around him, and she closed her eyes. It had been so long since he held her.

"Katherine, I have to tell you someth—"

"Nope, not tonight. No confessions." She leaned back so that she could touch her fingertips to his lips. "Step back. Let Hammet do whatever it wants. If you can't bear to see it shut down, resign. Let Brian make the final decisions. He's been doing that anyway."

Dennis scoffed. "Brian. He hasn't the heart."

"He's exactly the kind of person you need to see this through. The only difference between Hugh and Wolfhound is that one is dying slowly," she said. "Please, let it all go."

Dennis broke away. "It's not just Wolfhound. It's..."

Katherine waved her hands as if that could wipe those words away. To his surprise, she laughed while she did so.

"We'll go in circles, Dennis. I don't want to know what else there is."

Dennis smiled, grateful that she had stopped him. He was going to tell her an ugly truth and she didn't deserve that. Katherine was lovely, but he didn't desire her. She was concerned, but he couldn't find it in himself to care. She was smart, but hers wasn't the counsel he needed. Nothing Katherine could say or do would heal him, but he didn't want to add her to the casualty list. He didn't want to hurt anyone ever again.

"It's all going to be fine, Katherine," he said. "Give me a month to sort things out. After that, I'll know where Wolfhound stands. I'll know where I stand."

"And what about where we stand?" Katherine asked.

"We will be together forever," he said, and that was the truth. "There's no question about that. Not now."

Katherine let her eyes roam over his face and then she kissed him. It was clear he didn't spark at her touch, but that was all right. Once Wolfhound was settled and they had time, she would make sure that changed.

"That's all I ever wanted," she murmured. When she stood

away and shook back her long hair, Dennis was mesmerized. It almost looked red in the soft light. He touched it and swallowed a sudden sob.

"You've always been wonderful, Katherine," Dennis said. "Any man would be lucky to have you.

"Then let's start something new. Right here at home. There's nothing we can't do together."

Dennis looked into her dark eyes, wishing they were lighter. He touched her hair and it was straight, no waves under his fingers.

"You're right. There really is nothing for me in Ireland anymore."

Katherine tried not to show how thrilled she was at the perceived promise of change, but Dennis read her perfectly. She really was easy to please. All he had to do was rip out his heart and his wife would be happy. The only problem was that she didn't know when to quit.

"I know it's hard to admit, but no one is irreplaceable. Not even you."

"You're right," Dennis said. "No one is."

"Except to me. You're irreplaceable to me."

She kissed him once more. Dennis kissed back, but without passion. It was too easy to stoke desire's embers to flame, and he didn't want that to happen. She would read too much into it. Not that it mattered what he wanted. Katherine had written the script, and he was just a bit player. Her fingers slid across his chest as she took her leave.

"I'm going to get into bed," she said. "Don't be long."

Dennis shook his head. She took that as a promise, but he was politely declining an invitation. When Dennis heard the French doors close, he settled himself on the lounge, and took out his cellphone. Brian had left a message.

On track. Let's talk.

Dennis closed his eyes. He didn't want to talk to Brian. He didn't even want to know Brian. For ten years the man had passed judgement on Dennis without saying a word. He just watched, waited, and analyzed every move Dennis made. Brian should have stayed in the army. He was a fine soldier, but business was not a battlefield. Risky strategies, bold charges forward without a thought for who or what might be sacrificed, was dangerous. He turned off his phone and stayed outside until he was sure his wife was asleep.

19

The woman standing next to Finn in the elevator had no shame, openly giving him the once over from the top of his shaved head to the toes of his heavy boots. When the elevator stopped, the brass doors opened, and their ninety-seconds of intimacy were over, he stepped out and she stayed in.

The woman, like this tall building, and the people whose corporate ladder never led to the top of anything, made Finn's soul feel claustrophobic. Not that he didn't appreciate those who made the modern world spin, he was just grateful that his life had taken a different turn. Finn was, however, impressed with the service. He wasn't more than one step out of the elevator when he was greeted by a young man with a bright smile.

He sat behind an impressive desk at the far end of the long hall. The blonde wood had been fashioned into a long straight plane before turning up at the end like a cresting wave. Golden letters spelled out the words *Intrepid Insurance* across the face of it; on the wall behind the desk was a golden circle with the initials of the company carved inside. The double I's looked like towering buildings, buffers against the vagaries of life.

"Impressive." Finn nodded at the desk.

"Some artist in Norway made it, so that's cool." Finn smiled at the man's genuine pride. "Who are you here to see?"

"I've received a notice of an insurance settlement, but I believe a mistake has been made. I'd like to speak to someone about that."

"Can I look?"

Finn gave over the envelope. The young man pulled the papers partway out and nodded.

"248F9. That's Maggie Davis. You can wait over there while I get her," the receptionist said. "What's your name?"

"Finn O'Brien, though I doubt it will mean anything to her."

"Company policy," he said. "It's part of the personal attention we give at Intrepid."

The young man pushed a button and somewhere in the bowels of the giant office a phone rang.

"WANT TO GO TO LUNCH?"

Maggie looked up. Zach was peering over the top of their shared cubical wall. All she could see were his eyes behind the bright blue circle frames of his glasses and a mop of dark hair. Yesterday he wore horn-rimmed tortoiseshell frames that made him look like a metro-sexual Clark Kent. When she first started working at Intrepid Insurance, Maggie cringed at the thought of spending her waking hours with him. He was flamboyant, dramatic, living in his own too-hip reality, and way too chatty for her taste.

Within the week she had changed her mind. Zach was nice, and smart, and fun. His wardrobe of weird glasses was nothing more than an *homage* to Elton John. Zach was an aspiring musician, Maggie was an underground club girl, and their bonding was a done deal.

"Earth to Maggie?" Zach perched a little higher and waved. "Lunch?"

"Sure. Where?" Maggie closed the file she was working on, and put it on a pile on the side of her desk. Her chair squeaked a little as she kicked back.

"I don't care. Cheap. Chinese?" he said.

Maggie countered.

"Mediterranean. The place over on—"

Before the debate began it was over. Maggie's phone rang, and when she was finished with the call she put on her jacket.

"Too late. Duty calls. But if you go out, bring me something. I'll pay you back."

“Even if it’s Chinese?”

“Even.”

Maggie walked out of her cubicle, down the hall, and found Finn seated on a low-slung chair in the reception area, the fingers of one hand tapping his knee.

"Mr. O'Brien?"

"Maggie?"

"That's me,” she said. "Come on back.”

She chatted as they walked. Finn answered in kind, saying nothing of import as they turned into a section of cubicles that, like the reception desk, and was artfully pieced together.

"Here you go, Mr. O'Brien."

Maggie held a serviceable chair for him. She took an equally practical one on the other side of her desk. When she was seated, Maggie pushed aside her keyboard, laced her fingers, and gave him a smile.

"How can I help you today?"

"Well, I have an interesting problem, and if it isn't a problem then it will be all the more interesting."

Finn handed over the envelope Meg had given him.

"These papers arrived for my mother. While I'm sure she would be delighted with ten million dollars, my uncle was a pensioner, retired, and he lived in Ireland. This legacy seems a bit out of line. The second question is, why would this come from your office here in Los Angeles?"

"People take out large life insurance policies as a way of creating an inheritance. Your uncle might have wanted to provide if your mother was in need."

"That wouldn't be the case."

"Well, then, he might have just been really generous," Maggie suggested.

"That would make him a grand fellow, indeed," Finn laughed. "Still, my money is on a mistake."

"Well, then, let's take a look." She pulled the keyboard in front of her and started to type, referring to the papers as she did so. "You know most people would take the money and run."

Finn laughed. "I promise, my mother will have no trouble accepting the truth no matter what it is —millionaire or not."

Maggie shot a smile his way, only to have it fade as she scrolled down the information on her computer screen. She tapped the keyboard again, paused, and then added a few more strokes.

"Well, I'm seeing some conflicting information, Mr. O' Brien."

Maggie pushed back her chair, gathered the papers, and tapped them on the desk. Her smile had returned, but this time it was guarded.

"I'm going to check with my boss. I won't keep you waiting long."

When Maggie was gone, Finn rested one foot on his knee and listened to the wheels of commerce turning. Intrepid Insurance took bets on the destruction of a building, the failure of a business, the end of a human life. It was like a ghoulish casino, gambling on a worst-case scenario, cashing in on the best. Everyone who paid their dollar was hedging their own bet. Tiring of the business of insurance, Finn pulled out his phone and checked his messages.

Cori was sitting through the department's mandatory sexual harassment education meeting and was worried about herself. She had flunked the initial test, disqualifying herself as an outraged feminist because she thought the examples of inappropriate jokes in the workplace were funny. Finn suggested she cheat. She suggested the department just give her the money they were spending on her 'education' and let her fellow officers tell any joke they like.

There was a text from Gretchen. They were due to have dinner that night and she wanted to know if he preferred burgers or hot dogs. She'd been on a three-day assignment with the LAFD, and not managed the grocery. Finn responded that he would take her out. She sent back a heart on fire. He knew it wasn't passion she was suggesting, just a firefighter's sign-off.

The third text was never read. Maggie was back, and with her was a woman much like the one in the elevator. She was attractive, well dressed, compartmentalized, efficient, and very obviously in charge.

20

"Mr. O'Brien, this is Ms. Whitfield, our Executive Vice President of Claims."

Finn started to stand but there was no room to maneuver, so he stayed put as she shook his hand. Her grip was just solid enough, and her smile pleasant. She rested her hip on the side of Maggie's desk, the only place left to sit in this small place. Maggie, herself, was back behind her desk.

"Maggie explained the situation," Jane Whitfield said. "An error like this is unsettling after your loss. We do apologize. Mr. Murphy is insured by us through an affiliate in Ireland, but it is a personal policy valued at ten thousand dollars. We took care of the notification because the beneficiary is here in the States."

"And, the beneficiary is my mother? Or was that also a mistake?"

Jane Whitfield started to answer, but was distracted when Maggie raised a finger. A quick look was exchanged, the kind that said she would be with the girl in a minute.

"Yes, she is, and I'm glad we can clear this up," she said. "Do you have any other concerns we can clear up?"

“I don’t,” Finn said. “Thank you for your time. I’m glad this is a simple thing.”

Jane stood and went past Finn into the common area. Finn did the same, offering Maggie a wave of thanks as he went.

“I hope you didn’t have to come too far,” Jane said.

“No, I work in Hollywood. It wasn’t a problem,” Finn said. “You can reach me here, rather than go through my mother.”

Finn offered her a card. Jane Whitfield glanced at it as he said:

"One of L.A.'s finest.”

“I do my best.”

"Well, detective, thanks again for being so understanding. We’ll make things right.”

“There’s just one more thing,” Finn said. “There are extenuating circumstances regarding my uncle’s death."

Finn glanced away from the woman, aware that Maggie was slowly typing, her gaze flitting between him and her computer screen. He looked for some sign that she needed his attention, but Ms. Whitfield touched his elbow. She also lowered her voice because the topic was a delicate one.

"The only problem would be if your uncle died by suicide," Jane said.

"He died in an accident." Finn said, giving no credence to Agent Lowery’s suggestion that everyone was a criminal suspect.

"I’m so sorry. No wonder you’re concerned about your mother. It must have been a shock. Don’t worry. I’ll personally see that this is taken care of." She looked over her shoulder. "Maggie, go ahead and forward me everything you have on Mr. Murphy. I’ll see to the claim, and you can take it off your schedule.”

"Ms. Whitfield, I think you should—" Maggie started to turn her computer screen, but Jane Whitfield wasn’t interested.

"It's fine, Maggie. We don't want to keep Detective O'Brien any longer than necessary." To Finn, she said, "If your mother doesn't get a check in ten days, call me directly."

"Thank you." Finn took the envelope back. "Until then, I'll hold onto this."

"There's no need. I'll be redoing all the documents." She reached for the envelope, but Finn tucked it under his arm.

"Still, I'm a careful sort," Finn answered. "I'll have the full file just in case there is ever a question about the settlement."

Jane Whitfield's hesitation was nothing more than a wink, but Finn saw it for what it was. The woman didn't want a mistake of this magnitude documented. To her credit, she was gracious

"Of course. I like things wrapped up neatly, too." Jane smiled. "I think you know the way from here, Detective O'Brien."

"That I do. Thank you for your time."

Jane Whitfield turned one way and Finn the other. By the time he figured out that he didn't have her number, Jane Whitfield was in her office behind closed doors. He went to Maggie's cubical. She was leaning back in her chair, talking to the man in the next office.

"Excuse me, Maggie."

She snapped upright. The young man ducked away.

"Mr. O'Brien."

Maggie smiled, but it was a wooden expression. She was looking over his shoulder, barely paying attention.

"Don't worry," Finn said. "She's back to her office."

Maggie chuckled. Finn heard a stifled laugh from the man in the next cubicle.

"Ms. Whitfield said to call directly, but she forgot to give me her number. Can you give it to me?"

"Sure, of course."

Maggie waited for him to open his phone before giving him Jane Whitfield's private number. He copied it and thanked her.

"I hope everything gets straightened out," she said. "You're the second mis-notification we've had this week. I hope we haven't been hacked."

"Sure, there's a lot of that going around these days, too," Finn said. "Many thanks."

"You're welcome," she said.

To Finn it seemed there was something more. When she stayed silent, Finn said:

"Ms. Whitfield has bigger fish to fry than this. 'Twas only a mistake, and I'm sure not yours." Finn pointed to a notepad on her desk. "May I?"

"Sure."

He tore off a piece of paper and wrote his name and number on it.

"Just in case you need anything else from me to wrap this up."

"Thanks, but I'm sure Ms. Whitfield will take care of everything. She's very thorough."

"Then we've no worries," Finn said.

"No, I suppose we don't," Maggie said.

When Finn was gone, Maggie looked at the number. She started to crumple the paper only to change her mind and put it in a drawer. Maggie opened the files on her computer again, and started reading in earnest. Zach came in before she had read much.

"You still want to go to lunch?"

"No, thanks," Maggie said.

"I'm buying." When that didn't get a rise out of her, he said: "Still want me to bring you something back?"

"I'm good, Zach," she snapped.

"Okay, I heard you."

Zach gave up. This job wasn't worth getting upset about, and if Maggie wanted to do that then she was on her. She relented a minute later.

"I'm sorry," she said. "Really. Come on don't be mad."

Zach turned around again and pulled the extra chair up to the desk.

"What happened? What did you do?"

"Nothing," she said. "But someone did."

"Then you're not in trouble, so everything is okay," he said.

"No, it's not." Maggie crossed her arms on her desk, and lowered her voice. "I think there's something wrong because there were two problems with the same company. Whitfield didn't even want to hear about it."

"She didn't want to hear about it in front of a client," Zach said. "And when did you get so sensitive anyway?"

"I don't know." She chewed on her lip and gave him a look. "I just don't want to be a pencil pusher. I mean, don't you actually want to go home and know you made a difference?"

"Uh, that would be a no," Zach said and they both laughed. "But knock your socks off. Just cut Whitfield some slack. I wouldn't want you blabbing in front of an outsider either."

"You're right. My bad." Maggie tilted her screen. "You want to see what I'm looking at?"

"Nope," he said. "But if you run out of stuff to stick your nose into, feel free to do my work."

"In your dreams," Maggie said.

When he was gone, Maggie realized Zach was right. She would talk to Jane Whitfield privately. She might get a pat on the back. She could even get a raise. And one of these days, she might even be the boss.

~

JANE HAD PLANS FOR LUNCH, but those plans had changed. Now she was searching for the paperwork on Hugh Murphy's settlement.

When she found it, Jane hit the print button, and cross-referenced personal and corporate policy designators. Both were issued a very long time ago under the Intrepid umbrella, but written by their Irish affiliate. Both the policies were valid, as she well knew, and both had been compromised by an inattentive clerk who transposed two numbers. Jane began to type instructions to the overseas claim office when Maggie knocked on her door.

"Yes?" Jane hit send and then gave Maggie her full attention

"I just wanted to say that I'm sorry, I didn't mean to make problems in front of a client."

"I appreciate that, Maggie," she said. "Anything else?"

Maggie handed her a sheet of paper.

"This is what bothered me. There has been a cross-over between personal policies and corporate. It's odd that there were two in the same company, the same day, and the same mistake."

"It's all good." Jane looked at the new information. "Thanks, Maggie. I've already sent a correction on Mr. Murphy. I'll just add this one."

"Do you think someone got into the system and is redirecting corporate payouts to personal accounts?" Maggie said, pleased that Jane was engaging.

"I don't think so, and it's nothing for you to worry about. It's probably a coding matter," Jane said. "So, is that it?

"I suppose," Maggie said.

"Great." Jane was clearly done with the conversation. But before Maggie left the office she said: "I appreciate the extra mile."

Maggie went back to her desk, sure that Jane Whitfield now

saw her in a different light. But behind closed doors, Jane Whitfield wasn't thinking about Maggie Davis. She was considering making a call to a man she hadn't talked to in ten years. Then again, why bother? She had already taken care of things on her end, so there really was nothing to worry about.

21

"Finn, look at you!"

Paul Craig, the L.A. medical examiner, brightened when Finn knocked at the door of his office. He got up, grabbing Finn's hand, pumping it as he clapped him on the back. He took a close look at Finn's face.

"How are you feeling? Nothing broken?"

"I fared pretty well, Paul. Everything is healing."

"And Cori. How is she doing? Better? Bruises only?"

"She's fine. We're both fine," Finn said.

"That's excellent. I had no idea Mr. Murphy was your uncle until you called. I would have contacted you sooner if I had. Perhaps you might have wanted to be with me while I tended to him."

"I'm glad you handled it personally, but no need for me to be here." Finn let go of Paul's hand and sat down. "The ATF doesn't want me involved, but I didn't think calling you would be stepping on anyone's toes."

"I suppose you're talking about Agent Lowery," Paul said. "All business, that one. By the book. Close to the vest."

"Then you've met him," Finn said.

"Hardly. I receive my walking orders via formal texts and email. Or his assistant calls," Paul said. "I don't trust people who have no personal time for the departed."

"The fed has its own protocol."

Finn held his tongue about his dissatisfaction with the agent. If he started with his litany of complaints, he would never stop.

"Be that as it may..." Paul dropped the conversation. There was, after all, nowhere to go with it.

"Do you have any idea when you'll be able to release Hugh to us?" Finn asked.

"Again, waiting for Agent Lowery. Hopefully, by Friday next week. I'm sending everything I have to him this afternoon."

"We've arranged with the funeral home. They'll be ready when you are," Finn said.

"We'll just do the best we can with what we've got." Paul said, his voice trailing off.

"Was there some reason you wanted to see me, Paul?" Finn said.

"You know me, Finn, I don't like to make waves, and I've been second-guessing my call to you," Paul said. "Now that you're here, though, I should bite the bullet, and be done with it. The heck with Agent Lowery."

"He'll never hear about this from me," Finn laughed. "He won't even take my calls."

"Well then, let's take a walk."

Paul, chatted about his wife and the vacation they were planning as they walked through the halls. The detective listened with half an ear as he looked through the windows of the autopsy rooms. In one, a big man in scrubs worked on a cadaver. The chest was open, the face was peeled away. Finn smiled at the doctor who grinned back and raised the cadaver's hand to wave at Finn. Finn responded in kind, forgiving the gentle hijinks of people whose work days were filled with death.

The next two rooms were empty, which surprised Finn since the morgue was full up. He put a finger to his nose and rubbed. The smell of death and formaldehyde slapped him smack in the face the minute he left the administrative offices. Even after all these years he wasn't used to it.

Finn caught up with Paul as he was calling the elevator. It took them to the basement where Finn followed him to the room where brains were stored. The containers were uniformed, marked, and neatly stacked. Finn had seen this room once before, and thought it was a fascinating, otherworldly, dystopian place. It was also an odd destination.

"Sorry for the surroundings, but no one will bother us here. Have a seat," Paul said.

Finn pulled a stool up to the long, well-used table while the ME went to a cabinet at the end of the room. When Paul returned, he was carrying two large clear plastic bags. Finn had often taken possession of bags like this in the chain of evidence, but he had never accepted a family member's effects. He needn't worry. Paul was not giving him Hugh's things. Those would go to Agent Lowery. But now, Paul held up one bag and said:

"These are your uncle's clothes: Pants, hat, underwear, shirt, jacket. I found bits of his passport. Nothing is salvageable. I have his keys and some change from inside his pocket, but I found something else."

He sat on a stool, opened the big bag, and retrieved a smaller one. He reached inside that one, took out two stones and put them on the counter. Finn turned one between his fingers, and held it to the light. It was irregular in shape and the surface seemed scratched and cloudy.

"Sea glass?" Finn put it back down.

"I don't think so, Finn," Paul said. "I found one embedded in the upper arm of your uncle's jacket. I found another in his ear."

Clearly excited, Paul scooped them up and put them back in

the bag. He opened the second large bag and went through the same ritual. This time he put three rocks on the counter. They were a different size and shape than the others, but had the same milky look.

"I thought it odd when I found them on your uncle. I assumed something had kicked up from God knew where. Then I found these." He nudged a rock with a finger, then looked at Finn. "I'm no expert, but I think these are uncut diamonds."

"Sure, what would my uncle be doing with such things?" Finn laughed.

"I think your uncle was near the person who was carrying them, and the explosion blew them into him," Paul said.

"The only one he was close to was the stewardess," Finn said.

"Exactly." Paul finger-poked the counter so hard the rocks jumped. "I found one of these loose and two in the remnants of a cloth bag in the pocket of the stewardess' jacket. I have the body measurements of Mr. Murphy and the stewardess. Allowing for the curvature of your uncle's spine and the height of the stewardess's heels, the side of your uncle's face would have been parallel with her jacket pocket. Breast pocket to ear."

Paul sat back, and raised his palms as if to say his work was done. Finn inclined his head, considering the stone in his hand. He picked up another one and looked closer. His ex had collected sea glass, and it was smooth, colorful, and frosted. These stones were different. They were geodesic and there was a clarity underneath the surface.

"What does Lowery say?" Finn said.

"I won't know until he goes through what I'm sending this afternoon."

"Well then, it will be a while before he gets to this," Finn said. "But surely you don't think my uncle was colluding with the stewardess. The man was eighty."

Finn pushed the stones toward the M.E.

"It's not my job to speculate," Paul said. "But I know the ATF is sniffing around your uncle. Smuggling is bad business, and I doubt age would have anything to do with it if he was a criminal."

"True, but if Hugh were a mastermind with a young blonde accomplice, and someone wanted to send a message, they would shoot them both and take the diamonds. 'Tis how it's done in the movies."

"I'm just saying something might be off," Paul said, still serious despite Finn's teasing. "And you should be prepared."

"I appreciate that," Finn said. "No matter what these are, they probably belonged to the woman. It isn't illegal to have such stones."

"As I said, I draw no conclusions." Paul shrugged. "But I've dealt with ATF before. If this looks like an easy road to go down, they will go down it. God help you and your family if you're at the end of it."

"I'm appreciative, Paul, but this is Lowery's business. There's nothing I can do about it." Finn slid off the stool. "When will you be giving this over?"

"He's sending a messenger by four."

"Then you've already done the inventory and forwarded it. He'll know what he's supposed to have in that package," Finn said.

"Yep. Locked in."

"Pity," Finn said. "It would be difficult to borrow a stone and have it checked out."

"Yes, it would." Paul commiserated. "Still, I suppose a jeweler could tell what these were from a photograph. I mean if I had to guess."

Paul left the rocks on the counter, got up, and turned his back on Finn. There was much to admire about the man, subtlety was not one of those things. So as not to disappoint,

Finn photographed the stones, and cleared his throat when he was finished. Paul turned around, scooped them up, and packed them away. Finn thought it a pity there was no one to appreciate his performance

"Well, I better get these back to Sally to pack up. We can't keep Agent Lowery waiting."

The moment they were out the door, Paul started chattering again. The M.E. had done what he felt he must do. Hugh's effects would be sent to Agent Lowery who would pass them along to Josephine Sterling, who would pass them off to a lab. All those folks would conduct their tests, use their mathematics to assign distances of bodies to bomb. That would put further distance between humanity and evidence. The stones would be logged and examined and, if it were true that they were uncut diamonds, Agent Franks would be assigned to run down from whence they came, to whom they belonged, and if there was anything illegal about possessing them.

By the time Paul said his goodbyes, Finn was behind another hour on the clock. He decided another hour would make no difference in his day, so Finn drove himself downtown, parked in front of the Jewelry Mart, and went into the building at 637 South Hill Street.

The huge open space was divided into individual stalls. Jewelers of every stripe hawked their wares. Any one of them could have looked at Finn's picture but there was only one person he trusted, so he declined the calls to look in the display cases that sparkled with diamonds, rubies, and emeralds, slim bands of gold and silver chains. He went straight for the beautiful blonde standing behind the counter at Euro-Art Jewelers. She smiled wide when she saw him.

"It's been a long time, Finn," she said. "What are you looking for today?"

"Just you, Lydia," he said. "You and your beautiful eyes."

22

Jane was tucked into the corner of the couch in her office, her feet up, her shoes off. She had given strict instructions not to be disturbed, yet here she was. Disturbed. Bothered. Frustrated.

It was late in the afternoon, but only ten minutes since Maggie had left another report about the Wolfhound policies. As she read it, Jane's corporate life passed before her eyes. She had met Brian Cain at a distiller's conference when she was tasked with getting Intrepid's Irish affiliate on track. The attraction was instantaneous, the relationship short-lived, but the business they had done together was brilliant, and unfortunately enduring. It gave Wolfhound administration peace of mind and put Jane on Intrepid management's fast track. Jane had all but forgotten about what she had put in motion, and now here it was, staring her in the face, ready to bite her in the butt. There was nothing illegal in what she had done, but there was a question of propriety.

Now Maggie was close to figuring it out, and that was the strangest part of all. Jane had pegged her for a box-checker who didn't give a twit about what she was actually doing. Now here she was with her teeth sunk in, her eye was on the ball. This new report had thirteen names, cross-referenced policy numbers, and dates of issue. Jane had put Maggie off with vague mumblings.

Interesting.

Intriguing.

Yes, something to look into.

Of course...on to the proper channels.

The proper channels wouldn't like this one bit, but they would love Maggie's charts and graphs. Setting aside the report, Jane picked up the bi-weekly payout schedule and approved every request. Just as she finished, there was a knock and her door opened.

"Maggie."

Jane tried to keep her pique under control. Maggie didn't notice her boss's tight smile, and the disappointment in her voice.

"Before I leave for the day, I thought I'd see if you heard anything."

"Tech said they think it's a glitch, not a hack," Jane swung her legs off the sofa and slipped into her shoes.

"Did you tell them it looks like deliberate reassignment?" Maggie asked. "So far I found seven in the same company and four in another that had policies written for —"

"Corporate will handle it, Maggie.

Maggie did a little head tick as if something had stung her.

"Okay, then. Sure. I'll wait. Do you want me to—"

"I want you to go home. It's late," Jane said. "Unless there's something else,"

Maggie shook her head. She murmured a goodnight and left the office. Reaching back to close Jane's door, she saw that Jane

Whitfield was watching her. When Jane's phone rang, she picked up the receiver.

"Can you hold for a minute?" she said.

Jane walked across her office, closed the door, and went back to her call.

"Sorry. Yes, this is Jane Whitfield."

"This is Sarah from corporate claims to advise that there's a hold on the policy you asked us to expedite."

The woman went on to provide a policy number. Jane didn't need to take it down. She knew it by heart. What she didn't know was that the case was on hold due to a government investigation. That was an interesting and unwelcome piece of information. Jane finished the call and was dialing the next one when she was interrupted again.

"Come in." When Maggie appeared. Jane put the phone down. This time she didn't try to hide her displeasure. "You are pushing it, Maggie."

"I promise. This is it. I won't bring it up again, but I don't think you're seeing the implications. If all the accounts were experiencing this problem, I would think it was a glitch, but it's only two companies. That's why I think these two are targeted, and someone big needs to look into it."

"In this office I'm as big as you're going to get," Jane said. "Do you understand?"

"Yes," Maggie said, but now there was an edge in her voice and that really ticked Jane off.

"Good. Then go home."

Maggie hesitated, but not for long. When she was gone, Jane crumpled into her chair and looked at the paperwork. There were three more names on the list. Three more 'mistakes' just waiting to happen. When she had collected her thoughts, Jane picked up the phone. When the call was answered, she said:

"Brian Cain, please."

She was directed to Brian's assistant who asked:

"Is this regarding our recent claim?"

Jane didn't hesitate.

"Yes," she said. "Yes, that's exactly what this is about, and I need to talk to him or his brother ASAP."

23

Shannon Shaughnessy liked tea, but could not bear the smell of coffee; alcohol was a take-it-or-leave-it proposition. At work, Shannon would sweep a flute of champagne off a tray, holding it with her left hand, shaking hands with her date's colleagues and competitors with her right. Eventually, and discreetly, her glass would be left on a table while her date made deals or they huddled in a secluded corner while the man spoke of the trials and tribulations of being 'him'.

Because she was a pro, Shannon knew how to keep her wits about her, recognize when her 'date' needed her to intervene, engage in a charm offensive, or just to put on a good show of being his beautiful, devoted companion. She was a modern geisha, a beard, a confessor. In her own time, she was just Shannon Shaughnessy who enjoyed a drink now and again. If there ever was a time for a good stiff one, it was now.

She sat cross-legged on her bed, dressed in cashmere sweat pants and a cheap t-shirt. She was barefoot, her face was scrubbed, and her hair was piled high on her head, caught up in a plain rubber band. Tendrils fell down her neck and around her cheeks. She rested her whiskey on her knee; her other hand was palm down on her sister's suitcase.

Beside that was Maura's messenger bag.

Shannon imagined Maura had been carrying her purse when she was blown to bits because only an envelope with a shred of a driver's license and a bit of a health card was given to her. The clothes Maura had been wearing were with the investigators, and that was fine with her.

She had collected Maura's bags that morning, signing the inventory list presented by a gentleman who looked about as interested in his job as a snail is in its own trail. Shannon put Maura's things in the back of her car and thanked God traffic moved. She didn't want to be idling, creeping forward by inches, aware that the things in her trunk belonged to a dead woman.

When she returned home, Shannon put them in the corner of the living room. Ten minutes later, she moved them to a closet. Within the hour, Shannon had opened the closet door more than once before going about her business. She filled her calendar with appointments, declined a date from a repeat customer who paid well but crossed the line once too often. She checked her investments. Shannon showered, washed her hair, and paid her bills. All the while Maura's ghost poked at her.

Open them.

Open them.

She had thought herself long rid of her sister, but now Shannon realized that Maura had never been far from her thoughts. Though she didn't want to admit it, Shannon had been excited by Maura's visit. She had written the script in full. Maura would appear on her doorstep, arms wide, asking for forgiveness for all her harsh ways. Shannon had laughed at herself. She was far too experienced in the ways of the world to think this would happen, yet dream it she did.

Now here Maura was, just not in the way Shannon imagined. She was not on the doorstep but in the heart of Shannon's home—all that was left of her anyway. The bits and pieces of body the coroner had gathered up didn't count. They were the earthly remains of the person. The story of the person Maura was, and the truth behind her trip, was in the things she had brought with her. If Shannon didn't open them, she might miss a message from her sister. If she did open them and there was nothing for her, the pain of childhood would be revisited in full. Between a rock and hard place, Shannon made her choice.

She took half the whiskey in one drink to fortify herself, touched the latches and drew back. She finished off her whiskey, and tossed the glass on the floor. It landed with a thud on the carpet. The crystal was so heavy and the carpet so thick, that no harm was done. Rolling her shoulders, she pushed a corkscrew curl behind her ear, and then put both thumbs on the latches.

"Do it, you cow," she whispered.

Taking a deep breath, Shannon pushed. The latches flew up, but the lid didn't pop. Shannon was amused. Ever efficient Maura hadn't over-packed. When the lid was lifted, Shannon breathed in a delicate floral scent. She preferred earth notes to her perfume, but she could appreciate Maura's choice.

Shannon lifted the lid and let it fall back.

Inside, her sister's clothes were folded into clear packing cubes. Shannon left those alone and unzipped the netting pocket in the lid. She took out a pair of black pumps. The heel was high and the vamp cut low. The shoes were a sexier choice than Shannon would have imagined for Maura. There was a pair of Italian moccasins that were beautifully made and practical. Shannon put the shoes back.

She took out a small hair dryer and sighed. Typical Maura. Did her sister not think Shannon would share her hair dryer if she was willing to share her home?

Shannon unzipped the smaller pocket, removed the make-up bag, and looked inside. Her sister carried the essentials.

That done, Shannon went for the packing cubes. The small one held Maura's lingerie. The contents were quite fancy for a no-nonsense woman: lace panties and bras, a silk night dress. The second held shirts and blouses, an ecru-colored shell and a polo shirt. Each item was quality and quiet. Shannon realized they had something in common after all, a love of finely cut clothing. In the third was a pair of jeans, black slacks, a skirt, and a sweater.

Shannon put everything back exactly as she had found it, and closed the case. Clearly Maura was not coming to the United States to party, nor was she planning to stay long. A week at most. It would have been interesting to see how they fared together for a week.

Affixing the latches, Shannon pushed the case to the end of the bed. She would decide what to do with the clothes later. Perhaps there was a man in Ireland who loved Maura, and would want something of hers. Or a woman. Shannon didn't even know where Maura made her home, and how many other well-cut clothes might be hanging in a closet. And what about furniture? Books? A garden that needed tending? Perhaps her sister still lived in the family home. It was possible that the only thing that changed in Maura's life when Shannon left was that she was rid of her sister.

She had not given Maura enough credit after their parents' passing. There was, indeed, a lot to do when a person died. Though she wasn't ready to forgive Maura, there was now a chink in Shannon's emotional armor that surprised her. Then again, it was easy to let down one's defenses when the enemy was already vanquished.

The messenger bag was soft-sided, so she pulled it onto her lap. It was a fine piece of leather work, more suited to a man than a woman. Like the suitcase, everything was in its place: pens, paper pads, a file folder, a laptop, and a journal. Shannon opened the laptop, turned it on, and found it locked. Had they been closer, Shannon might have guessed the password. They had not been, so she could not. The computer went back in the bag to be dealt with later.

Business notes were in the file, a report along with a financial spreadsheet. Maura's work was meticulous. There was a rough draft of a press release for a clothing company, and another for a tech firm. Clipped to the top of the tech release was a business card. Shannon would forward the work and tell them what had happened.

Before she put the file away, something caught her eye. The company name on the card did not match the report. Taking it from under the paper clip, she saw that it belonged to Dennis Cain, CEO of Wolfhound Distillery. Shannon flipped it over. A local address was written on the back. Shannon put the card back and returned the file to the bag, making a note to contact Finn O'Brien and let him know that, indeed, Maura was working for Wolfhound.

Finally, she removed Maura's journal. It was a beautiful book, covered in oxblood leather. Maura's initials were stamped in gold at the bottom right on the cover. The edges of the pages had been painted in gold leaf, and there was a green silk bookmark attached.

Shannon was not a journal keeper. The important things in her life burned bright in her heart and mind, and would not be forgotten. Ruminating about the past did no good; writing about a future that was impossible to predict was a waste of time and ink.

Maura, obviously felt differently. In this fine book Shannon had no doubt she would be treated to many deep thoughts, judgements about the people her sister worked with, and perhaps a note or two about family. The first she had no interest in, and the last she wasn't sure she was ready to read. Shannon put the little book on the bedside table.

Sliding off the bed, she put both the suitcase and messenger bag away, scooped her glass off the floor, and went to the kitchen. She poured herself another whiskey for a spot of courage.

Admiring the twilight, and aware of the profound silence in her home, she went back to the bedroom. She put the glass on the bedside table, pulled back the duvet, and got into bed. Once settled against a mountain of pillows, covered by her duvet, Shannon picked up her sister's journal.

"Let's see what you've been up to, Maura, my girl."

She opened to the first page, noted the date, and reached for her glass. Shannon never took the first sip. A picture slipped from between the pages. The image didn't register immediately. When it finally came into focus, her hands began to tremble. She dropped her glass. Ignoring the whiskey soaking her duvet, Shannon pushed herself into a sitting position. Heart pounding, she picked up the photograph, turned it over, and read what was written on the back.

"Holy Mother of God, Maura," she whispered. "What have you done?"

24

"Holy Moly, O'Brien!"

Cori put one hand on her partner's shoulder, and with the other she pushed the muzzle of Finn's gun down until it was pointing at the ground.

Finn pulled away, angered at her reprimand. His eyewear was in place, his ears were on, and they were alone on shooting on the range, yet Cori was acting as if he were in need of instruction.

“What are you doing, woman?”

"You're not thinking there, buddy boy."

Cori lowered her eyes, but Finn didn’t take the hint. He doubled down, and tried to shake her off. Cori tightened her grip forcing him to reassess. That’s when he saw his rookie mistake. He had turned toward Cori with his weapon up and his finger still on the trigger.

Finn gave her a curt nod, moved his trigger finger, and engaged the safety. When his weapon was holstered, he ripped the protective ears off his head and horseshoed them around his neck. Cori removed her gear and fluffed her hair over her ears. She gave him a crooked smile.

"It's bad enough that I'd look like a week-old pear in my coffin. A hole in my head would be damn unattractive."

"There would be no hole in your head," Finn said. "Sure, I think I would have taken out your elbow."

"Now there's a happy thought," she said. "Just keep that thing safe until you've got someone deserving in your sights."

"Apologies. No excuse."

Dismayed as he was by his own stupidity, there was a silver lining. It was Cori with him on the range. Any other officer would jump at the chance to report him, to call him out, or put him down.

"Don't go beatin' yourself up," Cori said. "Even the preacher sins now and again."

"Sinning does less damage," Finn said.

"Depends on the sin. Just be careful. We've had enough accidents to—"

"It was a mistake, Cori. Leave it at that."

Finn walked around her, done with a discussion of his failings. She rested her tongue in her cheek, waited a beat, and then followed along. She was getting a little tired of walking on the eggshells her partner was leaving in his wake.

Finn put his ears and goggles in front of the duty officer, Cori piled hers on too. The man behind the desk sorted through the gear, making eye contact with Cori, sympathizing with her situation. She gave him a tight-lipped smile.

Finn went to the cubby where he had left his jacket. Cori joined him, pulling her own out and putting it on.

"Want to tell me what's going on?" she asked.

"'Tis been a bad day from the time I opened my eyes," he said. "I sliced my jaw with the razor, my new neighbor went for a run and left her car behind mine making me late. Captain Fowler is not happy with me."

Finn wasn't telling her anything she didn't know. Finn's attitude sucked. Whatever sympathy he had garnered because of his injuries and the loss of his uncle, had worn thin. Captain Fowler himself had ordered Cori to take her partner to the range so he could work out the kinks. Now here they were. The kinks still in place.

"We're all carrying a double load of laundry these days, so buck up," Cori said. "Come on. I'll buy you a cup of Joe."

Cori gave his shoulder a whack to get him moving. Before they made it out the door the desk officer called:

"Hey, you two want your targets?"

They looked at the range. It was clear that Finn's target had survived his assault quite nicely. Cori on, the other hand, made the kill shot each time. She waved off the offer, and leaned toward her partner.

"The trick is imaging. I'm always aiming for my ex," Cori said.

"He won't be bothering you from the looks of it. Next time I'll think of Agent Lowery, and there will be nothing left of that paper."

Finn opened the door for her, and he was laughing so that was a hopeful sign. They took their time walking across the grounds to the Academy Cafe. The hedge in front of the low-slung building was sculpted into four letters: LAPD. The 'D' was grown over so it looked like a solid green rectangle.

Cori opened the door, and Finn caught it before it closed. The cafe was small and utilitarian, unchanging since the day it was built. The walls were painted yellow and the booths were upholstered in black pleather, worn to grey on the seats. The place was spotlessly clean, and, at this time of the day, quiet as a tomb. At one table, a female sergeant scratched her head over the paperwork spread out in front of her. Two men in grey sweats were hunched over BLTs, eating in a silence that seemed comfortable.

Cori pointed to a booth and slid in; Finn tossed his jacket into the corner and did the same. He ran a hand up his arm. The sleeves of his t-shirt were short. His bruises had the same yellow cast as Cori's. He rubbed his leg where his wound was itching. Cori scratched her forehead and when she laughed it was deep and throaty.

"We're itching like a dog with fleas," Cori began only to be interrupted by the waiter.

She ordered clam chowder, Finn ordered coffee. When they were alone again Finn put his hands over his face, and then dropped them by his side.

"And you look like a hound that missed dinner."

"I'm feeling like being the hound would be a step up," he said.

Finn's coffee was delivered. He leaned one arm on the table and took to turning his cup in slow circles. Cori's soup was put in front of her. She smiled at the waiter and then gave her partner a push.

"Time you talk about it, 'cause I'm getting a tad annoyed with all this brooding.I got Jack Rabbit ears, O'Brien, so let's fill 'em up."

"We've had Hugh's remains cremated," he said. "That didn't sit well with ma. It's hard to know how to deal with her."

"It was the right thing considering." Cori said. "Are you all going to take Hugh back to Ireland?"

"We're talking about it."

Cori took the pack of oyster crackers, pressed it from the side, and smiled when she heard it pop open.

"You're a cheap date, Cori, if soup and crackers make you that happy."

"In my next life I'm going to be high maintenance." She crushed her crackers and spread them on the soup. "So, what other burrs you got under your saddle?"

"It's Agent Lowery, Cori. The man didn't have the courtesy to call me before talking to my mother, nor return my call when I wanted to ask him about it." Finn took a deep breath. "I've a hard time forgiving him for that."

"You're ticked because he didn't ask your permission to talk to your mom? Good grief."

Cori reached for the second package of crackers, popped them, crushed them. Her soup now looked like a sponge.

"He interrogated an old woman," Finn insisted. "If he's treating my family like this—a fellow peace officer—what treatment is he giving the others? A heads up, is all I'm saying. Someone should have been with her and—"

"Bull."

Cori's spoon hovered over her bowl, but her eyes were on Finn.

"First, your mom isn't some frail, little old lady. Second, you would have done the same thing to Lowery's mom, and third, he didn't cuff her and give her the third degree. Your mother made the decision to handle him on her own."

"She only did it because she didn't want to bother me," Finn groused.

"All mothers say that." Cori sniffed and tossed her hair. She said mother stuff all the time and didn't mean a word of it. "If something strange had gone down, she would have put him in his place. That's when he would have contacted you and told you she was uncooperative."

"You're right. You're right." His sigh told Cori he was not done with his complaining. "Still, I know he asked ma six ways from Sunday whether Hugh had been a terrorist. He pounded on it, an..."

Cori gave him a look that warned him to rethink his rant.

"All right. Agent Lowery questioned her about such things."

Finn edited his complaint. "If he had told me he was seriously pursuing that nonsense, I would have asked her myself without all the badge flashing and Agent Franks looming."

"And why would he take your word? If he knows anything about you —which I am sure he does— it's that you had trouble with the department. Anyway, you're calling the ATF kettle black when you're the pot. You photographed evidence, confirmed the diamonds, and now you're sitting on the information. That's real noble of you."

"I've no desire to get Paul in hot water," Finn said. "And I'll do nothing with that information unless it's used against Hugh. Lowery has the evidence now. It's up to him to figure out what it means."

"Nice try, but that's lame." Cori snorted. "Look, two rules: we don't investigate family, and we don't stick our nose into another cop's business without an invitation."

Cori pushed aside her soup. She went for her purse, but instead of threading it over her shoulder to leave, she held it close.

"Listen to me. Your uncle looked like the sweetest guy on earth, but we saw him for three seconds. That's three seconds out of a lifetime. You didn't know him, and your mother remembers a brother she loved. Lowery is right to investigate his way."

"I will not believe anything bad about the man," Finn said. "He gave up everything for the love of a good woman. That keeps a man on the straight and narrow."

Cori bit her tongue to keep from laughing—or screaming. The love of a woman had nothing to do with how a man turned out. Finn's wife had deserted him, and Cori's man left her with a baby and nothing else.

"Then maybe it's the dead wife who got on somebody's bad side," Cori suggested. "A lot happens in a lifetime."

"Sure, haven't I thought of all this myself?" Finn said. "That's why I've checked in with the Garda in Ireland to ask them to look into Hugh and his family."

"You're cruisin' for a bruisin' if Lowery finds out. Still, since you've already done the deed, what have you got?"

Finn, pulled out his phone, scrolled through it and found what he wanted.

"Nothing from the Garda yet, but I've a list of everyone who was on the plane, in the hangar, even the woman who cleaned the Platinum offices. I've talked to the pilot and his wife."

Cori cradled her chin in her upturned palm, listening to Finn recount what his rogue investigation had uncovered.

"The pilot admitted to having an affair with the stewardess, but denied knowledge of the diamonds," Finn said. "Still, they had done three runs together. Two of them to Zimbabwe."

"What did the wife have to say?"

"The last time she tried to divorce him, he went crazy," Finn said.

"Crazy enough to kill three people and destroy a plane?"

"Possibly. He radioed a May Day, landed the plane, and then was found sabotaging the landing gear to make it look like he had managed the impossible. He believed that if she thought him close to death, she would take him back—which she did."

"I'm surprised Platinum Wings hired him with that on his record," Cori said.

"There was a job in between, but I know nothing about that yet. Still, think about this. The divorce is about to be final, maybe the girlfriend is breaking up with him. It could be he was involved in a smuggling operation. That man's got a lot coming down on him, so what could be better than a disaster?"

"Look-over-there is always a popular ploy," Cori agreed.

"And the cockpit door was closed. If the fuel tank hadn't

been impacted, Mustafa wouldn't have been hurt at all. The bomb takes care of the girlfriend and the wife is terrified."

"What about the diamond-toting stew?"

"She's been with Platinum Wings for a while. No trouble. Before that she was in the Peace Corps and stayed on to work for an NGO."

"Let me guess. Africa." Cori said and Finn nodded. "What about regular routes for her since she signed on with Platinum?"

"There are no regular routes. Platinum goes where their passengers tell them to go," Finn said. "But she and Mustafa have been to Zimbabwe twice."

"Good to know you're not really investigating any of this," Cori said.

"Consider me a fact-checker," Finn said.

"And if you find something Lowery missed, he's really going to love you for showing him up."

Finn put away his phone.

"I promise, if I find something truly alarming, I'll pay Lowery a visit."

"Okay, since we're confessing to coloring outside the lines..."

Cori's eyes twinkled and it was clear she was about to bust her buttons. She scooted a little closer to the table and confessed.

"I was at the courthouse researching something else, and I took a peek at filings against Platinum Wings."

"Cori...." Finn gave her the side-eye even as he smiled.

"So sue me," she answered. "Anyway, there are two lawsuits against Platinum Wings: One personal against the owner for sexual harassment. The other is a negligence suit. A D-list actress cut her face on a flight, and says it ruined her career."

"What's her name?" Finn asked.

"I didn't recognize it. The point is, a big settlement –and the notoriety of either one– could put them out of business. Two would be the kiss of death. So, what if the plane gets blown to bits and Platinum collects the insurance? That might be enough to settle both actions, and start again."

"Good to know you're steering clear, Cori," Finn chuckled.

"I'm just a curious citizen. All I'm saying is that there are bigger fish to fry than Uncle Hugh, so leave it be. Nobody is coming after him or your mom."

"You're right," Finn said. "Besides, the man was Irish and he made whiskey. Logic says he would drink himself to death before he blew himself up."

The waiter came and took her soup bowl. Finn gave him the coffee cup. It was still half full.

"And what about Maura?" Cori asked. "If there could be a pissed off pilot in the cockpit, there might have been a madwoman in the cabin."

"I'm waiting on the Garda for that," Finn said.

Finn swung out of the booth, stood up, and dropped a few dollars on the table. He raised a hand in thanks to the waiter. Cori walked ahead of him. Since the only dog she had in the fight was a mongrel's curiosity, she let it all go as they retraced their steps across the grounds. Both agreed that Finn would drop her at her car, but neither of them would bother going back to work.

Cori invited him to dinner. Finn declined. He had plans to hit Mick's for a drink, chat up Geoffrey, and then see if his landlady would allow him an hour in her *sento.* Finn dug into his pocket for his keys only to come up with Shannon's business card.

One Night.

Finn felt a stab of regret and a hint of sorrow at the sight of it. No matter how much money she made, Shannon was still alone and for sale. Finn pocketed the card, palmed the keys, and before he got in the car, he answered a call from the Beverly Hills Police Department.

There was a problem that needed his attention.

25

Finn gave Cori a choice: go with him, or be dropped at Wilshire Division as planned. Given that Finn was already making the exit to the 10 freeway, the route that would take them through Beverly Hills, it wasn't much of a choice.

They cruised down Santa Monica Boulevard and turned the corner at Oakhurst Drive, a wide boulevard lined with houses that looked like hotels. In the middle of the block was the house they were looking for, and the only one with a cherry top parked in front. There were no emergency vehicles on site, which was good. There were no neighbors gathered in front of the place, pointing, and whispering, shocked that something horrible had happened. That was even better.

Their destination was a brick and stucco white two-story home. Stately leaded windows graced both sides of the front door and were framed by black lacquered shutters. The front door was black, and a gold knocker shaped like a lion's head with a heavy ring between its teeth was affixed to it.

The detectives parked on the street, crossed it, and walked up a brick path heading toward the door. The lawn on either side of them was sloped and meticulously manicured. The flowerbeds were lush with shrubs, bushes, and artistically placed flowers. The few trees on the property looked as if they had been growing undisturbed for generations. There was a long driveway parallel to the path they walked that led to a three-car garage. In front of that, there was a carport that had been created by extending the roofline of the house. Under the carport was a vintage Aston Martin, the back of it crumpled well and good by a Mercedes sedan.

"Someone had a good time," Cori said. "No skid marks.

"'Tis Mr. Cain's pride and joy. The Mercedes is Shannon Shaughnessy's," Finn said.

"She knows how to make an entrance," Cori said. "Can't wait to make her acquaintance."

They took the shallow steps to the porch and, because they had been summoned, Finn opened the front door without knocking.

"Looks like Scarlett O'Hara should be coming down that thing," Cori said, eyeing the curving staircase.

It dominated the entry hall, and led to an impressive second-floor landing. Up there, the walls were covered in shimmering wallpaper the color of champagne. Underfoot, black and white marble squares were set on the diagonal. There was a round table in the center of this rotunda, polished and shining. On it stood a vase of flowers, the stalks reaching toward a crystal chandelier that had been fashioned to look like birds in flight.

There were three doors off the entry. The one straight on led to a short hall and a kitchen beyond. The dining room was to the left – gray walls, white wainscoting, black lacquered furniture—and on the right was a living room. They went for the living room, pausing in the doorway to get the lay of the land.

On the couch, her back to them, was Shannon Shaughnessy. In front of her was a uniformed officer. He was listening to

Shannon talk, but was seemingly unimpressed with what she was saying. He knew that there was seldom a right side in a domestic disturbance, but Shannon was sure she held the high ground.

"He killed my sister. I'm telling you, he's a murderer. You have—"

She stopped talking when the man's eyes shifted. Shannon flipped around, to see what he was looking at. The mess of her hair, her pallid skin alight with freckles, and startling green eyes made her look like a madwoman. When Shannon caught sight of Finn, she shot off the couch. She didn't get far. The cop caught her arm and put her back down on the deep sofa.

"Let me go, you *bouzie*. Sure, aren't you a bad egg."

She ripped his hand away only to find Finn's hand on her other shoulder.

"You best be doing what the officer wants, Ms. Shaughnessy."

"But...Finn..."

Her head flipped from one man to the other. She breathed like a bull, nostrils flaring. If she could have pawed the ground Finn had no doubt that she would have dug a trench through the fine wood floor.

Cori went around the couch and stood on the other side of her. The woman turned her head left and right, and then landed her gaze on the officer in front of her. Seeing she was cornered and escape was impossible, Shannon gave in. She did not, however, give up. She took Finn's hand in both of hers and held it to her breast, forcing him down so that he balanced on the balls of his feet. She lowered her voice, talking fast, taking him into her confidence.

"Finn, I know what happened to that plane. That man upstairs, Finn, he blew up the plane. He killed your uncle. He killed my sister. I don't know how he did it, but I know why. I'm telling you—"

"Say nothing more, Shannon." Finn put his other hand over both of hers and gave them a pat. He looked at the officer. "Will you give us a minute?"

"Sure thing. My partner's upstairs."

"Alone?"

He shook his head.

"The residents are up there. Mr. and Mrs. Cain."

"Are they in need of medical attention?" he asked.

"They didn't want it," he said.

"Then you see to upstairs; we'll see to Ms. Shaughnessy," Finn said.

"If they press charges, I'll have to take her in," the officer said.

"I know," Finn said. "Let's see if we can work this out between them first."

The officer left, relieved to be passing Shannon off. When he was gone, Finn said:

"Let go, Shannon,"

She released his hand. Finn pushed himself up, and sat next to her on the sofa. Cori took a fancy chair covered in gold fabric, its arms and legs were carved like those of a gryphon complete with clawed feet.

Shannon looked younger without her make-up. Her big eyes were wide and childlike under her pale lashes. She wore a t-shirt that was stained. Her pants were soft, and her shoes were not shoes at all but fuzzy slippers. She hadn't thought before she left the house. A woman like her, cool as could be, must have been driven to madness to be seen in public like this.

"You've made some trouble, Shannon," he said.

"Not me, *boyo*, not me. But there is trouble to be had. I know why Maura is dead and it is a cold, cold thing." She swung her head and narrowed her eyes as she looked at Cori. "Who are you?"

"Detective Anderson. Detective O'Brien's partner."

Shannon narrowed her eyes to get a better look at Cori's face.

"You look like shit."

"Well bless your heart," Cori said. "You've got a potty mouth on you."

"Detective Anderson was at the airport, Shannon," Finn said. "Show some respect or you're on your own."

"Sorry," she said, and tossed her hair. There were tears in her eyes. She blinked them away. "Sorry. Truly."

"We're good," Cori assured her.

"Now to business, Shannon," Finn said. "We'll do what we can to walk you through this, so just answer our questions. Did you run your car into Mr. Cain's?"

"I did."

"Anything else?"

"I hit him," she said. "Perhaps more than once."

"Ah, Shannon." Finn shook his head. "Why would you do such a thing?"

Shannon reached into her pocket and handed Finn a photograph.

"Maura had a child, Finn. A child."

Finn looked at the picture. It was recent and beautiful. Maura sat cross-legged on the floor, her back up against an overstuffed chair. Light streamed from somewhere, making her look like a Madonna. She was shoeless, dressed in jeans and a fisherman knit sweater that was intricately cabled. The big turtleneck cradled her chin.

Like her sister now, Maura's face was fresh and clean. Her head was tipped so that her long hair fell over one shoulder. Where Shannon's hair was bright red/gold, Maura's was more like the deep dark red of sunset. Her smile was glorious as if she hadn't a care in the world save one, and that one was sitting in her lap.

A child, pudgy and soft as children are before they learn to walk, smiled, and reached for the camera. Its lips were a sweet pink bow, its eyes were big and wide. He knew the sounds that would come from those lips. Gurgles and coos. In Finn's life it had been his little sister, Meg, he carried about at that age.

He looked up when Shannon sniffled. Her cheeks were wet with tears, but her expression was defiant, her chin raised, and her eyes flat and dark. Each word she spoke was like a knife slicing through her lips.

"She had a child, and the man upstairs is that babe's father."

"Shannon, this child could be anyone's," Finn said.

"I've got her journal, Finn. She was coming to see Dennis Cain. She wrote to her baby that she was going to bring da home," Shannon said. "Do you think he'd want his wife to know? Do you think he wouldn't do anything to stop Maura from ruining his life? He has money. He could do it. He did do it because he was shamed."

She took the picture back, swallowing a sob as she looked at it. Then her eyes cut back to Finn.

"He killed your uncle, too. Don't be forgetting that, Finn O'Brien. Distant though they were, they were ours and that bastard took them from us. From this child."

Shannon took his hand again. She looked deep into his eyes.

"Make him tell the truth, Finn," she said. "And then make him pay. Lock him up. Throw away the key."

"You want revenge, Shannon?"

"I want justice, Finn."

26

Finn climbed the grand staircase wondering why some men felt the need to live in a home big enough for ten families and grand enough for a king.

Not that Finn didn't appreciate the beauty of the place, but his admiration was for the craftsmen who turned the spindle and the artist who inlaid the wood. He wondered if Dennis Cain appreciated the art he lived with every day, or if he was simply satisfied with the show of wealth. Not that it mattered. It was the bed he had made, and Finn could only hope he was comfortable in it.

On the landing, he followed the track of wall covered with family pictures: Dennis Cain, a woman Finn imagined to be his wife, two children, and a dog. The boys grew to men in the course of ten feet; the dog eventually disappeared from the pictures. Some photos were taken in Ireland and others in the U.S. The wife and children looked happier in the states. The gallery was carefully curated, but none of the pictures were posed or professional as Finn would expect. The family was naturally close, admiring of one another, comfortable in their skin.

One picture, in particular, caught Finn's eye. Mrs. Cain was very young. She stood next to a truck filled with boxes. A group of people was gathered around her, staring into the camera. Finn could not tell if they were hostile or hungry. Afghanistan? Pakistan? Turkey? There was no indication of what country she was in, only that she was in a desert and was wearing fatigues. It was an interesting photo to be hanging on this wall of privilege.

Finn paused once more. This time he was looking at a picture of Dennis Cain and his wife looking exceedingly happy. Their arms were around one another, her head was on his shoulder, and the sun was setting over a beach behind them. It was difficult to imagine so content a man straying. Then again, why not? Men did. Women did. There were no saints on earth, and devotion dissolved in the face of desire. Neither God nor good intentions could weed nature out of a body. What wasn't in a civilized human being's nature was to kill the way Maura and Hugh had been killed. A bomb was way too dramatic, too cold, and calculated. Crimes of passion happened in private moments; the weapons of choice were a knife, a gun, and a beating. Rage of that sort was up-close and personal.

Still, Finn was a cop and cops made no assumptions. Human nature was confounding because there were exceptions to every rule, to common sense, and to logic. Since the hour was getting on and the pall in the house was cloying, Finn moved on.

Glancing through an open door, he saw a lavish bedroom decked out in dark green and peach colors. He passed another bedroom. This one was blue and white. On the walls were the trappings of a child growing up: baseball plaques and posters of race cars. When he came to the third door, he saw the one room he envied in this fine house.

This was a man's domain: cherrywood wainscoting was on the bottom third of each wall, dark paint above. A plaid sofa, deep chairs, brass lamps, and a fine solid desk decorated the space. There were bookshelves lining one wall. Behind the desk was an oil painting of Wolfhound Distillery. The desk faced a wall of windows on the right and French doors leading to a balcony straight on. Through one bank of windows, Finn saw greenery. If he were to sit at that desk in the leather chair, he might be able to imagine that it was Ireland he was looking at, but it wasn't. The green wasn't the bright color of spring. This was darker and dense like a forest. It matched the mood of the people in the room.

Two cops – the officer from downstairs and his female partner – stood watch over Dennis Cain and his wife. Mrs. Cain sat in a barrel chair facing the door. One elbow was crooked on the arm of the chair, her fist raised to her jaw, one finger extended against her cheek. Her other arm was draped across that of the chair. She was well turned out in a tailored blue shirt, and black slacks. Her dark hair was pulled back in a long ponytail but it was unkempt. She was attractive, but not beautiful in the way Maura had been. She was sexy, but not sexy as Shannon was. Though her figure was slim she was not delicate. She was also coldly, frigidly, unbearably angry. The look in her eyes was as hard as granite. There was no sign of hurt or remorse, no questions or disbelief as he would have expected. Her eyes flicked toward Finn. He didn't interest her much, so she went back to staring at her husband.

Dennis Cain was collapsed on the sofa, bent over, holding an ice pack to his jaw with one hand while he cradled his head in the other. His white shirt was torn. He wore jeans. He was shoeless. Either the man didn't sense Finn's presence, or he didn't care that he was there. Finn quietly summoned the officers. The three of them moved into the hall.

"Did they say anything about pressing charges against Ms. Shaughnessy?" Finn asked.

"He says not," the male officer said. “He just wants the lady out.”

"And Mrs. Cain?" Finn asked.

"She hasn't said anything," the female officer responded.

"Since they don't want to make any more of a scene, you might as well be on your way," Finn said.

"If one of them changes their mind, call it in to Murray and Farmer. Beverly Hills isn't that big. We can be here fast."

"I doubt there will be a need, but thank you." Finn looked at the two miserable people in the office, before asking a favor. "Would you ask Detective Anderson to take Ms. Shaughnessy away?"

"You got it," Officer Murray said before adding: "Be safe, and thanks for coming out."

“Happy to help,” Finn said, knowing that domestic disturbances were the worst calls—volatile, and unpredictable—and the officers were happy to be away without an arrest.

He waited until they started to descend the stairs before going back to talk to the unhappy couple. Neither had moved, not a word had been spoken.

"Mr. Cain. Mrs. Cain."

Dennis Cain straightened up at the sound of Finn’s voice. He took the cold pack from his cheek and put it on the table, his expression was a mixture of curiosity, anger, and despair. When he took a good look at Finn and realized who he was, everything changed.

“What are you doing here?” he said. “This has nothing to do with the airport.”

"I'm sorry to see you under such circumstances, but the Beverly Hills police requested that I come. Ms. Shaughnessy asked them to call me because..."

“You know her?” He tossed his head. He snorted. “What is this? Are you two trying to pull a fast one?”

"My family knew the Shaughnessy family in Ireland. Circumstances at the airport brought us together. It was pure happenstance that we were there at the same time. If you like, contact Agent Lowery. He will attest to these facts."

Dennis Cain seemed unconvinced. It was not Finn's job to cater to him. It was not Finn's job to be there at all, and yet here he was.

"Mr. Cain, I can try to help you settle this matter, or I can call the officers back. Whichever you prefer. The fact of the matter is that Ms. Shaughnessy has said that you had a personal relationship with her sister. She is saying that you have a reason for wanting her dead. She's upset, and the best thing would be to talk to her."

"Forget it. I'm not saying one word to that crazy bitch," Dennis said. "And those allegations are absurd, not to mention slanderous. I told the officers and I told her as much when she stopped hitting me. Now, if you don't go, I will file complaints against those officers for dereliction of duty. They should never have let you in here. Get out, and tell that woman to back off, or I will take care of —."

Before Dennis Cain could complete his threat, his wife interrupted.

"Who exactly are you?" she asked.

Finn looked at Dennis Cain, giving him the option to answer his wife.

"This is Detective O'Brien, Hugh's nephew. My wife Katherine."

Finn offered a small smile, a nod. She did not reciprocate. Dennis lay back against the sofa cushions. Whatever fight had been in him was now gone. His jaw was swelling and his skin was starting to show the blue/purple of a large bruise.

"Do you have any jurisdiction here?" Katherine asked.

"Technically?" Finn asked. She shrugged as if to say that she didn't need chapter and verse, just an idea of who she was dealing with. "Any officer of the law would have jurisdiction in time of need. I'd like to think I can help sort this out as a friend."

"Is that woman gone?" Katherine asked.

"My partner is with her outside."

"Good."

Katherine's attention landed on her husband. Their eyes locked for a beat before Dennis said:

"We don't want any more trouble."

"But we could change our minds about pressing charges, Dennis," his wife said. "I think we should keep the option open."

"If I need to control the situation, I'll do it in civil court."

"Oh, for God's sake. She assaulted you. She should be held criminally accountable. Suing her isn't worth your time or money." Katherine turned her head a click, roping Finn into the conversation. "The woman burst in here and went for Dennis. I had to pull her off. I didn't know who she was, or what she wanted. She was screaming bloody murder. She was out of her mind."

"She was distraught. Her sister is dead. Her sister—" Dennis said.

"I don't care," Katherine said. "Her sister was a slut."

Katherine stood up and took a step forward. She crossed her arms and tossed her head. Where to go? What to say? Before she could decide, Dennis said:

"That baby is not my chi—"

"Of course, that is your child."

Katherine Cain's disdain was deep. Her words were barbs that would stick forever in the fabric of her husband's conscience. She caught sight of Finn, and controlled herself. It appeared Katherine Cain was not one for public displays.

"A phone call, a civil meeting asking Dennis to do right by the baby, is all that was necessary, but that woman wanted more than a decent settlement. Maura Shaughnessy wanted you, and the baby, and the business. She was coming here to take my family. Now she's dead. Problem solved. We'll send money to whoever is responsible for that child." Katherine dropped her arms, and her voice became a primal growl as she advanced on her husband. "But I will not have it, or that person downstairs, in our lives. Is that understood?"

"Mrs. Cain. Please sit down." Finn put himself in front of the woman. She turned on him, and Finn wanted none of her fury. Still, for Shannon and Maura, he said: "Please."

Katherine Cain hesitated, and then did as he asked. Finn pulled up a ladder-back chair, keeping equal distance from both of them.

"We have a shared interest in finding out what happened to that plane," Finn said. "Whether you like it or not, we will all need to cooperate to make that happen. That is simply fact."

"Here, in this house, we are talking about my marriage and my family," Katherine said. "I will do whatever it takes to keep those two things intact, including prosecuting that woman if she persists, no matter what my husband says. Your job as a 'friend' of hers is to take her away and make sure she never comes back. Any problems between Dennis and her sister are now moot."

"I think not," Finn said. "Ms. Shaughnessy believes Mr. Cain had something to do with the bombing. The motive being his affair and the child."

"Half our neighbors know that's what she thinks since she was screaming at the top of her lungs."

Katherine fidgeted in her distress, shaking her head, scratching deeply at the soft skin of her inner wrist. A slight tremor ran through her body. She took three quick breaths, licked her lips, and said:

"The idea that Dennis could make something like that happen is ridiculous. He wouldn't know a power supply from a switch. Besides, how would he have gotten a device on the plane? He was in Los Angeles. That plane came from Ireland."

"Were you in town also?" Finn asked.

"I resent that question," she shot back.

Dennis Cain sat up a little straighter, suddenly engaged in the conversation. He opened his mouth to speak and shut it again. Finn was well aware of his reaction, but he kept his eyes on the woman.

"I am curious about the specificity of your speech. Not many women would call out a power source and a switch."

"My father was an electrician. I was in the army. And I know how to Google. There isn't much you can't find out these days, not to mention there are ten million people who might make the same reference."

Katherine Cain's lips twisted in her frustration and disgust. Suddenly, Dennis shot up from the couch. If he was angry it didn't show, but he was weary beyond bearing and agitated.

"Okay. We're done. Just stop," he said. "I signed off on Hugh's trip, I didn't know Maura would be on that plane. From what I understand, she showed up at the Platinum terminal in Ireland, the airline confirmed she worked with Wolfhound. Someone vouched for her, but it wasn't me."

"Did anyone at Wolfhound know about your affair?"

"Brian. My half-brother. He is the CFO of the company. He handles daily operations in Cork, I take care of things here with our American partners."

Katherine snorted. "You told Brian? You don't even like him."

"I didn't tell him."

"He saw you with her? Oh, God. You were doing it at the office?" Katherine tossed her head, and Finn could only imagine what was running through her mind.

"Brian heard us talking, nothing more," Dennis said. "I'd just terminated Maura. I thought it best if she worked elsewhere. I wanted to make things work with you and me."

"And she didn't tell you she was pregnant?" Katherine said.

"No."

"When was the last time you had contact with Maura?" Finn asked.

"I don't know. Eighteen months ago, I suppose," Dennis said. "The last time I was in Ireland."

"But she still worked for Wolfhound," Finn pressed.

"Whatever work she did was not with me." Dennis's temper flared. "And just so we're clear, I know that I don't have to tell you a damn thing. For the sake of transparency, for my wife's sake, I will tell you this: Maura was not going to take no for an answer. She threatened to tell Katherine about our affair if I didn't approve her contract as a consultant. I did what she asked, and left Brian to deal with any fallout. He can be quite persuasive. It was my understanding that Maura was taken care of."

Dennis stopped talking. He thought again.

"Let me rephrase that. Brian told me Maura couldn't get work. I thought it was because she could be headstrong. Now that I know it was because she was pregnant. It makes sense that she would want to keep ties with Wolfhound. I suppose she was hoping that once I found out there would be a future for us."

Dennis bit his lower lip. His gaze wandered to a neutral space. This led Finn to think the man, himself, might have harbored some hopes of the same future. He regrouped, looked at Finn, and dispelled that notion.

"Look, it didn't matter what I thought, I felt I owed her something."

He didn't say more. It was the same old story. Still, he was right. He owed Maura something for the time they had spent together, for her hopes, for the promises he had made. Maura's reward was a job. To Finn that would be salt in a wound to be close to Wolfhound, but not to Dennis.

"Maybe Maura didn't know she was pregnant when she left the company. Maybe she was being proud or brave in not telling me," Dennis said. He looked incredibly sad. "Who knows what goes through a woman's mind? I would have helped her had I known. I wouldn't have killed her."

Dennis took a tentative step and then another. He put his hands on his wife's shoulders and drew them down her arms.

"I'm sorry. So very sorry for all of it."

He pulled her up and into him. He buried his face in her hair, still murmuring even as she backed out of his embrace.

"You're fooling yourself about Brian being the only one who knew," she said. "Everyone in the distillery probably did, and they were laughing at me. All the while I was working my butt off to help you and that damn company."

"Katherine, no. It wasn't like that." He reached for her again.

"Don't touch me, Dennis."

She moved, but he couldn't let it go.

"Brian and I may not be the best of friends, but he wouldn't do that," Dennis said. "He understood. He agreed to hire her as a consultant to placate her. He did that to protect me and the company."

"Protect Wolfhound," she said in disgust. "Isn't that always the way? I was such an idiot to think things would be different if we didn't live in Cork."

Katherine Cain threw her head back, took a moment, and then said:

"Well, gentlemen. I can't say it hasn't been fun, but I'm done. Dennis will see you out, detective."

27

In the near darkness Dennis Cain looked after her. Finn stayed silent until he heard the door close. Then Dennis turned to him.

“This is the last time I will see you unless it’s required by law, but I will tell you this: I loved Maura, and I didn't know about the baby. I didn't know she was coming here. I didn't know she would be on that plane. Maybe things would have been different if I had.”

"Would you like to speak to Shannon? It might help,” Finn said.

"Who exactly do you think it would help?"

Finn ceded the point. Dennis Cain was sad and ashamed, Shannon righteously furious, Katherine dark and disgusted. It wasn’t Finn’s job to sort it out.

"I'll be saying goodnight then," Finn said.

“Tell Maura’s sister that my attorney will work something out for the baby,” Dennis said.

“One more question if you don’t mind. For me, personally,” Finn said. “The day this happened? When I asked you about the woman on the plane? Did you suspect that it was Maura?”

Dennis Cain looked at Finn for a long while. His expression never changed, but a wave of emotions ran through his eyes. It went so fast, that the only thing Finn could identify was fear. Then Dennis proved more a man than Finn thought he could be.

"My brother told me when we heard what happened, and not before. It wasn't any of your business at the time," Dennis said. "Now, get out."

Finn walked down the hall thinking the pictures now looked sad. Even if Dennis and Katherine Cain survived this misery, they would never smile at one another the same way. Dennis Cain was a different man in his wife's eyes in the same way Bev was someone Finn no longer knew. He wished he could tell the Cain's that, in time, great sadness faded to regret, and that regret was an annoying thing but it was not fatal.

He took the sweeping staircase with a pace tempered by the slow tumble of his thoughts.

Mrs. Cain: It isn't every day we air our dirty laundry...

How much dirty laundry did they have to air?

Mr. Cain: I didn't know she was coming on that plane. Maybe things would have been different.

He admitted to knowing she was on the plane, but only after the fact. Finn somehow doubted that. He used the words *that plane,* not *the* plane. It was a small difference, but one that could mean many things.

Perhaps Dennis Cain knew something others didn't about that specific flight. Some knowledge of a threat? Perhaps it wasn't a threat against Maura, but someone else. And if he had known, would he have stopped it if he knew Maura was a passenger. Perhaps he would have let it go and been relieved at the outcome.

Finn dismissed that thought. Cain may have failings, but Finn doubted the man was a murderer. Nor was he so callous that he would not intervene if he knew of a plot against the people on that plane. It was Mrs. Cain who had the courage and the experience.

Armed service, indeed.

He strode over the checkered marble and out the impressive front door, stopping briefly to take account. Shannon's car was now on the street, and the woman herself was sitting with Cori on the curb. The women were bathed in the soft glow that came from the lights around the Cain's house and shadowed by the colors of twilight.

Finn stepped off the porch, detouring to the carport. He felt more pain looking at the damage done to the Aston Martin than looking at Dennis Cain's swollen jaw. As much as the man might aspire to a full Irish heart, he would never own it if he had no understanding of Irish women. They loved greatly, but did not take being wronged lightly. This was proof of it. He looked over at Shannon's Mercedes. It had fared better, but not by much. She wouldn't have a care for the cost of repair because satisfaction was priceless.

Finn walked across the drive toward the women. They looked like mismatched sisters —Cori with her teased blonde hair and Shannon with her riot of red. Both were long-legged, beautiful, and sat on the curb like queens. No hands to the head, no shoulders sloping, no tissues being passed to wipe away tears. Shannon had her pound of flesh for now. The rest—the bombing and the baby— would be resolved in good time. The one thing Finn knew for sure, was that Shannon would only give up when she deemed Dennis Cain had done right by Maura and her child.

Before he reached them, Cori got up and waved at the tow truck coming down the street. When it parked, Shannon went to speak to the driver. Finn looked away, his gaze sweeping over the wide street. The big houses looked like art canvases with their fancy lighting and beautiful gardens. He had no doubt that heaven would look like this except those streets would be paved in gold and there would be saints behind the fancy doors, not gilded sinners.

He noted the great expanse of land between houses, the hedges and mature trees. No one would have heard a dust-up, as Mrs. Cain feared. In fact, she could probably shoot her husband and bury the body without anyone knowing or, perhaps, caring.

Finn got to the edge of the property just as the tow truck driver finished securing the car and drove away. The women watched him leave before converging on Finn.

"So?" Cori asked.

"So, Shannon is free to go," Finn said. "Do not come back to this place, do not seek out Dennis Cain in any other place, or it won't go so easy for you."

"I'll go where I pleas..." Shannon began, but one look from Finn and she switched tracks. "Fine. I'll not come here again, but aren't you going to arrest him?"

"For what, miss?" Finn said.

"For what he did to Maura," Shannon said. "For leaving her to have a baby alone—"

"That's not a crime, Shannon. He says he didn't know she was pregnant."

"No man is that stupid—" Shannon said.

"Oh, honey, that's a big fat lie," Cori said, and even Shannon smiled. Still, she was like a dog with its toy, unwilling to give up the thing she had dug her teeth into.

"But he killed her. Even if he didn't put the bomb on that plane, I know he made it happen to cover his arse. Frickin' rich man. I know what rich men can do."

"An affair isn't proof of anything, but poor judgment," Finn said. "And that's the end of it for today."

Cori made the first move toward the car. Finn started to

follow, but Shannon took his hand, holding on tight, giving it a little shake to make sure he paid attention. Yet, when he did, she found herself at a loss for words and hung her head. Finn put his hands on her shoulders.

"Shannon. Listen to me. We've all things to be regretful of, but fists and fights do no good. It might even be harmful if you want to have any contact with Maura's baby. Do you understand?" Her head went up and down. He turned her around. "Good then. We'll give you a ride home."

Cori opened the door for her. Shannon got in the back, Cori took shotgun, and Finn was behind the wheel. Before she buckled up, Cori swiveled around.

"My guy has got something on the stove if you're interested," she said. Finn looked over his shoulder.

"Food and friends might be what you're needin'."

When Shannon smiled, Finn gave her no opportunity to change her mind. None of them looked back at the Cain house. It was only when they had been driving a while that Shannon said:

"Finn? The baby?"

"We'll find him," he said.

"And Maura?"

"I won't let it go," he promised.

Cori cut her eyes his way, but Finn didn't see 'the look'; the one that warned him to mind his business and let the rest of the world mind theirs.

When it came to Hugh Murphy, Maura Shaughnessy, and a baby waiting half way around the world for its mother to come home, Finn O'Brien would be relentless. That was a pity because none of them were his responsibility nor his fight. He had almost thrown away his life and career to protect a homeless man; throwing himself under the bus to make things right for family and friends was a no-brainer. Still, there was a lot of muck in this pig pen and everyone knew what happened when you laid down with porkers—everyone but Finn O'Brien.

He must have heard her thinking, because he glanced her way and gave her a smile.

All was well. 'Tis a happy ending coming. Don't worry.

Cori put her eyes forward. The oncoming traffic lit up her face.

Men could be so lame. Then again, women weren't exactly rocket scientists when it came to matters of the heart, so the playing field was pretty even. In the end nobody was ever going to have a clean win, but everyone would get beat up trying to get it.

28

The Groundling had a rep for great music, but the club itself left a lot to be desired. It was housed in one of five storefronts butted up against a cracked and dirty sidewalk on an unimpressive stretch of Ventura Boulevard. The unit on the end was occupied by squatters, so that really didn't count as a store. Three were empty leaving the club to provide the only sign of life, and then only after nine at night.

Above the door was a hand-painted sign. The artist had misspelled Groundling, leaving out the 'L'. That was okay with pretty much everyone because the paint was so dark you couldn't see it once the sun went down anyway. Luckily Zach had given Maggie very specific directions: go to Ventura and Bonin and look for the place with a bouncer the size of a gas pump.

Maggie didn't really want to go clubbing; she wanted to keep working on her 'special project' as Zach called it. He had done his best to dissuade her, but Maggie was all in and wouldn't listen. He told her nobody would want to hear what she had to say if she turned into a bitch. Then he said: you need to hear some music and dance.

That was Zach's answer for everything.

She put him off, only to change her mind when she got home.

Maggie had a creepy feeling the last few days. There was nothing specific she could point to that would cause this, there was only the sense that somewhere in the cosmos the wrong eyes were on her. Since she and Zach were friends, since that creepy feeling was getting worse, she went to The Groundling.

It was now ten-thirty on a 'school night' and Maggie was sitting at a round table with her chin on her fist, listening to good music, and watching Zach dance like a maniac. When the music stopped, he stumbled toward her, hands to his chest, breathing hard.

"OMG, I can't believe you're not dancing. Mags, how can you sit there?"

He plopped himself at the table, smiling, sweating, his hair plastered to his head. His glasses slipped down his nose, so Maggie snatched them. She handed him a napkin to wipe his face while she polished his lenses.

"Isn't this group awesome?" Zach laughed as she handed his glasses back. He reached for her drink, but her glass was empty. "I'll buy you another one."

"I'm good. Really. I have to go."

Maggie put a hand out to keep him from getting up. He fell back in the chair, his arms limp by his side.

"That's funny. You're not even here, and you have to go," Zach said. "You were supposed to leave work at work."

"I'm just not feeling it. Sorry." Maggie gave him puppy-dog eyes, hoping that would help him accept the inevitable. "Next time, I promise."

The music started again. He tossed his head back and screamed.

"I hate working!" Zach threw himself half over the table. "I hate you working! You're turning into Whitfield. Let's quit. Come on. Let's do it. We'll quit. Now. Right now. Pinky swear."

He held out his pinky. Maggie laughed and swatted his hand away.

"You're an idiot. How are you going to pay for your fancy glasses if you don't work?"

Maggie thought he was incredibly cute. And smart. And it was a mystery why the chemistry didn't go past him being an awesome friend. Tonight, she would have loved to go home with him, crawl into bed, and shake her feeling of dread. But friends were too hard to come by to ruin everything because she was having an anxiety attack.

"I'll find me a sugar mama!" He threw out his arms then wrapped them around his body and gave himself a hug.

"Yeah. Let me know how that goes." Maggie started to stand, but Zach caught her wrist.

"You'll be sorry. Someday when you need me, I won't be there." He tugged on her arm. "Come on. *Making Hay* is coming up. They're only playing this one night."

Just then the guitarist went on a riff that threatened to break her eardrums. Maggie put her lips really close to Zach's ear and screamed:

"No!"

The riff ended, and the sudden silence startled both of them. Maggie laughed and took it down a notch.

"Give me a few days. I'm going in early tomorrow, and I'll be done."

Zach let her go.

"You've been going in early every morning. You have lunch at your desk," Zach complained. "Come on Maggie. If you're starting to drink the Kool-Aid, it's my job to knock the cup out of your hand."

"End of the week. That's a promise."

Maggie gathered up her things, smirking and shaking her head. She adored Zach, but things had changed. She was seeing her future, and she wasn't in love with it. Zach wasn't relationship material, and she wasn't going to find a solid guy at The Groundling. If the perfect man never showed up then she was on her own. There were worse things than turning into Jane Whitfield. She was successful. She could take care of herself. Maggie was finding out that she was cut from the same cloth. She patted Zach on the head, and kissed his cheek.

"All will be revealed in good time," she said. "I'm not being mysterious but if I'm right what I'm working on could be a big deal. It could mean the difference between a job and a career."

"In Insurance?"

"Why not?" Maggie hugged her jacket. "You should be happy for me."

"Just promise that you won't leave me in that cubicle when you're the top dog. I want a real office."

Maggie laughed. "I'm headed all the way to corporate with this. I'll take you to Chicago with me."

"You really have gone to the dark side," Zach said. "But, okay, Chicago's cool."

"Chicago won't know what hit it when we get there." Maggie gave his shoulder a pat. He grasped her hand, suddenly serious.

"You know I would help," he said.

"Forget it. I want all the credit," Maggie said.

"I would never—"

"I'm joking, and I'm tired." The music started again. She raised her voice. "And I'm going home."

Zach threw her a kiss. He was back on the dance floor by the time she was out the door. Behind her, the music pounded, but it was a low, dull, repetitive resonance that she felt rather than heard. Maggie took her keys out of her purse and headed to her car.

There was a cool summer breeze. Maggie shivered a little, and hurried down the block. She got behind the wheel of her car, locked the doors, and turned on the overhead light. In the passenger seat was the work she had brought home. Eleven names were checked off. She had twelve more to go. Once she had double-checked everything, Maggie was going to the regional manager because Whitfield had lied when she said she sent the information to the higher-ups. Maggie's report had ended up in Whitfield's trashcan. Either the woman didn't care that the system had been breached, or she was jealous that Maggie found the problem. Either way, Maggie was done with playing by the rules.

Flicking off the light, she started her car and drove back to her apartment. It took her five minutes to find a parking space. When she finally did, Maggie was exhausted. Once inside she changed her clothes, but before she drew her curtains Maggie lingered at the window, looking out onto the dark, quiet street. There were ten buildings on the block just like hers. Giant rectangles divided into three rooms where people like her counted themselves lucky that only a third of their paycheck went to rent. She wasn't living in a ghetto; she just wasn't living.

In the apartment across the way, two people were fighting. She hiccupped a laugh. Things could be worse, she supposed. The good news was that things were about to get better for her. She went to bed planning her move to Chicago and how to use the money that would come with a promotion. There would be a retirement account and travel. She would go somewhere fun. Somewhere interesting. She would go to Paris. It was all going to be so good.

29

Shannon was sprawled in an Adirondack chair that had once been painted yellow and at another time red. Now the chair was blue, but the blue had worn off in places to show the red and the yellow. Finn sat in a green chair. In front of them was a round metal tub filled with charcoal, Cori's poor-man's fire pit. The backyard was a square of sun-parched grass: bald in patches, overgrown with crabgrass in others. The flowering shrubs were big, and healthy, but the fresh buds shared space with withered blossoms. There was a plastic push-toy near the garage wall, four balls of various sizes—one partly deflated— and a blow-up kiddie pool. Cori's place was a far cry from Dennis Cain's fine mansion, and Finn preferred it.

"You've nice friends, Finn," Shannon said.

"And you've not even met Geoffrey yet."

"And he would be?"

"A charming man from Trinidad who owns my watering hole, Mick's Irish Pub," he said. "I keep the darts going and such."

Finn stared into the charcoal fire, happy to be lazy after such a day, happier still that Shannon was calmed down. He put his

Guinness bottle to his lips only to find it empty, so he let it rest on the grass, keeping his fingers upon the neck. It was getting late. Everyone was tired, but too comfortable to move.

He looked toward the kitchen in time to see Cori give Lapinski a kiss as he handed her a dishtowel. Shannon followed his gaze.

"They'll do well together." She inclined her head toward the house. "And are you fine with that, Finn?"

"I am."

Finn wouldn't discuss his feelings for Cori, when he, himself, could not define them. She was his friend, his partner, and closer than a lover could be. Thomas was a friend to them both, and a fine man. If Cori was happy, Finn was happy, for he had nothing to offer her now. If he regretted that down the road, it would be his regret.

"You are all lucky then. It's fine to be in love, better to have such good friends." Shannon let her head roll across the back of the chair. "I'm sorry your woman went off the deep end."

"It happens," Finn answered.

If he had no desire to speak of his affection for Cori, he certainly would not speak of Bev. She was not a wife, not a lover, not a friend, but a wild person with no real care for herself. He was going to call it a night when Shannon's voice floated toward him once more.

"I'm no *hoor*, Finn," she said.

Finn smiled. Her protestation was sweet because she could not bring herself to say the word 'whore' outright even if she wasn't one. Not that it was any mind of his. Still, he was happy to hear this. He liked Shannon. He admired her passion. He would hate to see it wasted on men who had nothing to give her except money.

"And what are you, Shannon?"

"Arm candy," she said. "A confessor. An ear for men with too many problems and too much money. I'm paid handsomely for my presence and counsel, nothing more. You would be surprised how lonely and unsure the rich are. "

From the corner of his eye, Finn saw her arm fall to the side. She let her own bottle of stout swing from her fingers. Her voice was still beautiful, but from the sound of it, Shannon Shaughnessy was as lonely as her clients.

"I am not lying. I do not lie," she said. "In that way Maura and I were alike."

"I believe you," Finn said. "Though it's not necessary for me to."

"'Tis, Finn," she said. "You must know who I am because I want that baby. I'll not let that man or his wife have anything to do with the child. I want you to know this, so you'll have no problem helping me find him."

"Shannon, there is a lot ahead of you. The Cain's have money—"

"As have I." She sat up and touched his arm, insisting he attend to her.

"And in the United States, the father is given priority in the courts—"

"And I'll go fight him—"

Finn spoke over her.

"Shannon, 'tis not a battle between you two, but a question of what's best for the —"

Before he finished, Cori and Lapinski joined them. They came toting barrel-backed plastic chairs.

"You two look serious," Thomas said, putting his chair across from them. He waited until Cori was settled before he sat down, but he spoke all the while. "Shannon, I'm telling you right now that if you need any help, I'm your guy. I won't take a dime."

"Lapinski, you'd give away the choir books before anyone

had a chance to sing." Cori laughed. "No one is going to arrest her for anything."

"Shannon is wanting Maura's baby as her own," Finn said. "I told her that in this country the father has priority."

"But the child is in Ireland. I'll not have two orphans in the family," Shannon said. "That man being a father is as good as having none at all."

"She's got a point," Cori said. "But growing up like that—when the wife hates you—would be hell on earth for that kid."

"Maura wrote in her diary that she tried to contact him," Shannon said. "He never answered her. The man is scum."

"He denies that, Shannon. There are always two sides. He might have blocked her and she wouldn't know it," Finn said. "And if Maura was coming for a showdown, why not bring the baby as evidence? There would be no way to turn away from that."

"Thank goodness she didn't," Lapinski said, and no one misunderstood him. The only way this tragedy could have been worse would be if that baby had perished onboard the Platinum Wings flight.

"I didn't tell Amber's father for almost a year after she was born," Cori said.

"Why did you wait so long?" Shannon asked.

"I was scared. I figured if he didn't want me, why would he want her? Then I was pissed off. I mean, if he treated me bad then maybe he would treat the baby bad," Cori said. "But I think the real reason was that I didn't want to share all that love with someone who was basically an asshole."

Everyone chuckled. Lapinski took her hand.

"And then I convinced myself that if he saw Amber, he would love me, and her, and we would live happily ever after," she said. "I'm here to tell you, Shannon, Walt Disney had it wrong. Not every story has a happy ending."

"How long before Amber told her boyfriend about Tucker?" Lapinski asked.

"I made her tell him right off. She did, and he left. It hurt her, but at least she knew where she stood."

"And she had you," Finn said.

"Yeah, she had me," Cori said.

"There are a zillion other reasons why a woman might not tell the father," Thomas said. "She could be ambivalent. Maybe he's violent. Maybe she never had any intention of letting him know. This works both ways, you know. Sometimes women get pregnant and walk away."

"We'll never know which it was, will we?" Finn said as he stared into the dying fire. "Cain didn't know Maura was pregnant."

"By his word." Shannon reminded Finn.

"True, but I'm thinking he doesn't have it in him to kill her," Finn said. "Not to mention he was here in L.A."

"Again, we've only his word," Shannon said.

"You know who else has money?" Cori's fingers intertwined with Lapinski and she gave him a little tug. "The wife. If you were Maura, and good old Dennis wasn't returning your calls, contacting the wife would be the next step, right?"

"That should be easy enough to trace," Thomas said. "You can get the phone records."

"If we could get a subpoena," Finn reminded them. "Which we won't be able to because this is not our job."

"But Lowery could get it. You'll have to tell him what went down tonight," Cori said.

"He'll want to talk with you, Shannon," Finn said.

"Call him now," she said.

"In good time," Finn said.

"But a woman, a mother, killing another woman with a

baby," Thomas said. "Your husband's baby no less. That would be cold."

"No colder than a mother killing her own children, and how often have we seen that?" Cori said.

"So, what do we do about this?" Shannon said, and all eyes turned her way. "I want Cain to pay, or the two of them if they deserve it."

"You'll have to settle for the satisfaction of smashing his car, Shannon," Finn said. "Still, I'd like to see Maura's journal. Maybe we can help track the baby down. "

“You've got Maura's phone number, right?” Thomas said. “I could have her address by...”

"Whoa. Whoa. Slow it down,” Cori said. "Shannon, sleep on this. Make a plan. Being a single mom is no picnic."

"I've got money," Shannon said.

"And time? And temperament?” Cori said. “I don't know you real well, but first impressions tell me that 'calm' is not your default mode. You've got to do some real soul-searching. That little thing might have better options in Ireland."

“There's a lot to think about, but I'm done in.” Finn got himself up, slung his jacket over his shoulder, and put an end to the conversation. “It's time we are going."

He and Shannon were saying their goodbyes and thank yous when Finn's phone vibrated. He glanced at it, and then opened the message. In Ireland, the Garda Michael Hedgecoe was working overtime. Finn opened the attachment the man had sent, gave it a cursory look, and then made one more request. Would Garda Hedgecoe have a look at Shannon Shaughnessy? Finn would do the same in the U.S. If she was going to pursue custody, he wanted to know all about her. He closed his phone, and found Shannon looking at him closely, but he deflected her attention by thanking Cori. It was Cori who walked him down the driveway. Thomas had Shannon in hand and followed behind.

"This is going to be like stacking dominoes," Cori said. "One block falling is all it takes to bury you under a pile of misery."

"It's already a mess and personal, so I'll see it through."

"Yeah, well sympathy is one thing, jumping in the snake pit is another." Cori paused. Finn stopped at the same time. "All I'm asking is, get that girl to slow down."

"I doubt she'll listen, but I'll try."

He gave Cori's shoulder a squeeze. Thomas handed Shannon off. She was alight with news of what Thomas was going to do: try to hack Maura's computer, track down an address, search hospitals where the baby might have been born. The soles of her fluffy slippers slapped the street as they went to the car. Finn and Shannon waved. Cori and Lapinski waved back, but Cori shivered as she watched them go.

"I think someone just walked over my grave," she said, and then turned toward him and patted his chest. "Or maybe it was O'Brien's grave they were dancing on. Sometimes it's hard to tell where I start and he ends."

"Not for me," Thomas said.

"Always said you were a smart one." Cori took his shirt collar between her fingers and gave a little tug. "I'm not telling you what to do, but think twice before you go stickin' your nose into the Shaughnessy sisters' problems, okay?"

"It's not much to look into a computer."

"It's not getting' in, Lapinski, it's being able to get out of this mess. That's always the tricky part."

30

The man stared into the mirror, and considered how he looked with a mustache. Before he could decide, his wife said:

"You look stupid."

He twitched his lips, and turned his head right and then left, hoping to see something that would prove her wrong. He didn't.

"You're right."

He ripped off the fake mustache, and tossed it onto the dressing table.

His wife was dressed for bed, but she was putting things right before she settled down. They were peas in a pod that way. They both loved to have everything in its place, and she was meticulous. She picked his jacket off the back of a chair and said:

"Cleaners?"

When he nodded, she went through each of his pockets, and when he looked up again, he saw that she was holding up something, waving it at him.

"If you're cheating on me," she said. "You could do it in a classier place than this hotel."

The man got up and went to see what she was holding. He laughed. Just looking at the napkin from the hotel made his head itch all over again. He took it, and threw it away.

"I had to pick something up. I was in and out in five minutes."

He sat down at the dressing table again. She put the jacket in the cleaner's bag and then went over and wrapped her arms around his neck. She kissed his cheek and looked into the mirror thinking that together they made quite a handsome couple.

"Then I know you aren't having an affair. Five minutes wouldn't be nearly long enough."

She kissed him again, and got into bed. He was back at the make-believe, futzing with his props. She took a magazine off the bedside table, opened it, but kept looking at her husband. Finally, she said:

"I don't think you need to do much of anything, honey. I mean, your face is kind of..." she crinkled her nose and then smiled. "It's confusing. Considering what you're doing, that's a good thing. Say you were an eyewitness, and you were looking at you, and *you* had to describe yourself to a cop. I mean, really. How would you?"

He tilted his head and took a long look. She was right. Everything about his face was just a little off. He wasn't handsome, but he wasn't a ghoul. Sometimes his hair stuck straight up and sometimes it lay flat against his head. When he wore his contacts, his eyes looked small and mean. When he wore his glasses, he looked kind and curious.

He pushed his cheeks up and let them fall. He tugged at the corner of his eyes where fine lines radiated toward his cheeks. He pulled his bottom lip up and clamped his teeth over it. He looked like a sponge. He smiled, and he could see why his wife liked his smile the best.

What she disliked was his extracurricular activities, but she had stopped harping on it long ago. Still, she tried to undermine his enthusiasm every chance she got. She went back to reading her magazine. He put away his make-up and brushes, and got in bed with her.

"Have I ever told you I love you?" he said.

"Yes."

She pretended to read.

"Have I ever told you you're brilliant?"

"Not often enough."

She flipped a page. He ran a finger down her arm.

"You want to come with me? Day after tomorrow. I've got a really interesting one. It's going to take some doing, but..."

She shut her magazine and tossed it on the floor. Turning toward him, taking his unmemorable, lovable face between her hands, she said:

"No. Not now. Not ever. This is your thing. I don't like it. I don't want to know about it." She snuggled down and so did he. "A lot of things could go wrong. You said you almost got caught last time."

"What are they going to do if they catch me? Shoot me?"

He pushed back her hair, and she fell in love with her goofy, adventure-loving, strange man all over again.

"It only takes one thing to go wrong," she said.

"Never going to happen. I know what I'm doing."

He kissed her forehead, he kissed her lips, but when he turned out the light, he turned away from her. She put her hand on his back, but he didn't stir. She rolled over, sorry that she had put a damper on things, but one of these days his 'fun' wasn't going to end well.

She fell asleep, leaving her husband to stare at the wall and wonder if she was right. Maybe he should quit. But there was the money to consider. It was too late to back out now, so let the games begin.

FINN PARKED his car across from his mother's house. Once in a while he drove by to check to see if her lights were off and the backyard gate was closed. Tonight, the backyard lights were on, so he pulled over.

It was quiet as he crossed the street and lifted the latch on the gate. He walked up the drive noting the neatly wound hose and the lemon tree heavy with fruit. But when Finn turned at the corner of the house, he saw that the lights had not been left on by mistake.

Dressed in her housecoat and slippers, his mother was sitting on the bench under the tree the family had planted after Alexander died. Her hair was cut short, and it still took him aback to see her this way. He missed the long braid, but she had only kept it long because his father loved it that way. Everyone in the family knew that cutting her hair signaled a turning point, one she was ready for even if they were not.

"Ma?"

She raised her head, and slipped her rosary beads into the pocket of her robe.

"You've found me out, Finn." He walked across the yard and sat next to her. "What are you doing sneaking about, not knocking on the front door?"

"I was in the neighborhood," Finn said. "I thought you'd left on the lights."

"You were checking on me."

"That I was."

He chuckled, and so did she.

"'Tis nice out here even though it's late. Peaceful."

"I suppose," she answered.

In the silence they heard a dog bark. A door slammed shut. In the distance was the white noise of freeway traffic. Finn's mother took his hand and squeezed it. Her plain gold wedding band glinted in the light.

"Alexander's been gone a long while," she said. "Such a long time."

"That he has," he said.

Finn still blamed himself for his brother's death. Forgetting to pick him up from school only to have a predator do the chore for him was a guilt he would always live with. Nothing his mother could say would change that.

"I hear his voice sometimes," she said. "Sitting here, I feel as if I could touch him. 'Tis a mother's memory."

She raised Finn's hand, shaking it so that he understood Alexander's memory felt as real to her as he did. She let his hand go and stood up. Finn's mother was a tall and regal woman. She put her hands in the pockets of her robe. Even though she tried to hide it, Finn saw these hands curling into fists.

"And then I think of Hugh. I can't feel him and I am so angry about that. I'm angry with our parents for sending him away. Worse, I'm angry with God for taking him as he did."

"I wish it could have been different," Finn said.

She turned on him, showing him a face that he had never seen before. She was a woman at a crossroads, but she wasn't looking for direction on which fork to take. She had already decided.

"Sure, I'm thinking of Hugh and Alex, but mostly my hatred is for the violence that took them both. One young, one old. It doesn't matter. I am sickened and my soul is dark."

"I know, ma," he said. "I'm so sorry there was nothing I could do."

"'Tisn't about you, Finn O'Brien. It was never about you. It's about God and my heart. God says we have free will, but why is it the evil ones who exercise it? The rest of us trust in God and I'm tired of trusting when this is what He gives my family. Not rewards but grief."

She came back toward, him, fast and sure. She sat down beside him and he saw a fever in her eyes.

"I want someone to pay, Finn. I want to tell these people who did these things what they've taken from me, and then I want them to burn in hell. God forgive me, that's what I want. I choose not to turn the other cheek. That is a sin, but I am choosing to do it. That's my free will."

"Ma..."

"Please, Finn. Please. Do this for me. Find them. Let me see them. Let me watch their punishment."

Finn closed his eyes. He shook his head. He could not give her what she wanted. Alexander's case was cold before he had taken his oath; Hugh's investigation was out of his hands.

"I can't, ma."

"You can," she insisted. "I've never asked you for anything, but now I am. Alexander was long ago, but Hugh, Finn. Do something about Hugh. Don't let me die without sending one of the *fooking* bastards who took my family to hell."

JANE WHITFIELD WENT to bed at eleven. She checked her email. She checked her office voice mail. She checked her cell. There were no messages.

She closed her eyes, but sleep wouldn't come.

At two in the morning, she picked up the phone and dialed the number for Wolfhound Distillery. It was ten in the morning in Ireland. She spoke to Brian Cain's assistant again, and this time she made it clear that she must speak to him immediately. That's when she found out that Brian was in Los Angeles. He wasn't taking calls from anyone, and Jane could leave a message with her.

Jane said that would be unacceptable, and a few minutes later she had the name of the hotel where Brian was staying.

Agent Lowery sat in his 'office'. It really was his daughter's old bedroom. He had intended to paint it when she moved out, but he never got around to it so the walls were still shell pink. There was an elliptical in one corner that he used now and again, a bookshelf and a large desk. It wasn't the most attractive room but it was serviceable. He had a fax, a printer, a computer, and a television. He didn't watch television much, but he used the heck out of everything else. Right now, he was waiting for a fax to come through from The Garda in Ireland, a full report on the origin of the Platinum Wings flight, the passengers, the pilot, the stewardess, and anyone else who had even looked at that plane. There were fifteen pages. So far five had been printed.

His phone rang as page eight began to print.

"Yep," he said, recognizing the caller as Agent Franks' "What did you get?"

"She wouldn't talk to me," Franks said. "And she wouldn't let Mustafa talk to me. She said she was sick of cops coming to ask them the same questions over and over."

"Have you been making a nuisance of yourself?" Lowery asked, holding the receiver against his shoulder with his cheek as he took out the printed pages and tapped them on the desk.

"Not me," Franks answered. "O'Brien. He went to the house once and called twice."

Lowery paused. He took the phone off his shoulder. When

the silence lasted too long, Franks said: "Lowery? Want me to go back and try again?"

"No, give them some time to chill," Lowery said.

"What about O'Brien?"

"I'll take care of it," Lowery said. "Go home. Tomorrow, check in on Sterling. See if she's got word on the timing device or sourced the explosives."

The call ended. Lowery took the final pages of the Garda report, added them to the ones he had, and stapled them together intending to read them in bed. Before he turned out the office light, though, he glanced at the cover sheet to look at the table of contents. It was then he saw that the report had been cc'd to Finn O'Brien.

He put the papers on the desk, changed his clothes, and told his wife to go to sleep without him. He was going for a walk. She said it was too late, but agent Lowery knew it was exactly the right time. He had to decide what to do about Detective Finn O'Brien, and it was best thought about in the open where he couldn't put his fist through a wall.

31

"Sorry, I'm late."

Brian's hand slipped across Jane's shoulders so quickly she barely had time to register it.

"You look wonderful, Jane. Every inch the executive," Brian said. "A far cry from ten years ago when you were just an agent hungry for business—even Wolfhound's."

"You haven't changed either. A soldier in a suit. I bet you're stuffed full of grand ideas."

Brian laughed, taking that as a compliment. He snapped his napkin and put it on his lap. The waitress appeared, a huge grin on her face, as she waited to hear what his pleasure would be.

"Have you ordered, Jane?"

"I'm not hungry," she said.

"You shouldn't drink on an empty stomach." He opened the menu, ran his eyes up and down. He handed it back and said to the waitress: "I'll have an ice tea, and bring an order of calamari."

The waitress was more than happy to bring him whatever he liked. She pranced away. Jane was still sullen.

"That will tide you over." He nodded at her glass. "Vodka, I imagine."

"You remembered." She picked up the glass and toasted him. "To old times when we were young, and randy, and reckless." She took a drink. "Were you going to tell me you were in town?"

"I wasn't planning on doing any socializing," he said. "And, frankly, I didn't know you lived here or that you had risen to such heights at Intrepid."

Jane moved her glass a quarter turn. She ran her finger around the rim. It wasn't just their history that made her nervous. It was the business that brought her here. Brian didn't like the silence.

"According to my assistant, you called in a panic and were quite rude. It's hard for me to imagine you panicked."

Jane ignored the banter. She was in no mood, and she found it oddly unattractive coming from him.

"What's going on, Brian?"

"You're going to have to be a bit more specific, Jane?"

"Wolfhound has filed two corporate claims. There's a government investigation that is holding up the processing and that is worrisome." Jane took another drink.

"The question is, what business is this of yours?" Brian said.

"I'm glad you asked that—."

Jane stopped talking when the waitress brought Brian's order. As soon as she was gone, Jane leaned into the table and lowered her voice.

"It seems a Mr. Hugh Murphy's personal policy was mixed up with your corporate portfolio which meant the corporate claim was going to be settled to his personal beneficiaries."

Brian's dark eyes flickered. Jane knew that look. She had his attention.

"And was it? Did you pay out ten million dollars?" Brian asked.

"First tell me why you had two claims in one day?"

"There was a problem with the plane on which two of our employees were traveling. Sadly, they both died. It happens."

"It does, but this time it's drawing more attention than either of us is going to want." Jane picked up her napkin. She ran it through her hands and then tossed it on the table. Unsettled, she said: "The person inputting the data used the wrong codes. Somewhere in Ireland, a beneficiary has been informed that Maura Shaughnessy left them ten million dollars. Hugh Murphy's beneficiary was in the U.S., and it went through my office."

"That's unfortunate." Brian picked up his drink, holding it steady, his jaw tightening. "But you caught it."

"If I had, it wouldn't be a problem. The insured's nephew came in asking about it."

"A police detective?" Brian asked.

"Yes. How did you know?"

"Dennis talked to him." Brian took a drink and then set his glass down, all his attention on her. "What did you tell him?"

"I told him it was a glitch," Jane said. "I expedited the payment on the personal policy, but I have no idea what's happening in Ireland. I only know that, pending the outcome of the investigation, both corporate policies are on hold. You're going to have to wait for them to settle—if they settle that is."

"That's not acceptable," Brian said.

"There's nothing I can do about it," Jane snapped.

"What about the second policy?" Brian said.

"I advised the office in Ireland of the mistake on the Shaughnessy policy, and they said they would see to it. I can't press further than that."

"Alright," he said. "I am aware of Maura's situation. I can track that down. But, it's a simple mistake. This doesn't seem to be a thing to worry about, now does it?"

"It wouldn't have been except for Maggie Davis. She's the expeditor who handled the beneficiary's questions. She pulled up Wolfhound's account and saw both of the claims. She thinks Wolfhound has been targeted and that hackers are settling corporate payouts on personal beneficiaries."

"An interesting conclusion that I'm sure you disabused her of."

"I tried but she keeps digging and cross-checking. Soon she'll know exactly what we did." Jane took a deep breath. "I don't want Chicago looking into this."

"Nor do I," Brian said. "If there is no further inquiry, then I am assuming the claims against Murphy and Shaughnessy will be settled."

"I see no reason why they wouldn't, but Maggie is putting toge—"

"Maggie be damned," Brian shot back. "Just shut her down."

"How about this, Brian," she said. "How about you get on the horn and cancel the outstanding policies. You don't need them."

Brian grabbed her wrist and twisted.

"Don't tell me what I—"

In that same second the waitress had the misfortune to reappear. This time when she looked at Brian Cain it was with alarm. She cut her eyes to Jane.

"Is everything okay here?" The waitress asked, and everyone knew she wasn't talking about the calamari. Brian let Jane go.

"Fine. Thank you," he said. "We'll just take the check."

Jane finished her drink while the waitress tallied it up. Brian handed the girl a credit card without bothering to look at the bill. She left without saying another word. Brian was composed once again.

"Please, don't be telling me what I need, Jane," he said. "I will look at our policies. There might be some I can cancel. Two will remain in force for at least another year and there is no negotiating that. You take care of your end, and I'll do what I can on mine."

He started to get up. She put out her hand.

"What are they investigating, Brian? I need to know."

"'Tis nothing to do with you." Jane took hold of his jacket, annoying Brian. People were watching, so he smiled but spoke through clenched teeth. "The plane blew up. They believe it was a bomb."

"Oh my..."

"For God's sake woman, whatever you're thinking stop it." Brian pulled away from her. "How it was done, if it was done, is no matter. There are no caveats in our policies save for suicide. You know that."

"I am already on the record asking to push one settlement through just to get it off the books. Do you know what that will look like if they see Maggie's information and find out a federal investigation is under way?" Jane asked.

"It will look like nothing as long as this is your only query," Brian said, done with their conversation. "Now shut down your girl however you have to. Do it today, Jane."

With that he was gone, and Jane was staring across the room at the waitress. She pushed her chair back and left the restaurant before the girl came over. The last thing she wanted to be asked again was if she was okay.

Jane Whitfield thought it should be fairly obvious that she was not.

"I'D WHISTLE if I knew how, detective."

Eileen Waters, Captain Fowler's new assistant, was that odd combination of personable and professional. Finn admired the energy she brought to the front office, Cori thought she was a hoot, but neither of them had much to do with her because there were only two reasons to be talking to Fowler's gatekeeper: either they had done something good or they had done something bad. Finn knew he'd done nothing good of late, so he had to assume the latter.

"You're a charmer, Eileen," Finn said.

"And you clean up real nice. A suit and everything. Have you been in court?" she asked.

"You caught me at my uncle's funeral."

She pulled a face. He assured her that it was a grand send-off, and then said: "Can you give me a hint as to what I'm walking into?"

"Sorry, my lips are zipped. All I can say is, he's really not happy," she said. "I could also say he's got on a very nice yellow tie today, but I don't think that will help you much, so get ready to pull up your big boy pants."

She waved him on, but Finn paused before he knocked on the captain's door.

"Is Cori in there, or it is just me in the dog house?" he asked.

"Just you," she said. "It's a shame. You've been a pretty good boy the last few weeks."

Finn laughed, and buttoned his jacket before opening the door to Fowler's office. The first thing he saw was the captain's yellow tie. The power of suggestion amused him. Fowler looked more like a captain of industry than a cop. Harvard educated, handsome as a movie star, he was a dedicated, by-the-book advocate for justice who still had some heart. The heart seemed to be missing at the moment. The captain's face above the fancy tie and his crisp white collar was set in a sober expression. He sat away from his desk, a question in his eyes as he noted Finn's suit, but he said nothing. Instead, Fowler's eyes clicked toward the corner of the large office. They were not alone. Paging through one of Captain Fowler's prized history books was a man Finn knew.

"Good to see you, O'Brien."

"Agent Lowery," Finn said.

32

Maggie fidgeted, uncomfortable being alone in Jane Whitfield's office. She put her head back and blew out a breath. She unclasped her hands and then clasped then again. She tossed her hair over her shoulder and licked her lips, and nearly jumped out of her skin when Jane Whitfield swooped into the office and spoke her name.

"Yes. Yes."

Maggie sat up straight. Swiveling her head as her boss closed the door. Jane's suit jacket was on and buttoned up. Her make-up had just been freshened, but she still looked awful: pale and agitated.

When she rushed past, Maggie thought she smelled liquor. Jane took a seat behind her desk. She adjusted a few things: a pen, a file, her computer monitor. Finally, she cleared her throat, put three fingers to her brow, and got down to business.

"Maggie, there is no easy way to tell you this, so I'm just going to say it. We're going to have to let you go."

"What? Why?" Maggie was half out of her chair. Jane waved her down.

"You have violated my trust. You went over my head with a problem that I was aware of and —"

"But you weren't doing anything about it," Maggie insisted.

"This problem is being handled. In this office. By me. On my schedule," Jane said, her anger barely under control.

"Well, I don't think it is," Maggie said.

"I beg your pardon."

"You heard me. You told me what I don't know and that's fair," Maggie said. "But I've tried to tell you what I do know. You want to sweep this under the rug because you wrote those policies."

Maggie rose. She got close to the desk, so close that she could see Whitfield was sweating.

"Why don't you just admit it, so it can be fixed?"

"That's it." Jane got up too. "You've been with this company for a year and a half. You graduated top of your class, but that's about all you had to recommend you. The only work experience you had was as a barista. You don't know anything about how real business works, especially at the level you're trying to crack. You're out of here."

"It's not going to be that eas—" Maggie's voice rose, but Jane cut her off with a warning.

"Be careful."

"No, you be careful. There are laws to protect people like me. You may have experience, but I know my rights. If you made a mistake, say so. If you're covering up—"

"That's enough. Enough."

Jane picked up the phone, dropped the receiver and picked it up again. She kept her eyes on Maggie while she made her call. When it was answered she raised her voice.

"I need security to escort an employee out of the building. Yes. Now."

"Are you kidding me?" Maggie said.

Jane slammed down the receiver and went around her desk until she was close enough to see the fear in Maggie's eyes. Good. She should be afraid.

"Intrepid has excellent lawyers and unlimited money to fight slander," Jane said. "If you want to have any future, drop this."

"Screw you."

"Go back to your desk. Someone will meet you, and take you out," Jane said. "I'll advise HR, and they will deposit your last payment before the end of the day."

Maggie stood still, seething, knowing that what Whitfield was doing was wrong. Deciding not to say something she would regret, Maggie left Jane Whitfield's office. She walked through a front office, past people who didn't make eye contact with her. When she got to her desk, she slammed open her desk drawer. Zach was in her cubicle a moment later.

"What are you doing? What's wrong?"

"Whitfield fired me." Maggie pulled out a brush and lipstick and slammed the drawer closed.

"Jesus, Maggie. Why? What did you do?"

"I did the right thing. Whitfield screwed up, and I sent the information to her boss."

"Oh God," Zach wailed. "What are you going to do now?"

Maggie rummaged around inside another drawer, closing it when she found a thumb drive. She put it in the computer, tapped the keyboard, and waited.

"Hurry. Come on," she said under her breath. "Got it."

She hit the keys again. Zach looked at her screen.

"Don't," he whispered. "Jesus, you're going to be in trouble."

"If you don't want to see, then go away."

Maggie rummaged through her top drawer, came up with a piece of paper with a phone number on it and started dialing. Before she finished, a female security officer showed up.

"Maggie Davis?" she said.

"Give me a damn minute," Maggie snapped.

That was the wrong thing to say. The woman moved in on her. Maggie showed her back, giving Zach a look and a cock of the head as she did so.

Zach tap-danced, trying to figure out what she wanted. Then he saw her eyes dart to the computer. He rolled his own in exasperation. Still, he put himself in front of the uniformed woman.

"I'll walk her out," he said, hoping to stall security so the download would finish.

"Sorry. Gotta be this way."

She pushed him aside. Maggie was dialing again, frantic to make a connection. The security lady was getting upset, herding Zach into the hallway. That's when he saw Jane Whitfield coming their way at the same time he heard Maggie say:

"Hello, I want to speak to—"

Before Zach could get a word out, Whitfield stormed into Maggie's cubical, grabbed the phone and slammed it down.

"You're done," she said.

Maggie picked up her bag and her purse.

"Fine. I'm going."

Whitfield blocked her way.

"Give me your bag."

Maggie started to object. Zach shook his head furiously, so she handed it over. Whitfield riffled through the bag, pulled out two folders, and looked through them. She pushed the bag back at Maggie, pulled the thumb drive out of the computer, tossed it in the trash and then let security take over. Knowing it was over, Maggie went with the uniformed woman.

"Do you want me to come with you?" Zach asked, fretting as he followed them.

Maggie stopped long enough to squeeze his arm. She lowered her voice.

"Bandwidth5. Just remember that, okay?"

"Let's go," the woman said, ending the conversation.

Zach watched them walk away, and when he turned around, Jane Whitfield was staring at him. Zach went back to his cubicle. It took him ten minutes to screw up the courage to stick his head into the hall and see if she was gone. She was, so Zach ducked into Maggie's office to see if she'd left anything behind.

There was nothing to see, but the computer was still on. Curious about what had been so important, Zack leaned over the keyboard. The screen lit up, but the machine had been asleep long enough to lock again.

"Zach."

He bolted upright at the sound of Jane Whitfield's voice.

"I was just shutting down, Maggie's computer," he said.

Her eyes went to the computer and back to him.

"You'll be taking over her accounts until we can fill this position," Jane said. "Unless you'd like to go with her."

"No. No. I'm good."

"Then I suggest you get back to work."

Jane went back to her office, closed her door, and got her bottle of vodka. She poured a stiff one and sat down in her big, executive chair. Taking a deep breath, Jane spun around slowly. Once, twice, three times. When she was face-forward again, Jane looked at the phone and thought about calling Brian. She would tell him that everything was taken care of.

Instead, she poured herself another drink and held off. She had no idea if that was true.

33

Lowery ambled across the office and perched himself on the side of the captain's desk. Finn knew this for what it was: a symbolic gesture of dominance that was Lowery's alone. Captain Fowler never would be part of such a theater; two men with rank against the one without. Lowery, however, was comfortable with such rudeness.

"Look, Detective O'Brien," Lowery said. "I didn't come here to mess with you. I just needed some help getting you on board because you're putting me in a bad position. I know you've been to see Mustafa and his wife. I know you've contacted the Garda. My people are working hard, and you're in the way. Captain Fowler and I further agree that there isn't anything you can do that we can't do better. Your captain and I agree that it's time you stop being a cowboy—or whatever rides the range where you come from."

Finn ran a finger up the side of his nose, and chanced a look at Fowler. The man was stone-faced, as unhappy a man as Finn had ever seen. There would be no help, so Finn spoke directly to Agent Lowery.

"Here is the problem as I see it, Agent Lowery. You're not doing these 'better' things very quickly, now are you?

"I've heard nothing. Shannon Shaughnessy has heard nothing. Your team has not even interviewed us, nor my partner, Cori Anderson. We were both there and we are trained officers of the law. Do you not think we might have some insights that would help your investigation?"

"You're on the list," Lowery said.

"Then the list is flawed. We should have been the first people spoken to," Finn snapped.

"When the tables are turned," he said. "We'll have coffee so you can fill me in on your game plan, and I'll tell you where you're wrong."

"I would have at least acknowledged your standing," Finn said, hard-pressed to keep the disgust from his face. "I certainly would have acknowledged your loss."

"Then I apologize for my lack of sensitivity," Lowery said.

"The fact remains, O'Brien, that you have been conducting a parallel investigation. That is unacceptable," Captain Fowler said.

"Captain, I—"

Fowler silenced him, raising his hand slightly.

"Your own work for this department has been neglected. You are damaging Agent Fowler's investigation, you ha—"

That was enough. The morning's peace, the blessings of the priest, none of it could keep Finn's ire from boiling over. He was half out of his chair, hands on the captain's desk, pleading his case, and unable to look at Lowery's smirk.

"And how have I damaged anything, captain? Name me one time that I have crossed the line? Perhaps, Agent Lowery could be specific with that information."

The agent's name was like bile in his mouth, but he tamped down the anger in his voice as he straightened up.

"Sure, didn't he interrogate my own mother without bothering to tell me? I only spoke to the pilot to ask if he had a word with my uncle. I've that right, especially when there is so little information coming from the people in charge. Am I to be discriminated against as a victim because of my job?"

"Sit, O'Brien," Fowler said.

Finn hesitated, but did as his captain asked. Lowery took the floor again. If Finn had been in charge of this meeting it would be Lowery in the chair of shame, and he would be doing the lecturing, but Captain Fowler let the agent have his head.

"This isn't as simple as a dead junkie on one of your street corners," Lowery said. "This is a federal investigation, with international repercussions. If the people — or person—we're looking for see confusion or misdirection because you're muddying the waters, they will exploit it. If they get away from us, it's not like some two-bit hood getting a pass."

Lowery had closed in on Finn, not quite finished with teaching investigation 101.

"We are methodical, we have technical investigatory channels you can only dream about. We have databases that you couldn't begin to understand."

He leaned very close. He spoke each word as if it were a sentence.

"We don't need your help. Period."

Finn and Lowery had eyes only for one another. Lowery raised a brow, waiting to see if Finn was listening. He was, and he didn't like what he heard.

"Perhaps, Agent Lowery, you could share a bit of what you've found in your mysterious databases," Finn said. "Just to make me feel a bit more comfortable."

Lowery smiled. He put his butt back on the edge of the desk, planted his feet, and put his hands in his trouser pockets. He looked so satisfied and superior that it made Finn sick.

"We've been in touch with the Garda, and they tell us that your uncle had no connections to any political group. He lived a quiet life as did his wife. Neither had any criminal record."

Finn's lips tipped. He would not say 'I told you so', but that information was so insignificant it wasn't worth acknowledging it.

"And the pilot?" Finn said.

"He has a history." Lowery was coy, but Finn would not let him off the hook so easily.

"I suppose you're referring to the history with his previous employer." Finn egged him on.

"Mustafa faking an emergency landing and tampering with the plane to impress his ex? Is that the narrative you're talking about?"

Lowery pulled up a little taller, enjoying Finn's disappointment.

"Or are you thinking about the job after that where he cold-cocked another pilot and broke the man's jaw? That landed Mustafa in rehab for a drug problem and anger management..."

Lowery paused. His eyes got big. Now he was having fun.

"And did you know Mustafa had done eighteen months for possession? He was smuggling coke then, but the guy who owns Platinum went to school with Jimmy Mustafa. He gave him a job despite his record. I think you figured out that the pilot and the stew had a thriving, if minor, diamond smuggling operation. But did you know the Bureau was on to them? Now you've stepped on our toes and the FBI's. What else are you planning to screw up, O'Brien?"

Finn colored. Lowery was right. He had only part of the pie, but Finn had a good piece of it.

"You haven't spoken to Shannon Shaughnessy," he said.

"The Shaughnessy women are not a high priority."

"Perhaps they should be," Finn said. "Your investigators

handed Maura Shaughnessy's journal off to her sister. If they had read it, you would know that Maura Shaughnessy had a child by Dennis Cain and was coming here to confront him. This was a personally volatile situation for the gentleman. You might have also learned that his wife was in the armed services. Murder has been committed for less."

Now it was Lowery's turn to be embarrassed. He had personally made the call to release the passenger's luggage after a basic eyes-on in order to get the families off his back. Someone had missed the journal and he would find out who it was, but hell would freeze over before he would admit a mistake to Finn O'Brien. Not that he had to worry about admitting anything. Fowler had his back.

"O'Brien. This isn't a pissing match," the captain warned. "When did you find out about this?"

"Day before yesterday, captain," Finn answered. "There was a physical confrontation between the Cains and Ms. Shaughnessy. Beverly Hills PD called me at Ms. Shaughnessy's request. They wanted to diffuse the situation and trusted a fellow officer to do that."

Finn looked at the ATF agent.

"Unfortunately, I had my uncle's funeral to attend. Agent Lowery decided to complain to you, captain, before I had a chance to share this information."

"We can do without the asides," Fowler snapped. "Agent Lowery, I'm sorry. My detective should have called you immediately."

Fowler put eyes on Finn even though he was clearly speaking to Lowery.

"My detective will have a detailed report in your hands by the end of the day. Detective O'Brien will then cease all contact with anyone involved in this matter. He and Detective Anderson will make themselves available at your convenience for interviews. If Detective O'Brien has any further information or questions, he will write it up and give it to me. If I determine it is appropriate, I will send it on to you."

Finn moved up in his chair.

"Captain, I have done nothing any family member wouldn't have done. I've told everyone that I was contacting them in a personal capacity. I have not crossed the line."

"And Mrs. Mustafa had your card," Lowery said. "You used your title when contacting the Garda in Cork. You knew exactly what you were doing."

"If anyone misunderstood it is on their head," Finn said.

"It doesn't matter. The Garda officer has been reassigned so as not to create any more confusion. The Mustafa's have been apprised of the situation and will not be taking your calls. Since you have a personal relationship with Ms. Shaughnessy, she is free to do whatever she likes," Lowery said. He turned toward Captain Fowler. "I think we're clear now. Captain—"

"I think not," Finn said. "Were it not for my connection with Ms. Shaughnessy, he wouldn't know that Dennis Cain had a motive for wishing her sister dead. The arrogance of this man, suggesting that no good has come—"

Captain Fowler stood up so quickly it took Finn aback. He came around his desk and gripped Finn's arm.

"I believe you're done, detective."

Finn pulled away, setting himself against his captain now. Realizing what he had done, he composed himself.

"Yes, captain. That I am."

Finn looked at Lowery. Thankfully the man was not smirking. Finn pulled at his tie to loosen it. He popped the top button of his shirt. Satisfied that the detective was under control, Captain Fowler moved Lowery toward the door.

"You have my number if there is anything you need."

Fowler opened the door. Finn heard the tapping of Eileen's keyboard and phones ringing. He saw a uniformed officer pass in the hall, and the two men in charge shake hands. It was business as usual. Finn was forgotten. Or so he thought. Lowery looked at him, wanting the last word.

"Just remember this, O'Brien. Our investigations make yours look like a tea party. This thing with Platinum? A private jet blowing up? Three dead? It's bad, but at the ATF this is small potatoes. That's—"

That was it.

With a great roar, Finn launched himself across the office, throwing the full force of his body at the agent, knocking Lowery off his feet. They spilled out of Captain Fowler's office, landing at Eileen's feet. She was quick, pushing back, sending her wheeled chair spinning toward the wall.

"O'Brien!"

The cry of Finn's name was Fowler's order to stop, but all Finn heard was the blazing sound of fury filling his head. Lowery grappled with Finn, pushing him off just far enough to catch his right leg in a scissor lock. Finn cried out against the pain as his healing wound broke open. It wasn't enough to stop him. He raised his fist and brought it down on Lowery's jaw, a solid blow that snapped the man's head with its force. Again, he raised his fist, but Lowery was swift and tough. He tightened his legs, pressuring Finn's as he raised his arm to block the coming blow. Finn cared nothing for the pain. All he could see was the man's narrow eyes, all he could hear were Lowery's insults.

Small potatoes.

Hugh, Maura, Alexander, and all the others who died by cruel hands were neither small nor insignificant.

Small potatoes.

The blows Finn landed were for his mother's pain, and Shannon's, and his own heart that, until this moment, he did not realize had been shattered long ago.

Small potatoes.

None of them were worth Lowery's time or effort. How shameful, evil, and misguided. If this horror wasn't worth Lowery's best effort, then Finn would take over. He would honor the dead no matter who stood in the way.

All this went through his head as they rolled against the desk and back to the open room. They grunted: Finn with the effort to beat some humanity into Lowery; Lowery with the hunger to put Finn down once and for all.

It seemed like a saloon brawl that lasted hours, but only moments passed before Captain Fowler had Finn in hand. He threaded his arms through Finn's, seizing him, yanking him back and up. Finn struggled against him. He swore, spitting his objections and outrage, but there was no way to break the hold and he was dragged back and away from Lowery.

People crowded into the doorway. Detectives, officers, and lay personnel had run toward the sounds of the altercation. Some had their weapons in hand, ready to deal with whatever they might find. The doorway was narrow and only a few could see in. They looked at Finn O'Brien, and he looked back, his anger still volcanic. Captain Fowler tightened his grip. Lowery crab-walked backward, using his elbows, not trusting Fowler to keep the enraged detective under control.

Eileen rushed forward to help him up, but Lowery shook her off. Slowly he got to his feet. His eyes never left Finn O'Brien's as he swiped his sleeve across his mouth. He looked at the fabric and saw blood.

"I'll get ice," Eileen said.

"I'm good."

Lowery shook his head, refusing her help. Fowler twirled Finn away and threw him into his office.

"Stay there." He shut the door. To the onlookers he said, "Get back to work."

There was a collective hesitation, a human desire to watch a train wreck, but Captain Fowler left no room for choice. The crowd dispersed—all except one. Cori Anderson locked eyes with Fowler, and he knew exactly what she wanted, and there was no way in hell he was going to give it to her. Cori had to make the choice: be pulled down to O'Brien's level, or obey orders.

"Anderson?"

Her hesitation was brief. When she was gone, Captain Fowler turned to Lowery, who was trying to make himself presentable. He looked at Fowler with the same disgust he had shown Finn.

"Keep that piece of shit away from me."

Captain Fowler answered:

"And if you ever come back here, show some respect."

Fowler turned his back on Lowery, confirmed that Eileen was all right, and then went to his office, slamming the door behind him

He looked at Finn O'Brien for a good long while without saying a word. The detective's hands were clenched, his face glistened with sweat, his stance was that of a man who, given half a chance, would finish what he started. Captain Fowler understood what had happened; what he didn't understand was why Agent Lowery triggered O'Brien. Finn knew. Lowery was the proverbial straw and Finn was the camel with a broken back.

He had shouldered the ostracism of the LAPD after he killed a fellow officer who was trying to kill him. He endured vilification in the press. He had been transferred and browbeaten in the hopes that he would quit. He had been tortured by his wife's departure. Through it all, he stood up against power, money and the people who had both. He believed in God. He treated all people equally. He had born his share as had Job. The difference was, Finn had a breaking point and Job had none. It was Lowery's dismissal of him, his experience, his family, and his history that Finn could not bear.

Fowler did a quarter turn and another, and then sat behind his desk. His jaw was set to guard against saying everything he was thinking.

The captain tapped a finger on the arm of his chair. He admired Finn O'Brien more than the detective knew. He had purpose, faith, and he was an honorable man. It was the latter that the captain found intriguing. The concept of honor was above reproach, but, in reality, it was also a slippery slope. No one could own the definition of honor. There was always higher ground to be had. Ring the bell of honor every day and soon it would sound tinny. No one would come to church.

"Captain?"

Finn stepped forward. Fowler held up a finger and wagged it. He wanted one more minute to collect his thoughts. When he had taken it, he said:

"Go home, O'Brien. Do not show your face until I tell you to. Is that understood?"

"Yes, captain," Finn said. "I'll just tell—"

"No," Fowler said. "I want you to get out. Stay out. Don't go near Lowery, his team, or any of the victims."

"Yes, sir."

"Leave your badge," Fowler said.

"Captain..."

"Leave it." Fowler shifted in his chair. "And your gun."

Finn hesitated, and then gave up his badge and weapon. Before Finn was out the door, Fowler said:

"He was wrong, O'Brien, but so were you. Get it together."

JANE WAS STILL AGITATED, still upset, still disbelieving that she had taken such a drastic step and fired Maggie. There was going to be fallout, of that she was sure. Maggie could bring a wrongful termination action, she could continue to contact corporate, she could...

Jane rubbed her temples. She was too upset to think of all the ways Maggie Davis could make trouble. That meant she, Jane, needed to be proactive. She called HR and instructed them to immediately fill Maggie's position and disable her email. Then she called Daniel in IT, and told him she wanted a copy of everything on Maggie's computer, and transfer all open claims to Zach. Jane was about to hang up when she thought of one more thing.

"Daniel? I need a transcript of last week's calls from extension 370. How long will it take you to get it? Okay. Okay. What about the calls placed today? Five minutes? Great."

Jane hung up, pushed back her chair. She thought about having another drink but instead paced the length of her office as she waited for Daniel to do his thing. Thank God for corporate ass-covering. Intrepid recorded every call going in and out. Right now, her ass was in the sling, and she wanted to know who Maggie was talking to.

Not that she had done anything wrong.

She had just pushed the envelope.

Who didn't do that now and again?

Jane went back to check her email. Daniel had been as good as his word. She pulled up her chair and clicked the file open. Maggie had made twelve calls between the time she came in that morning and the time she was escorted out. Eleven were claims related. Jane dialed the last number and when it was answered she heard:

"LAPD, Wilshire Division, how may I direct your call."

Jane hung up.

"Shit. Shit. Shit," she said, and then Jane Whitfield put a call into Brian Cain.

.

34

"One more. Come along, my friend. Geoffrey, are you hearing me, man?"

Geoffrey Baptiste spread his arms and put his hands on the bar. Under his black and red beanie, his long dreads swayed across his shoulders as he wagged his head. His skinny shoulders seemed ready to poke through his too-big shirt. His face was dark as night, his eyes were clouded, and when he spoke, his words sounded like a dirge.

"O'Brien, O'Brien, O'Brien. You not bein' smart. Dats whiskey you be swiggin'. Ain't water, O'Brien."

"Don't I know, Geoffrey. 'Tis Wolfhound Whiskey." Finn raised his glass and tipped it this way and that. "A most beautiful thing. Like drinking gold, 'tis. And I'm in need of one more, so kindly fill my glass to the top this time."

"You be owin' me de gold, for many already. Five, O'Brien. I never seed you drink dis way."

"I never had reason until now."

Geoffrey made a dismissive sound. O'Brien had plenty of bad days but this looked to be the worst, and the barkeep had no idea what to do with him.

Finn put one elbow on the bar, and rested his head on his hand. He was tired in heart and soul, but he was not drunk. If he had tied a good one on, he would be lost in a blessed two-day, dead sleep. Alas, he was at Mick's Pub and still conscious.

Geoffrey sighed. He licked his lips. He looked over Finn's head. It was good that he had so few customers, because Finn needed his full attention.

"Be that as it may, Geoffrey, I applaud you. Having the good taste to keep this ambrosia behind your bar 'tis brilliant—and oddly appropriate— if I do say so." Finn's body did an odd sweep, as if it wasn't sure whether it should try to stand or not. "And I will applaud you further if you simply fill my glass once again, and leave me to wallow in my misery."

Geoffrey sniffed, he clicked his tongue, and then he reached behind him, took the bottle off the shelf, and poured a generous shot.

"I don' be smart, O'Brien. Didn' know'd I even had dis bottle. Guess the Jumbie put it der."

"What in the hell is a Jumbie?" Finn motioned for Geoffrey to keep pouring. Geoffrey obliged, but only by a bit.

"Boogieman, O'Brien. He put dis in my bar, and come for you wit it. He gonna git you in de end. Mark my word, bad 'tings happen when de Jumbie put de eye on you."

Geoffrey put the bottle beside Finn. He rested his skinny arms on the bar, and stuck out his non-existent ass. All the rings on his fingers and the bracelets on his wrist sparkled and winked.

"O'Brien, you gonna tie one on big time. I see dis. But don' be doin' it here, okay. Okay? Go home. I don' wan' no trouble wit de law. You be hearin' me, O'Brien?"

"We're good, then, Geoffrey." Finn waved the glass under his nose and then took a drink. "No trouble with the law. I'm not the law anymore, so you can't get in trouble with me."

Geoffrey rolled his eyes. It was useless to talk to the man, so he went back to his chores. Finn turned on the stool and set his eyes on the dartboard in the corner. Someone had stacked the darts in the bullseye. Had Finn been playing, he would have thrown that score. He was the dart master of Mick's Pub, and no one could beat him. Now there were two other people in Mick's, but they were not worthy of his challenge. Or at least Finn didn't think they were. Nor did he want to find out.

"'Tis depressing in here, Geoffrey," Finn said.

"It be fine before you show'd your face." He shook the water off the glass he was washing, set it aside, and dunked another. "You bring de dark cloud. Dark as night. You be in a bad, bad place." He washed, and shook, and set the second glass out to dry. "You gotta go, O'Brien. Go home. I got no time to be watchin' out for you."

Finn inclined his head thinking that Geoffrey's advice wasn't bad. He had been sitting on the stool for three hours. The good news was that he had spent his time wisely: thinking without speaking, speaking without thinking, raging without making sense, lyrically reminiscing about his family. He even managed a bit of philosophy which included 'this too shall pass' and 'a pox on all their houses'. To the former he added, 'but only after I get my pound of flesh', to the latter 'and I will spit on their graves'. Then he asked for another whiskey.

Now sitting with his back to the bar, his moody thoughts his own, he was quiet and Geoffrey was happy for it. He was happier still when the front door opened, the Guinness sign fritzed, and Cori arrived.

She gave Geoffrey a nod. He gave her a look that told her he was grateful that the cavalry had arrived. She walked across the room, her heels sounding hollow on the hard floor. Finn heard her— he probably recognized the sound of her walk—but he didn't look her way even when she pulled out the stool next to him.

"Hey there, buddy."

She put her purse on the bar.

"Are you sure you're wantin' to be seen with me, Cori?"

Finn tipped his glass her way. He was sloppy. Cori handed him a napkin, which he immediately tossed.

"I threw in with you a long time ago, so this isn't going to make matters worse." She slid her eyes to Geoffrey. "Got any ice tea back there?"

"I can do dat."

He headed off to the kitchen. Cori gave Finn a long, cool once over.

"Aren't you lookin' all cattywampus, O'Brien."

"I've no energy to figure out what it is you're saying, Cori," Finn said. "So, if you're telling me I'm a fool take it back. If you're telling I'm looking fine, then say it plain."

She twisted in her seat and rested her head on her upturned hand.

"You don't have the brain cells to figure it out." She nudged the Wolfhound bottle. "Kind of pouring salt on the wound with this stuff, aren't you?"

"Dennis Cain may be acting the maggot, but he's got the touch with whiskey—" Finn drank. "Or Uncle Hugh did."

"Oh, baby," Cori sighed. "Are you going to pull out your dead uncle and wave him like a flag just so you can go into battle? Southerners love a lost cause, but we ain't got nothin' on the Irish."

"We are cousins in that way, are we not?"

Finn chuckled and swung around so that they were both hunched over, heads together. When Geoffrey brought Cori's ice tea, she moved Finn's bottle. He moved it right back. Then he set it away from her.

"Sure, 'twas a gift from Geoffrey. I'll pay a pretty penny for, but it was a gift nonetheless."

"Okey-dokey."

Cori dropped her hand, and ran a trill on the wood with her fingers.

"Here's the deal, my friend. You're a big boy, so do what you want. But just so we're clear, I'm not here to sympathize, or to hold your hair back when you barf and then tuck you in to sleep it off. I think you're an idiot. You're on unpaid leave, so you're going to have to watch your pennies. Worse, you just gave every cop on the force a reason to rethink the slack they were cutting you. Any goodwill on that score is backsliding. Last, but not least, you have left me guilty by association and with a shit-load of work."

Cori turned square to the bar and took a drink of her ice tea. She looked at Finn's image in the mirror behind the bar. Finn did not look back.

"Apologize, O'Brien. Apologize to Fowler and to Lowery if you've got to, 'cause you're about as useful as tits on a boar hog sitting here drinking away your sorrows. Salvage something."

"They are my sorrows, and I'll deal with them as I will." Finn finished off his drink. "You wouldn't understand such sorrows."

Cori heaved a sound that was somewhere between a laugh and a cry of outrage. She swung her head his way, looked at him long and hard, and then got up.

"You bastard," she said. "From the minute I told the brass I would hook back up with you, I've had nothing but sorrows. I didn't think you deserved all the shit they were heaping on you. I admired what you did for that homeless guy. I admired your strength, and your loyalty, and your ethics. And sometimes you're funny. But make no mistake. I agreed to be your partner because I knew you were a good, solid guy, not because I thought you were God."

She took her purse off the counter and put the strap over her shoulder.

"You don't stand that high, my friend, nor do you wallow in a hell any worse than anybody else."

She opened her purse and took out her wallet. Finn put his hand up to stop her.

"I'll pay for the drink," he said, shamed by her but not enough to apologize to anyone.

"I wouldn't have you pay to have my toenails clipped."

She leaned close and got in his face.

"You aren't better than every other cop, O'Brien. You aren't more sensitive than any other human being on this planet. When you meet an asshole like Lowery, you suck it up, you don't get into a pissing match. Otherwise, you know what you are?"

"An *eejit*?"

"If that's Irish for an asshole like Lowery then, yeah, you're one of those." Cori put twenty down. "You tie one on, and then go home and sleep it off. After that, have some coffee and decide if you want to be some guy who is pissed off at the world and burns bridges he hasn't even finished building, or do you want to be the other guy."

"And which guy would that be?"

"The one who's worth other people sticking their neck out for."

She wasn't gone more than a minute when Finn settled his bill, picked up his bottle of Wolfhound whiskey that Geoffrey had put in a bag, and took his leave. He left his car parked, not worried about a ticket since it belonged to the department. His mind worked, but in the way a man who has had his share of liquor will.

Understanding of his own failings —and forgiving them—he still harbored some pique toward Cori and Fowler. But he gave them a pass for certainly he loved them both. The idea that he would not be bringing his mother heads on a platter almost made him weep –or perhaps it was the warming of the whiskey in his veins that made him feel teary.

Finn kicked at a stone and it popped across the sidewalk. He could do nothing. He was useless. He could not even remember Alexander's face, nor Hugh Murphy's for that matter.

And yet...and yet...

Finn paused to get his bearings only to see that Fate had taken him to the place he needed to be. Stumbling once, he squared his shoulders, righted himself, and walked down the block to the condo in the middle of the street. The building was a modest four units. Finn knocked on the front door of the one in the back on the right. He could smell onions and garlic cooking. He knocked again. This time the door was opened and there was Gretchen looking fetching in her uniform pants and white wife-beater. There was nothing more appealing than a beautiful woman in a man's work clothes. Finn grinned.

"I'm in need of comfort, Gretchen," Finn said.

"Do you deserve it?"

"Ah, Cori has been busy, has she not?" Finn put his shoulder against the jamb. "Sure, she's not happy with me."

"I'd say that's an understatement." She leaned against the jamb too. Finn inclined his head, and held up his bottle.

"I've brought cocktails, Gretchen."

Her stomach rippled as she laughed without making a sound. She shook her head. She sighed.

"Aw, what the hell. I've always been a sucker for a man in a suit."

She tugged on his tie, and pulled him close. Finn was smiling when their lips met, but by the time his arms went around her, he was dead serious about showing her how much he appreciated her hospitality.

They parted briefly: Finn to put his whiskey on the dining

room table, Gretchen to turn off the stove. By the time they made it to the bedroom they were in a frantic race, tangled in a jumble of clothes and limbs, their lovemaking that of a desperate man and a woman who understood that you could fight fire with fire.

When they lay together, watching the evening turn to night, Gretchen was nestled under his arm, waiting for Finn to speak. His hand ran over her bare shoulder, his eyes were fixed on the ceiling.

"I've never been without my badge," he said.

Gretchen put her arm over his chest, tilted her head back and put her lips on his cheek.

"And what would you do if you had it?" she said.

"My job, but nothing about my uncle," Finn said. "The captain would be watching me like a hawk."

"But you'd still want to do something about your uncle, right?"

"Yes, I would be wanting that," he said.

"Well, then, what can you do without the badge?" She ran a finger down the side of his face. "You're off the clock. Nobody watching you. As long as what you're doing is legal, seems like the sky's the limit." She propped herself up. One finger now traced the muscles braiding up Finn's arm. "Or I suppose you could just hang around in bed all day feeling sorry for yourself."

Finn looked into her eyes and saw mischief and truth. She raised one brow and he finally understood what she was suggesting. As Finn turned on his side, he took her hand and kissed it.

"If I were with you a week in bed it would be heaven, my girl," he said. "But it's your mind I am finding particularly attractive at this moment."

"I aim to please," she laughed. "Maybe it would do you good

to just be a guy with time on his hands. You can go where you want...talk to whoever you want..."

"I can think of so many ways to pass the time." Finn fell back, pulling Gretchen on top of him as he did so. "How can I ever thank you for such wise counsel?"

"I think you know."

Gretchen giggled and put her long legs on either side of his. He kissed her face, her lips, her eyes, only to pause to ask a favor.

"And when I'm done sincerely thanking you, might I beg a ride back to my car?"

This time Gretchen laughed out loud, and buried her face in his neck.

"It will cost you," she said.

"Happy to pay the price," he answered.

And then they didn't talk anymore.

DENNIS AND KATHERINE CAIN finished their early dinner. Katherine went to her book group, or at least that's where she said she was going. She had been going out every evening, sometimes offering an excuse, sometimes not. That was fine with Dennis. If distancing herself made her feel better, then he was happy for it. If she was seeing another man, then he, Dennis, deserved her infidelity. As for him, he was grateful for the silence and the space in the empty house.

Dennis sat in the rooms where his sons had grown up, thinking that he had done a good job of raising them to men. They were decent people who would be disappointed in the things their father had done, but they wouldn't condemn him. Not even when they learned the worst.

He sat at the dining room table, wondering about Maura's

child. Shedding a tear for her, and feeling guilty for it; feeling guiltier still when he admitted that it was a relief she was gone. She had intended to upend his life before he was ready, and that would have been hard to forgive.

In the bedroom he shared with Katherine, Dennis lay on the bed, hoping to discover the great love he used to have for his wife. All he found was admiration for her, sorrow for the hurt he had caused, and shame that it was Maura he thought of when he touched the sheets or turned his head on the pillow.

In the backyard, the water in the pool shimmered under the big moon. The beautiful trees made him think of the evenings he spent with Maura, their shared love of Wolfhound, her fiery passion for everything including him. He wasn't the man either of the women in his life deserved. He should have been honest with both of them. He hadn't been. He would probably be a better person on his own.

Since he could find no peace in the home he shared with Katherine, Dennis went to the one- room that was his alone. He turned on the banker's lamp as he sat down to work at his desk, pulling his papers into the little pool of light.

Mrs. Farrow had sent a request for a meeting with Harry to discuss the parameters of the offer that Brian had submitted. Dennis had left the formal proposal in his brother's hands, because the one thing they agreed on was Wolfhound and its future.

Brian offered seventeen million. Dennis knew it probably wasn't enough, but Harry was willing to work with them. All in all, Dennis was pleased with the job Brian had done. They would retake control immediately upon acceptance of the offer, paying off the outstanding monies owed for the long-term advertising and promotion that was already purchased, retaining independent sales contractors in the U.S. for a year before re-evaluating their employment. The Wolfhound name would revert and they would not hold Hammet to any non-compete directives. All they had to do was come up with half the buyout in cash. Brian assured him it would be no problem. Dennis texted Mrs. Farrow, copying in Brian, accepting the date and time of the meeting.

Next was the overview of the new equipment. The specs on the machinery were amazing, and Dennis found that spark of excitement he thought was long gone. He had always loved the nuts and bolts of the business. Brian had been right to make the investment. It would pay off soon enough.

Dennis looked at the sales reports, and his enthusiasm sobered. Their bottom line was precarious at best. Wolfhound 24, while anemic, was keeping them afloat as was the gift box division that Hammet had begun two years earlier.

Finally, Dennis took the last file. On the front was a Post It. Neatly written in Brian's hand was the message: countersign.

Dennis looked at the first pages and signed. He looked at the second set of pages. He looked again, not quite understanding what this document was. Slowly, it dawned on him what he was looking at and he didn't like what he saw. He read it through once more.

It was mid-morning before Dennis decided what to do. He hadn't slept. Katherine had come home late and gone to their bedroom, not bothering to seek him out. He didn't wake her when he left the house. He took the file with him.

BRIAN LOOKED AT HIS MESSAGES, returning again and again to the information Jane had sent regarding Maggie Davis.

He now knew everything there was to know about the young woman who was causing so much trouble. Jane was at the end of her rope. He thought she was smart enough not to be ruffled by a thing like this. He thought Jane was tougher. She wasn't. She needed his guidance, she said. What she meant was she needed him to take care of the problem.

Brian understood that. If this woman continued on the way she was, it would do no one any good. He considered a few options, weighed the benefit of each and how the outcomes would affect Wolfhound, because, like his brother, he would do anything to protect the family business.

35

Finn made notes on the bombing and its aftermath as he remembered it: the plane, the people, the environment, the response. He went over Garda Hedgecoe's report with a fine-tooth comb, and found what he was looking for: the Garda's final analysis was that the Platinum plane had not been breached in Cork. That meant the device could only have been put on the aircraft in San Francisco, so that is where Finn went.

Like Los Angeles, the Platinum Wings facility was on a private road a distance from the main airport. Like Los Angeles, the terminal was one of a handful of buildings facing a private runway. Like Los Angeles, the side panels of the glass door leading to the terminal were etched with the Platinum Wings logo. Finn shivered when he opened the door. The memory of that disaster was fresh, but he tamped it down and said his hellos to the young, beautiful, blonde woman behind the desk. She turned her computer screen and folded her hands. Her time was his.

"Good morning. How are you?" she said.

"Fine, thank you," he said. "I'm hoping for a bit of information."

"Of course," the woman said. "My name is Deborah and you're…?"

"O'Brien. Finn O'Brien."

She indicated the chair, but it was a moment before he sat comfortably. It wasn't just that his leg hurt, it was that he felt half-dressed without his badge. Finn chuckled, hesitating, a little shy of the situation because he knew that he was an imposter. Yet there was no way to get what he wanted, if he didn't play the game.

"So where is it that Platinum Wings will take you?" Deborah said.

"I'm thinking of bringing my family over from Ireland for a visit. I'd like to make it a special trip, but I'm wondering how this might work. The cost and such."

"How many passengers are you anticipating?"

"Two only," he said.

"And where would they be embarking?"

"Cork," he said.

Deborah's head went up and down, the smile never left her rose-colored lips. She was working on the computer again, typing as she listened.

"Excellent, we can definitely handle that. And the destination would be San Francisco?"

"No, I'd like them to arrive in Los Angeles. Is that possible?"

"Of course," she said. "Anything is possible. What is the date of travel?"

"We've not quite worked that out," Finn said. "I'd like to understand how a private charter works before I make the commitment."

"Of course." Her fingers hovered over her keyboard. She inclined her head and her blonde hair swung to her right shoulder. "Many people don't realize that we are competitive with commercial flights if you factor in the level of comfort and ease of scheduling."

"I was thinking to fly them directly to Los Angeles."

"Of course, if you like," she said.

"But if I wanted to divert to San Francisco so I might say hello before they go on to Los Angeles, could that be done?"

"There are no schedules except the one you set, Mr. O'Brien. We can accommodate any travel plan. If you wanted us to divert to Minneapolis and then to Los Angeles, we could do that too." She laughed a little, and her eyes twinkled. "But that would cost you more."

"I would expect that," he said. "And your crew? You're not hiring second-rate pilots who can't get a job with the big airlines, are you?"

"Only the best," she said, and Finn wondered if the woman knew of Jimmy Mustafa's resume.

"And security? How do you vet your staff and ground crew?"

Deborah's smile faltered. She asked:

"Is there some specific concern you have, Mr. O'Brien?"

"No, 'tis only that I'm the cautious type. My family is very dear to me."

"Well, I can tell you that safety is our top concern. We do complete background checks on everyone who comes within ten feet of our planes. Our ground crew is limited, and we keep nine on rotation. They are employees, not contract workers. Ninety percent of them have been with the company for five years or longer. Even the catering is delivered to the ground crew so they are the only other people onboard besides the flight crew."

"That is very impressive, indeed," he said. "Is it possible for me to look at your operation?"

"Of course."

She led Finn into the waiting area, and he was transported back to Los Angeles. The sofas and chairs, the lamps and rugs, were exactly the same. Were he to open the door to his left he would see a marble bathroom; the door on the right would lead him to a bedroom suite.

Yet the longer he stood there, the smaller the world became. Finn looked at the big window and saw the fireball; he felt again the glass biting into his face, stabbing into his leg. When he looked at Deborah, he saw another young woman thrown up against the wall, the buttons ripped off her shirt, blood on her face, still determined to do her job as she told him 'there is someone I need to call'.

Deborah hadn't noticed his distress. Done expounding on the facilities, she led him outside. The runway was empty.

"I imagine all your planes are in the air. How many do you have?"

Finn turned a tight circle, searching for camera placement, estimating the distance to the hangar, not caring where the planes were. Deborah stayed close. There would be no way for him to engage anyone else.

"We have a fleet of nine planes. Three are based in New York. Three here in San Francisco and three in…" She paused and rethought. "I'm sorry, we have eight planes at the moment. Two in Los Angeles."

"I would think your services would be in great demand in Hollywood," Finn said. "Why only two?"

"One of our planes is out for maintenance," she said. "I'm sure it will be back online soon."

"I see. And your ground crew?"

"There." She pointed to a large hangar past catering facility.

"'Tis very accessible to the public."

"We have cameras, a direct line to airport security, and other measures that I'm not at liberty to talk about. Many of our passengers also bring private security," she said. "Perhaps if you could be more specific about your concerns, I could address them."

"No, I've nothing specific. I just wondered if anyone could enter a plane since you've no TSA." He raised a hand indicating the wide-open space. "There is no fence, nothing to keep someone from wandering onto the runway, perhaps onto the plane."

This time the woman laughed.

"That could never happen. Our flight crew is fully trained to deal with any security event, even hostage situations. No one who doesn't belong will get by them..."

Finn nodded, thinking, putting the pieces together, connecting the dots. Jimmy Mustafa and the stewardess, highly trained as they were, would have the advantage of being masters of their aircraft. Either could have planted the bomb, or they let someone they knew inside and it was that person who did the deed.

Still, why destroy their ride? Especially one that was so convenient to their extra-curricular activities? That left someone accessing the plane with their permission, or they had been inattentive and away from their posts.

Still, there would have been cameras. Unfortunately, he couldn't access the video without authority. Still, since the plane was on the ground, the mechanics would have been about and seen anything out of sorts.

"Mr. O'Brien?"

Finn was startled, unaware that he had been staring at the terminal while Deborah was speaking.

"Yes? I'm sorry. Daydreaming. Terrible habit."

"No problem," she said.

Finn suddenly felt her good humor had been put on notice.

Before he could put his finger on the subtle change in her attitude, she touched his elbow lightly.

"Shall we go back in? I have a brochure that will show you the interior of the planes, and give you some idea of price." They walked slowly, chatting amiably. "And what is it you do, Mr. O'Brien?"

"I'm in public service."

He opened the door for her.

"That's interesting."

She went ahead of him.

"It can be," he said.

"And what branch of the government do you work for?"

"I'm in security," he said.

They were back at her desk. This time she adjusted her computer so that he couldn't see any part of the screen. She started to type.

"Well, then, that explains the questions," she said amiably. "I'm happy to say, you couldn't do a better job yourself when it comes to Platinum Wings security."

Finn smiled. Her fingers hovered over her keyboard.

"And how did you hear about us?" she asked.

"Through a friend."

Deborah raised her eyes, waiting for something more specific.

"A Mr. Cain," Finn said.

She typed; typed and smiled. Finn looked at the cameras in the small room. He didn't notice Deborah pause, and her smile falter. By the time he had eyes on her again Deborah had recovered. She gave him a beautiful brochure. He took a quick look, and his lips twitched when he saw the prices. Dennis Cain had been generous indeed with Uncle Hugh.

When she requested his contact information Finn thanked her, said he would be in touch. When he was gone, Deborah sent an email to the head office about the man who wanted to bring his family over from Ireland.

DENNIS AND BRIAN met in the restaurant of the hotel where Brian was staying. Between them were the papers that were waiting for Dennis's signature.

"We have a meeting with Harry in a few days. He's expecting us to put up our good faith money in escrow," Brian said.

"But this way, Brian? This is how you're managing the money?" Dennis waved his hands. "Never mind, I don't want to know. Don't tell me. I have to think about this."

"You didn't think about it all those years ago, why should you start now?"

"I didn't understand then. I didn't really grasp the implication. It was a concept. It was—"

"It was strategic. We hedged our bet. Some risks pay off."

Brian slapped his hand down on the papers. He took a pen out of his pocket and held it out to Dennis.

"Just sign the friggin' things. Sign them now, and we've taken Wolfhound back."

When Dennis didn't move, Brian took his brother's hand, and put the pen in it. He held tight, so tight it hurt Dennis.

"I told you one day we would need it and now is the day," Brian said. "And if you try to tell me you knew nothing about this. If you dare walk it back, I swear I will kill you."

Brian sat back. Dennis looked down at the agreement. He saw Brian's signature, and space for his own. The gravity of all this was overwhelming. He put the pen down and said:

"I can't."

With that, Brian launched himself across the table, took Dennis's hand, slapped the pen against his palm again, and pushed until his brother's fingers were wrapped around it. When the tip of the pen was on the paper, he looked straight into his brother's eyes.

"Bullshit. You had every idea," Brian said. "Just one more. Sign it."

36

Finn took his time taking off his jacket and putting it in the car as he surveilled the terminal office. While the glass on the front door of the terminal was smoked to guard against the sun, it wasn't opaque. He could just make out Deborah standing behind it, watching him. This told Finn two things.

First, what happened in Los Angeles did not stay in Los Angeles. Even though the explosion at the airport had barely made the papers, Platinum Wings had their employees on high alert. His inquiry into flights from Ireland, security, and his reluctance to leave his contact information, were red flags, and he should not have been so obvious. Still, it was always better to stand on a foundation of truth and build a shaky story around it than create one out of whole cloth.

It was also clear that Deborah was proactive. She had his name, could identify the car, and was probably waiting to see if she could get the license plate. It wouldn't take long for all this to filter back to Agent Lowery, so Finn needed to take his next steps as quickly as he could.

He got behind the wheel, made a tight turn, and headed

back the way he had come. Pulling to the side of the road, Finn waited a full fifteen minutes to give Deborah time to lose interest. When he deemed it safe, Finn turned the car around, drove past the terminal, and parked by the maintenance hangar near a truck that had seen better days and a well-kept SUV.

The building was exactly like the one where he first encountered Agent Lowery. There was a massive amount of space, but no aircraft. That didn't mean the building was empty. There were boxes, machinery, tools, and luggage dollies stored alongside the walls.

A narrow door stood open revealing a bare-bones loo, and another opened onto a small glass-walled office. Inside that there was a metal desk, two chairs, and a bookshelf brimming with binders, repair manuals, and a vase with fake flowers.

The walls were papered with a big calendar, schematics, notes, and weather charts. Rolled-up blueprints were stacked in a pyramid on the utilitarian desk, and behind it there was the requisite framed picture of a Platinum plane, new and shiny, just off the assembly line. The smell of grease and oil identified this as a working place and inside were the working men who noticed Finn before he noticed them.

"Can we help you?"

The air was still so the voice Finn heard was crystal clear. Still, it was difficult to pinpoint where the sound had come from. Finally, his eyes landed on the two men sitting in an enclave carved out of a stack of boxes, a lathe, and a half-built engine. Both men were sitting on folding chairs: one was a lawn chair and the other was low to the ground and made for the beach. The older man amply filled the lawn chair. He was big, but not gone to fat. He sported the 'high and tight' cut of a Marine, but it had been some time since his service because his brush was white. He was clean-shaven and master of his kingdom.

The man sprawled in the beach chair was younger and loose

like a puppet, all arms and gangly legs. His hair was long and lank. His arms were covered in tattoos of no great artistic value. Both of them wore white coveralls. The younger man's, were too big. The older man wore his like a uniform. He was sharp-eyed; he was the man to talk to.

Finn put on a friendly face as he walked toward them, dividing his gaze between them to be polite. The younger one smiled. He was eating a sandwich. The big man was nursing a soda.

"Name's O'Brien," he said, standing at a respectful distance. "I've heard that you might be looking to add to your team."

"James," the big man raised a finger indicating the younger man. "I'm Marv. You a mechanic?"

"I know my way around an engine."

"Have a seat."

Finn chose an empty crate, turned it over, and sat himself down.

"Want something to drink?" James asked. Finn smiled at the man's voice. It was as high as a boy's.

"Whatever you've got," Finn said.

Marv reached into a battered cooler behind his chair, picked up a can of cola and tossed it Finn's way. He popped it, and shook the spray off his hands before he took a drink.

"Thanks. 'Tis a long day."

"Where've you been so far?" Marv asked.

"Actually, you're the first I'm talking to. My cousin's friend works here, and she thought I might talk to him about employment."

"Who are you looking for?"

"To be honest, I've no idea. She just said he was here. She mentioned his name, and I've forgotten it. I think it was something like..."

"Gerber," James said. "I bet it was Gerber. Does that ring a bell? Greg Gerber. Tall. Brownish hair. Big guy..."

James' eyes wiggled to Marv and back again to Finn. Though the other man hadn't moved a muscle, James had obviously been reprimanded. His voice trailed off like a child realizing that he had said a bad word in front of his grandmother.

Finn took another drink, and then laughed a little as if embarrassed.

"How I could forget that name, I don't know," Finn said. "Sure, 'tis like a rhyme. Is Greg about then? I'd like a word with him."

"No. He's not," Marv said. "And wouldn't matter if he was. I'm the one who does the hiring around here. What paper are you carrying?"

"Paper?"

"AMT certificate. Are you an avionics technician? Maintenance? What?"

"I've no certificate, but I'm a fine mechanic. I work hard. Point me to a problem and you've no worries. I'll fix it."

"It don't work that way, buddy. FAA's gotta pass you through. It's no joke working on an aircraft," Marv said. "Some people don't understand that, do they James?"

"Nope, Marv. They sure don't."

James stuffed his mouth with the last of his sandwich. Marv gave a slow nod. Whatever had happened to Greg Gerber was not good, and if Finn had to guess James had narrowly avoided the man's fate.

"I take my work seriously, no matter what the engine powers," Finn said.

"That's a good thing." Marv crushed his can, crumpled his napkin, and put both in a bag as he talked. "But if you're that careful, I would have thought you'd have done your homework.

No mechanic worth his salt doesn't know what certification he needs."

"Agreed," Finn said. "I was needing a job because I just moved here this month. My cousin said Greg could fix things. My bad."

"Yeah, well, she had part of that right. Greg could fix anything; he just didn't want to stick with engines."

Marv stood up.

"It sounds like your parting with Greg was not a happy one. Is there anything I should be telling my cousin? I wouldn't want her to stay friends with him if he were sketchy," Finn said, feeling his momentum waning.

"If she was my cousin, I'd tell her to steer clear," Marv said. "But she's not my cousin, and I don't talk about business unless it's the brass asking. James."

"Yep."

James hopped to and Finn could have sworn he stood at attention.

"Let's get to it." Marv turned to Finn. He was a good guy. Upstanding. "Look, check back after you're certified. We run lean here. Only nine of us, three on three, but you never know. People move on. Some get their butts kicked out. You just never know."

Finn stood, too. He picked up the crate he'd been sitting on, turned it upright and put it back where he had found it. He crumpled his empty can too. Marv put his hand out for it.

"Appreciate it. I'll do that."

Finn smiled at the younger man, and gave a nod to the older as he said his thanks. He was pleased that his gamble had paid off. He hoped to simply get a handle on what type of crew worked on Hugh's plane, instead he got what every cop hoped for: a person of interest.

37

Parked off to one side of the runway was a sleek white plane, smaller than the one Hugh had flown to the U.S. The only identifying mark on it was a number and that gave Finn pause. Had another aircraft been parked on the side of the runway, close enough that a competitor could have tampered with the Platinum craft and gone unnoticed? Perhaps the perp had breached the wrong plane, and the bomb was meant for another aircraft. Both theories were farfetched, on a par with Dennis Cain blowing Maura to kingdom come over a baby, but stranger things happened in this world.

Finn's next stop was the catering building. Inside, a young woman with a clipboard was taking inventory. Finn asked his questions, she had only one answer: come back Thursday when the boss is here.

He walked back to his rental, perched himself on the hood, and let his boot heels hit against the tire as he considered what he had accomplished. He now knew Platinum Wings ran a tight ship, but not tight enough, and Greg Gerber was an asshole who warranted further investigation. Finn took out his phone. A quick search of the name Greg Gerber in San Francisco brought up twenty listings. Finn dropped his hand, looked toward the horizon, and thought of calling Cori. She could have a name and address for him in a flash. She wouldn't give it to him, of course, but she could do it.

Just as Finn was deciding it was time to find a pub for lunch, James walked out of the hangar. His coveralls were gone, giving way to jeans that rode low on his nonexistent hips and a T-shirt that had seen better days. He carried a backpack and walked like a man with a lot on his mind.

"Done for the day, are you, James?"

Finn expected a wan smile and a wave in return, but to Finn's surprise James walked over and leaned against the car.

"Yeah, not much to do. We're not expecting a flight until tomorrow," James mumbled. Marv's pissed anyway."

"Sorry, if I made him angry," Finn said.

James's head wobbled, one of his shoulders sloped.

"It's not you really," he said. "It's the whole thing."

James picked at a hangnail. Finn noticed he wore a wedding band.

"Life can be a trial," Finn said.

"Yeah, Marv gets really mad when he thinks about Greg. He was not a great guy, I can tell you." James kicked at the ground. "I'm really stupid, you know. I thought Greg was so cool, but boy I was wrong. You should tell your cousin, man, she needs to just cut him loose."

"I'm sorry I brought him up," Finn said, ignoring the tingle of anticipation that was running through him.

"You wouldn't know about it." James went quiet. Worried the conversation would end there, Finn gave the man a little encouragement.

"What is it he's done? I mean if he's dangerous, I should tell my cousin. I wouldn't want her to come to any harm."

"Naw, nothing like that." James put his hip up against the car door. He lowered his head. Finn did the same. "It's just that Greg thinks he's a player. I mean, there was stuff. It was just bad."

"Like what?" Finn asked.

"Like he was ordering extra parts and reselling them. He made a nice chunk of change on the side." James rubbed his fingers together. "I mean real money."

"Sure, that's not good," Finn said, treading carefully. "Did that cause problems. I mean problems that would compromise the aircraft? Is that what upset your boss?'

"Nothing like that. He ordered the right parts, just too many."

James leaned back a little. He picked and picked at his nails, unsettled, uncomfortable. The man carried a stone-load of guilt.

"Were you helping him, James? Are you afraid Marv might find out, and it will mean the sack for you?"

"I didn't even know, but I was kind of the one that turned him in. I couldn't find the right number of gaskets. I showed Marv. Marv— he's a pretty straight guy and likes to run things just right—he started checking into the problem and found out that Greg had been doing that shit for a long time. But then there was something else that Marv doesn't know about, and it's really bad. I think it's really bad."

James threw his hands up. His head swiveled like he'd been slapped.

"Aw, man... I figured if Greg was gone, I wouldn't even think about it anymore. I feel so bad, you know? It was really funny when he did it, but it's not funny now. If anyone finds out that I knew, I'm toast."

"I've no skin in the game, James," Finn said. "Telling me might ease your mind."

"I haven't even told my wife. I think it might have been some really bad shit."

James put both hands to his face, rubbed it hard, and then tossed back his hair.

"Okay. Okay," he said. "Here it is. Greg let some guy on one of the planes. Then the plane had a problem, and I don't know, I'm thinking maybe the guy who got on did something bad."

James moved like his feet were being held to the fire. Finn had no desire to put it out, so he waited for James to start dancing around again. He didn't have to wait long.

"Friggin' A, I just started sleeping again and when I think about that day, I get nightmares. I got no proof of anything. Just this feeling. Ever have just a bad feeling in your gut?"

"Surely I have," Finn said. "What is it that's making your stomach churn?"

"Well, here's the thing. Nobody is supposed to go on the planes except us, but Greg let this dude on."

"Why would somebody want on the plane?" Finn asked.

"This guy said his partner left some important papers—like really important—and he wanted to put it on the plane to kind of embarrass him so he wouldn't do it again. I could see it. I done stuff like that. Anyway, I heard all this from Greg 'cause I was on a chore for Marf. When I come back, Greg's got the guy all decked out in coveralls and ready to go, so who am I to say anything?

"Greg scored a grand just for getting the guy up the stairs and back, so he could leave the stuff his partner forgot. I thought it was funny too. I even took a picture of them, like they was having a party or something." James shook his head. "You've gotta tell your cousin, Greg is shit."

"Do you still have that picture of him and this man? I'd like to show my cousin so we know we're talking about the same person." Finn held his breath knowing this was the make-or-break moment.

"I don't know. Maybe."

James pulled the phone from his pocket without thinking, involved in his own misery, wanting to share all the shame with someone. Finn saw a young woman as skinny as James on most of the pictures.

"I hope Marv doesn't find out," he muttered. "I'll never work again if Marv finds out."

"He'll not be finding out from me," Finn said.

"I appreciate that man." James stopped scrolling and held out his phone. "Here. That's him."

Finn took the phone, so he could get a closer look at the picture. One man was loutish: his face, his posture, his big hands, and feet. The other man was indescribable: his hair, his features, his posture, were all ill-defined. Finn couldn't even tell If the man was smiling, but he was holding a briefcase cradled in his arms.

"Mind to share this, so I can show my cousin?" Finn asked.

"Naw man, go ahead."

Finn smiled. Consent was a wonderful thing. It would be important when this came to court, which he had no doubt it would. Both of these men would be held accountable for Hugh's death.

James took his phone. He shared the drop. Finn accepted it.

"Shall I tell Marv?" James said. "I mean, it's probably nothing, but it could be something. What happened to that plane was bad..."

Finn slid off the hood of the car, pocketing his phone.

"If it were me, I would wait and see how things play out."

"Ya think?" he said. "I got a wife. She's pregnant. I don't want anyone to think I was with Greg. Know what I mean?"

"I do," Finn said. "But if anyone comes asking about that day, tell the truth. For now, hang tight."

"Thanks man. Thanks." James put his phone away. He hitched his backpack. "And I think you're right. I don't know anything for real. I don't know who this guy was. If anyone asks, Marv will give them Greg's information and they can go to South City and find him. Not my problem. All I did was take a picture."

"I wouldn't worry about it. Can't be anything too bad, now, can it?"

"How do you figure?" James asked.

"If he didn't mind having his picture taken then he couldn't be much of a criminal, could he?"

"Oh man, I never thought of that," James said, smiling now. "And besides, what's done is done, right?"

"Right." Finn put a hand on James's shoulder. The man's bones were bird-like. "Just do your job, and take care of your family."

"Yeah. Sure. And if you get your papers, come on back. I wouldn't mind someone to talk to. Marv really isn't much of a talker." James stuck out his hand; Finn shook it. "Thanks, man."

James walked lighter when he left. Finn waved, and watched the truck until it had disappeared. He looked back at the hangar, having no doubt that Marv still worked diligently. There was nothing to be gained by speaking to him again, so Finn tapped Greg Gerber's name into his phone once more. This time he added, South San Francisco. There was only one in that city.

Next, he texted Thomas Lapinski, attached the picture James had taken, and asked:

Guy with the briefcase? Location? Name? Anything. ASAP.

Once that was done, Finn hopped off the hood, dusted off his butt, and got into his car. He set the GPS and went on his way, a happy man.

~

THOMAS LAPINSKI WAS PLANNING his cross-examination of a middle manager at a box manufacturing plant who took perverse pleasure in humiliating and degrading women over fifty for their performance on the line. Since it turned out that he wasn't exactly nice to women under fifty, and a hundred percent of those working the line were women, Thomas had plenty of witnesses to put on the stand to testify against the man on direct. The cross was just the icing on the cake.

Since he was ahead of the game, Thomas allowed himself to be distracted by the shimmy of his telephone as a text came through. He read it, tapped on the file, and looked at the picture. Lapinski smiled. Finn was definitely giving him a challenge with this one. There wasn't much to recommend the man in the picture, and face recognition software wasn't infallible. Still, Thomas turned to his computer, fired up his special software, and went to work.

He loved a challenge.

JOSEPHINE STERLING HAD her shoes off and her feet up on her desk while she read *Detonator*, the magazine of the International Association of Bomb Technicians while she ate a turkey sandwich that she had brought from home and drank an ice tea she got out of the vending machine. The sandwich tasted great; the only tea in the whole drink was the word printed on the can. Still, it was good.

It was after two, she was on her lunch hour. Even if she wasn't, this was her domain and she could damn well do what she pleased, so she kept her feet up when Marta came into her office.

"Hey, Agent Sterling. Got the mail." Marta rifled through the armload of paper, took out three files, added two memos, and put them on the side of Josephine's desk. "Not much today."

"Thanks," Josephine said.

"You're welcome."

Marta left, and Josephine finished both her reading and her lunch. She went to the ladies' room to wash up. Before she made it back to her office, Josephine was called away to deal with a problem in the lab, pulled away from that problem to have coffee with an ex-colleague, and, after that, there was a meeting she had all but forgotten about. Unfortunately, it would be another four hours before she sat down at her desk and went through the mail.

CORI STUCK her head into the front office and asked Eileen:

"Captain wanted to see me?"

Eileen inclined her head. Cori walked to his door and gave a knock on the jamb. Fowler looked like a purebred on race day, all spit and polish, sitting like a soldier at attention. He raised a hand, inviting her in. He didn't ask her to sit.

"Where's O'Brien?"

"Got me, captain," Cori said.

He paused his reading and looked her in the eye. She looked right back because she was telling the truth. Even if she wasn't, she would look him right back because Cori Anderson was a firm believer in lying if you had a damn good reason.

"If you hear from him, find out exactly where he is," Fowler said.

"Anything else?"

"Don't tell him I was asking. Is that understood?"

"It is, captain."

Cori left the office, throwing a thanks at Eileen. She had no problem with Fowler's request. Her nose was out of joint too.

O'Brien had disappeared without telling her where he was going.

She was working double-time to cover his work.

And there was the other thing.

She missed Finn and wanted him back where she could keep an eye on him.

38

There was an older model Toyota in the driveway of the small house. No toys to be seen, so no children were about. The garage door was open. It was built for two cars, but the space was filled floor-to-ceiling with boxes and furniture; trash and tools.

This house was no different than any other in the quiet neighborhood, except it was ill-kept. Far down the way was a gardener loading his mower onto the back of his truck. There might be some mothers home, elderly folks watching TV, but for the most part Finn imagined the people who owned these places were at work.

As he walked to the door, Finn watched for a curtain to move, a face to appear in a window, some sign that he was being met with suspicion. Finn did not discount the possibility that James had given Greg Gerber a heads up that someone was looking for him.

Finn got to the front door without incident and rang the bell. The place was small, the chimes were loud, and, when no one came, Finn didn't wait long to ring again. Finally, he rapped on the cheap, hollow door. He knocked louder the second time, and then gave up.

He was three steps into the yard about to head toward the back of the place when the door opened. Greg Gerber was, indeed, a big man. He was also an unhappy one.

"What the hell do you want?"

"Greg Gerber?" Finn said.

"Who's asking?"

"I didn't think your bell was working," Finn tried the charm offensive first, smiling and apologizing, opening his hands as he walked back to the porch. "Sorry for the knocking."

"I was in the can," the man grumbled. "You better not be selling anything."

"That I'm not." The toe of Finn's boot was on the threshold. His smile widened. "I would like to talk to you about Platinum Wings. I was just over there speaking to..."

"That little shit. Goddamn James. I got nothing to say about that friggin' job."

Greg flipped the door hard. Finn straight-armed it, and Gerber was caught off guard. It bounced back hitting his shoulder. The man recovered quickly and ferociously.

"Screw you, buddy."

He grabbed for the door again, but Finn was faster. His boot met the wood, the door splintered, and Finn was on Gerber before he knew what hit him. The surprise of it, Finn's weight and righteousness, had him on the ground in the first second and in a chokehold the next. Finn slammed the door shut with his foot, and tightened his hold to keep the man in line. Gerber gagged. His hands clawed at Finn's arm, but there was nothing to be done.

"I'm sorry for this. I truly am, but I'm needing some information." Finn pressed against the man's neck, staying just shy of the pressure that would render him unconscious. "I haven't time to court you, so you'll listen. When I am finished talking, you will tell me what I want to know. Is that understood?"

Greg Gerber gave up, relaxing as best he could, trying to get a breath. Finn gave him credit for quickly realizing the futility of his situation. Slowly he pulled his arm away, and rolled the man over. Finn put his knee on Gerber's middle.

"You a cop?" Gerber asked.

"It doesn't matter who I am," Finn said. "You let a man on a plane that was headed to Los Angeles. He paid you. I want to know who he is and what he put on the plane."

"Screw you if you're not a cop."

Finn rolled his eyes. He had hoped the man was smarter than this. He pressed his thumb into the man's neck knowing exactly how hard to compress the nerve to make Gerber buckle. He yelped, and tried to roll away. He didn't get far.

"I said you were to listen and then answer my questions," Finn said.

"Stop! Stop!" Gerber screamed, but Finn had no intention of stopping. He pressed harder knowing now that Gerber's reflexes were completely compromised.

"That plane blew up." Finn raised his voice against Gerber's cries. "Three people are dead. You will hang for it unless you tell me who the man with the briefcase was. Are you hearing me, friend? Three dead."

Greg Gerber stopped screaming. Finn eased up on the pressure, sat back, and rested on his haunches. He stayed close should the man resist again, but the fight had gone out of Gerber. It was replaced with a sickening fear and disbelief.

"Blew up? A friggin' plane blew up?"

"In Los Angeles. After it was serviced by you in San Francisco," Finn reached into his back pocket for his phone, touched the screen, and put the picture in front of Gerber. "Remember this? Now if you didn't put a bomb on that plane, then I'll assume it was your friend with the briefcase.

Gerber turned his head. Finn shoved it closer and pulled on the man's shirt.

"Look at it."

"It wasn't me!" Gerber wailed.

"Then perhaps it was both of you. Some con? A way to get money out of Platinum? I don't care what went wrong, I only want to know which of you did it and why."

Greg shook his head. Finn stood up, backing off far enough to let the man get to his feet. Gerber tugged at the elastic on his sweat pants, and at the hem of his shirt. His hands twitched, and his head shook again and again as he tried to wrap his brain around what Finn was saying.

"No, man. No. Hell, no," Gerber said. "I didn't have anything to do with any plane blowing up. I didn't even know about it. How do I even know that's true?"

He stumbled to the sofa, a cheap thing covered in fake leather, cracking at the seams, the plastic hide peeling off the arms. Finn stayed close, at the ready in case the man tried to leave before Finn wanted him to. A small, ugly dog threw itself at the screen door and was barking up a storm. Finn gave it one look and no more.

"My uncle is dead, a stewardess, and another woman," Finn said. "Now who was the man who paid you for access to that plane?"

"I don't know." Finn made a move. Gerber put up his hands, his voice rising an octave. "I swear, that's the truth. He showed up that day. That's all. I never seen him before."

When Finn made no other move, Gerber lowered his hands.

"Marv and James were gone, I was working, and this guy comes up to me already talking. He made a lot of noise about his partner coming on the plane, and him forgetting some important stuff in the briefcase, and how the guy was a jerk and needed to be taught a lesson."

"And?"

"I told him I would put it on, but he said he wanted to do it himself," Gerber said. "I was like you can't do that. Then he says can he do it for a grand, right? Shit. I mean a grand? I'm like 'I can make that happen'."

"How did you get him past the stewardess and the captain?"

"Those two?" Gerber made a noise that was none too complimentary. "They hump in the cockpit. They're running stuff too. No skin off my nose. Besides, you think they paid any attention to us? Stick up their asses..."

Gerber put a hand to his neck. Finn had no doubt it hurt. Gerber said:

"If that guy was carrying a bomb, how was I supposed to know? He wasn't like some bad guy; he was just normal. And a guy doing something like that? He's gonna sweat, right? Know what I'm sayin'? There'd be something wrong."

"How did it go down then?"

Finn moved a step to the side and two back, making the man focus on him. He could hear the little dog skittering to follow him, barking all the while.

"I told you," Gerber wailed. "He comes by. We yuck it up. James comes back, and I've got the guy in some coveralls. The dude wanted a picture to give it to his partner, so James takes one on the guy's phone."

"Then why does James have the picture on his phone?"

"He had a new phone, man. He wanted to try it out." Greg put a hand to his head. "He takes the picture, and he's showing me how we can transfer it without even typing anything in, but then the plane comes. We figured we'd do it later, but we never did."

"Then what?"

"James handles the fuel. I'm supposed to take the food from the caterer. It was perfect. I get this guy in and out and nobody notices. He leaves the briefcase. When the plane takes off, he hands me a thousand bucks, and he's gone."

"How did you not hear about what happened?" Finn asked.

"Marv fired me like an hour later." Gerber shrugged and fell back. He dragged a hand through his hair as if he were exhausted. "I had a side gig going, and that's why I got canned. It wasn't much. Man, I worked my butt off for that outfit, and he just cuts me loose."

"No good deed goes unpunished," Finn said, the irony lost on Gerber. "I want a name."

"I don't kn..."

Finn was on him in a flash: knee on the man's huge thigh, hands around his throat.

"I want a name, and I want it now."

This time Gerber found his strength, pulled Finn's hand off his neck, and pushed him away.

"Get the hell off me. I don't know." When Finn stood back, Gerber pushed himself to the edge of the couch cushion, stopping just short of launching himself at the detective. "I don't know who you are either, and if you don't get out of my house, I'm calling the cops."

With that, whatever advantage Finn had was gone. Greg Gerber was nothing more than a nickel-and-dime opportunist. Platinum was well rid of him and Finn had no authority.

"I'll be sharing this information with the police if I find you've lied to me."

"Get the hell out."

Finn walked out of the sad little house where Greg Gerber appeared to live alone with only a mean little dog for company.

He got into his car. The gardener down the way was gone. The street was still quiet. Finn rested his elbow on the window's ledge, tapping the top of the car with his fingers. He had learned a lot, yet nothing at all. Just as he was thinking this trip was folly, that he should just pass the picture and information on to Lowery, his phone vibrated.

He opened the message from Thomas. It said:

You're welcome.

After that there was a name and an address.

Finn started the car, released the brake, and headed into San Francisco. As he drove, he changed his mind about sharing information with Lowery. He was going to give the man and his mother the bomber instead.

39

Diseased as the heart of San Francisco was, the bones of the city were still beautiful. It was the flesh and muscle of it that were deteriorating.

Finn's destination was the Civic Center. He threaded his way down sidewalks clogged with homeless tents. Syringes littered the street. Human feces were in evidence. Men in various stages of undress sat on the sidewalk or lay in the tents. Some were blissfully unaware of the world around them. Others were pulled into fetal positions on the hard ground, content in heroine's embrace. One man begged Finn for something: money, food, who knew? Lifting his palm might only be a reflex.

Finn learned long ago there was a difference between the homeless and the hopeless. Real homeless had truly fallen on bad times, and their energy was spent clawing their way back to society. Then there were criminals who loved the life of unaccountability and worked the system. Finally, there were the crazy souls in need of help that no one seemed willing to give. Cities groaned under the weight of these people, while politicians ordered Finn and his like to stand down. He walked through them now without conscience. He didn't want to put hands on them for any reason, he only wanted the man who had paid Greg Gerber a thousand dollars to get onto a Platinum Wings plane with a briefcase full of explosives.

That man was Stuart Gowdy. He was of medium height, medium build, and had medium brown hair. Stuart Gowdy, a man whose face was so unmemorable it was almost indescribable. Unless, of course, Thomas Lapinski was working his magic. He had found a name and a work address for the man, and Finn could only hope both were legitimate.

He broke through the siege of tents when he reached his destination. The promenade of open space leading to the domed city hall, the jewel in the city government's crown, was clear of encampments. Some truce among the dispossessed and the decision-makers left the lawns and surrounding areas pristine. Finn veered left toward a four-stories high block of concrete that looked like a poor relation next to city hall's grandeur. Its only adornment was a golden seal of state above the door.

Inside Finn put his jacket on the security conveyor along with his phone, and was waved through the metal detector. He put his jacket back on, thanked the officers, and walked to the directory. There he found that the offices of the GSA were on the third floor.

The third floor was not much different than the first. He trod over grey linoleum that had been worn down the center over the years. The walls in the long hall were painted white that was fading to grey. There were doors on both sides of him hewn out of dark wood, covered in layers of stain and lacquer. Every other door had a pebble-glass window on the top half. Each of those windows was stenciled with gold letters spelling out the department and designation. Finn went to room 302, GSA, Tenant Services, and opened the door, ready to take on whatever was to come, but the office was empty.

A dark wood wall divided the space. The top half was made of the same pebble glass like that on the entrance door. The sliding window from which a receptionist would inquire as to a person's business was open, but there was no one to greet him. Finn put his head through to get a look at the working area.

Directly beneath him was a built-in desk for the receptionist. Two more desks were positioned in an open space, and there was a private office, the door of which was neatly labeled with the words: Stuart Gowdy, GSA Manager, Section 32.

"Hello?" Finn called with no expectation that anyone would answer him.

He opened the door that led from the reception room to the back offices. On the reception desk were a closed planner, a mug, and a computer. The chair was pushed close, the receptionist who had left her space so tidy was gone for the day. Of the two desks that were in the common area, one appeared to be unused. On the other was an open book, the cover showing a bare-chested Scott and a beautiful woman in a flowing dress. There was a picture of a family on one side and a stack of papers on the other. Finn opened the drawers and found what one would expect of a workstation: tape, pens, more forms, hand lotion.

Finn checked the time. It was four o'clock. Banker's hours for the GSA personnel.

He pushed the door of Gowdy's office with one finger. It met no resistance. Out of habit, he checked behind it just in case, and then turned his attention to the office itself.

Single sheets of paper were tacked to a bulletin board, bound reports, spiral notebooks, three ring binders were all neatly labeled and filled wall-to-wall bookshelves. There were stacks of paper on the floor and on the credenza behind the desk. The desk was bigger and newer than those in the outer office as were the electronics. There was a very fancy keyboard and two large computer screens. Both screens were dark. From the credenza, Finn picked up a wedding picture. The frame was the kind of thing a woman would pick out and a man would feel obligated to display.

The woman beside Stuart Gowdy was attractive, happy, and proud. She wore a ballgown wedding dress and short veil. Two sets of older people flanked them. It was a charming photograph, but Finn assumed nothing. A simple family man did not pay people to get on a plane with a briefcase that held a bomb. Yet a man who could commit such a crime, could easily lead a double life. Some people were adept at hiding their true selves, and using others as camouflage without a hint of conscience.

He picked up a three-ring binder, but as he started to page through it, the door of the outer office opened and closed. Finn put the binder back on the desk. He heard a few footsteps; then nothing. A murmur; then nothing. The person in the reception area was unhurried, having no idea anything was amiss. Finn fell back a foot, not hiding himself but wanting to have the first-eyes-on. His heart raced. A roar of white noise filled his ears. He shook his head to be rid of it, and held his breath to slow the heartbeat.

The man on the phone was just outside the office. He was happy. He laughed as he said goodbye. Ten seconds later the man Finn hunted walked through the door. He was as unimpressive as his picture. In one hand he held a cup of coffee, in the other a brown paper bag.

He saw Finn a second after he crossed the threshold, and he reacted as anyone would: surprised, wary of a man who did not belong. What he didn't seem was frightened.

"Stuart Gowdy?" Finn said.

"Who are you?"

"I'm a man who wants to talk to you about a briefcase and an airpla...."

That's all Gowdy needed to hear. He threw his coffee at Finn's face, and Finn's head snapped to the side. The coffee was hot but not scalding, yet the surprise took him aback. The liquid landed in one eye and covered his cheek, sliding down Finn's neck, soaking into his T-shirt. The paper bag followed. Finn raised one arm and knocked it aside. All of this gave Gowdy just enough time to bolt through the office, out the door, and into the hallway. Finn got to the door before it fully shut, but he was not fast enough to catch Gowdy. He looked up and down the empty hallway, cursing himself for letting him get away.

Then Finn caught sight of the emergency exit door closing at the far end of the long hall and gave chase. He rammed through the door. His boots fell heavily on the metal landing. Below, Gowdy was moving fast but he was untrained in the art of flight. He was taking too many steps on the turn to the next flight to the next flight of stairs, and that was slowing him a little. Still, Gowdy was a good length away, and he didn't have far to go to reach the street.

Finn hurtled over the railing hoping to gain some ground, but his foot hit a riser. He slid down three stairs, cursing as he fell. He righted himself, finishing the last flight in record time, but Gowdy was out the door before Finn once again.

Finn swore he heard the man laugh.

40

Finn burst onto the street, going right by default, but Gowdy could not be seen on the long stretch that led to the busy corner. Finn's head snapped left. The intersection that way was closer and less busy, but it was still a sprint to get there. Knowing he was losing time, Finn took a moment to regroup.

When he did, he took off at a trot toward the corner that was closest. He dodged a woman who was looking at her cell phone. She had a few words for him as he passed too close for her comfort. Finn slowed his step, conserving his energy, not wanting to overshoot his target and miss Gowdy.

Like an empty office, a long, sparsely traveled street had its share of interesting things to find, so Finn started to take note. He dismissed the building from which they had come. It ran the length of the block. There was a gated service entrance, and two more emergency exits: one behind him and one ahead. He went to the one ahead and pulled on the door. As expected, it was locked from the outside. Finn's best guess was that Gowdy had made it to this intersection, but there was no way to tell for sure.

Finn's next target was the buildings on the other side of the street.

There was a cafeteria on the corner, but the people going in and out showed no sign of distress. There was a cobbler, but the shop was closed. The window was clear so Finn could see the counter inside, the shoes lined up waiting to be fixed. Nothing about it set Finn's teeth on edge. Next to the cobbler was an empty storefront.

If Gowdy was gone, he was gone. At least Finn could give Lowery a name, and GSA would give the agent an address. One thing was sure, the man was no ordinary GSA employee if he could manage to disappear so quickly. Still, while hope was a shallow river, Finn's boat floated upon it so he didn't give up. He looked at the other side of the street again and realized he'd given no consideration to what was on the sidewalk.

There was a newsstand that was locked tight behind a metal grate. There was also a cluster of tents: one was bright blue and new, another was no more than a tarp stretched across two shopping carts, and the third was very worn and very small. A man could live in the first, take shelter in the second, and in the third he could do no more than huddle if he weren't too large. There was also a pile of cardboard, a chair, and blankets.

As he was looking, contemplating his next step, Finn saw a man sitting within the jumble. His hair and clothing were the color of the tarp, his face was so worn it had taken on the look of weathered cardboard. He was motioning to Finn so he crossed the street.

The man was younger than Finn first thought, and it was hunger, not drugs, that gave him his gaunt appearance. He was wrapped in a dirty blanket. His tennis shoes had no laces. There was a dog by his side, silent and watchful. The man put out his hand. Finn put a five on his palm. The dog raised its hind leg and scratched behind his ear.

"He gave me ten," the man whispered.

Finn dug in his pocket again. This time a twenty passed between them. The man smiled. His teeth were good. It wouldn't be long before they weren't. He put the money in a jar next to him and then covered the jar with a box. He pointed to the small tent.

"Hold the dog," Finn said.

The man showed no sign of worry. What would happen would happen; he had done his part and would eat well that night. Finn walked to the small tent, opened the flap, and saw that his money had been well-spent.

Stuart Gowdy sat with his knees pressed to his chest, his skinny arms wrapped around them. His tie was a bit askew, but other than that he looked none the worse for wear. He raised his head and looked at Finn, seeming as comfortable sitting in a homeless man's tent as he would having lunch at the deli. To Finn's surprise, the man made no move to rush him. Instead, he laughed, unwound himself and crawled through the opening, pushing Finn back as he did so.

"Oh, man, that was crazy, but you got me. I didn't even know we were still going. Good job. You're amazing whoever you are."

He gave Finn a pat on the shoulder, turned toward the homeless man and said: "Thanks, buddy, but I know you sold me out. I would have done the same."

With that, he walked away. Stunned, Finn watched him for no more than a second before the rage overtook him.

"Gowdy, you bastard!" Finn roared.

The man turned, but kept walking. Once again, he morphed. He was unhappy, peeved, even a bit angry as if Finn was now a bother.

As Finn rushed him, Gowdy changed again. Now he was confused. Suddenly, it dawned on him to be afraid. He backed off, his hands out to stave off an attack. The dog with the itch barked once. The homeless man got to his knees to watch.

"Are you crazy?" Gowdy screamed. "Stay away from me. What's wrong with you?"

Finn threw himself at the retreating man, grabbing him by the collar, yanking him back.

"Help. Somebody." Gowdy screamed as he flailed. "Call the police."

Finn wrestled him to the ground. When he had his knee on the man's chest, and Gowdy's arms spread over his head and pinned to the concrete, Finn growled:

"I am the police, and you're a dead man."

41

The sun was going down by the time Zach knocked on Maggie's door. There was a chill in the air, but it was nowhere near cold enough to be bundled up in sweat pants, a sweatshirt, thick socks, and a scarf the way Maggie was. Her hair was unwashed. She wore no make-up to cover the dark circles under her eyes. Zach thought her hands were shaking, but she stuffed them into the kangaroo pockets of her shirt before he could be sure.

"Are you sick?"

Maggie shrugged as she shut the door with her hip.

"Want a drink? Some coffee? I've got both."

"I think I'll take the drink," Zach said.

Maggie went into her small kitchen. She came back with a bottle of Scotch, and two glasses of ice. Her pour was generous. She handed him a glass. He looked around, sat on the sofa, and eyed the mess of papers littering the coffee table and the floor.

"It looks like you've been busy." He picked up a page while he took a drink. His face fell. He looked at Maggie. "Is this what I think it is? You shouldn't have all this stuff."

Maggie was in the easy chair, pulled into a ball. She took half her drink in one gulp.

"Maggie, look at me."

Her lashes fluttered. She took a deep breath, put her head back, and smiled sadly at him.

"I know I shouldn't have kept it, but I was working at home when Whitfield canned me. I just didn't return it," she said. "Sometimes I look at it and think, 'screw it'. I should just get another job and forget the whole thing. But I know what Whitfield did was wrong, and this is evidence."

"Evidence of what?"

"Fraud, Zach. A huge fraud on the backs of little companies. I'm not sure how it works, but Whitfield's deep in," she said. "Listen to this."

Maggie accessed her messages and held her phone toward Zach. Whitfield's voice was the next thing he heard, and it sure wasn't her office voice.

I got the letter from your lawyer, Maggie. You have no idea what you've done. It's out of my hands now, but watch your back, or...

The message ended there, but Zach didn't need to hear anymore. The intent was clear. Maggie put her phone aside. Zach set his drink down, tossed the paper on the table, and put both hands to his head. He took a minute, and then dropped his hands, letting his arms rest on his knees.

"Okay. Okay. This isn't good. What's the deal with a lawyer?"

"Mr. Brown?" Maggie said. "He specializes in whistleblower cases."

"Do you have to pay him?"

She shook her head. "Not unless there's a settlement, then he gets part of it."

"Did you know he was going to send something to Whitfield? Who else did he talk to? I mean do you even know how this all works?"

"No. I mean, not really. I thought maybe he would just listen and..." Maggie blew out a breath. "When I was in his office I understood what he was saying, but I thought it would take a while for him to do anything. He said he needed more information. I didn't know he was going to give Whitfield notice."

"Well, it's out there now," Zach said. "Can you work while you do this? You're going to need money."

"He said it would be better if I had a job, because it wouldn't look like I just wanted money."

Maggie picked at the upholstery on the arm of her chair.

"Then you better get one soon 'cause you're not going to be getting a reference from Whitfield. Jesus, Maggie." Zach bit his lip, he looked out the window, his right leg was jumping up and down like it was keeping time to a particularly frantic riff. "This is going to look like a revenge thing no matter what."

"That's what you think of me?"

"Don't put words in my mouth, Mags." He didn't mean to snap at her, so Zach regrouped. "I'm just trying to put this in perspective. I mean, this kind of thing can go on for years. It might make the news. Maggie, why did you want to do this?"

Maggie got out of her chair, and slammed her glass on the coffee table. She paced and gestured, angry and afraid.

"I didn't want to do it, but I know what I know. Sometimes there's just something you have to do. I mean, what would you have done?"

"I don't know," he wailed, but he was lying. Zach did know what he would do; he would turn a blind eye. "Walk away, Mags. Write a letter to Whitfield and tell her it was a mistake."

Maggie looked at Zach, really looked for the first time. He was kind and sweet. He was not brave, but he was there for her. She pushed the coffee table away from the couch to give her room, and then she knelt down in front of him. She put her hands on his knees.

"But what if this is the right thing to do? I just..." Maggie paused. She was fairly vibrating with anxiety. "Zach, I want to be a good person. I want to make a difference. If I tell you how to get the files off my computer, would you? You won't have to look at it. You won't have to know what's there."

Zach took both her hands in his. He was sad, because she looked so hopeful.

"I'm not your guy, Mags; not for something like this. I'm sorry you can't count on me, but you can't."

Maggie held his hands tighter and gave them a little shake. She smiled, but it was an expression of resignation.

"I can count on you for the big things," she said. "You came when I needed you. You listened to me. You worry about me."

"But I won't be a superhero with you."

"Then how about you pick up the pieces if I run into Kryptonite," Maggie said.

"I can do that, but I'd rather not have to."

Maggie smirked, let him go, and gathered up the papers off the floor.

"So?" Zach asked.

"So, I'm going for a run, and you're going to order some food."

"And..."

"And I'll figure it out, Zach." She tapped the pages on the table until they were in a neat pile. "I won't forgive myself if I don't do something, and I probably won't forgive myself if I do and ruin my life."

"Some choice," Zach said.

"Whatever I do, it's not going to be half-assed." She stood up. "Besides, I've got someone else who might be able to help. You know that cop who came in about his uncle's policy? He said I could call him, so I did. I'm waiting for him to get back to me."

"What can he do?"

"I don't know, but I need as many people in my corner as I can get."

SHANNON SHAUGHNESSY TURNED heads as she walked into the coffee shop. A beautiful woman was always of interest, but one dressed in an evening gown so delicate that it made her look as if she was made of air, was unusual for a burger joint. The diners noticed the velvet coat over her shoulders, the jewel-encrusted sandals, the red hair knotted at the nape of her neck and pinned with pearls.

The people who were mid-bite, the ones who had been studying the plastic menus, a guy who was headed to the John when she came in, all fell silent as she passed. A waitress tripped and dropped a glass. Shannon didn't notice, nor did she pay attention to the ensuing whispers, the speculation as to whether she was a movie star no one recognized. Thomas Lapinski watched her come, and when she was close he pushed himself up and off the plastic-covered booth in greeting.

"Oh, sit man." She waved him down.

"You look beautiful, Shannon."

"Work clothes, Thomas," she said, giving him a glorious smile as she slid into the booth.

"I'd hate to see your dry-cleaning bills. Can I get you something?"

"No, I've a full meal waiting for me at the Four Seasons." She put her coat on the seat beside her, but kept her jeweled satin bag close on the table. "I used to expect great things from a fancy hotel's kitchen, but it is all chicken in the end."

"Anyone special tonight?"

"A lovely gentleman who lives well on the benefits of a trust, but is afraid of his elderly mother who holds the purse strings.

She will cut him off if she finds out he's gay, poor man.,'tis difficult not living in the open. I've a great affection for him." Her lashes fluttered. She gave a soft snort and her eyes twinkled. "I suppose, though I'm a bit of a hypocrite. I never told my family how I made my way."

"Did you tell Maura?"

"No, I did not." Shannon laughed outright "She scared the piss out of me, Thomas."

"I've never heard a woman speak like that, and make it sound like genteel conversation."

"It's the sign of a true professional in my line of work. So, have you something to show me?"

"I wish it was more."

"I appreciate whatever you've found, Thomas."

"Then let's get to it." Thomas pulled one sheet of paper out of a pile. "This is a copy of Maura's passport. Do you recognize the address?"

Shannon looked at the Xerox and shook her head. Her sister had been a beautiful woman. Even in a passport picture, Maura looked lovely. Shannon set it aside. A property report was next showing Maura as owner of the house in which she had lived.

"The address is not familiar, but she was still in Cork." She tapped the paper with her long nail. "'Tis a nice house, isn't it? The baby will have a yard to run in when he grows."

Thomas smiled and moved the property report out of the way before he went on.

"I didn't find a landline number. When Lowery gives you back her cell, I'm sure you'll find the information you'll need to locate your nephew."

He paused when the waitress appeared to refill his cup. He touched her hand when it seemed the cup would overflow. Shannon was that distracting. Flustered, the waitress apologized and went on her way.

"And what of her computer?" Shannon asked.

"Still working on it, but I do have this." Thomas handed her the next Xerox: a birth certificate.

"Aidan. That's a fine name." Shannon smiled and her eyes lingered on the baby's name. "Maura didn't name a father."

"Which means the only way to verify paternity is a DNA test, Shannon. Cain doesn't want anything to do with Maura's child, so it seems you're free and clear if you decide to pursue adoption."

"Unless he comes back another time wanting to claim him."

"There's always a chance," Thomas said, "I doubt that's an option as long as he's married."

"And where is the baby?"

"I haven't figured that out yet."

Thomas put the last three pictures on the table. Shannon held her purse tight in her lap to give him room.

"I've confirmed the house is empty. That means Maura did not get a sitter for Aidan. There are no grandparents to call on, the Cain brothers are here in the U.S., so that leaves either a friend or a service. I'd put my money on a friend watching the baby, so I did a search. I came up with quite a few professional pictures of Maura, but these look to be social. I think she would leave your baby with a friend, not a colleague, don't you?"

Shannon picked up a picture of a group of people all approximately the same age as Maura. Her sister looked relaxed, like she was having fun.

"See this woman next to Maura?" Thomas pointed at the woman in question.

"They have their arms around one another," Shannon said wistfully. "More of a hug than she ever gave me."

"Do you recognize her or any of them?" Thomas said.

Shannon tapped her nail on one of the photos.

"I think that's Michael Carney, a friend from school. The woman I don't know."

Thomas collected the photographs. "I'll track down Michael Carney then, and if I run across the woman too, all the better."

"And then what?" Shannon asked.

"And then I'll give you the information, and you will call them. You're the aunt. It's Ireland. I think that would be best."

"I think so, too, Thomas. I can navigate," she said. "Just point me to the star."

Shannon touched the chignon at her neck and pushed a pearl pin in tighter. The beads on her dress caught the light and twinkled. Her bare shoulders seemed to sparkle too. Thomas thought she looked like a fairy. She opened her purse and took out her phone to check the time.

"I'm late," she said.

"I hope he won't dock your pay."

"I don't work by the hour, Thomas." She gathered her coat, truly amused. "But I'd best be picking up as many gigs as I can. It would do Aidan no good to have me running off every evening."

"You're a fine woman, Shannon."

She slid out of the booth, draping her velvet coat over her arm. Holding her jeweled purse to her breast, she leaned over, and kissed Thomas on the cheek.

"Debatable, Thomas, but I try."

She swept away in a cloud of expensive perfume, as unconcerned with the stares that followed her out as the ones that had followed her in. When she was gone, the waitress came with the check.

"Sorry it didn't work out," she said.

It took Thomas a minute to figure out what she meant. When he did, Thomas laughed.

"It will—eventually."

42

Finn O'Brien was back in Stuart Gowdy's office. The man, being who he was, had a key to the emergency exit, so they were able to skirt security at the front of the building. They walked up the flights of stairs more slowly than they had gone down.

Now the miserable man was sitting in his very own chair behind his desk, shaking his head. It was well after six and a deep quiet had descended on the government building. Finn sat opposite him, watching, and waiting. He did not prod the man. Having come so far for the truth, he was willing to wait for the information he wanted. They were both exhausted, but Gowdy was crushed.

The man was pale, his eyes were drained of color, and there was a red welt rising on his cheek where he had fallen against the edge of the newsstand. There was also a look of distrust in his eyes, because the shock of what had happened was wearing off.

"How do I know you're a cop?" he said. "How do I know any of this is true?"

Finn kept his eye on the man, as he fished his phone from

his pocket. He placed the call, put it on speaker and when the operator answered, identifying the LAPD, Wilshire Division, Finn whispered:

"Ask for Detective O'Brien."

"I'd like to speak to Detective O'Brien, please," Stuart said.

"I'm sorry, Detective O'Brien is unavailable. Would you like to speak to his partner?"

Finn shook his head, but Gowdy paid no mind.

"Yes, I would," Stuart said.

"Transferring you to Detective Anderson, have a good day."

The line went dead for a moment before it was picked up.

"Detective Anderson, Wilshire, how can I help you?"

Stuart sat up taller, aware that Finn had not expected him to engage. Now it seemed the detective didn't want him to.

"Yes. Yes. My name is Stuart Gowdy. I'm trying to confirm if someone named Finn O'Brien is a cop."

"May I ask why you'd like that information, Mr. Gowdy?" Cori asked.

"Just is he, or isn't he?" Stuart said.

"Well, Detective O'Brien works out of this division, but he isn't..."

Finn interrupted. Not wanting Gowdy to hear that he had been suspended, he took the phone off speaker.

"Cori, it's me," Finn said. "I'm here with Mr. Gowdy, and I'm needing you to confirm my association please. I've forgotten my credentials at the hotel."

There was a moment of silence and Finn knew well that Cori was gnawing her lip, trying to decide between saying what she should and what he wanted her to.

"Perhaps you could tell me a something about your association with the gentleman, Detective O'Brien?"

Finn glanced at Stuart. The man was watching him like a hawk, so Finn didn't take Cori to task for playing games.

"Mr. Gowdy had unauthorized access to the Platinum plane here in San Francisco. I'd like to speak to him about that."

"I see. Then, yes," Cori said. "Put him back on."

Finn put the call back on speaker.

"Mr. Gowdy, I can confirm that Detective O'Brien works out of Wilshire Division. Is there any other information I can provide you?"

The man shook his head before realizing he had to speak.

"No. Thanks. That's what I needed to know."

"Thank you, Detective Anderson," Finn said. "I'll be back tonight. Perhaps you could pick me up at LAX, and I'll fill you in. American Airlines. Flight 2540 at 9:10." Finn listened and then said: "Yes. I'll meet you at the curb. Thank you, Detective."

Finn ended the call, careful to keep his expression neutral.

"I want your badge number," Stuart said.

Finn looked over the desk, picked up a pen, and wrote his badge number on the corner of a file folder. He pushed it toward Gowdy.

"That's all I'll be giving you," Finn said. "It's your turn."

Gowdy took a deep breath to compose himself before he looked Finn in the eye.

"You won't believe it," he said. "I don't believe it."

SOMEONE HAD FLIPPED a switch in the bullpen at Wilshire Division. Everyone was busy at this late hour. Leads were being run down, reports shared, and interviews conducted. Cori had been between phone calls when Finn's came through. Part of her wished she had missed it, but she hadn't.

Not wanting to give herself a chance to change her mind, Cori immediately got up and went to Fowler's office. Eileen swiveled her chair, and called after Cori.

"He's out of here in five minutes for dinner with the mayor. Be quick."

Cori found the captain standing in front of a small mirror adjusting his tie. He looked at Cori's reflection as she put a piece of paper on his desk.

"O'Brien is in San Francisco." She put the information on the desk. "He wants me to pick him up."

"Thank you, detective," Fowler said.

Cori hesitated, "And?"

"And I'll take care of it."

"But—"

"I said I'd take care of it." Fowler shrugged into his jacket. He looked disappointed to find Cori still there.

"Is there anything else, Detective?"

"Nothing Captain," she said. "Have a good one."

Cori walked away. Instead of going back to her desk, she went outside and planted herself in the alley, her back up against the wall of the building. She punched in nine of the ten numbers that would connect her to Finn. Her thumb hovered over that last digit, but she couldn't press it.

Cori understood what her partner was doing, but he was jeopardizing his job for the second time in his career. The first time his stand was righteous, this time it was ego that drove him. He and Lowery were two fighting cocks. As much as she cared about her partner, she couldn't get in the ring with him on this one.

Resting her head against the wall, Cori pocketed her phone, and closed her eyes. Finn wasn't due for a few more hours. A lot could happen in those hours, but whatever it was, it would have to happen without her, and she regretted that deeply.

Five minutes later she was straightening her desk. She had cancelled dinner with Lapinski, because her mind would be on Finn. She wanted to think about his choices and her own.

Maybe she would warn him despite orders to the contrary. Both the captain's orders and Finn's request made her a liar one way or the other, and that was just one itch too many. Before Cori could gather her things, the phone on the desk rang again.

"No, Detective O'Brien isn't here," she said none too kindly. A second later, she caught herself. "I'm sorry. Long day. Do you want to leave a message?"

Cori dragged a legal pad toward her, wrote down a name—Maggie Davis—a number, and a message: *this is about his uncle's insurance policy.*

43

Josephine Sterling, made it back to her office after six, disgusted that the art of conducting a meeting was a thing of the past. She'd never heard so much bull in her life.

She eyed the stack of files on her desk, thought about taking them home, but decided against it. She was desperately in need of some R & R even if it was just a good night's sleep after a couple of hours of watching television with her cat. Not one to leave work undone, Josephine decided to give each one a look in preparation for the next day. Fifteen minutes, tops, and she was out of there.

The first report was on the fire in the marina that sunk one of the tourist boats and killed fifteen people. There had been an explosion before the fire, but there was nothing nefarious about the incident. A burner in the kitchen blew, there weren't enough emergency exits, and people died. Case closed.

The next piece was an agency-wide announcement about a celebration in commemoration of the establishment of the agency.

Yay.

Inside the third was a single page report from the ATF National Repository. The piece of metal from the Platinum site that Josephine had tagged as part of a watch was exactly that. Not only had they managed to raise a serial number, they had pieced together additional metal shards and found a few other tidbits.

Josephine smiled, appreciative of such impressive work. She scanned the images, and faxed them to Agent Lowery, and then she went home to her TV and her cat.

Agent Lowery was in the kitchen when he heard the fax machine whir. He wandered into his home office, and watched the pages come through. Like Josephine Sterling, the information impressed him. The watch parts found in the debris indicated that this was the timing device. The timepiece was expensive and exclusive.

He looked at the wall clock, and saw that it was late. He would follow up in the morning. Right now, he had work to do. He put on his jacket and kissed his wife on the cheek. She patted his hand and said:

"Be careful."

Her warning was reflex. She was so engrossed in her TV program that she barely noticed him leave the house. He wondered how long it would take her to notice if he didn't come home.

His first stop was to pick up Franks. While they drove to the second stop, Lowery told him about the watch. Franks said, 'it's about time'. Lowery drove on, wondering if Agent Franks' jokes would ever get any better.

MAGGIE HAD CUT her run down to four miles but that still gave Zach plenty of time to order food. She felt a ton better, almost happy, and she was hungry. She had zoned to some great music, worked up a sweat, and there was someone waiting for her at home. Even if it was just Zach, it was nice to know he cared enough to stick around.

Maggie was flying when she turned the corner and started down the long block to her apartment. She was a third of the way down when she looked up and saw Zach in the open window watching for her. Two of the street lights were out, but when he finally saw her, Zach called out. She couldn't understand what he was saying, so she waved and started across the street. That's when she was hit.

The car came out of nowhere. The impact was brutal, throwing Maggie forward head first. She hit hard. Zach screamed, and ran for the door, rushing into the street, falling to his knees beside her. His arms flailed; his cries rose. Maggie was broken and bleeding, the car was gone, and he had no idea what to do. Suddenly, there was a woman kneeling next to him and a man seeing to Maggie. The man was on his phone calling for help, the woman put her arm around Zach and told him it would be okay.

Zach wanted to say something too, but all he could do was cry.

FINN WAS the last one off the plane. He said his thanks to the stewardess and hit the breezeway, still bothered, fascinated, and appalled by what he had found in San Francisco. If what Stuart Gowdy told Finn were true, then the person who was responsible for the explosion that killed Hugh and Maura was still out there. Gowdy was only responsible for unknowingly putting the bomb on a plane. The information was incredible, but as slippery as a gold ring dropped down the drain, lost in the wet, and the dark, and the sludge.

Late for his plane, Finn had dashed for the airport, taking all the information Gowdy was able to give him. He'd spent the short flight wishing he could access the internet.

Tired, distracted, Finn traversed the terminal to the escalator that would take him to the lower level of LAX. Zoned out men and women kept pace with him, families with strollers slowed him down, but Finn hurried along as best he could. On the lower level, he zig-zagged, dodging those waiting for their luggage. He went outside where more people milled around, frantic to find their rides, catch their buses, or claim their cars in the parking structure. Finn stopped at the curb. He dialed Cori to let her know he had arrived. She didn't pick up. He was leaving a message for her when he was attacked.

The two men were fast and sure. One threaded his beefy arm around Finn's throat while the other took hold of his wrist and slapped him with cuffs. Finn was face-planted on the hood of a car waiting at the curb. Startled, the driver threw himself into the traffic that was circling the airport. A van slammed on its brakes. Other cars honked. No one stopped to see what the problem was, but many slowed to watch.

The hand on Finn's head pressed his cheek into the car hood, the force of it twisting his mouth so that he couldn't speak. It blinded him in one eye. Through the other he saw at least one person filming with their phone. A child came close enough that Finn could see the little boy's nose running. His mother scooped him up and away a second later.

The next thing Finn O'Brien saw was the torso of a man clad in a polo shirt and a blue windbreaker. His chest expanded with a deep, long-suffering sigh before he bent down, his hands cupping his knees, and squared off with Finn.

"Welcome home, O'Brien."

"Agent Lowery," Finn muttered, and then raised his head just enough so that his mouth could work properly. "I assume 'tis Agent Franks fondling me."

Lowery raised a hand, and Finn was yanked upright. He looked over his shoulder.

"I win," he said, working his jaw to ease the pain Franks had inflicted.

"I don't think so, buddy," Lowery said. "In fact, you just cashed out."

WHEN FINN WOKE, he was lying on something that passed for a bed at MDC, the federal detention center in downtown Los Angeles. He knew what the outside of the building looked like: a towering white structure stitched with narrow, sealed window; so narrow and high it would be impossible for a man to escape through them. However, Finn had never been inside MDC. Now he was intimately familiar with the booking room, the shower room, and the cell where Lowery had arranged for his overnight stay. It was clean, uncomfortable, and, he hoped, restricted. Cops were not favored guests no matter where they were incarcerated.

Throwing his legs over the side of his 'bed' Finn stood, stretched, and walked the few steps to the metal sink. He splashed water on his face and looked in the reflective metal that passed for a mirror, trying to see if there was any damage to his cheek. There was none. He grabbed the orange jumpsuit he had discarded on a shelf the night before, and stepped into it, one leg a time. As Finn dressed, Agent Lowery's litany of his offenses played through his mind.

Interfering with a federal investigation.

Intimidation of witnesses.

Impersonating an officer.

Spitting on the sidewalk.

Telling an improper joke.

Existing.

Finn had remained silent, knowing anything he had to say would simply add fuel to Lowery's fire. They both needed a night's sleep —good or otherwise. Buttoning up his jumpsuit, wishing he could have another shower, Finn sat back on the bunk.

Having neither watch nor phone, all he could do was wait for the routine to begin. Thankfully, he didn't have to wait long.

"O'Brien."

Finn heard his name and the sound of a key in the door at the same time. It was opened by a guard, spit and polished, who had no skin in any game other than a pension. He waited for Finn to come to the door, and then handed him his clothes and his phone. Finn checked the phone. There were messages, but no time to retrieve them. The guard said:

"Get dressed."

Finn would have liked to have shaved, but he settled for what he could get. Finished dressing, he knocked on the door and the guard opened it, escorting him to an interrogation room where Agent Lowery waited.

"Sleep well?"

"I've done better." Finn pulled out a chair and settled himself at the metal table. The room was mic'd, he was sure; the cameras were a no brainer. "Should I be asking for an attorney?"

"Depends." Lowery twirled his paper cup.

"I suppose there's not another cup of coffee to be had, is there?"

"No."

Lowery gave him a tight-lipped smile, taking inordinate pleasure in finishing his brew. He was having a high old time stretching out the time, but Finn knew the game and he didn't want to play.

"Where does this leave us then? In a pissing match, or will you get out the thumb screws," Finn said.

"Charging you would be a waste of the tax payer's money. The thumb screws would be a waste of my time." Lowery pulled his chair closer to the table. "I am just tired of you getting up in my territory, and you're tired of me being an asshole about it, so let's call it a draw."

"It's apparent I've no one backing me up, so I suppose I've no choice," Finn said.

"If I were you, I'd thank your partner for saving you from yourself," Lowery suggested. "You were damn clumsy in San Francisco."

"Deborah," Finn said. "Smart girl."

"She could have been dumb-as-a-stone and tagged you. But here's the thing, none of us are stupid no matter what you think. I understand that you've got major skin in this game, but so does everyone. You don't think the other families are having a bad time? And what about the Platinum employees who lost colleagues? They are scared to death to get on their planes. At some point you've gotta look in the mirror and ask what makes you so damn special?"

"You've a point, Agent Lowery." Seeing himself through Lowery's lens was not pretty, but Finn still believed his actions were for the best. "You've no heart in this, Lowery. It's all forms and forensics. 'Tis harsh for those of us who are waiting."

The agent sat back. One hand was in his lap, the other was on the table. He turned his fingers into his palm and then unfurled them again. He was silent for a long while before he said:

"That's a low blow, O'Brien."

Lowery's lips twitched. He seemed to be warring more with himself than Finn.

"You don't know a damn thing about me, but I'm willing to share. My agency has marginalized me. I'm old. I want things done right. They want stars, and I ain't one. I think you had a similar experience, but that's neither here nor there." Lowery said. "One thing we can agree on is that we both want this to come out right, and it won't if you keep getting in the way. When I present the case to the U.S. Attorney, he's going to need a clear path to prosecution and that includes evidence. Untainted evidence. No matter what you have found, no matter how good your intel, it is useless without ATF protocol. Are we clear?"

"We are," Finn said.

"Then let's hear it. What did you find up north?"

FROM DEBORAH'S insistence that Platinum Wings security was foolproof, to James' confession of complicity, to Gary Gerber's payoff, and Stuart Gowdy's breach of the plane, Finn laid it all out. He called up the picture of Greg and Stuart and sent it to Lowery.

"That briefcase looks like it fits the bill," the agent said. "Now the question is why?"

This time Finn pulled up a website on his phone and showed it to Lowery.

"Dark Quest. It is a hyperrealistic RPG." Finn said.

"What's that?"

"A role playing game, Lowery. All those people dead for a game," Finn answered.

Ten minutes later, Lowery was digesting Finn's information. His fingers tapped the table as he processed the information.

"So, this company—Dark Quest?—they arrange these

fantasy scenarios that are played out in real life and real time, and anyone with enough money can be James Bond. Is that right?"

"Correct. But Dark Quest is a little different," Finn said. "Their customers write their own scripts. Stuart Gowdy put in a request for an assignment, and he was matched him with someone who had made a similar request. Gowdy received a storyline from his matched player. It included specific directions. Both players pay a handsome sum to be involved. If Gowdy did not accomplish the task, he forfeits his fee to the other player and Dark Quest takes a percentage. If the game is successful, Dark Quest keeps both fees."

"So, the game they were playing was what? Hijacker? Terrorists?"

"Secret agent. Gowdy was to smuggle government papers onto a plane carrying 'Irish dissidents'," Finn said. "I've the name of the hotel where he picked up the briefcase. The key card to the room was handed off in a paper bag in the breakfast area, the room itself was on the second floor. Gowdy didn't see who left the case, nor did he open it."

"So, who rented the room?"

"Is it your entire job you're wanting me to do, Lowery?" Finn said, hoping to soften the agent. He thought he managed when he saw a twitch at the corner of Lowery's mouth, but all the man said was:

"Don't get cute."

"Then in answer to your question, I've no idea," Finn said. "With no badge, the hotel would have told me nothing."

"But the mechanic and some GSA fool were happy to spill their guts? What did you do, say please?" Lowery held up his hand, changing his mind. "Never mind. I don't want to know how you did it. Just cut to the chase."

"Okay, Gowdy goes away from the airport happy, thinking

he's a big man for completing his task. He texts a number to confirm completion, and sends a picture of the briefcase on the plane as proof. He gets a virtual medal. The other person is alerted that the mission is accomplished."

'That is some crazy shit." Lowery shook his head.

"Gowdy is expecting a visit from you," Finn said. "The man had no idea that he had been carrying a bomb."

"I'm not going to fall all over you for this, O'Brien, but good work."

"Flowers would be nice."

Finn was rewarded with a chuckle just before the agent took out his phone. When Agent Franks was on the line, Lowery stood up, walked away, and filled the agent in. Franks would take the first flight out to San Francisco. An itinerary would be forthcoming—

Before he finished, an officer who looked much like the one who had taken Finn from his cell, walked in. Lowery held the phone away from his ear, listened to the man, and then sent him on his way. Lowery finished giving Franks his marching orders and looked at Finn.

"Looks like your ride is here."

Once more the door opened, and this time Cori was there. She wasn't smiling.

"He's all yours," Lowery said.

"Not sure I'm wantin' him back." She cocked her head at her partner. "Let's stop bothering the nice man, O'Brien."

Finn looked at Lowery for permission to leave.

"Go. But stay on your side of the street."

Finn took his jacket, and followed Cori into the hall. She was more than a step ahead of him, but he caught up with her once they were outside.

"Agent Lowery said I should thank you for saving me from myself."

"You going to take his advice?"

"I am," Finn said. "Thank you, Cori."

"You're welcome." She smiled and put her hand on his shoulder. "Now let's go."

"I'm still on suspension. I wouldn't want you puttin' your neck out for me again, Cori."

"You haven't quite burned this bridge yet," she said. "Besides, this isn't official."

"Where are we going?" Finn asked.

"The morgue," Cori answered.

44

"Where is he?" Finn asked the M.E.

"My office. I couldn't get him to leave," Paul Craig said. "He saw the accident, and he was at the hospital too. He's not related to the deceased, but he made such a ruckus they told him where they were sending her. I thought I was going to have to get security, but then he said he was going to call you. I told him I would. Can you talk to him, please? I mean, I sympathize, but I really need him gone."

"And his name again?" Finn asked.

"Zach is all he gave me," Paul answered.

Finn looked at Cori, she looked back at him. She didn't have a clue.

"And the deceased?" Cori asked.

"Maggie Davis," Paul said.

"I think I took a call from a Maggie Davis." Cori snapped her fingers trying to remember, but Finn was already on it.

"Twenty-something. Dark hair? About five-five?" Finn asked.

"That's her," Paul said.

"The girl from Intrepid Insurance." Finn's jaw set. He took a breath. "How did she end up here?"

"Hit and run. She was assigned to Doctor Connor." Paul stuck his hands deep in the pockets of his white coat, looked at Zach, and shook his head. "We don't see many people willing to storm the citadel for our patients. She must have meant a lot to him."

"We'll see to it from here," Finn said.

"I appreciate it."

Paul went on his way; Finn and Cori went into his office to see about the man who was hunched over in a chair in front of Paul's desk. Finn called his name. When he turned, Finn recognized him as the cubical man with the glasses. He stood up, nearly knocking over the chair as he did so.

"Mr. O'Brien. Maggie's dea..."

"I know. I'm sorry for it," Finn said. "This is my partner, Detective Anderson."

"Condolences," she said, wishing there was a better word.

"What is it we can do for you, Zach?" Finn asked.

"Maggie called you like three times. You said she could call if she needed anything, but you never called back." He took a step forward and one back. He wrung his hands. He pushed up his glasses. He got in Finn's face. "If you had talked to her, she wouldn't be dead."

"Hey, now." Cori took his arm and moved him away. "Accidents happen. You can't blame Detective O'Brien."

"That's the point. This wasn't an accident," Zach said. He pointed at Finn."And it happened because of him."

THEY SAT AT A ROUND TABLE, at a Mexican food restaurant two blocks down from the morgue. Carnitas had been stewing all night and the smell inside the place was rich, dense, and comforting. A woman brought them glasses of water and menus.

They set aside the menus, but Zach could not get enough water. He was calmer now, but he was still hunched, still mourning, still unsure of how he had found himself in this place with these people.

"I know what I saw. That car didn't stop. I don't even know where it came from."

"What did it look like?" Finn asked.

Zach sighed, worn out. It had been a very long night. He sat back in his chair. Both hands were still around his glass and he dragged it across the table, keeping it with him like a security blanket.

"White, I think. Yeah, white. A sedan. I can't tell you the make or the model. I was watching for Maggie. She went out for a run, I ordered dinner, and it was getting cold. She waved and I could see she was smiling, so she was feeling better. "

"Did you see who was driving? A man? Woman? Was there more than one person in the car?" Cori asked. Zach shook his head.

"I was on the third floor looking down, and I was looking at Maggie," Zach answered. He raised a hand and swept it in front of him. "Bam. Just like that this car takes her out. I saw her face. She was like... surprised. Like, she was saying 'whoa what just happened'."

"It could have been a drunk driver or someone who was high," Finn said. "Impaired drivers don't have good reaction time."

"No. No, wasn't like that. That car hit her square," he said. "And two other people saw the guy run over her deliberately when she was already hurt. It's in the report. Look it up. Whoever was driving wanted to kill her."

Zach blinked back tears. He looked at the ceiling.

"I loved Maggie. I mean, she was my best friend, and I was hers. It wasn't fair after all she's been through." He looked at Finn and then at Cori as if they should understand what he was talking about.

"Zach, why did you ask for me? This really is best left to the investigating officer," Finn said.

"She was trying to get ahold of you because of work. She got fired because she found a problem with your uncle's life insurance policy and then she found more problems with our other policies. I think that's why someone wanted her dead, and I think maybe it was our boss."

"Zach," Finn said. "I met the woman, and I've good radar for something amiss."

"Well, your radar was off. Whitfield threatened Maggie, and now Maggie is dead."

Zach took a minute to regroup. Anger, frustration, fear, and guilt jumbled up in his brain. Finally, he put his hands flat on the table and when he spoke his words were measured.

"Maggie asked for my help, and I told her no. She wanted your help but you didn't call her back."

"I didn't know, and I'm sorry for it," Finn said. Explaining his suspension would give Zach no comfort.

"Have you contacted her family?" Cori asked.

"I don't think she has any," Zach said.

"She must have an emergency contact," Finn said.

"I guess," Zach said. "But what If Maggie doesn't have anyone? How does she get buried? Do I have to do that? What about the stuff in her apartment? What about..."

"We'll help you manage," Cori said. "One step at a time."

"Zach, what was it Maggie wanted to speak to me about exactly?" Finn asked.

"She was going to be a whistleblower. She had an attorney, but she was having second thoughts and wanted to talk to someone who knew the law. Since all this started with your uncle's policy, she thought you could advise her."

"Whistleblower is big stuff,' Cori said.

"The thing is, I think she was right. She's got all sorts of stuff in her apartment that makes it look like Intrepid was involved in a fraud. The companies she was looking at have too many corporate policies insuring individuals. She thought she would get promoted if she told management. Instead, she got fired. Then she got dead."

They sat together, considering the narrative: a young, ambitious woman, big business, big money, a convenient accident. Finn broke the silence.

"If Maggie's last wish was for me to have a look at her information, then we'll have a look," Finn said. "Can you get into her apartment?"

"Yes," Zach said, and for the first time he smiled. "Yes, I can."

45

It was déjà vu all over again for Dennis Cain. He was in a fancy elevator, dressed in a fine suit, and headed to a meeting at Hammet Industries. The only thing that was different this time was that Brian stood by his side, ramrod straight, eyes forward, pleased that soon he would be going back home.

Brian took the lead when the elevator opened. Pamela, the receptionist, said hello as she always did. Brian did not. Dennis murmured a greeting, but didn't make eye contact. The brothers breezed past Mrs. Farrow who offered a curt 'good morning'. Harry waited as he had waited the last time they met. He welcomed them both with firm handshakes.

"It's a happy day for you and Wolfhound," he said

The Cain brothers sat on the couch; Harry in the king's chair across from them. The man was pleased because this was a good deal all around. Wolfhound had been an annoyance, a rare failure for Harry, and the initial sale had been a thorn in the Cains' side.

"The board has agreed that we will let Wolfhound go for

twenty-two million. All said and done, including reversion of the name rights," Harry said.

"'Tis fair," Brian said. "I think all of us agree on that, do we not, Dennis?"

"Yes," Dennis said.

Harry's smile faltered a bit. He looked more closely at Dennis, noting he was not himself. Still, whatever was between the brothers was of no interest to him.

"I'll be straight. They didn't like it. Breaking even is not what we usually do," Harry said.

"What tipped the decision in our favor," Dennis asked.

"Compassion," Harry said. "Two of our members didn't want to visit anymore misery on your company after the accident."

"Compassion, or are they wanting to be rid of us so there is no liability?" Brian asked.

Harry laughed, and Dennis looked at his brother. He was vile, but Harry was no better. Dennis hated that these two were making light.

"Some things are better left unspoken," Harry said. "Now, if this is acceptable to you, we can begin the process. Our legal department is ready to move forward. Dennis?"

"I have everything in order." Brian answered before Dennis could speak. "But I'd like to delay two to three weeks."

"If there's a problem with the money, I need to know now."

Harry's tone changed. He did not like being played the fool, and if this paltry deal fell through that's exactly what he would be.

"We're waiting on a check from the insurance company. The money is due to be transferred by the end of this week," Dennis said. "I simply want to have a cushion, so that we fulfill our monetary obligation in full."

"Impressive that the airline has moved so quickly to settle with you."

"'Tis not the airline," Brian said. "Though we'll be happy when they settle too."

"Then someone on that plane must have been very important," Harry noted.

"Key men always are," Brian said.

"Ah," Harry said. "I see."

Dennis knew the man didn't really see. Even if he did, he doubted Harry would care. In fact, Harry might even be impressed.

SHANNON SHAUGHNESSY SAT in a bar in West Hollywood waiting on her date, a woman with a lot of money but no friends. Every month she and Shannon had a late lunch, and then wandered through high-end furniture stores. The woman never bought anything, she just liked to dangle the idea of a big commission in front of lowly salespeople. Shannon thought it a cruel hobby; the woman thought it fun. Shannon got paid, the woman went home, and Shannon thought no more of her.

Each month, though, Shannon did wonder why the foul women spent money for her company and not another who charged less. In fact, it would have been cheaper yet to hire an assistant who would be at her beck and call all day. Since this was only a fleeting thought, Shannon continued doing what she was doing: pressing the buttons on Maura's bent and twisted phone, praying that it would come on long enough to have a look at her address book, but it was dark behind the smashed screen.

The man who had given it to her could offer no information on whether or not the ATF had accessed the chip, or whether they had downloaded files that might help Shannon find her nephew. She did not waste precious time trying to get blood from a stone. That man was no more than a clerk, after all.

"You're here. Good."

Shannon looked up and smiled at her client. The woman was nicely turned out in a sleek red dress with a flounce that landed just above her knees. The frock was Givenchy, and Shannon thought it a bit young for the woman. Still, who was she to judge?

"Always on time," Shannon said.

She slid off the barstool, walking ahead of the woman as they followed the maître 'd to their table. Shannon's client enjoyed the heads turning, fooling herself that she was the one being admired. The waiter appeared the moment they were seated, taking their linen napkins and placing them upon the ladies' laps.

"What have you there?" the woman asked.

"My sister's phone," Shannon said. "She was killed when her plane exploded."

"Pity," the woman said as she opened the menu. "I'm thinking salmon today. What are you thinking?"

Shannon put the phone in her bag, and said nothing. To say what she was thinking would be bad for business.

BRIAN CAIN WAS happy that his work was almost done. Soon he would be gone from this place. He was happier still when he saw that his assistant had been working late. He jotted down the information she had provided, double-checked it, and when he finished, Brian erased the message.

When that was done, he packed his bag with his suit and good shoes, his fancy shirt and toiletries. He put his light jacket on over his T-shirt, checked out of his room remotely, and left the hotel.

Downstairs, he went to self-parking, found his rental, and tossed his bag in the trunk. It wasn't a bad drive from downtown L.A. to Dennis's home. He would say his 'special goodbye' to his brother and his wife, and be gone, back to Ireland, safe at home.

When he reached Beverly Hills, Brian pulled into the driveway of Dennis's monstrous house, got out, and rang the doorbell. It was Katherine who answered. She looked more composed than the last time he had seen her. Dennis came down the stairs just as Brian kissed her cheek. The brothers shook hands.

"Good of you to have me over for a farewell drink," Brian said.

Polite mutterings were offered.

Couldn't let you go without...

Appreciate all you've done...

Sorry you couldn't stay longer...

"Might you let me use your phone. Mine doesn't seem to be working properly."

"Sure, not a problem."

Dennis pulled his phone from his pocket and handed it to his brother. Brian inclined his head as if embarrassed.

"Tis of a personal nature," he said.

Dennis and Katherine disappeared into the living room. When Brian was sure they were out of earshot, he made his call. When it was not answered immediately, he had a moment of panic. That was unusual for him, but this bit of business was important. If it wasn't wrapped up now, he would have to rethink everything.

Then he heard her voice, and Brian Cain relaxed.

~

"O'Brien! Ms. Cori! You be lookin' fine today."

Geoffrey called out the minute they opened the door to Mick's. Cori and Zach headed to a table while Finn went to order refreshments.

"Who be dat wit you, O'Brien? He be a baby."

"Old enough, Geoffrey," Finn said. "'Tis been a long afternoon and we're needing two black ones and a vodka cranberry for my partner."

Finn put the money on the counter. Geoffrey swiped it up.

"Be getting' to it dis minute, O'Brien."

"Thanks, Geoffrey. And I'm liking the beanie. Pink looks good on you."

Geoffrey grinned. Finn headed for the corner table where Zach and Cori were already pouring over the information they had taken from Maggie's apartment. It was all they had taken. Everything else would have to wait for someone close to Maggie to deal with the remnants of her life—or someone else who would investigate her death.

Zach was beside himself inside the place. Crying quietly while he took what they had come for. Even Finn and Cori took a moment: Cori because she couldn't help but imagine Amber coming to such a horrible end, Finn feeling responsible because he hadn't been there for the girl.

"What have I missed?" Finn pulled out a chair and joined the conversation.

"I was showing Detective Anderson, the problem with Mr. Murphy's policy. It was just a matter of transposition. Someone mixed up a personal policy number with a corporate one. Both policies had been taken out in his name. Both on the same day. The corporate policy had a payout of ten million dollars upon death, and the other one ten thousand. It turns out that the same thing happened, on the same day, with the same company for Maura Shaughnessy."

"Why would there be corporate policies at all?" Finn asked. "Hugh was retired and Maura was a consultant."

"Someone at Wolfhound could have forgotten to cancel the corporate policies when employment ended," Zach said. "But as long as the premium was paid, the policy would be in force."

"It's a possibility," Finn mused. "Mr. Cain admitted he hadn't thought of Hugh's retirement until years later."

"And Maura?" Cori asked, leaning back so Geoffrey could serve them. He hustled back to the bar and they put their heads together again. Zach shrugged.

"I only know what Maggie told Whitfield. She thought corporate claims in the millions were being settled to personal accounts. The beneficiary gets a ton of money and the books are closed showing a settlement."

"'Tis an interesting theory," Finn said. "But Maura's policy bothers me. Why keep her covered at all? Wouldn't that raise a red flag?"

"She would only be a name in a computer. No one at Intrepid would know if she was a full-time employee or not," Zach said.

"Maybe Dennis Cain kept her covered for the kid's sake," Cori said. "That baby would be set for life with ten mil if he was the beneficiary of the policy."

"Except it doesn't work that way," Zach said. "If there hadn't been the original problem, Wolfhound would be the beneficiary because these were key man policies. They're special. They cover people considered essential to the business. Invaluable even."

"So the money goes to Wolfhound, and Dennis controls Wolfhound, which means he controls the money. He could dish it out to Maura's kid without anyone knowing, including his wife."

"And Hugh's settlement goes into the coffers," Finn said. "What business couldn't do with an extra ten million dollars?"

"If Maggie had left it there, everything would have been okay."

Zach dug into the file one more time. He put a spreadsheet in front of the detectives.

"Wolfhound has ten key man policies in force, and only twenty-five employees. They had one pay out in 2010, another in 2014 and now these two. Four settlements in that span of time is crazy-weird, not to mention it's usually only the top brass who are covered by these policies," Zach said. "The only exclusion is suicide."

"Well, lookie there," Cori tapped the paper. "Jane Whitfield. She wrote all of them."

"It seems that Wolfhound has found a way to have an influx of cash on a regular basis," Finn said. "Do you know how the first two key men passed, Zach?"

"Maggie was looking into that the day she got fired. She was trying to download the information to take with her, but Whitfield stopped her." Zach said. He looked from one detective to the other. "Do you think she was on to something?"

"I think she walked right into the outhouse," Cori said. "This stinks bad."

"She wasn't thinking anybody got murdered, though," Zach said. "I know that for sure. She had a theory that the codes were being changed online. That way the claims would be settled, but the people wouldn't actually be dead. No one would know the difference at Intrepid if the proper claim mechanism was triggered."

"Zach," Finn said. "Can you give us the information on the policies that were paid out— names, date of demise, policy numbers—that sort of thing?"

"I can pull that together from this information," he said.

"Good. When it's done, give it to Detective Anderson."

"Okay, but why?"

"Because we're going to see this through," Finn said. "But we're going to it the right way. Cori will coordinate with the investigating officer. She'll talk to the D.A., get warrants and get into Intrepid's files."

"Intrepid won't know what hit them," Cori said.

SHANNON'S CLIENT WAS GONE, but she was still in the restaurant bar sipping tea, and fielding calls from the agency about her appointments. That very night she was due at a small gathering at a famous director's Malibu house. Her date was a shy actor whose agent was popping for Shannon's services in the hopes of making the lad look more a player than he was. She finished her tea, and agreed to another appointment.

"Doing okay, there, Shannon?" the bartender asked when she was done with her call.

"Sure, I'm done. Thank you." She pushed her tea cup toward him.

"Your friend was on a tear today, wasn't she?"

"That she was." Shannon slid off the high chair. "But she's no friend of mine. Business only."

"Funny what we do for money?" he said.

"And love," Shannon said.

"You got that right."

She gave the bartender a good tip, and, once she was outside, did the same with the valet before he went to retrieve her rental car. It was brought around in record time.

The valet had just closed the car door for Shannon, when her phone rang. Intending to turn down any more engagements, she was surprised to find that it wasn't her agent calling. Instead, it was a man inviting her to a meeting in Beverly Hills. Mr. Cain, it seemed, had a change of heart. He wanted to talk about Aidan.

Stunned, Shannon sat behind the wheel until the valet knocked on her window, needing her to move. She smiled at him and did just that. While she drove, she made two calls.

The first was to her agent, to inform her that she would not be able to go to Malibu that evening. What followed was a tirade of threats, an avalanche of pleas, and finally an offer of more money if she would relent.

"Catch yourself on," Shannon admonished the woman, before she hung up.

The second call was to Thomas. He didn't answer. She left a message. She was off to the Cains by invitation and would call him and Cori and Finn later.

FINN PUT a few bills on the table for Geoffrey. Zach was gathering his papers when Cori's phone rang. She mouthed the word 'Lapinski' and turned her back to take the call. But what he wanted wasn't personal. When she hung up, she said:

"Shannon Shaughnessy's on her way to the Cain house. She left a message for Lapinski. Says she's been invited."

Finn raised a brow. He took out his own phone and started to dial.

"Are you going to stop her?"

"'Tis not up to me." When his call was answered, he said: "Agent Lowery. I've a bit of news I think you should know."

Cori smiled, amused to see that her partner was finally playing by Lowery's rules. The conversation was short. When Finn ended it, he gave Zach a pat on the back.

"Cori, will you be seeing Zach to his car?"

"I can do that. What about you?" Cori asked.

"Agent Lowery and I have a date."

"Wow, talk about kiss and make-up," Cori laughed. "Where's he taking you?"

"Beverly Hills," he answered.

AGENT FRANKS HAD IMPRESSED LOWERY. He had spent his time in San Francisco well. Now Lowery was in possession of copies of the hotel registration card where Dennis Cain had stayed, the time he checked in and out, a statement from the maid who had serviced the room, and one from Stuart Gowdy who, according to Franks, was still a mess and a half but cooperative. The last piece of the puzzle was a certificate of authentication from Windmere Watches in Switzerland, a firm even older than Wolfhound Distillery.

Agent Lowery put all these things in his case file and left the office. First stop was the judge's chambers to get his warrant, then he would pick up Finn O'Brien. Hopefully, the detective could work his magic on Shannon Shaughnessy before she made any more trouble. The last thing Lowery wanted was anyone getting in his way

46

Shannon parked across from the big house, admiring the architecture and the landscaping. Both had gone unnoticed the last time she had been at the Cain's home.

Setting her purse crossbody, she flipped her hair over the strap. It was heavy for such a little thing but it held the tools of her trade, and a lady never left home without them—except for the night she read her sister's journal. That night Shannon had left everything behind when she went to confront Dennis Cain, including the memories of every hurt between her and Maura.

Chin up, shoulders back, Shannon crossed the street, and, at the front door, took the great golden ring in the lion's mouth, raised it up, and hit the metal plate. Her heart pounded, partly with excitement and partly with dread: excitement that Dennis Cain was doing the right thing for Maura's son; dread that he might change his mind. When no one answered her knock, Shannon pushed the bell. Still nothing.

She stepped off the porch, and went part way down the brick walk, stopping to light a cigarette. She took a long drag, trying to calm her rising anger, wondering if this was a sick joke. Shannon tossed her head. She put the cigarette to her lips again and this time, when she blew out a plume of smoke, she decided she would not allow Mr. Cain to toy with her.

She walked up the drive, past the two cars, and went through the gate into the Cain's backyard. It was a lovely place, but it was as quiet as the front of the house.

"Hello!" she called. "Where are you, Dennis Cain?"

Shannon walked to the edge of the pool, smoking, contemplating the sparkling water, thinking she would like to drown Dennis Cain beneath it. She was just taking the last puff when she heard.

"Ms. Shaughnessy?"

The voice came from the direction of the house, and it took Shannon a minute to tag the man standing in the shadows of the pergola. Shannon put her free hand to her brow to cut the late afternoon sun. She flicked her cigarette into a pot where a tomato plant wilted.

"Sure, couldn't you have waited by the front door? It was you, who called me —."

Shannon checked herself. Pique would do no good. "I am sorry. I didn't mean to be sharp. 'Tis kind of you to meet with me."

"No offense taken," he said.

For each step she took forward, he took one back, moving into the cool dark of the house. Shannon stepped over the threshold. It took a minute for her eyes to adjust, but when they did, her smile faltered and faded. The man in the house was unknown to her, but she recognized the two people on the couch well enough: Dennis and Katherine Cain.

Shannon was still trying to make sense of what she was seeing when her phone started to ring. She opened her purse and turned away to take her call. Before she could say hello, the man's hand covered hers.

"I'll be taking that," he said.

Shannon pulled back. He was stronger than she, and Shannon had no choice but to let it go. She turned, sharp words on her lips, but they were never spoken. Shannon Shaughnessy was distracted by the gun pointing at her stomach.

"SHANNON'S NOT ANSWERING," Finn said, keeping his eyes on the road, admiring of Lowery's navigation through rush hour traffic.

"I hope you don't have to play referee when we get there," Lowery said. "The woman is a handful."

"I appreciate you bringing me along."

"You can keep the Shaughnessy woman in hand," he said. "I don't want her interfering with my business—or you either."

"I know I've no standing, but I am curious about what it is you'll be doing."

"I'm taking Dennis Cain into custody for the Platinum Wings bombing."

Lowery kept his eyes on the road, as he handed Finn a file.

"The first page is a copy of the hotel registry in San Francisco. Cain checked in and out within eight hours. Easy trip from LAX to SFO, plant the briefcase, get back on the plane, and be home in time for the meeting at Hammet. The maid gave us a description."

"It's vague," Finn noted.

"Good enough for government work. Franks is getting a picture. He'll pin her down."

Lowery indicated that Finn should turn the next page.

"That's Gowdy's log-in information to Dark Quest. Franks is still in San Francisco, but he's run down the company and talked to the CEO. He's cooperating. He confirmed Cain was the other player via the game code. He gave us a phone number and credit card information, but I know the account will go back to Dennis Cain," Lowery said.

"And how can you be so sure."

Again, the twirl of a finger. Finn turned to the last page. It was a fax cover sheet from a Swiss firm. Attached to that was an ownership certificate for a timepiece.

"Agent Sterling found a metal fragment that she thought might have come from a watch casing. She put together a few other shards, and sent them to the repository. The report just came back. That metal was from a vintage *TAG Heuer* with an oscillating pinion. The company makes top of the line watches, artillery pins, all precision timing devices."

Lowery turned off the freeway. They would be at the Cain's house in a few minutes.

"*Heuer* also manufactures collector pieces that are signed and numbered limited editions. This particular watch was originally sold to a Mr. Shamus Cain in 1938. In 1952 it was passed on and the registration changed to Mr. Collin Cain. In 2012 the watch was inherited and registered to Mr. Dennis Cain.

"That watch, O'Brien, was the timing device on the bomb. With a little digging, I'm confident we can find a picture of Dennis Cain carrying that fancy briefcase Stuart Gowdy put on that plane."

"Impressive, Agent Lowery," Finn said. "I'm appreciative."

"No problem."

Lowery turned onto Oakhurst Drive. Finn put aside the file. It was almost done. Finn might not be bringing his mother Dennis Cains' head on a platter, but he and Shannon would be there to see Agent Lowery do it and that was just as good.

47

"It is nice to officially meet you, Shannon."

"And you would be?" Shannon asked.

"Brian Cain."

"There's a family resemblance," she said.

"As with you and your sister," he said. "I knew Maura well. Not as well as Dennis, unfortunately."

He moved his gun to usher her into the living room. Shannon clutched her purse, squared her shoulders, and walked past him with her head high. Everything looked as it had when she burst into the house all those days ago, except this time no one would be putting up a fight. There was a bullet hole in Dennis Cain's head; a bloom of blood on Katherine Cain's chest.

"So, then, you've killed your brother and his wife."

Shannon was cautious of every word she spoke and the tone she used. She knew too well that a calm man was more dangerous than an angry one, and Brian Cain was calm.

"It couldn't be helped," he said.

"Was it you who called me, then?"

"Maura was smart too." Brian smiled. "'Tis a pity the world is going to be without the Shaughnessy sisters, but so it must be."

As he spoke, Shannon took note of her surroundings, hoping to identify the place that would give her a fighting chance for survival. The couches were deep, the cushions soft. Once sitting, she would be sucked into them, unable to move quickly. The tables in the room were small and delicate. They would offer no protection. She looked at the gryphon chair. It was solid and upright.

"Mind if I sit?" Shannon said. "I've gone a little weak in the knees."

"We've not much time, just so you know," he said. "I've a plane to catch."

"Sure, we wouldn't want you to be late." She crossed her long legs. Her purse was in her lap, her fingers on the gold latch. It felt cool between her fingers. "But if I'm headed to my eternal rest, I would like to know why."

Brian moved a step or two. He was confident yet, but not overly so. He didn't get too close to Shannon.

"It is a bit absurd, really," he said. "It should never have come to this, and I am sorry."

"I don't mind meeting St. Peter with a good story to tell," Shannon said.

"'Twas family business. My brother sold Wolfhound a few years ago, I wanted it back but hadn't the money. I figured a way to get it."

"Ah, money. Such a bother," Shannon said. "And how did blowing up a plane help you get that money? I assume it was you doing the deed."

"I arranged it," Brian said. "The hardest part was securing the explosives, but I've friends from my military days. One here in the U.S. accommodated me for a price. Instead of a nonstop from

Cork, I detoured to San Francisco, collected the device, handed it off, and then I could only hope for the best." Brian smiled. "I'm sure you would be impressed if I had the time to tell the full tale."

"I've no doubt, *boyo*."

Shannon forced her body to relax. One finger twirled in her hair. She smiled, but it was wasted energy. Power, not sex, was his thing.

"So, tell me, then, Brian Cain. What good was killing an old man and my sister?"

"Are you familiar with key man insurance?"

"Can't say that I am," Shannon said.

"A key man is a person of such importance that, should he— or she- die, the company which employs them would be compensated greatly for their loss. Dead, old Hugh was worth ten million dollars to Wolfhound."

"And Maura? Was she collateral damage?"

"Maura was a gift. I learned just at the right moment that she was also an honored Wolfhound key man. There are others who are covered—they don't know it, of course—but Maura was convenient," Brian said. "I've a friend who put the policies in force a long while back. For Wolfhound, it was a savings account. Our employees were old, we insured them, they passed, and Wolfhound received a settlement. It was their legacy to a company they loved."

"You're telling me the old guard wasn't dying off quickly enough, so you helped them along? A bomb on a plane, two taken out at once," Shannon said. "Is that it, you *bodach*?"

"I'm no pig, Shannon?" he laughed. "I am a savior. It is the small things that have bedeviled me. I thought no one would ask after Hugh or Maura. It seems I was wrong on both counts."

"Your brother? His wife? You're leaving a bloody trail." Shannon motioned to the bodies. "Why was this necessary?"

"It was a tumble of small things that took on a life of its own.

O'Brien asking questions, the girl at the insurance company doing the same. I had no choice," he said. "I need that money, and I wanted no more questions."

Shannon barked a laugh, and it was as genuine as her disbelief of what she was hearing. She shook her head.

"You are fine-looking," Brian Cain. "But you're an idiot, my boy. The law will be finding you out. If not for the bombing, for these two here."

"On the contrary. I won't have killed anyone. You will," Brian said. "You are a violent, vindictive woman. There is a police record of you attacking Dennis and his wi—"

"You bastard."

Shannon set her spine and pressed her knees together so he wouldn't see her shake. Her eyes darted to the dead people on the sofa, to the entrance to the room, and to the front door beyond it. Her fingers opened and shut the clasp on her purse. Brian's eyes went to her hand. He was annoyed by the snapping, so she latched it tight, and held his gaze.

"I am not afraid to do what must be done," he said. "You will have shot poor Katherine and Dennis, and then turned the gun on yourself. Every bit of evidence in the bombing points to Dennis, I've made sure of that. The icing on the cake is that my brother is also a key man. Wolfhound will thrive."

"Don't get too cocky, my friend. Finn O'Brien will never think I've done this thing. He will never stop looking for the truth. And that little girl at the insurance company? Another loose end. You're a dead man walking, don't you know."

"The girl is dead; a traffic accident. Ireland has no extradition to California because it is a death penalty state. By the time O'Brien puts it together, I will be safe at home."

"And the person who wrote these policies?"

"Afraid of her own shadow, and understanding what I'm capable of." Brian walked toward her. He hunkered down so he could look Shannon in the eye. With his free hand, he pushed back her hair. "You, Shannon, are the bow that ties up the package. The wronged, grieving, hysterical woman who attacked these fine people once before returns to finish the job..."

Brian sighed. He put his hand on the arm of the chair and pushed himself up.

"This will be the talk of Beverly Hills, and I will be shocked when I hear of it."

"They'll trace the gun," she said.

"'Tis a souvenir from Katherine's days of service. She was a good soldier. She put up a fight. But there is nothing that points back to me," Brian said. "And now, Shannon, I truly must finish up."

He took a step back and raised the gun.

"Stand up."

Before Shannon could do as he asked, in that split second before he pulled the trigger, two things happened to distract him: the doorbell rang and Katherine Cain moved.

48

Brian was on Shannon fast, stowing the gun in his belt, tangling one hand in her hair and putting the other to her throat.

"Make a sound, and I will break your neck."

He yanked her up, dragged her through the living room, threw her into a closet, and slammed the door. She landed hard, freezing where she fell, not wanting to move until she had the lay of the land. On the other side of the door, a chair was hooked under the knob, locking her in. All of this had taken no more than a few seconds.

Slowly she untangled herself, ignoring the pain in her neck, and the cut on her knee. She put out her hands, gauging the size of the space. Three feet wide and perhaps five feet long. Two garments hung above her. A man's coat, and a woman's sweater. She had fallen on a vacuum robot, a small round thing, harmless unless you fell just the right way— which she had. There were two rods leaning against the back wall, but they were aluminum and of no use as a weapon.

She stood up carefully, and ran her hands over the walls near the door. There were no switches, but something grazed her head. It was a string. She pulled it, and a bare bulb shined dimly overhead.

Kicking aside the little vacuum, Shannon put her back up against the far wall, and slid down to the ground. She pulled the strap of her purse over her head, and held it tight against her stomach. No matter what was happening outside the door she knew he would be back, and she best be ready. A man like Brian Cain didn't go away nor did he go down easy.

"NOBODY'S HOME."

Agent Lowery stood at the edge of the porch watching Finn walk around the white sedan in the driveway. The detective opened the door, put his knee on the driver's seat, reached over, and popped the glove compartment. When he was done, he backed out and called 'rental' to Lowery. Finn walked to the front of the car and ran his hand across the bumper and the grill. He hunkered down to look at the tires. Lowery came to the edge of the porch.

"You'd do well to impound that car," Finn said. "Damage here. Perhaps blood. Some fibers. I'll bet you a whiskey this is the car that hit Maggie Davis."

"I didn't peg Dennis Cain for a psycho," Lowery said.

"Don't be counting your chickens," Finn said. "'It was Brian Cain whose name is on the rental agreement."

"Doesn't mean he was driving the car," Lowery said.

"Doesn't mean he wasn't," Finn countered.

He went to the Audie and checked it out. Both cars could look white on a dark night. This one was registered to Katherine Cain. Lowery went back to the front door. He was ringing the bell a second time when Finn joined him.

"'Tis a large place. Perhaps they can't hear us," Finn said.

"Maybe they don't want to hear us," Lowery said. "You want the back or the front?"

"I've seen the front. I'll go 'round back."

They parted ways, Lowery to wait for someone to answer the front door and to look through the windows hoping to catch someone's attention, while Finn went to the backyard.

He noted the pool and lounges set close together with a small table between them. The umbrella was tipped to break the morning sun not the afternoon. The BBQ was covered. The pots of tomatoes on the upper patio were dry and hadn't been watered in a long while. Someone had used it as an ashtray. There was a film of dust on the table and chairs on the upper level.

He tried the French doors and found them locked. Finn cupped his hands on the glass and peered inside. He saw the family room and the kitchen. He could just see the edges of the living room. What he didn't see was people.

BRIAN CAIN WATCHED AND WAITED. The men outside had done what they could. They rang the bell, they looked through every window save the one that was draped in the living room.

Even if Shannon screamed, she would never be heard, locked in the closet as she was. It was Katherine Brian worried about. He had thrown himself on top of her, clamping a hand over her mouth, even though she made no noise. What he had seen was probably a death twitch, but he was leaving nothing to chance. Brian checked her pulse. It was so weak as to be almost undetectable. Positive that Katherine could not call out, Brian moved to the window, pulled at the edge of the drape, and saw that the two officers were getting in their car. The detective left his door open for a moment, looking back at the house. Brian held his breath, breathing easy only when Finn O'Brien closed his door and the car pulled away.

"We can go to the Beverly Hills courthouse to get a warrant," Lowery said when they were half way down the block.

"Fine," Finn said.

Lowery slid his eyes toward his passenger. Finn O'Brien was chewing his lower lip.

"What?"

"Sure, something's not sitting right, Agent Lowery."

"Well, think about it while I —" Lowery began. Before he could finish, Finn shot upright. He turned and looked back at the Cain house.

"Turn around. Turn around now. Shannon's in that house, and if she's in there, so is Cain."

"How do you know?"

"There was a cigarette in a pot, Lowery. The Cains don't smoke, but Shannon does. This one had a gold filter like hers. It was fresh. Go back."

Lowery didn't need more, nor did it matter any longer whether a federal agent or a city detective was calling the shots. Both were sure that the urgency was real, and the stakes were high. The tires screeched as the agent pulled a 180. He pulled up to the curb, slamming on the brakes when his car was only inches from the red Mercedes. They both looked at the big, quiet house. Drapes were drawn across one big window, and the others were dark. Lowery shook his head. It was hinky before, it was downright ominous now.

"The curtain," Finn said.

Lowery looked in time to see the edge of the drape swaying slightly. Whoever had been watching them, had now abandoned their post. Lowery had his gun in hand when they got out of the car. This time Finn led the way, and Lowery was a step behind giving cover.

SHANNON OPENED HER PURSE, emptied the contents, and tossed it aside. She turned off the overhead light, and then settled herself in the corner. The mannequin she had made from one of the aluminum poles and the coat that had been hanging above her was in front of the door. It would be the first thing Brian Cain saw. If the sight of it gave him pause before he found her, she would have a chance. That was more than Maura had.

FINN WENT LEFT and put his back up against the wall beside the Cains' front door. Lowery did the same on the right. This time they did not announce themselves.

Finn took off his leather jacket and wrapped it around his left hand. He locked his eyes with Lowery and raised a finger on his right hand. Then another. Both knew what would happen on the count of three. Glass would break and they would only have a few seconds to reach inside, find the lock, and open the front door. If they were wrong, there would be hell to pay.

It would be a small price, though, if they found Shannon alive.

SHANNON HEARD the chair hit the wall as it was thrown aside. The knob of the closet door was turning. Shannon pushed deeper into the shadows, her back hard against one wall and her feet tight against the other. When the door opened, Brian Cain moved cautiously. He was not fooled by her mannequin and he tipped it aside, revealing himself in bits as he came for her: his brow, his nose, his shoulder. Her mouth went dry. Shannon's left-hand shook, her right did not, and that surprised her.

Brian spied her. In the dark, the man's eyes glittered like a night creature. He smiled and reached for the string hanging from the ceiling. Shannon heard the click. The light went on as he said:

"They've gone Shannon. No one to save you now."

"By your word only, Brian Cain," Shannon answered.

FINN WAS FINISHING his count to three when they heard the shot. Lowery got low. Finn broke the window by the door, reached in and threw the lock. It took a second to open the door and another to enter the house. Unarmed, unthinking, Finn ran through the great rotunda, feet pounding on the black and white marble. Lowery followed and both men stopped short when they saw the carnage in the Cain's home.

Dennis and Katherine on the couch and Shannon Shaughnessy standing over the body of Brian Cain. In her hand was a revolver, so small it could fit in a purse. She looked at Finn O'Brien and Agent Lowery with clear eyes. When she spoke, her voice was strong.

"Sure, the Cain boys were such *bloody feckers*, weren't they Finn?"

With that, Shannon Shaughnessy walked toward them, handed over her gun, and went outside for a smoke.

49

Finn walked the streets of Cork alone, the sounds of the bells of St. Anne of Shandon still ringing in his ears.

An hour before he sat at his mother's side, Meg on the other, as the priest spoke of Hugh Murphy, a man he had known in life. There were others in attendance. Some from Wolfhound who had worked with Hugh, and others who were Hugh's in-laws and friends. They offered condolences at the man's passing, expressed shock at Dennis's fate, and disgust at Brian's evil ways. Finn's mother thought it a proper send-off for her brother and an excellent ending for the Cains.

Finn had not been thinking of the Cain family, or Hugh, or what had brought them to Ireland during the ceremony. He was done with them all. There was only one thing on his mind, so he left his mother and sister to Hugh's in-laws and went on his way.

Fifteen minutes later, he reached the stone row house that was his destination, rang the bell, and waited. He knocked. Finn turned to look at the street, wondering if he had mistaken the day and time.

"You're an impatient sort, Finn O'Brien. You think I've an elevator in this old place?"

Finn turned at the sound of Shannon's voice. Before he could greet her, she was on the front stoop, putting her arms around him, her curls and waves covering his face like a cloud. She gave him a final squeeze, and then held him away to take a good look.

"Seems a lifetime ago since I laid eyes you, does it not?"

"It does Shannon, but you've not changed in all these days," he said.

"So, you say," she laughed. "Sure, I barely remember when I had time to put make-up on, and I've not had a cigarette in months. You take your life into your hands being in the same house with me. I'm a misery, don't you know."

"I'm a trained officer of the law," Finn said. "I think I can manage."

"You've your badge back then, have you?"

"And even a thanks from Agent Lowery for assisting."

Sure, there is a god," Shannon said. "Come and meet Maura's son."

With that she drew him inside her home, and he saw that it was not what it appeared. On the outside it was history, on the inside it was Beverly Hills. The hardwood floors gleamed, the carpets were lush, the furniture modern. In front of the window was a playpen filled with toys in which a little boy played quietly.

"Aidan." Shannon picked the child up and held him to her shoulder, showing him off. The little boy took no notice of Finn as he touched Shannon's face, putting his tiny fingers on her eyes, her nose, her lips. She kissed them. Finn put a hand on his back.

"He's a fine one, Shannon."

'That he is."

Neither of them mentioned the resemblance to his father.

The Cain's were history. Finn might recall it now and again; Shannon would have to decide whether to share it.

"Will you be having coffee? Tea?" Shannon said.

"Coffee," he answered.

Shannon put the little boy back to play. He gurgled and chattered in the way babies will as she went off to get Finn a cup. He sat upon the long sofa, keeping his eyes on the little boy whose hair was the dark red of his mother.

"I thought you'd be in the house with the yard, Shannon, but here you are in the city."

She came out of the kitchen and handed him a mug before sitting cross-legged on the sofa next to him.

"I couldn't be living there knowing it was Cain money that bought the house," she said. "Truth be told, too much isolation isn't good for someone like me. This was a good compromise."

Shannon let her eyes linger on the boy. If there had been any doubt in Finn's mind that Shannon would come to regret her decision, it was gone now.

"So," she said, "Did you sort it out then? All the mess?"

"Are you sure you want to know?"

"I think since I've killed a man over it, I should know," she said.

Finn couldn't argue with that so he told the story of a young insurance executive, Jane Whitfield, and an all-too handsome military man, Brian Cain, who was working in the family business. Jane wrote the multiple key man policies and her company took notice of her industry. They promoted her. Brian was a patient man and he funded them.

"Brian assumed at least one elderly employee would pass each year or two, the policies would be claimed, and Wolfhound would have a reliable cash infusion."

"But the old *feck*—" Shannon paused. Cigarettes weren't the only thing she was trying to give up. "The old ones kept going, is that it? Nobody dies, no money."

"And without the money, Wolfhound fails. Dennis sold out to Hammet when times got bad. When the brothers had a chance to buy it back, Brian accelerated things. He needed money and he saw a chance to get a two for one. He suggested Dennis offer Hugh a trip and told Maura now was the time to confront Dennis n his home ground."

"So, Dennis Cain truly had no idea that his brother was going to kill two people to get the money?" Shannon said.

"No. But he had to know when Brian had him preemptively sign two more claim forms for employees who were still alive."

Shannon sighed. She twirled a strand of hair around her finger as she looked at her nephew.

"It hurts my heart to think Aidan will one day ask after his mother. It will be a sad story. The man left a damn bloody trail."

Finn set aside his cup, got up and went to the play pen. He leaned over and held out a foam ball to Aidan. The little boy took it and then handed it back to Finn.

"He counted law enforcement being stretched thin in the U.S. Not to mention he'd been quite brilliant framing Dennis and you. He came pretty close to getting away with it."

Finn left Aidan to his toys and went back to sit with Shannon. "I'm happy you survived him. And Mrs. Cain too."

"She is a fighter, and I know that first hand," Shannon said.

"If she hadn't, we would still be thinking Dennis had blown the plane. Katherine Cain gave Brian the watch without telling her husband. She felt bad he never received anything from his father. Brian never registered it, so the company still thought it belonged to Dennis. He used the watch to frame his brother."

"Brian was meticulous," she said.

"He even doctored his brother's Irish passport. Brian's

picture; Dennis' information. He used it to sign at the hotel. Agent Lowery found it among Brian's things."

"At the risk of sounding naive, wasn't trying to kill the three of us at the house a bit much. Why not leave it at the girl from the insurance company?"

"A soldier's clean-up mission. Every death would have had a logical explanation. Between framing his brother, choosing the victims, and setting up the macabre game with Stuart Gowdy it was an impressive plan."

"And it did him no good, now did it?"

At that moment, Aidan pulled himself up and screeched gleefully. Finn picked him up. The little boy felt solid in his arms, and for a moment Finn felt Maura's spirit with them. He glanced at Shannon and saw she was thinking of what might have been too.

"And why was it you had a gun with you, Shannon?"

She collected the coffee cups, casting a smile his way as she took them away.

"You think a rich man is not as cruel and unpredictable as a poor one?" she said. "'Twas a legal carry, Finn. My purse and my heart feel lighter these days without it."

Finished with her chore, Shannon went to the front door. She opened it and reached for a stroller.

"Come, It's a lovely day. Let's walk."

Finn followed her outside and put the little boy into his stroller. They walked slowly, through the busy neighborhood as if they did it every day.

"What will happen to Wolfhound now," Shannon asked. "Sure, the money that would buy it back is no longer available, is it?"

"Legally, there was no reason to withhold it. The premiums were paid and the company is liable."

"'Tis a ridiculous world, Finn."

Finn had no answer for her. He agreed in full. Still, Shannon was curious about one more thing.

"Who will run the place now?" Shannon asked.

"Mrs. Cain, if you can believe it."

"Ah Finn, how fickle is a woman's heart?" Shannon laughed. "Deny your husband while he was alive, embrace his passion when he's dead. It must be a great guilt she carries."

"At least it will remain in the family," Finn said. "And you, Shannon, how is it with you?"

"Good, Finn. Truly it is."

They turned a corner and headed to a park with grass the color of spring, shade trees, and children running about. Shannon took a blanket from the stroller, and handed it to him. They settled down and Aidan climbed between them.

"I'll be forever grateful to Thomas for finding Maura's friend. The woman was so sad to hear what happened, but happy that Aidan would have family to raise him. I don't know how long it would have taken me to find her on my own."

"Will there be a problem with adoption?"

"My lawyer says no," Shannon said.

"And will you work?"

Shannon shook her head.

"I did well, Finn, so we've no worries," she said. "And there is Maura's insurance, and she had funds. Those I'll save for Aidan. If I do go back to work, I won't be spending my time entertaining rich folk, I'll tell you that."

Shannon held onto the little boy and let him bounce a bit as she looked over the park. Finn rested on one elbow, picking at the green grass, teasing Aidan with the blades

"I wonder, Finn, is it cruel of me to think that everything turned out for the best?" She looked closely at him. "I've never been so happy, and yet it comes at such a great price."

"It was none of your doing, Shannon. I think Maura would

be happy that her child is with you."

"But Maura and I weren't family, not really. We'd not a word between us for years, and before that, none were kind."

"Is it guilty you're feeling for your happiness?"

"Yes," Shannon said.

"It will pass," Finn said, "but only if you allow it."

"'Tis hard to do," Shannon said.

"But it can be done." Finn sat up. "If there's anything I know about the Shaughnessy women, it's that neither one of you likes to lose a fight."

Shannon threw back her head and laughed.

"That is the truth," she said. "And I would not have managed any of this without you. I can never thank you enough."

Finn got to his knees. He reached for Aidan and gave the little boy a hug before he handed him back to Shannon.

"'Tis family you fought for when you could have turned your back. Maura sees that."

"You've a great deal of faith, Finn O'Brien," she said.

"Sure, it would be a sad world without it."

He stood up, letting his eyes rest on Shannon and her child, for that's what Aidan was now. Maura would always be remembered, but it would be Shannon who guided him to manhood and that was a lucky thing. With Maura, Aidan's future would have been a tug of war: Maura on one side, Dennis on the other and Katherine Caine determined to keep them apart.

Finn kissed the top of Shannon's head. She was smiling when she looked up, as if she felt herself surrounded by love for one perfect moment. Then her smile faded a little. She had seen enough men leave her, some she cared for and others she didn't. But Finn she would miss more than any other.

"You're off then, are you?"

"We leave tomorrow morning," Finn said. "I best be collecting my mother and sister."

"I'm glad you came to see about us," Shannon said.

"I am, too. You're an amazing woman, Shannon," he said. "And a fine sister."

He took his leave with a few more words, wishes of good luck and happiness. But Finn hadn't gone more than a few steps when she called to him.

"Sure, don't be a stranger, Finn O'Brien," she said. "For Maura's sake. For ours."

Now it was his turn to smile. Maura was a memory. He would never return to Ireland for her. His heart was with Gretchen and Cori, and yet more than a bit of it was being left with this woman.

"'I'll be no stranger to you, Shannon Shaughnessy," he said. "If you and Aidan should ever need me, I'll come."

Shannon put her fingertips to her lips. She sent him her kiss before she pulled her little boy close.

Finn walked away knowing Shannon Shaughnessy would never have need of him. She would carve a path for her and Aidan fearlessly and choose her own happiness. Finn's life was elsewhere; Shannon, on the other hand, was home.

DEAR READER,

I would like to ask a favor. Would you leave an honest review of ***Distant Relations*** *at the online store where you purchased this book? Just click on write a review, and tell other readers what you liked about it. Thank you from the bottom of my heart for this support. I greatly appreciate it.*

Rebecca

Don't stop now!
HOSTILE WITNESS starts on the next page!

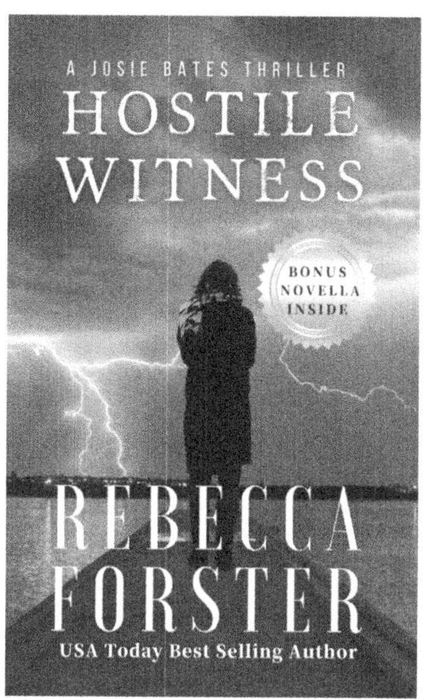

CHAPTER 1

"Strip."

"No."

Hannah kept her eyes forward, trained on two rows of rusted shower heads stuck in facing walls. Sixteen in all. The room was paved with white tile, chipped and discolored by age and use. Ceiling. Floor. Walls. All sluiced with disinfectant. Soiled twice a day by filth and fear. The fluorescent lights cast a yellow shadow over everything. The air was wet. The shower room smelled of mold and misery. It echoed with the cries of lost souls.

Hannah had come in with a bus full of women. She had a name, now she was a number. The others were taking off their clothes. Their bodies were ugly, their faces worn. They flaunted their ugliness as if it were a cruel joke, not on them but on those who watched. Hannah was everything they were not. Beautiful.

Young. She wouldn't stand naked in this room with these women. She blinked and wrapped her arms around herself. Her breath came short. A step back and she fooled herself that it was possible to turn and leave. Behind her Hannah thought she heard the guard laugh.

"Take it off, Sheraton, or I'll do it for you."

Hannah tensed, hating to be ordered. She kept her eyes forward. She had already learned to do that.

"There's a man back there. I saw him," she said.

"We're an equal opportunity employer, sweetie," the woman drawled. "If women can guard male prisoners then men can guard the women. Now, who's it going to be? Me or him?"

The guard touched her. Hannah shrank away. Her head went up and down, the slightest movement, the only way she could control her dread. She counted the number of times her chin went up. *Ten counts.* Her shirt was off. Her chin went down. Ten more counts and she dropped the jeans that had cost a fortune.

"All of it, baby cakes," the guard prodded.

Hannah closed her eyes. *The thong. White lace.* That was the last. Quickly she stepped under a showerhead and closed her eyes. A tear seeped from beneath her lashes only to be washed away by a sudden, hard, stinging spray of water. Her head jerked back as if she'd been slapped then Hannah lost herself in the wet and warm. She turned her face up, kept her arms closed over her breasts, pretended the sheet of water hid her like a cloak. As suddenly as it had been turned on the water went off. She had hidden from nothing. The ugly women were looking back, looking her over. Hannah went from focus to fade, drying off with the small towel, pulling on the too-big jumpsuit. She was drowning in it, tripping over it. Her clothes – her beautiful clothes – were gone. She didn't ask where.

The other women talked and moved as if they had been in this place so often it felt like home. Hannah was cut from the pack and herded down the hall, hurried past big rooms with glass walls and cots lined up military style. She slid her eyes toward them. Each was occupied. Some women slept under blankets, oblivious to their surroundings. Others were shadows that rose up like specters, propping themselves on an elbow, silently watching Hannah pass.

Clutching her bedding, Hannah put one foot in front of the other, eyes down, counting her steps so she wouldn't be tempted to look at all those women. There were too many steps. Hannah lost track and began again. *One. Two...*

"Here."

A word stopped her. The guard rounded wide to the right as if Hannah was dangerous. That was a joke. She couldn't hurt anyone – not really. The woman pushed open a door. The cock of her head said this was Hannah's place. A room, six by eight. A metal-framed bed and stained mattress. A metal toilet without a lid. A metal sink. No mirror. Hannah hugged her bedding tighter and twirled around just as the woman put her hands on the door to close it.

"Wait! You have to let me call my mom. Take me to a phone right now so I can check on her."

Hannah talked in staccato. A water droplet fell from her hair and hit her chest. It coursed down her bare skin and made her shiver. It was so cold. This was all so cold and so awful. The guard was unmoved.

"Bed down, Sheraton," she said flatly.

Hannah took another step. "I told you I just want to check on her. Just let me check on her. I won't talk long."

"And I told you to bed down." The guard stepped out. The door was closing. Hannah was about to call again when the woman in blue with the thick wooden club on her belt decided to give her a piece of advice. "I wouldn't count on any favors, Sheraton. Judge Rayburn was one of us, if you get my meaning.

It won't matter if you're here or anywhere else. Everyone will know who you are. Now make your bed up."

The door closed. Hannah hiccoughed a sob as she spread her sheet on the thin mattress. She tucked it under only to pull it out over and over again. Finally satisfied she put the blanket on, lay down and listened. The sound of slow footsteps echoed through the complex. Someone was crying. Another woman shouted. She shouted again and then she screamed. Hannah stayed quiet, barely breathing. They had taken away her clothes. They had touched her where no one had ever touched her before. They had moved her, stopped her, pointed and ordered her, but at this point Hannah couldn't remember who had done any of those things. Everyone who wasn't dressed in orange was dressed in blue. The blue people had guns and belts filled with bullets and clubs that they caressed as if they were treasured pets. These people seemed at once bored with their duty and thrilled with their power. They hated Hannah and she didn't even know their names.

Hannah wanted her mother. She wanted to be in her room. She wanted to be anywhere but here. Hannah even wished Fritz wouldn't be dead if that would get her home. She was going crazy. Maybe she was there already.

Hannah got up. She looked at the floor and made a plan. She would ask to call her mother again. She would ask politely because the way she said it before didn't get her anything. Hannah went to the door of her – *cell.* A hard enough word to think, she doubted she could ever say it. She went to the door and put her hands against it. It was cold, too. Metal. There was a window in the center. Flat white light slid through it. Hannah raised her fist and tapped the glass. *Once, twice, three, ten times.* Someone would hear. *Fifteen. Twenty.* Someone would come and she would tell them she didn't just *want* to check on her mother;

she would tell them she *needed* to do that. This time she would say please.

Suddenly something hit up against the glass. Hannah fell back. Stumbling over the cot, she landed near the toilet in the corner. This wasn't her room in the Palisades. This was a small, cramped place. Hannah clutched at the rough blanket and pulled it off the bed as she sank to the floor. Her heart beat wildly. Huddled in the dark corner, she could almost feel her eyes glowing like some nocturnal animal. She was transfixed by what she saw. A man was looking in, staring at her as if she were nothing. Oh God, he could see her even in the dark. Hannah pulled her knees up to her chest and peeked from behind them at the man who watched.

His skin was pasty, his eyes plain. A red birthmark spilled across his right temple and half his eyelid until it seeped into the corner of his nose. He raised his stick, black and blunt, and tapped on the glass. He pointed toward the bed. She would do what he wanted. Hannah opened her mouth to scream at him. Instead, she crawled up on to the cot. Her feet were still on the floor. The blanket was pulled over her chest and up into her chin. The guard looked at her – all of her. He didn't see many like this. So young. So pretty. He stared at Hannah as if he owned her. Voices were raised somewhere else. The man didn't seem to notice. He just looked at Hannah until she yelled 'go away' and threw the small, hard pillow at him.

He didn't even laugh at that ridiculous gesture. He just disappeared. When Hannah was sure he was gone she began to pace. Holding her right hand in her left she walked up and down her cell and counted the minutes until her mother would come to get her.

Counting. Counting. Counting again.

Behind the darkened windows of the Lexus, the woman checked her rearview mirror. Damn freeways. It was nine-friggin'-o'clock at night and she still had to slalom around a steady stream of cars. She stepped on the gas – half out of her mind with worry.

One hundred.

Hannah should be with her.

One hundred and ten.

Hannah must be terrified.

The Lexus shimmied under the strain of the speed.

She let up and dropped to ninety five.

They wouldn't even let her see her daughter. She didn't have a chance to tell Hannah not to talk to anyone. But Hannah was smart. She'd wait for help. Wouldn't she be smart? *Oh, God, Hannah. Please, please be smart.*

Ahead a pod of cars pooled as they approached Martin Luther King Boulevard. Crazily she thought they looked like a pin setup at the bowling alley. Not that she visited bowling alleys anymore but she made the connection. It would be so easy to end it all right here – just keep going like a bowling ball and take 'em all down in one fabulous strike. It sure as hell would solve all her problems. Maybe even Hannah would be better off. Then again, the people in those cars might not want to end theirs so definitely.

Never one to like collateral damage if she could avoid it, the woman went for the gutter, swinging onto the shoulder of the freeway, narrowly missing the concrete divider that kept her from veering into oncoming traffic. She was clear again, leaving terror in her wake, flying toward her destination.

The Lexus transitioned to the 105. It was clear sailing all the way to Imperial Highway where the freeway came to an abrupt end, spitting her out onto a wide intersection before she was ready. The tires squealed amid the acrid smell of burning rubber. The Lexus shivered, the rear end fishtailing as she fought for control. Finally, the car came to a stop, angled across two lanes.

The woman breathed hard. She sniffled and blinked and listened to her heartbeat. She hadn't realized how fast she'd been going until just this minute. Her head whipped around. *No traffic.* A dead spot in the maze of LA freeways, surface streets, transitions and exits. Her hands were fused to the steering wheel. *Thank God. No cops.* Cops were the last thing she wanted to see tonight; the last people she ever wanted to see.

Suddenly her phone rang. She jumped and scrambled, forgetting where she had put it. Her purse? The console? The console. She ripped it open and punched the button to stop the happy little song that usually signaled a call from her hairdresser, an invitation to lunch.

"What?"

"This is Lexus Link checking to see if you need assistance."

"What?"

"Are you all right, ma'am? Our tracking service indicated that you had been in an accident."

Her head fell onto the steering wheel; the phone was still at her ear. She almost laughed. Some minimum wage idiot was worried about her.

"No, I'm fine. Everything's fine," she whispered and turned off the phone. Her arm fell to her side. The phone fell to the floor. A few minutes later she sat up and pushed back her hair. She'd been through tough times before. Everything would be fine if she just kept her wits about her and got where she was going. Taking a deep breath she put both hands back on the wheel. She'd damn well finish what she started the way she always did. As long as Hannah was smart they'd all be okay.

Easing her foot off the brake she pulled the Lexus around until she was in the right lane and started to drive. She had the address, now all she had to do was to find friggin' Hermosa Beach.

~

"For God's sake, Josie, he's a weenie-wagger and that's all there is to it. I don't know why you keep coming in here with the same old crap for a defense. Want some?"

Judge Crawford pushed the pizza box her way. It was almost nine o'clock and they had managed to work out the details on the judge's sponsorship at the Surf Festival, discuss a moot court for which they had volunteered, polish off most of a large pizza, and now Josie was trying to take advantage of the situation by putting in a pitch for leniency for one of her clients.

She passed on the pizza offer. Judge Crawford took another piece. He was a good guy, a casual guy, a local who never strayed from his beach town roots in his thirty-year legal career. His robes were tossed on the couch behind them. His desk served as a workstation and dining table. In the corner was his first surfboard. New attorneys called to chambers endured forty-five minutes of the judge reliving his moments of glory as one of the best long boarders on the coast. Three years ago, when Josie landed in Hermosa Beach, she got the full two-hour treatment but only because she knew a thing or two about surfing from her days in Hawaii. She'd spent the extra hour with Judge Crawford because he knew a thing or two about volleyball.

Josie Baylor-Bates had been big at USC but when she hit the sand circuit she'd become legendary. Everyone wanted to beat the woman who stood six feet if she was an inch, played like a professional, and won like a champion. Few did, but they started trying the minute the summer nets went up. Of course USC and Judge Crawford's surfing days were both more than a few years ago, but still their beach history tied them together, made them friendly colleagues, and gave them license to be a little more informal about certain protocols – including the judge speaking his mind about Josie's current client, Billy Zuni: the surfing-teenage-beach bum with a mischievous smile and penchant for relieving himself in city owned bushes.

"That's a gross term," Josie scoffed as if she'd never heard of a weenie-wagger before. "And it is not appropriate in this instance. I've got documentation from their family doctor that Billy has a physical problem. He's tried to use the bathrooms in the shops off the Strand, but nobody will let him in."

"That's because Billy seems to forget he's supposed to lower his cutoffs *after* he gets into the bathroom, not before," the judge reminded her. "Nope, this time he's got to stay in the pokey. Hey, it's Hermosa Beach's pokey. Five cells and they're all empty. Billy will have the whole place to himself. It's not going to kill him, and it may do him some good. I'm tired of that damn kid's file coming across my desk every three months."

"Your Honor, it's obvious you are prejudiced against my client," Josie objected, pushing aside the pizza box.

"Cool your jets, Josie. What are you going to do, bring me up on charges for name calling?" Judge Crawford laughed heartily. His little belly shook. It was hard to imagine him on a long board or any other kind of board for that matter. "Listen. I understand that kid's got problems. You're in here like clock-work swearing he'll be supervised. I know you check up on him. Everyone at the beach knows that, but you can't do what his own mother can't."

"That's exactly the point. Jail time won't mean a thing. What if I can find someone who'll take him for a week? Will you consider house arrest?"

"With you?" The judge raised a brow.

"Archer," Josie answered without reservation.

Judge Crawford chuckled. "Not a bad idea. Sort of like setting up boot camp in paradise. That would make Billy sit up and take notice. I don't know anybody who wouldn't toe the line just to get Archer off their back."

Josie touched her lips to hide a smile. Judge Crawford steered clear of Archer after a vigorous debate on the unfortunate constitutions of judges facing re-election. As Josie recalled, words such as wimps and sell-outs had been bandied about freely. It wasn't that Archer was wrong, it was just that the opinion was coming from a retired cop who wasn't afraid of anything, who got better looking with age, and could still sit a board while the judge. . . Well, suffice it to say the judge had been sitting the bench a little too long.

"Archer might do Billy some good," Josie pushed for her plan.

"Or scar him for life." Crawford shook his head and pushed off the desk. "Sorry, Josie. It's going to be forty-eight hours this time and community service. Best I can do."

"I'll appeal. There are a hundred surfers down on the beach changing from their wet suits into dry clothes every morning. Half of them don't even bother to drape a towel over their butts. The only reason you catch Billy is because he's stupid. He thinks everybody ought to just kick back – including the cops."

Crawford stood up, put the rest of the pizza in his little refrigerator, and plucked his windbreaker with the reflective patches off the door hook as he talked.

"That's cute. You still think you're playing with the big boys downtown? Josie, Josie," he chuckled. "What's it been? Three years and you still can't get it through your head that Billy Zuni and his little wooden monkey wouldn't rate the paperwork for an appeal. Let him be. They'll feed him good in Hermosa."

"Okay, so I can't put the fear of God into you." Josie shrugged and got to her feet.

"Only if you're on the other side of a volleyball net, Ms.

Bates. Only then." Judge Crawford ushered Josie outside with a quick gesture. She waited on the wooden walkway as he locked up.

The Redondo Courts were made up of low-slung, white-washed, Cape Cod style buildings with marine blue trim. All the beach cities did business here. It was a far cry from down-town's imposing courthouses and city smells. Redondo Beach Court was perched on the outskirts of King Harbor Pier where the air smelled like salt and sun. Downtown attorneys fought holy wars, and life and death battles, while standing on marble floors inside wood paneled courtrooms. Here, court felt like hitting the town barbershop for a chaw with the mayor. Some-times Josie missed being a crusader. The thought of one more local problem, and one more local client, made her long for what she once had been: a headline grabber, a tough cookie, a lawyer whose ambition and future knew no bounds. But that was just sometimes. Mostly, Josie Baylor-Bates was grateful that she no longer spoke for anyone who had enough money to pay her fee. She had learned that evil had the fattest wallet and most chaste face of all. Josie could not be seduced by either any more.

"You walking?" Judge Crawford called to her from the end of the path.

"No, I drove."

"Want me to walk you to your car?" the judge offered.

"Don't worry about it. This isn't exactly a tough town, and if another Billy Zuni is hanging around I'll sign him up as a client."

"Okay. Let me know if you and Faye are in on that sponsor-ship for the Surf Festival."

"Will do," Josie answered and started to walk toward the parking lot. The judge stopped her.

"Hey, Josie, I forgot. Congratulations are in order. It's great that you're signing on as Faye's rainmaker."

Josie laughed, "We're going to be partners, Judge. I don't think there's a lot of rain to be made around here."

"Well, glad to hear it anyway. Baxter & Bates has a nice ring, and Faye's a good woman."

"Don't I know it," Josie said.

Faye Baxter was more than friend or peer; she was a champion, a confessor, a sweetheart who partnered with her husband until his death. Josie was honored that now Faye wanted her, and Josie was going to be the best damn partner she could be.

Waving to the judge, Josie crossed the deserted plaza, took the steps down to the lower level parking and tossed her things in the back of the Jeep. She was about to swing in when she caught the scent of cooking crab, the cacophony of arcade noise, the Friday night frantic fun of Redondo's King Harbor Pier and decided to take a minute. Wandering across the parking lot she exited onto the lower level of the two-storied pier complex.

The sun had been down for hours but it was still blister-hot. To her right the picnic tables in the open-air restaurants were filled. People whacked crabs with little silver hammers, sucked the meat from the shells, and made monumental messes. On the left, bells and whistles, and screams of laughter from the arcade. Out of nowhere three kids ran past, jabbering in Spanish, giggling in the universal language. Josie stepped forward but not far enough. A beehive of blue cotton candy caught her hip. She brushed it away and walked on, drawn, not to the noise, but to the boats below the pier.

These were working craft that took sightseers into the harbor, pulled up the fish late at night; they had seen better days and were named after women and wishes. The boats were tethered to slips that creaked with the water's whim and bobbed above rocks puckered with barnacles. Josie loved the sense of silence, the feeling that each vessel held secrets, the dignity of even the smallest of them. The ropes that held these boats tight could just as easily break in an unexpected storm. They would drift away like people did if there was nothing to tie them down or hold them steady.

Josie leaned on the weather worn railing and lost her thoughts to the heat and the sounds and the look of that cool, dark water. At peace, she wasn't ready when something kicked up – a breeze, a bump of a hull – something familiar that threw her back in time. Emily Baylor-Bates was suddenly there. A vision in the water. The Lady of the Lake. Yet instead of the sacred sword, the image of Josie's mother held out sharp-edged memories. Josie should have walked away, but she never did when Emily came to call.

Even after all these years she could see her mother's face clearly in that water. Emily's eyes were like Josie's but bluer, wider, and clearer. They shared the square-jaw and high cheekbones, but the whole of Emily's face was breathtakingly beautiful, where her daughter's was strikingly handsome. Her mother's hair was black-brown with streaks of red and gold. Josie's was chestnut. Her expression was determined like Josie's but...but what?

What was her mother determined to do? What had been more important than a husband and a daughter *A good daughter, damn it.* What made her mother – even now after all these years she could barely think the word – *abandon* her? Why would a woman cast off a fourteen year old without a word, or a touch? There one night, gone the next morning.

Suddenly the water was disturbed. Emily Baylor-Bates' face disappeared in the rings of ever widening concentric circles. Startled, Josie stood up straight. Above her a group of teenagers hung over the railing dropping things into the water. They laughed cruelly thinking they had frightened Josie, unaware that she was grateful to them. The water was mesmerizing, the memories as dangerous as an undertow. Emily had been gone for twenty-six years. *Twenty-six years*, Josie reminded herself as she strode to the parking lot, swung into her Jeep, turned the key, and backed out. The wheels squealed on the slick concrete. She knew a hundred years wouldn't make her care less. Time wouldn't dull the pain or keep her from wanting to call her mother back. On her deathbed, Josie would still be wondering where her mother was, why she had gone, whether she was dead, or just didn't give a shit about her daughter. But tonight, in the eleven minutes it took to drive from Redondo Beach to Hermosa Beach, Josie put those questions back into that box deep inside her mind. By the time she tossed her keys on the table and ruffled Max-The-Dog's beautiful old face, that box was locked up tight.

The dog rewarded Josie with a sniff and a lick against her cheek. It took five minutes to finish the routine: working clothes gone, sweats and t-shirt on, and her mail checked. Faye had dropped off the partnership papers before leaving for San Diego and a visit with her new grandson. The tile man had piled a ton of Spanish pavers near the backdoor for Josie to lay at her leisure. The house of her dreams – a California bungalow on the Strand – was being renovated at a snail's pace, but Josie was determined to do the work herself. She would make her own home; a place where no one invited in would ever want to leave.

In the kitchen, Josie checked out a nearly empty fridge as she dialed Archer. It was late, but if he were home it wouldn't take much to convince him that he needed to feed her. Josie was punching the final digits of Archer's number when Max rubbed up against her leg, wuffing and pointing his graying snout toward the front door. Josie looked over her shoulder and patted his head, but Max woofed again. She was just about to murmur her assurances when the house seemed to rock. Snarling, Max fell back on his haunches. Josie let out a shout. Someone had thrown themselves against the front door, and whoever was out there wanted in bad. The new door was solid, the deadbolt impossible to break, but the sound scared the shit out of her. The doorknob jiggled frantically for a second before everything fell quiet – everything except Josie's heart and Max's guttural growl.

Bending down, Josie buried one hand in the fur and folds of his head. With the other she picked up the claw hammer from the tool pile. Standing, she smiled at Max. His eyebrows undulated, silently asking if everything was all right now. For an instant Josie thought it might be, until whoever was out there flew at the door with both fists.

"Damn." Josie jumped. Max fell back again, snapping and barking.

Clutching the hammer, Josie sidestepped to the door. She slipped two fingers under the curtain covering the narrow side-window and pulled the fabric back a half an inch. A woman twirled near the hedge. Her head whipped from side to side as she looked for a way into the house. Her white slacks fit like a second skin, and her chiffon blouse crisscrossed over an impressive chest. A butter colored belt draped over her slim hips. Her come-fuck-me sandals had crepe-thin soles and heels as high as a wedding cake. This wasn't a Hermosa Beach babe and Josie had two choices: call the cops or find out what kind of trouble this woman was in. No contest. Josie flipped the lock and threw open the door.

The woman froze; trembling as if surprised to find someone had actually answered. She started forward and raised her hand, took a misstep and crumpled. Instinctively, Josie reached for her. The hammer fell to the floor as the woman clutched at Josie's arm.

"You're here," she breathed.

Close up now, Josie saw her more clearly. The dark hair was longer than she remembered. The heart-shaped face was still perfect save for the tiny scar on the corner of her wide lips. Those long fingered hands that held Josie were as strong as they'd always been. But it was the high arch of the woman's eyebrows and her small, exquisitely green eyes that did more than prick Josie's memory; they shot an arrow clear through it. It had been almost twenty years since Josie had seen those eyes, and the face that looked like a heroine from some Russian revolutionary epic.

"Linda? Linda Sheraton?"

"Oh, God, Josie, please help me."

THE WITNESS SERIES

HOSTILE WITNESS Book #1

Including bonus novella, Hannah's Diary

A prominent judge is brutally murdered; a 16-year-old girl is accused. Josie Bates may have to defend her with her life.

SILENT WITNESS Book #2

When Archer is accused of murdering his stepson, Josie finds her faith tested as she defends the man she loves.

PRIVILEGED WITNESS Book #3

The wife of Josie's first love is dead; his disturbed sister is accused. Josie is drawn into a world corrupted by lies, power, and abuse.

EXPERT WITNESS Book #4

Josie disappears leaving Hannah and Archer to come to grips with the ruthless attorney she used to be, and those who hope she's done for good

EYEWITNESS Book #5

A latchkey kid Josie cares about is accused of a triple murder. The justice she seeks is buried in a history half a world away.

FORGOTTEN WITNESS Book #6

A madman's ramblings put Josie Bates on a collision course with the United States government that wants to stop her at any cost.

DARK WITNESS Book #7

In a remote wilderness Hannah's life hangs in the balance. To save her, Josie invokes a fierce and primal law: survival of the fittest.

LOST WITNESS Book #8

On a cargo ship, a powerful man is dead. On shore, a man from Josie's past pleads for help that could cost Josie Bates her life.

FINN O'BRIEN THRILLERS

SEVERED RELATIONS Book #1

Detective Finn O'Brien follows a trail of shattered relationships to find out why two children and their nanny are dead.

FOREIGN RELATIONS Book #2

More than one person wants a foreign woman dead, two countries want her forgotten, and Finn O'Brien wants justice.

SECRET RELATIONS Book #3

Finn tracks a serial killer as he navigates a shadowy world of illegal immigrants where life is cheap - even his own.

INTIMATE RELATIONS Book #4

Finn is out of his element when a brutal murder sucks him into the world where art and tech make strange and deadly bedfellows.

DISTANT RELATIONS

To find out why his uncle and childhood sweetheart died in a fiery explosion, Finn goes rogue to find justice.

MORE THRILLING READS

BEFORE HER EYES

Searching for a murderer, Sheriff Dove Connelly is dragged into a world where nothing is at it seems.

THE MENTOR

A terrorist bombing puts fledgling U.S. Attorney Lauren Kingsley in deadly danger and even those closest to her are suspect.

BEYOND MALICE

Amanda Cross defends her estranged sister against a murder charge only to uncover a truth that could destroy both their lives.

KEEPING COUNSEL

Attorney Tara Linley's client has a killer smile that hides a psychopath's insanity. When he crosses the line no one is safe.

CHARACTER WITNESS (not Witness Series)

Kathleen Cotter thinks her eccentric client is a nut, until she uncovers a trail of lies and corruption that threaten to make this case her last.

Thank you for adding my books to your library! Check out my website for even more exciting reads.

Rebecca Forster lives in Southern California. She is married to a superior court judge and has two grown sons. She has written over 40 books.

Sign up for Rebecca's spam-free mailing list, get a free gift and never miss a new release.

www.rebeccaforster.com

Made in the USA
Monee, IL
13 August 2022

10930513R00203